THE ROGUE PRINCE

THE ROGUE PRINCE

PRINCE

SKY FULL OF STARS, BOOK ONE

LINDSAY BUROKER

FOREWORD

Hello! Oh, my. That was perky, wasn't it? Hello. Yes, hello, and thank you for picking up the first book in my new Sky Full of Stars series. It's a spin-off series set ten years after the events in my Fallen Empire books. If you haven't read those stories, it shouldn't be a problem. We've got new heroes stepping forward for these adventures, and there will be plenty of new side characters, as well. But for fans of the original series, we *will* get a few peeks at the old gang along the way. I aim to please all of my readers. Perkily.

Before you jump in, please let me thank those who've helped me put together this first book: my beta readers, Sarah Engelke, Cindy Wilkinson, and Rue Silver, and my editor, Shelley Holloway. I would also like to thank Tom Edwards for the cover art. I asked him if he could make a cool-looking spaceship that happens to be reminiscent of a turtle (you'll soon be introduced to the *Snapper*), and he didn't bat an eye. It's possible I'm one of his more "special" clients, but he's a professional. All these great people are.

Now I'll stop blathering and let you jump in. Read on!

CHAPTER ONE

A bleep came from the sensor panel, and Jelena Marchenko slid her sparkly purple stallion mug to the side. A holodisplay popped into the air, showing energy and life signatures in the target installation, and nerves fluttered in her stomach. Their destination wasn't visible on the *Snapper's* cameras yet, but it would be soon. They would land in one of the craters or canyons on the dark, pockmarked side of Alpha 17 Moon, and they would begin their infiltration.

"We there yet?" Erick Ostberg asked, shambling into Navigation and Communications in his socks and rumpled pajamas, his short blond hair sticking out in so many directions it looked like he had slept in a wind tunnel. He yawned, showing off all his teeth. Anyone who thought Starseers were mysterious and powerful warriors had never seen Erick in his asteroids-and-spaceships pajamas.

"We've arrived at our first destination," Jelena said. "You might want to get dressed."

"Right," Erick mumbled, yawning again as he started to turn around. The sensor display caught his eye, though, and he paused, frowning. "That doesn't look like the sprawling industrial city of Gizmoshi."

"It's not."

Jelena took a deep breath, bracing herself to explain this side mission she had planned. At twenty-four, Erick was almost six years older than she, and even though she was the acting captain of their freighter, he had seniority in her family's business, and as the engineer, he could find a way to stop this "mission" before it ever started. She had to be persuasive here. Even though she'd often talked Erick into adventures when they'd been kids on her parents' freighter, ever since he returned from college, he'd been less likely to go along with her whims.

His brow furrowed. "Wait, did you say *first* destination?"

"That's right." Jelena glanced at the big view screen that stretched across the front of NavCom, making sure there weren't any terrain features coming up that she would need to pilot them around. Alas, the bluish gray surface of the moon remained relatively flat, aside from all the craters left by asteroids, so there was no excuse not to look Erick in the eye…"I've decided that we'll stop before reaching Gizmoshi. For another pickup."

She'd wanted to drop off their cargo *before* this side trip, but it was the middle of the night for the city's inhabitants, and nobody at the warehouse had answered the comm when she tried. And she dared not delay any longer than necessary, not when her parents and *their* freighter were only two moons away.

"*You've* decided?" Erick was frowning at the facility on the sensor display now, appearing much more awake. "Do your mom and Leonidas know about this decision?"

"Not yet."

"Uh huh, and what cargo are we picking up?"

He eyed her suspiciously, his face crinkling the way it did when he was concentrating on using his mental powers, his telepathy most likely. Jelena could feel the pricking at her mind as he tried to read her thoughts, but she had also been training as a Starseer for the last ten years, and even if her specialties were communicating with and healing animals, she could keep people from poking around in her head.

"Animals," she said.

Erick groaned and rolled his eyes, his usual reaction to her obsessions. "Animals you can pet and fondle before we drop them off? Where are they going? Gizmoshi?"

"I'm not sure yet, but somewhere farther away would be safer, I'm sure. In case their disreputable owners come after them."

"Jelena, you're not making any sense. Unpack your brain."

Right. She was going to have to tell him everything if she wanted his help. Even though she was willing to do this alone, it would be easier with a partner-in-crime. No, not crime. She refused to think of this as anything other than noble and righteous.

"Through various sys-net groups I monitor," she said, "I've become aware that Stellacor, Inc. is keeping all manner of lab animals caged up in their Alpha 17 facility. As if experimenting on them isn't bad enough, the conditions are horrible. They violate the Tri-Sun Alliance regulations for using animals for science." Her lips thinned in her usual irritation that the Alliance allowed experiments at all, but at least there were laws about humane treatment.

"The dark side of Alpha 17 isn't in the Alliance, and the Gizmoshi side is only nominally so," Erick said. "*Most* of Aldrin's moons are a wild free-for-all." He waved toward the rear of the ship, probably to indicate the green gas giant behind them.

"That's not an excuse for people doing despicable things."

"Half of the system is doing despicable things. It's the half that's resisting being swept up into Alliance control. They like that the regular laws aren't enforced out here. They'd rather make their own regulations."

"They can regulate however they like, so long as they're not being cruel to animals." Seeing his mulish expression, Jelena kept herself from launching into one of her rants. Erick was fond of animals, but not to the extent that she was, and lecturing him had never been the way to get his help. "I could use your engineering brain for this," she said, waving to the co-pilot's seat. "I'm sure the facility will have a security system of some sort, even though I can't imagine that many people come way out here to bother them."

According to the public record, the Stellacor corporation owned hundreds of square miles of the undeveloped side of Alpha 17, and aside from their laboratory complex, there weren't any cities or even structures for as far as the eye—or the ship's cameras—could see.

"You want me to help you commit a crime?" Erick asked.

"If the Alliance laws don't extend out here, then it can't be a crime." She smiled sweetly.

"I'm sure the locals have *some* kind of law," he muttered, the words turning to a groan at the end. "I just realized what all that pet food stacked in one of the cargo hold cabinets is for. I figured your parents had gotten it because they'd lined up some kind of legitimate animal transportation gig for our next trip."

"No, I bought the feed with my allowance money. You can't rescue animals and then not have munchies for them."

Erick groaned again. "Your satellite slipped its orbit, Jelena."

Despite his words, he slid into the seat beside her. Jelena started to feel triumphant—he was going to help her!—but he reached for the communications controls.

"What are you doing?" She grabbed his wrist before he could hit a button.

"Comming your parents."

"Because you miss them and want to make sure nothing is going wrong in the *Star Nomad's* engineering room while you're gone?"

Erick gave her a flat look. "Because I'm sure you don't have permission to do this, and I'm even more sure that they wouldn't approve."

"That's part of being eighteen. If I did things my parents approved of, it would be weirder than the suns orbiting their planets."

"You *just* talked them into getting a second ship to expand the family business and letting you run freight missions. Why do you want to jeopardize that? They're going to know you're not as mature and reliable as they thought." Erick twisted his wrist and tried to pull it from her grip, but she squeezed harder.

He was taller and stronger than she, but she usually won when they sparred in the *Nomad's* gym. Erick had always been more interested in refining his mental talents—not to mention tinkering with machines and working with her grandfather to create Starseer tools—than in learning to fight, whereas her stepfather, former Cyborg Corps commander Leonidas Adler, hadn't given her the option of bowing out of training sessions. He'd been determined that she be capable of taking care of herself, and her mother had agreed, often joining in on the family sparring sessions.

"I can push that button with my mind, you know," Erick said, and did so. The holodisplay flashed to life next to the sensor display. He blinked, and the contact information for the *Star Nomad* popped up.

"*Erick,*" Jelena growled, tightening her grip. When she'd been imagining the trouble she might face this night, it had involved dealing with the facility's security, not with angry parents. That part, she'd assumed, would come later. If at all. They need not find out, if Erick didn't tell them.

"This is for your own good," he said. "I'm not going to let you sabotage yourself. You've been asking for a ship and to be allowed to do runs for two years. You wanted a chance to prove yourself capable of helping out with the family business. This is your chance. It's ridiculous to seek out trouble the first opportunity you get."

Jelena had told her parents she wanted to help with the business, and that wasn't *untrue*, but even more, she wanted the freedom to be her own person and to do more than just run freight. She wanted to use her gifts to help those in need. And maybe, just maybe, she would be recognized for helping those in need and that would earn her a place in the Starseer community, a community that had ostracized her family because Grandpa's brother had tried to take over the entire system ten years ago.

That wasn't Grandpa's fault, and it certainly wasn't *her* fault. She wanted to be invited to get to know those with gene mutations such as she had, mutations that allowed humans to develop mental powers far beyond the norm. Mutations that made her different. She was glad she had Grandpa and Erick to talk to, but she longed to find others who understood what it was like to be a Starseer.

She released Erick's wrist, and he faced the comm display, maybe thinking she had given up. She tapped a control and brought up another display, this one connected to the sys-net group she'd mentioned. An image of a dirty, bleeding dog with all its ribs showing popped up, the animal stuffed into a cage too small for turning around or standing up fully. It was one cage among many in rows and stacks, each with an abused animal inside. There were pigs and monkeys and cats, as well as dogs. Seeing the pictures again made tears come to her eyes, and she wanted to hide them away, but Erick needed to see them.

"A guard who used to work there posted these," Jelena said. "He said it'd gotten really bad lately, since something big shook up the company a month ago, and that the animals are being almost completely neglected now. He wished he'd had the courage to do something before he quit."

"Jelena," Erick said with a pained sigh. This time, it didn't sound like it was a sigh at her antics, but one of defeat. He cared about animals too. She knew it. He'd been the chicken wrangler on the *Nomad* for years.

He twitched a finger, and the comm display winked out.

She didn't smile or clench a fist in triumph, not this time. Seeing the animals had stolen her capacity for buoyant feelings, at least for now. All she could feel was determination.

"You'll help me?" she asked.

"In and out, no delays," Erick said.

"That's exactly what I have in mind. I want to be gone before they even know we're there or who we are. Then we fly straight to Gizmoshi and deliver our cargo. We'll be there by the time Xing's warehouse opens in the morning, and then we'll rendezvous with Mom and Dad after that. They don't even need to know we took a side trip."

Erick snorted. "Is being delusional part of being eighteen too?"

"If it is, it's a good thing I have a college-educated, twenty-four-year-old along who is wise to the ways of the universe. And who can crack security systems and thwart any mechanical obstacle out there with a mere wave of his hand."

"All right, all right, enough flattery. If you really want to show your appreciation, get me a pack of *Striker Odyssey* cards."

Jelena thumped him on the shoulder. "Deal."

• • • • •

Jelena rode her thrust bike through the wide airlock hatchway and onto the ledge where she had landed the *Snapper*. It was halfway down a cliff in a deep canyon that cut through the moon three miles from the facility. She didn't know if approaching through the canyon and landing inside of it had kept her ship off the radar, but she hoped it had. If nothing else, it was the middle of the night local time, so maybe everybody inside would be sleeping.

Jelena shifted on her seat to make sure she had everything while she waited for the airlock to cycle again and for Erick to come out. He was bringing a stack of hoverboards and several inflatable escape pods that could house the animals on what she hoped would be a quick, short trip back to the ship.

"Staff? Check."

She patted the holder built into the back of her thrust bike, making sure her Starseer staff was securely attached. Part tool and part weapon, the staff looked and felt like wood, but the enhanced material could deflect everything from chainsaws to lasers and blazer bolts. It always felt slightly warm in her hand, almost humming with its embedded energy, and it was tuned to her so that when she gripped it, the Kirian runes engraved in the side glowed a soft silver, the power syncing with her brain waves and helping enhance her focus.

"Spacesuit with twelve hours of oxygen in the tank?" She patted the tank on her back and the helmet fasteners, though the suit would have already alerted her if anything was amiss. "Check. Water and meat-flavored ration bars for the animals?" She patted the satchel magnetically sealed to her suit. She had pet treats in with the feed, but these were easier to carry and packed a lot of calories in small bites. "Check. Explosives…"

She didn't open the satchel to check, but she could feel their outline. She'd taken them from Leonidas's small armory on the *Nomad*, though she wasn't sure yet if she would use them. Liberating animals she could justify as something noble. Willfully destroying private property…That would be taking this to another level. But didn't she have to strike some blow against Stellacor? If she blew up the area where they'd been keeping the animals and left a message—a warning—that there would be repercussions if they did it again, wouldn't that be more effective than simply taking the creatures? Maybe it would keep them from getting another batch of animals to torment.

"*Explosives?*" came Erick's voice over the comm as the outer hatch opened. He flew out on his bike, the faceplate of his helmet turned toward her, a couple of built-in lights driving back the shadows on the ledge. "You're bringing *bombs?*"

"Just little ones. For blowing little holes in walls. I've got fence cutters too. Just in case we need help getting into—or out of—the facility."

He joined her, his bike floating a couple of feet off the ground, the hoverboards and pods also floating behind him, bobbing slightly as he stopped. "Help getting out of the facility, because the owners are chasing us all the way back to the ship?"

"You like being chased. You love a good race."

"A race over a course against other thrust bikers. Not across a moon with angry people shooting at us and with three clunky escape pods trailing behind." He jerked a gloved thumb over his shoulder. "Do you think we'll need that many? Twenty people are supposed to be able to float around in space for days in one of these."

"There are almost two hundred animals caged there, according to the guard's report."

"Two hundred?" Erick blinked and looked back toward the cargo hold, though the hatch had now shut, and they couldn't see it. Jelena knew the contents well and that stacks and stacks of gray shipping containers rose to the high, arched ceiling, taking up two-thirds of the space. "Do you think there's room for that many?"

It would be tight, which was why Jelena had wanted to drop off their legitimate cargo first, but she shrugged, smiled, and said, "I figured they could have your cabin."

"Funny."

"We'll work something out."

"Jelena...how closely did you look at the blueprints you gave me?"

"I looked at them." That's when she had decided she could use Erick's help.

"This isn't exactly a low-tech facility." He unzipped a pocket, pulled out his netdisc, and brought up a holodisplay showing the blueprints. "I think there may be a forcefield in addition to the wall around the compound." He waved a finger through the display to point at things, highlighting them in blue as he did so. "Did you see this? And this, this, and this? Also, our sensors picked up drones flying around over everything." Two dozen more highlights appeared, little dots moving above the facility.

"What's your point?" Jelena asked, though she suspected she knew. Any thoughts she'd had of simply riding up and snipping some barbed wire to get in were being quashed.

"This place is secure. Very secure."

"That's why I invited you to come along."

"Invited, right. I believe the word is manipulated."

"I'm glad they had vocabulary classes at that fancy university you attended. Look, you've disabled ships' shields from a distance before. What's a little forcefield? Can't you break their generator?"

Erick shifted on his bike, looking up and down the canyon and back at the *Snapper*, its bulky, green turtle-shaped outline almost invisible against the backdrop of the dark cliff behind it. Nobody would call the craft sleek, and it wouldn't win any races, but she loved that it, if one used one's imagination, looked like an animal. Erick had pointed out numerous other freighters in the price range her parents had been looking at, but after they'd helped the previous owner out of a jam, and the *Snapper* had become available, Jelena had fought hard for it. The ship had soul.

"Did you look up what the company does?" Erick asked quietly, apparently not thinking of the *Snapper*.

"Of course I did. They grow human organs from stem cells and sell them to medical facilities for transplants. There's absolutely no reason they need to experiment on animals for that."

"You're not a scientist. You don't know that. They could be working on some other things, too, other things to help people."

"You're not backing out on me, are you?"

He sighed. "No. If those pictures were true, then I don't disagree with you on this, but if the company is doing something good for sick people, well, just don't forget that, huh? Maybe their methods could be better, but if the ultimate outcome saves lives…"

"I'm sure they make a *lot* of money selling those organs, I doubt anyone here is altruistic. If they were good people, they wouldn't treat the animals that way. And from what the guard said, they don't treat their human workers that well either."

He shook his head slowly, his expression bleak behind his faceplate.

Jelena tried not to feel affronted by his doubt, but she knew he wouldn't be questioning her mother or Leonidas if *they'd* decided on this mission. More likely, he'd be asking if he could help blow things up. For someone who liked to create and fix things, his green eyes gleamed like wet emeralds in the sun when he got a chance to fire weapons or light explosives.

Trying to sound encouraging, she leaned over and gripped his shoulder. "Come on, Erick. We can do this. We're *Starseers*. Practically superheroes."

"Superheroes? Do you still wear that underwear with the ponies on it?"

"That's none of your business. And they're unicorns."

He snorted.

"That reminds me," she said, waving toward his torso, "are you wearing your pajamas under your spacesuit or did you change into something a little fiercer?" She imagined their foes throwing back their heads and laughing if they were caught and stripped of their suits for an interrogation.

"Fiercer? Like what? Should I have added a cape? And a sword?"

"A sword? Who carries around swords anymore?" She waved at his staff, similar to hers, in its holder behind him. "That's the appropriate weapon for a Starseer."

"Glad to hear it."

She noticed he hadn't denied having the pajamas on underneath his suit. Ah, well. They would just have to avoid being caught and interrogated.

"Are you ready?" she asked.

"Yes." He patted a toolbox he'd attached to his bike.

"Good." She started to urge her bike into movement, but paused. "Thanks for coming with me, Erick."

He truly had no reason to go along with her whims, other than the fact that he worked for her parents. Since her mom was the captain of the *Star Nomad* and co-owner of the business, Erick was used to obeying *her* orders, but it wasn't as if that power transferred down to Jelena. He'd been like a big brother to her ever since he'd first come aboard the ship to train with Grandpa, tolerating games far too young for him because she'd been the closest person to his age aboard, even if he would have preferred spending time with Uncle Tommy or Abelardus, the Starseer who'd lived with them for a time. But those two had moved on eventually, and Jelena and Erick had become closer after that.

She liked having a big brother, especially since he still played games and had a goofy streak, though she sometimes wondered what it would have been like if Thorian—once *Prince* Thorian—had stayed aboard the ship too. Only two years apart in age, they had become playmates and best friends after her biological father had died and during the time she had been separated from her mother. Unfortunately, after Grandpa's crazy brother had been defeated, Thor had gone off with Dr. Dominguez and those secretive Starseers who wanted to use him to bring the empire back. In the beginning, her family had visited, and she'd kept in touch with Thor, but she hadn't heard from him in the last four years, and she had no idea what he was doing these days.

"You're welcome," Erick said. "Don't get us killed."

"I didn't get us killed during any of our years of childhood adventures, did I?"

"No, but I have scars."

"Most people can't get a scar from a pillow."

"A pillow thrown by an android might as well be a rock."

"Moonpuff."

She grinned at him and drove her thrust bike toward the edge, tilting it upward as she flew off. The thruster power increased, the seat thrumming beneath her, and the nose rose toward the starry sky and the top of the canyon.

Erick zoomed past her, zigzagging like a drunk in a race.

"You think *I'm* going to be the one to get us killed?" she asked, worried he would lose the hoverboards and their loads. She imagined the inflatable pods pitching over the side and crashing to the canyon floor. Though it would be a slow crash, since the moon claimed only twenty percent of standard gravity.

"Just testing to make sure everything is attached securely." He waved back at her and continued weaving and zigzagging until he reached the top of the canyon. All that being mature and adult when commenting on her plans must have been wearing at him.

He did wait for her at the top, and they flew across the pockmarked moon side by side. From above, the craters hadn't appeared so large, but now as they rode around and over them, they made the bikes seem small, their riders miniscule.

Jelena tried not to feel insignificant underneath the millions of stars glittering in the black sky all around them. She also tried not to think about the lack of air outside, even though the text and graphs that ran down the sides of her helmet's liquid Glastica display reminded her of it. Unlike with combat armor, these suits couldn't stand up to anything like bullets or blazer fire. If they were punctured, she and Erick would be in trouble. Superheroes, she'd jokingly called them. Yes, they had some mental powers that most people didn't, but they were just as vulnerable to death as any human being.

"We're probably visible to their sensors," Erick said as they flew closer, the black wall around the compound coming into view.

"Can you break them?"

He'd broken enemy ships' systems from a distance before, often to help the *Nomad* escape pirates or competitors who weren't above ruthless tactics. Running freight between planets and moons that were solidly under Alliance control was usually a safe proposition, but once one flew farther from the core worlds, the system grew much dicier. The pay for running freight out there could be impressive, too, and Mom and Leonidas weren't too conservative to be tempted from time to time. After all, Grandpa was a powerful Starseer who could often convince enemies to leave them alone. And if that didn't work, Leonidas would happily engage in combat with anyone who tried to board the *Nomad*. He might be fifty now, but he still had all his cyborg implants, and he could put fists through walls—or skulls.

"If I had a lot more time to study the facility, I probably could," Erick said, his helmet swiveling toward her.

From her angle, Jelena couldn't see his eyes through the faceplate, but she could imagine the reproof in his gaze. She should have given him the blueprint and told him about everything earlier, but she'd been worried that, with more time to think about it, he would grow certain that he needed to tell her parents. He'd almost told them, as it was.

"Maybe they'll think we're tourists."

"Tourists cruising across their private property."

"I didn't say we were conscientious tourists. Let's keep going and be prepared to improvise. If we have to, we can abort." Temporarily, Jelena added silently. If they found out they were outmatched, she would take what they learned and come up with a more sophisticated plan. She admitted being a little daunted by all of the security measures Erick had found. She hadn't expected a laboratory to be equipped like some medieval Earth fortress poised on a contested border.

"All right," Erick said. "Your animals are being kept near the outside of the compound, aren't they?"

Jelena nodded. "In a warehouse on the southwest corner." She didn't add, *according to my source.* She didn't want to give Erick another reason to worry, but all of the information they had *could* be false. The Stellacor people could have even planted it, though she couldn't imagine why they would want to lure animal crusaders down to their facility.

The walls seemed to loom taller and taller as they sailed closer on their bikes. Jelena wished there were some mountains or boulders to hide their approach. Even though the moon was dark, with the only lights clustered around the facility, she felt vulnerable and exposed. And—she frowned as something twanged at her senses—she felt something ahead of them.

"I thought so." Erick slowed down his bike. "Forcefield."

Jelena couldn't see anything, but she could feel it. An invisible dome covering the compound.

Erick would have to handle it. She had no way of lowering a forcefield unless she knew where the button was and could find some animal inside that she could telepathically convince to push it. Technically, she could speak telepathically with people, too, but she found touching the minds of strangers extremely uncomfortable and usually reserved that intimacy for close friends and family. Besides, Grandpa had always emphasized that using one's talents to manipulate people was ethically questionable, unless it was clear those people were enemies and dangerous.

Erick lowered his bike to the ground and planted his boots on either side of it. His helmet drooped toward his chest. "I'll try to trace the power to its source and see if I can figure out where the on/off switch is."

"Good. Thanks." Jelena wouldn't have the foggiest idea how to do that.

She shifted in her seat while she waited, feeling useless. And even more vulnerable than before. Now that they were closer, she could sense with her mind the drones. They were zipping about on patrol routes, cameras recording footage around the compound. What would she do if guards were sent out to tell them to leave? Or to *force* them to leave?

She looked toward the southwest corner of the compound. From her position, she couldn't see anything except the wall, but she concentrated on sensing life on the other side. She struggled to see inanimate objects with her mind, but she had no trouble detecting the bodies of living, breathing creatures, human and otherwise. They were close enough now that she could brush against the awareness of many animals, and she lifted her head like a hound catching the scent. She'd found the warehouse. The information hadn't been false.

"They're there," she whispered, looking toward Erick.

"Who? Guards?"

"The animals. They're where they're supposed to be." Jelena could tell that most of them were sleeping, but a few were awake, and she sensed their discomfort and how some of them were in pain. She blinked before tears could form—she wouldn't be able to wipe them while she wore the helmet.

"Ah." He sounded distracted. He was probably still tracing the forcefield to its source.

"All we have to do is get through the forcefield, over the wall, and break into that building."

"*All.*"

Jelena concentrated on that area again, trying to sense if there were any human guards in there with the animals. She brushed the mind of a dog and lingered because it started, sensing her distant touch. She shared soothing feelings with it, even as she grimaced because she could feel its discomfort in its cage.

Her cage, she corrected, getting more of a sense for the dog. Of the sores on her body, the hunger gnawing at her stomach, the bewilderment at being kept in this dark place, the fear of when she was taken out into the light, to other rooms in the facility, to places that would bring more pain—

"Jelena?" Erick touched her arm, and she flinched.

"Yes," she said.

"Stay with me here. There are people awake in there, and I think someone might have noticed us."

"It's dark in the warehouse with the animals. I don't think anyone is there with them."

Yellow flashed in front of them, and they both jerked back. For a second, the outline of the forcefield was visible to the eye, the dome covering the entire facility, from the ground to above the two towers near the center of the compound.

"Did you cause that?" Jelena asked when darkness returned.

"No, I hadn't touched anything yet. There's not a simple on/off switch. It's a software program. I could possibly destroy the generator and the forcefield altogether, but I don't think we want to make enemies here—or alert them to our presence so soon."

"Are you sure you didn't trip something?" Jelena eyed the top of the wall facing toward them, imagining a parapet that people could walk along and shoot from.

"Positive. It could have just been—" His helmet tilted.

Not certain why he'd stopped, Jelena opened her mouth to ask, but she realized the sensation she'd felt earlier was gone.

"It's down," Erick said, turning his bike's thrusters on again, the stack of hoverboards flowing after him.

Jelena nudged her bike forward, too, though wariness made her hesitant to roar forward at full speed. "It just went down? You didn't do that?"

"It wasn't me. It's probably for them." He pointed toward the stars.

It took Jelena a moment to spot lights against the starry sky, a ship approaching. For an alarmed moment, she thought her parents might have found out what she was up to and that the *Nomad* was coming to get them. But the facility wouldn't have dropped their forcefield for some strange freighter.

"Late for a delivery or a pickup," she mused, then gunned her thrusters when she realized Erick was rapidly pulling away from her. She didn't want to miss her chance to get to the wall before the forcefield was turned back on.

"Maybe their crew didn't feel like diverting for illicit activity," Erick said without looking back. He seemed determined to get to the wall before that ship arrived.

"You were more polite and less sarcastic before you went away to school," Jelena said, alternating between watching the approach of the ship and the terrain as she flew over it. "And I thought we discussed that we couldn't possibly be doing something illicit in a place where there aren't any laws."

"I mostly remember discussing swords and capes. And ponies and unicorns." He reached the wall and paused, looking up. Considering flying over? That would be simpler than cutting—or blowing—a hole.

"Because I'm a good friend, I'll do you a favor and not tell any women you date that you can't keep from thinking about my underwear."

"Should I ever find someone to date me, I'm sure I'll be grateful."

"Didn't you tell Leonidas you were meeting a girl in Gizmoshi after we dropped off the cargo? You specifically asked if we could spend the night there."

"I am supposed to meet someone, but it's not for a date. It's a couple of crew mates from *Striker Odyssey*. We're going to have a beer at a pub, link our netdiscs, and practice some maneuvers so we can kick the Elder Squadron's butts the next time we're in the combat arena."

Jelena digested this as she caught up with him at the base of the wall. "You told my dad you have a date when you're going to meet a bunch of gamers?"

"I didn't want him to think I was...uhm. Well, you know he's not impressed by games."

"He's not impressed by my horse obsession, either, but he still loves me."

"You're his stepdaughter. If he didn't love you, your mom would kick him in the asteroids."

"True, but I don't think you have to lie to him about women."

"It's not any worse than lying to him about secret side missions."

"I haven't lied about anything." Jelena pointed to the top of the wall. "Let's try going over. Maybe their arriving ship will keep them distracted."

"I wish that were true," Erick said, looking past her toward the corner of the wall.

Two men with blazer rifles were running toward them, taking huge bounds in the moon's low gravity. Startled because they weren't wearing spacesuits, Jelena gaped at them, but then she realized that the bland, emotionless faces belonged to androids. Androids who, judging by the way they slung those rifles toward Jelena and Erick, had orders to kill them.

CHAPTER TWO

Jelena grabbed her staff from its holster as she parked and hopped off her thrust bike. She was tempted to use the vehicle as a shield, but didn't want it damaged—they had to haul rescued dogs away with that bike, damn it. Besides, she didn't have a Starseer staff for no reason.

She sprang away from the bike as the androids ran closer, grimacing when, thanks to the low gravity, it turned to far more of a *spring* than she'd intended. She was still in the air when one pointed his blazer rifle toward her chest.

Shield, she thought, a mental order for the staff. It didn't need words, but using them helped her with her focus. She needed all the help she could get now, with adrenaline charging through her veins.

The android fired, and a crimson bolt streaked toward her.

"Careful, Jelena," Erick barked, glancing at her and lifting a hand, as if to help.

As her boots touched down, the bolt bounced off the invisible barrier extending from either side of her staff. It was part mental construct and part a gift from the tool. The android fired again, bolts streaking toward her face. She kept her concentration, trying not to think about anything except keeping her shield up, but a quick thought darted through the back of her mind, that these androids were shooting to kill.

"Watch yourself," Jelena said as the other android fired at Erick. She didn't want him getting in trouble because he was worrying about her. "Your crew mates need your help to kick those virtual butts."

The android shooting at her stopped, his expressionless face not giving any hint about whether he was alarmed that she could deflect his bolts or not. He simply raced toward her, then leaped for her.

Jelena threw herself to the side, rolling as she'd done thousands of times in practice with Leonidas. But this was different. The spacesuit and the light gravity made her awkward, and fear made her hurl herself farther than she intended. The android flew by her, which was good, but she didn't have a chance to crack him on the back with her staff as she wished. It would take a lot of damage to down an android, and their opponents would never grow weary, not the way she and Erick would.

When Jelena jumped to her feet, the android had already landed, turned, and was leaping for her again. This time, she planted her feet, even though her instincts made her want to keep dodging, to avoid those lightning fast hands and the harm they could do. An android would be even stronger than Leonidas, and she had seen what *he* could do. She wished he were here now and regretted not trying to elicit her parents' help in this.

Jelena jammed the butt of her staff into the ground and angled the tip outward. Airborne, the android could not halt its path, but he twisted in the air, trying to avoid striking the tip of her weapon. She shifted it to the side, keeping the butt on the ground to brace against his weight, but making sure it caught him.

A jolt ran up her arm as his side struck the tip of the staff, but silvery energy crackled in the air around the weapon. Her emotions—right now, her *fear*—powered it as much as her conscious thought. The energy flare was far greater than usual, and branches of lightning streaked out and around the android. Crashing into the staff might not have damaged him, but he stumbled back under this secondary assault. He tilted his head, as if with curiosity.

Jelena took advantage of what seemed like hesitation, or at least a pause for consideration. For the first time, she went on the offensive, gripping the staff in both hands and attacking. The android leaped back, avoiding a combination of swings and jabs. With his superior speed, he might have grabbed it out of the air, but he was eyeing it warily. She hoped the energy had done some damage to his system. Now, if she could just strike him again…

The wall rose behind the android, and she kept pressing, trying to back him up. He might have trouble maneuvering if he bumped against it.

But he must have realized the same thing. He raised his rifle, at first looking like he might try to shoot again, but instead, he gripped it in both hands. The next time she jabbed with the tip of her staff, instead of backing away, he stepped in and used the rifle to block her, trying to knock the weapon aside. But the touch once again elicited a surge of energy, the air crackling around the staff and the rifle, lightning branching up the android's arms. Jelena channeled some of her own mental power into the staff, trying to enhance its effects.

The android stumbled back, dropping the rifle. She lunged after him, jabbing her staff into his chest.

Maybe some circuit of his had shorted out, because he seemed temporarily stunned. She connected solidly. More lightning leaped between them, and he stumbled back again, crashing against the wall, his arms spread.

She pressed the tip of the staff against his chest, again trying to enhance the energy flowing out of it. She wasn't a toolmaker, the way Erick and her grandpa were, and she didn't understand how the power worked, but after ten years of training, she had no trouble using it. She imagined the energy shorting out all the android's circuitry and frying his neural network. She wasn't rewarded with anything so satisfying as smoke coming out of his ears, but his silvery eyes grew dim, and he stopped moving.

Jelena stepped back, and the android tipped over with the grace of a coat rack toppling. Though she wasn't positive he was permanently out of commission, she turned to check on Erick.

He stood by the bikes, the butt of his staff resting on the ground beside him as he watched. The torso of the android that had been attacking him lay under his boot. An arm rested a few feet away, cut circuits still sparking. She wasn't sure where the head had gone. The pieces had been neatly severed, as if by some giant saw blade.

"You did that with your staff?" Jelena asked, wondering if she should feel betrayed that hers hadn't come with such abilities, at least insofar as she knew.

Erick grinned behind his faceplate and held up a tool the length of his arm. "Plasmite torch. You're not the only one who brought tools."

"Showoff."

"That's why the ladies flock to me." Erick jogged over to her android and fired up the tool, the orange blade flaring oddly in the missing atmosphere. He must not have trusted that her damage had permanently destroyed it because he severed the head.

Jelena turned away. Even though androids were machines, their resemblance to people made her uncomfortable. "Do they? I didn't realize any of the crew mates meeting you at that pub were women."

"One *does* have long hair."

"Well, that's almost the same thing, isn't it?"

She looked toward the corner the androids had originally run around. What would she and Erick do if living, breathing guards were sent out? They couldn't cut up real people.

The ship that had been approaching was no longer in sight. Had it landed? Somewhere inside? She stretched out her senses to check behind the wall. Yes, there it was in a courtyard out front, extending an airlock tube to a building.

"The forcefield is back up," she noticed.

"I know," Erick said, his tone turning grim as he strode back to his bike. "Let's get your animals and hope nobody inside is keeping track of those androids. I'll work on trying to figure out how to get the forcefield down while we work."

Jelena slung a leg over her bike, fired up the thrusters again, and flew toward the top of the wall as she checked for life—guards—along it. She couldn't navigate with her staff in her hands, so she wouldn't be able to deflect weapons fire while riding, at least not without risking falling off.

There wasn't anyone striding along the wall, but when she eased her bike above it, she came face-to-face with a giant artillery gun. With her heart trying to lurch into her throat, she steered around it. It was one of dozens of massive weapons along the wall, and her earlier thoughts of ancient fortresses guarding borders came to mind again. Why did a research facility need such defenses?

"I bet they don't invite kids in on field trips," Erick muttered, bringing his bike even with hers as he peered up and down the wall and into the compound.

"What?" Jelena asked.

"When I was seven, my school went on a field trip to a hospital. There was a research wing with all these dead fetuses and mutated organs in jars."

"That's disgusting."

"To a seven-year-old, it was magnificent. I got to touch a heart with two extra chambers."

Jelena had been much more excited about touching horses at seven. That seemed far more normal. Her younger twin sisters had been the same way at that age. For the most part. Nika might not have been that horrified by a grotesque mutated organ.

"There are a couple of people going down that tunnel and into that building to meet the people from the ship," Erick said quietly, waving toward the front half of the compound. All of the twenty or thirty buildings were connected via hard tunnels or flexible tubing.

"Our warehouse is that way."

Jelena pointed in the opposite direction, hoping the arrival of the newcomers would distract the guards, and that they would forget that a couple of androids had wandered out to check on something and hadn't returned. She also hoped nobody was looking up at the walls. All it would take was a glance for someone to notice them, especially with the bulky hoverboards trailing Erick's bike. But as far as she could tell, nobody was outside the facility.

Erick turned his bike along the wall and headed in the indicated direction. He was careful not to touch anything, and Jelena followed his example. Who knew what alarms might light up if they bumped one of those guns?

They descended into the interior as soon as they could, slipping into an alley between the wall and a building, and Jelena felt slightly more at ease, even though there weren't nearly as many shadows as she would have preferred. Harsh lights shone down from the walls and every building corner, stealing hiding spots.

A flash came from the front of the compound. It wasn't the force-field this time. Maybe something to do with the ship being unloaded? Jelena wondered what kind of cargo was coming in and imagined a fresh delivery of hapless animals, but she supposed the odds leaned toward something more prosaic, like food and water for the researchers. She thought of the explosives in her satchel, and couldn't help but fantasize about destroying the supplies of the people who let those animals go hungry.

"That's it, right?" Erick said, stopping at the corner of a building and looking across to another one.

With drab gray walls and no windows, there was nothing to make it stand apart from the rest of the structures they had passed, but Jelena could sense the animals inside. "Yes."

A tunnel led into the building, but she didn't see a way in from the outside. Would they have to cut a hole in the wall? If so, all the air would escape, and some alarm would surely go off. Worse, the animals would be in danger. She couldn't imagine getting the pods inflated and all of them inside before they ran out of air.

"Let's go around to the back," Jelena said, nudging her bike into the lead. "See if there's a door."

"Wait." Erick gripped her arm and waved her back against the wall. His helmet tilted upward.

Jelena looked and, out of habit, listened, though she wouldn't be able to hear anything in the nonexistent atmosphere. One of the drones flew overhead in a lazy circle, and she froze. She hadn't seen them since they'd approached the wall, so she'd forgotten about them. Had they been put on pause while the ship approached?

It passed out of view without slowing down, continuing on some pro-grammed route.

"Did it see us?" she whispered.

"No way to tell." Erick released her arm.

Jelena kept an eye toward the sky as she drove out into the open, then along the wall of the animal building. She rounded a corner and her grip tightened on the handlebars when she spotted a back entrance. It looked more like a spaceship hatch than a door, and she hoped that meant there was an airlock that they could get inside without venting the building's air.

"Cargo door," Erick said, driving up to a control panel and examining it. He avoided stepping in front of a small hole that might have been a camera.

"Can your smart, computer-loving brain convince that panel to let us in?" Jelena asked.

"If not, my smart plasmite torch can." He tapped the case where he'd secured the weapon.

"You sound like Leonidas."

"Really? I'd assumed he would just punch his fist into the panel."

"He would, but it would be a smart fist."

Despite his threat to pull out the tool, Erick withdrew his netdisc instead. He brought up the holodisplay, tapped in a couple of commands, and held it up to the panel. "My decryption program is going to have a chat with it."

"I didn't know you'd taken hacking courses while you were away at school." As far as she remembered, Erick had always been more fond of working with physical components rather than dithering with software.

"There were a few extracurricular activities. And I have a sys-net buddy who specializes in this sort of thing."

A green light came on, and the hatch opened into an airlock chamber. Good. It was large enough to accommodate their thrust bikes. Even better.

As Jelena flew in, she glanced skyward one more time. There weren't any drones hovering overhead, but she feared this had been too easy, aside from the androids. Could this be a trap? But who could have expected them? As Erick closed the hatch behind them and cycled the lock, she prayed to the three suns that their luck would hold, that drones weren't delivering footage of their intrusion—or of them beating up the security androids.

It didn't take any fancy software for Erick to open the interior door. There was indeed atmosphere inside, as the animal sounds that greeted her ears told her. The lights came on automatically, and whimpers, grunts, mews, and hoots followed.

Jelena didn't even have to reach out with her senses to feel all the life around them as the dogs, pigs, cats, and monkeys awoke. But they awoke in pain and in fear, cringing back as far as they could in their cages. Jelena sent out waves of reassurance and shared images of grasslands and forests, places where they might run free and not need to fear experimentation. She had the sense that not all of them had ever seen grass or trees. Had they been born and bred in some lab? Solely for this fate? Even if that was so, they seemed to understand what she shared, some genetic memory recognizing the idea of freedom.

Despite her resolve not to cry, tears pricked her eyes at the helplessness and hopelessness that they all felt. And not all of them, she realized as she scanned the warehouse, were alive. Some animals had died in their cages and not yet been removed by whatever cold-hearted bastard tended this place, if this could be called tending. She didn't see water dishes anywhere and sensed the animals' thirst, as well as their hunger.

"All Earth-descended animals?" Erick asked, glancing at the cages that lined the wide aisle stretching before them as he pulled the inflatable pods off the hoverboards.

"I think so." Jelena headed to the closest cages, hoping they weren't bolted down so she could simply move them into the pods without worrying about finding keys for doors until later. "If the experiments are for the benefits of humans—" she sneered as she spoke, finding no justification for the way the animals had been treated, no matter who was to benefit, "—then they'd need to use animals that share a lot of our DNA. The creatures native to the system are weird, the ones that weren't introduced by us and modified to survive here. Not that the mutants aren't weird too."

"Nothing wrong with being a mutant," Erick said dryly, no doubt thinking of his own genes.

The colonists who had landed on Kir long ago had come from Earth, the same as the rest of the humans settling on the habitable planets and moons in the Tri Suns System, but those who had become the Kirians hadn't realized from afar how much radiation their planet held. Their colony ships had only been made for the one-way trip, so the residents had been stuck on the planet for generations, until resources were gathered and an infrastructure built that could once again make spaceflight possible. In the meantime, the scientists among the colonists had tinkered with people's genes, trying to change them so they could better survive on their harsh planet. Many had died. Those who had lived and had offspring had been able to tolerate the radiation, but the genetic tinkering had caused a few side effects.

A sore-covered dog with patchy fur whined hopefully at Jelena. In a surge of anger over the animal's state, she waved at the cage lock, snapping it off with her mind. Telekinesis wasn't her specialty, but she could do enough. Especially when properly motivated.

Even when the door swung open, the dog did not come out. She coaxed it with her mind, and finally it—she—limped out, barely able to stand. She pulled her into her arms, careful not to put pressure against her wounds, and soothed the shivering body. She glared down the aisle at other cages, snapping the locks on those too. Her throat tightened at the sight of several of the animals not even moving in response, barely alive.

It looked like the situation had grown even worse since the guard posted those pictures. Surely, Stellacor couldn't be doing legitimate experiments on the animals when they were in so poor a condition.

"Uh," Erick said, from where he was inflating two of the pods. "Might be better to leave them caged until we get them back to the ship."

Jelena sighed. "I know. I'm just..."

"It's horrible, I know," Erick said with sympathy in his voice, and a hint of the indignation she felt as he glanced toward the animals. "We'll get them all out."

Not all of them. For some it was too late. But she couldn't chastise herself for that. They would get the ones that they could. It was better than nothing.

She set down the dog, which stayed close, leaning against her leg. She pulled out a couple of her ration bars, tore them open, and fed the animals trundling out, but she dared not spend much time on that. Mostly, she left bits of bars on the floor to help entice out the ones she freed.

Then she went to detach cages from the wall, using the laser knife on her multitool to cut them away from their mountings. Erick had the first pod inflated, and she hurried to load their living cargo into it. The animals had been forced to defecate in their cages, and she was glad she couldn't smell anything through her helmet. Washing them and cleaning the *Snapper* would be her fun project while Erick was off not meeting women. Otherwise, it would be hard to explain to her parents how their newly acquired freighter had come to smell like a sewer.

Erick inflated a third pod and worked alongside her, quickly moving cages while glancing often at the door that led to that tunnel and the rest of the facility. He lined up the hoverboards behind his bike, checking heights and deflating the pods slightly to be sure they would fit through the cargo doors in a chain. They were meant to be lifeboats in a spaceship emergency, not shipping containers.

A clang came from beyond the tunnel, and Jelena froze. Was someone coming?

Several monkeys hooted, and she winced at the noise. She used her power to soothe them, assuring them there was nothing worth chatting about right now. She hoped she wasn't lying to them.

"There are people in the next building over," Erick said, not pausing in his work. "I think they're unloading the cargo from the ship."

"Can you tell what it is?" Jelena asked, thinking again that more animals might have been brought in. If the cargo was being stored so close to this warehouse, wasn't that possible?

"No." Erick shook his head, but he was so busy working, she wasn't sure if the no meant he couldn't tell or didn't have time to pause and use his mind to look. "I have figured out which building houses the forcefield generator. We need to make sure we have time to visit it on the way out."

Jelena grunted as she hefted a monkey cage down. She'd forgotten about the forcefield. If they got all of these cages loaded but then couldn't get back to the ship, this whole adventure would be for naught.

The first dog she had freed, along with several others, followed her as she carried the cage to the pod and Erick stacked it inside. She was glad that he, with his more mathematical mind, was doing the loading—he would get far more to fit than she would have.

"That's the last animal that's still alive," she said, then reluctantly convinced the free ones to go into one of the few larger cages in the pod, one that only had a couple of scared puppies for occupants. She hated to lock them back up, even for a short time, but the ride back out might be bumpy, and if the cages toppled, she didn't want any unprotected bodies in the middle.

The first one she'd freed paused to lean against her leg again, and she gave the dog a pat.

"Go on in there, girl. We'll get you to a better home soon."

"Just give me two minutes to make sure the pods are secure on the hoverboards, and I'll have this train ready to go," Erick said. "We'll ride to the building with the generator. It would probably take me about ten minutes to overload something or figure out which circuit to cut. At this point, it may be easiest if you use your explosives to simply blow up the generator." He gave her a significant look through his faceplate.

"How did you know I brought explosives large enough to blow up buildings?" She had specifically promised she'd brought *small* bombs.

"You're not as convincing as you think."

"I managed to get *you* here," she pointed out.

"Because I was *sleeping* until you sprang this on me."

"Well, you won't do that again when I'm piloting."

He snorted. "Probably not."

Another clang came from the other building.

"I'm going to take a quick peek in there," she said, since Erick was still working.

He frowned at her. "Use your mind, not your eyes. And don't get caught."

Jelena waved an acknowledgment and trotted toward the tunnel, surprised he hadn't tried to dissuade her. But then, he *had* known her since she'd been eight.

She stopped at the entrance, resting her gloved hand on the wall next to it. There was a window in the center of the door, and she could make out the outline of the tunnel that led to the next building and another door at the end. Faint illumination filtered through that window, but it didn't look like many lights were on over there. Not like in the animal warehouse. She was glad nobody was near the tunnel, or they might have wondered at the lights at their end.

Taking Erick's advice, she reached out with her mind. She sensed the vague dimensions of another large warehouse and two men in a far corner that contained counters and appliances. Refrigerators? Erick would know. Could it be some kind of station where the scientists did some of their experiments? The men were moving items into the area from a hoverboard. She didn't sense any animals or anything else living besides them. There was no reason for her to linger. Still, curiosity plucked at her mind's eye as she struggled to identify what the men were moving. Some kind of long crates, it seemed.

"Probably just food being unloaded," she muttered to herself, though the emotion she sensed from the men made her believe that wasn't the case. She couldn't read their thoughts, but they seemed uneasy about something. About what? She tried to see the world through their eyes, as she'd done with the animals, but their minds made her uncomfortable, as touching the thoughts of strangers often did, and these people seemed particularly unpleasant.

This interior door had a simple knob on it, no fancy control panel. She tried it, and it turned. Unlocked.

Jelena glanced back at Erick. He was almost ready to go, but looking through the window would be easier than trying to use her mind to see everything that was going on.

"Just a quick peek," she repeated softly and eased open the door.

She paused, fearing some alarm might go off, but nothing happened. Another clang came from the building, the men bumping one of their crates against something metal. No, that had been a hatch shutting. There was only one man in the warehouse now. The other had gone back for more cargo. There, even if the person spotted Jelena, which *wouldn't* happen, she should be able to handle one man.

She padded down the tunnel and peered through the next door's window. All she saw were floor-to-ceiling racks of boxes and equipment. She bit her lip, knowing she should go back. But it wasn't as if she and Erick could escape without detection when they were going to blow up the forcefield generator building. If the man noticed her…the detection would just come a little earlier.

The doorknob turned again, and she eased out into the warehouse. She stepped carefully, aware that sound *would* travel in here.

She made it to the end of the aisle and poked her helmet around the corner. Finally, she could see that lab area she had sensed, and she spotted the man too. He was using a hand tractor to lift something out of the long, rectangular shipping container she'd sensed. It was one of several that they had stacked by the counters. She would only stay long enough to see what he was unloading and then go back to help Erick.

Something rose out of the container, enveloped and lifted by the power of the hand tractor. The lighting wasn't very good, and the man blocked part of her view, but her breath caught when she spotted a shoe and someone's leg. A stiff leg that did not move as it—and the rest of its body—was lifted. Jelena stared, her mind slow to accept what she was seeing. The worker walked the body—the *corpse*—over to an open door on the wall. Using the hand tractor, he slid the corpse into a long, refrigerated chamber.

It's like a morgue, Jelena realized.

Were the corpses for more medical experiments? Had they been purchased legally, assuming there was such a thing, or was something shady going on in that warehouse?

The man closed the door and moved the crate somewhere outside of Jelena's angle of view.

"You check the organs before you put him away?" someone asked, the second man.

He walked into Jelena's view, and she almost scurried back, afraid he would see her. But wouldn't movement be more likely to draw his eyes? Her side of the warehouse was dark, so they shouldn't see her if she stayed still.

"He looked fine," the man with the hand tractor said, using the unit to pull another shipping container over.

"You know Radnov wets himself if we take up storage units with corpses he can't use later."

"If he wants perfect corpses, then maybe he should get them from a medical supply facility instead of buying them from gangsters."

"Yeah, *you* tell him that."

The two men worked together to open the lid of another container. Belatedly, Jelena realized she could be recording the audio and the video with her forward helmet cam. To what end, she didn't know, but she whispered a command to turn it on and record. Maybe if she could post what was going on here, both with the animals and these corpses, it would raise some awareness of the corporation and their questionable research practices. Maybe, with enough public outcry, the medical facilities buying organs from them would stop using them, and the corporation would have to change its practices.

Wishful thinking perhaps, but she recorded the men moving another corpse into a locker, this one belonging to a young woman who didn't look any older than Jelena. She hadn't seen much of the first corpse, but remembered that he had been young too. Awfully young to be dead. Gangsters, the man had said. Were they killing people for some bounty? A bounty put out and paid for by Stellacor?

The men opened a third container.

"This one has a blazer hole in her chest," one man said. "Radnov's going to be pissed that she got frozen and brought in."

"It might have missed the heart. Just put her away, and let the scientists figure it out."

"Doesn't look like the prep was done well, either. The organs are probably blocks of frozen meat by now. Going to be impossible for them to sell."

"Not our problem. We're just the dock workers."

Jelena would have scratched her head if her helmet hadn't been in the way. Why would Stellacor be selling dead people's organs when they could grow their own from stem cells? More demand than supply? Did growing them from scratch take a long time? Were they having people *killed* so they could get young, healthy organs to sell when their own labs couldn't meet the demand?

Jelena? Erick's soft voice sounded in her mind instead of over her comm.

Yes? She answered the same way, not wanting to speak aloud with the men over there. She kept recording.

Your new friends are waiting for you. He managed to sound dry even when speaking telepathically, and she was sure he knew exactly where she was.

I'm coming. I just—

An alarm blared, making her jump.

"What the—" one of the men blurted as they both spun, looking around.

Jelena jerked her head back, wincing. She couldn't tell if they had seen her. She ran back toward the door, trying to keep her footfalls light, though the wailing of that alarm ought to drown them out.

"Hurry," Erick said, over the comm this time. "That's for us. The natives have realized we're here."

CHAPTER THREE

Jelena sprinted through the tunnel to the animal warehouse, then whirled back toward the door. She yanked out her multitool and flicked on the laser cutter. She melted the unsophisticated lock on the knob, hoping that would delay pursuit, and raced over to join Erick. He was already on his thrust bike, the inner airlock hatch open. As soon as he saw her, he flew into the airlock.

The alarm wailed just as loudly in this building, and she could feel the animals' fear. They were locked into three pods now, sealed inside to protect them from the lack of atmosphere outside. It was dark, and they were afraid. Jelena tried to soothe them as she flung herself astride her bike, nearly knocking her staff out of its holder. One of the pods and hoverboards was magnetically attached to the back of her bike. Two trailed after Erick's.

"Sorry," Jelena blurted. "But I had to see. They're doing something—"

"Later," Erick said curtly, tapping the panel. "We'll have to go out one at a time. There's not room in the lock for both bikes and their pods. Give me one of your bombs. I'll try to blow the forcefield while the lock is cycling for you. Just push this to activate it."

"Got it," she said, hurrying to dig out one of the bombs, though she hated the idea of separating.

Erick and his two pods disappeared behind the hatch, and a *thunk-kert-hunk* sounded as the airlock activated.

"It wasn't your snooping," Erick said from inside, his voice coming over her helmet comm.

"What?"

"They found the androids, and someone thought to look at the security footage. That's when they sounded the alarm."

"Footage of our fight?" Jelena asked, sensing Erick growing farther away. He was outside the building now, flying away.

"Yes. They may know what we are."

What we are. Such a strange way to say it. As if they weren't human.

"Superheroes in unicorn underwear?" she suggested.

Erick didn't answer.

Jelena hit the button to open the inner hatch. It hadn't taken long for the airlock to work. Maybe she could still catch up to him and help.

A bang and a thunderous clang sounded behind her. The door being thrown—or blown—open.

Cursing, she flew into the airlock. She couldn't see much behind her with the hoverboard and pod attached to her bike, but she sensed four people racing through the warehouse. *Armed* people. The pod could withstand being hit with small pieces of space debris, but she had no idea if it could endure blazer fire.

Once inside the airlock, Jelena tapped the same buttons that Erick had. The hatch did not respond promptly, as if it had to think about whether it wanted to obey or not.

The sprinting men were already halfway to her. One lifted a rifle.

Jelena flung the image of an animal into his mind, a livid wolf with a mouth full of fangs, the creature leaping for his throat, angry at being part of some lab experiment. The man shrieked, dropped his weapon, and raised his hands to his throat. He whirled toward where he believed the attack was coming from. His colleagues crashed into him.

"What are you *doing*?" one blurted, tripping and flailing.

The hatch finally shut, and Jelena didn't hear the response. She bounced on her bike seat, silently urging the airlock to hurry up and vent the atmosphere. She hit another button, trying to override it and open the outer hatch without waiting. The controls bleated a discontented noise at her. She growled. This hadn't taken so long for Erick, had it?

A thud sounded behind her, and she leaned forward, eager to race out. But the outer hatch didn't open. A squealing of metal came from the one behind her. She sensed the men right on the other side. Damn, had they overridden the controls?

Whimpers and plaintive howls came from within the pod. The walls muffled the sounds, but Jelena still heard them, and they tugged at her heart. She couldn't let those brutal men recapture the animals.

The hatch was wrenched open an inch, light slashing into the dim airlock. She dug into her satchel, pulled out one of the bombs, and thumbed open the protective cover over the detonator. The hatch squealed and opened a couple more inches.

She slid off her bike and moved around the pod. Maneuvering in the chamber, which had seemed delightfully large before the pods had been inflated, was cramped and she could barely reach the hatch.

The butt of a rifle thumped against the hatch, visible through the slim opening.

"Throw your weapons out and put your hands up," someone ordered.

Gladly. Jelena tapped in a fifteen-second delay and pressed the detonator. She turned the bomb sideways, thrust it through the gap, and tried to throw it into the warehouse, far enough away that the explosion wouldn't threaten her or the animals. Unfortunately, it must have struck one of the men, because a thud sounded, followed by a clank as it fell to the floor right outside the hatch.

Men swore and fled away from it. Jelena hammered at the control panel, trying in vain to get that hatch to shut—and the outer one to open. But the guards must have jammed it in their attempt to override it.

Jelena grabbed her staff and closed her eyes to concentrate. Her first thought was to hurl the bomb deep into the warehouse, but that would leave her still needing to find a way out. With her staff's help, she created a barrier similar to the one that had deflected the android's blazer fire. She curved and stretched it, trying to turn it into something akin to the dome-shaped forcefield that protected the compound.

Jelena? Erick asked into her mind, surprising her and almost making her lose her concentration. *Where are you? I was able to get the forcefield down.*

Not now, she thought back, aware of the last second ticking away on the bomb.

An explosion roared and brilliant light flared inside the warehouse. Jelena squinted and gasped as something hammered into her shield. She threw all her concentration into maintaining the barrier, holding the staff out in front of her as if it alone could deny the power of the bomb. A whoosh of air sounded, and a draft tugged at her spacesuit. Abruptly, all sound halted. The light remained, burning red through her closed eyelids, but then it, too, disappeared. Pieces of the hatch—or was the entire building falling apart?—beat down on her shield.

The light finally lessened, and Jelena risked opening her eyes. The hatch was gone, as was the ceiling of the airlock and part of the ceiling of the warehouse too. She wasn't sure where the men were. Had they made it back to the tunnel? Or were they stranded outside of the structure, exposed to the cold harshness of space? Maybe they'd died in the explosion.

That grim thought filled her with horror. This had been about rescuing animals, not killing people. She and Erick had joked about whether or not this was a crime, but surely killing people would be considered a crime anywhere in the system. By the three suns, she hoped they had gotten to safety.

The rear hatch was contorted, halfway ripped off its hinges. Jelena climbed back on her thrust bike and nudged it into motion, eyeing the pod as she flew out, making sure her barrier had indeed protected it and that it wasn't damaged. It didn't seem to be. She could sense the animals inside, terrified but still alive.

I promise your lives will be better soon, she whispered into their minds, even though they couldn't understand words. *You won't have to fear anything anymore.*

"Jelena!" Erick barked over her helmet comm.

After the silence, the syllables boomed into her brain.

"I'm right here." She looked both ways, trying to locate him as she noted the carnage her explosive had caused. The entire back half of the warehouse had been destroyed. Wrecked cages lay everywhere, scattered among warped pieces of metal and plastic, some still falling slowly in the low gravity. "Where are—"

"Look out!"

His words came with an image, two compact spaceships zipping across the compound and toward her position. Though Jelena could not see them yet, she trusted Erick's warning and gunned her thrust bike. She flew toward the back wall, lifting the handlebars to head over it.

As soon as she rose above the level of the buildings, she spotted the ships. They were flying straight toward her, and she groaned, knowing they would be far faster than her bike. She cleared the wall, but she would never make it back to the canyon before they caught up with her.

"I could use some help, Erick," she said, turning toward the canyon. The pod, bumping and wobbling behind her, blocked her view of the ships, but she sensed them back there.

Erick came into view ahead of her, the other two pods trailing behind his bike. For some reason, he was staying still, looking back toward her instead of fleeing.

Jelena opened her mouth, intending to tell him to get going, to split up so their pursuers wouldn't know who to chase, but he pointed behind her. She had to veer to the side to see around the pod and back to the ships. She was in time to witness one pitching to the side and crashing into the other one. They hadn't been shielded, and she imagined she could hear the warping of metal, even if there was no sound out here. The crash took both of them to the ground.

"Did you cause that, Erick? If so, you're my hero." Jelena pointed her bike toward the canyon again.

"Does that mean you're going to get me a cape?"

"I'm already buying you *Striker Odyssey* cards. Isn't that enough?"

"Seems paltry for what we've been through tonight." He turned his bike to match her speed as she caught up with him.

"I *am* on an allowance, you know. My funds are limited."

"That's disappointing."

"Tell me about it. Maybe we can tie a sheet around your neck, and it'll be *like* a cape."

Erick's helmet twisted to the side, and he didn't answer. Jelena followed his gaze and spotted someone in a spacesuit running after them. Arms pumping, the person carried a huge blazer rifle and an even huger second weapon. It looked like a grenade launcher. Jelena couldn't believe how fast the figure's legs churned, covering the ground with great bounds.

"That's a person. I don't want to hurt—" Erick waved back in the direction of the crash.

Maybe androids had been flying those ships, so he hadn't hesitated to damage them. Jelena thought of the men in the warehouse, the ones she wasn't sure had escaped the explosion.

"I understand," she said. "I'm sure we can outrun him."

Already, the dark slash of the canyon was visible ahead. Less than two miles, and they could descend to the ship.

"Her," Erick said.

"What?"

"That's a woman."

Jelena glanced at the figure again, awestruck by its—*her*—speed. "You're sure it's not an android?" she asked, even though that wouldn't have made sense. An android did not need to wear a spacesuit.

"I bet she's a cyborg. Look at how she's keeping up with us." He looked down at his speedometer. "That's amazing."

"She's falling behind," Jelena said. "We'll make it. As soon as we get in, we'll take off. We can sort out the animals later."

"There's another ship taking off from the compound," Erick said, his voice going grim again.

"We just have to make it inside. The *Snapper* is armored like an assault tank."

"With the speed of a turtle."

"A fast turtle. We'll be fine." Jelena hoped she was right.

"Zigzag," Erick said. "The ship is coming up behind us. A human pilot."

"You may have to crash it anyway. If we get caught, those people aren't going to hesitate to kill us." She remembered the way those androids had shot to kill as she obeyed Erick's order and picked an erratic route across the pockmarked terrain.

"Of course not. We broke into their facility and stole something." Erick sounded like he regretted going along with her now.

Jelena clenched her jaw. She might regret that this hadn't gone better, but she couldn't regret choosing to come. Those people deserved some kind of karmic revenge for working for this vile corporation, damn it.

A blast of white energy slammed into the ground scant meters behind them. Moon rocks hurtled up, pelting the back of the pod and flying over Jelena's head. She'd already been zigzagging, but she made her route even more erratic and unpredictable.

She glanced back, spotting the ship right behind her—and the smoking crater that blast had left in the moon. It was as large as the natural ones caused by asteroid collisions. That had been an energy cannon. She had few delusions about creating a barrier that could withstand a direct hit from one of those.

In addition to the ship, the cyborg was still chasing them. But she had fallen back. Jelena might have laughed because she had to run around the massive crater the ship had made, but all of her humor had fled. The cyborg could still be a threat once they reached the canyon. On foot, she might catch them while they were loading their cargo. She could fight them, delay them while the ship came down and fired on the *Snapper*.

"We'll go in different directions when we go into the canyon," Jelena said. "You go straight to our ship and get your cargo in. I'll try to lead them away and then catch up with you."

Another e-cannon blast interrupted Erick's reply. It slammed into the ground just in front of them, tearing away the edge of the canyon, and flinging rock into the air.

Erick went left, and Jelena veered right. If they had been riding on wheeled bikes, they both would have crashed into the new hole torn into the ground.

Without hesitating, Jelena flew over the rim and down, streaking along the wall, almost scraping the pod on the rocks. Reminded of her precious cargo, she gave herself more room.

The ship flew over the edge right behind her. She dove for the bottom of the canyon, whipping past cliffs and piles of rubble, searching for terrain she might use to slow her pursuer. The ship flew over her and fired down from above. She veered sharply, barely avoiding an energy blast that streaked past her. It slammed into a rubble pile at the bottom of the canyon, and the dust of pulverized rocks exploded into the air.

She flew into the cloud, using the camouflage it provided to turn around. Erick would only need a minute to get his cargo and himself into the hold, and then he would need her there to pilot. She couldn't let herself get drawn too far away. She couldn't let herself get killed, either.

Gunning the engine, calling for all the power the bike could muster, she sped along the bottom of the canyon, back in the direction of the *Snapper*. With some satisfaction, she glimpsed the pursuing ship still going the other way. Sadly, it soon realized it wasn't following her anymore, and it did a loop, flying up, then upside-down, and finally twisting and diving back down into the canyon. The ship was slower than her bike, at least in maneuvering in the tight passage, and she'd gained time. She hoped it was enough.

Up ahead, she spotted the ledge where the *Snapper* rested. Erick stood outside, waving his staff as if he were a ground guide ready to help her park. She would have preferred he already be safe in the ship, but his bike and the two pods weren't in sight, so he must have already gotten them inside.

Before Jelena reached the ledge, another e-cannon blast streaked through the air, missing her and the pod by less than a foot. She could feel the heat from it through her suit.

She glanced back in indignation that those people were firing upon their own lab animals. Didn't they want them back? She reached out with her senses, trying to find the pilot. There were three people in the ship's navigation compartment. There, that was the pilot. A woman flying with intent as her cohort prepared to fire again. The pilot was concentrating hard, knowing that flying through the canyon took precision. One mistake, and she could wreck their ship.

Jelena was almost to the *Snapper*, but knew she and Erick would be easy targets when they were out on that ledge. The ship was gaining ground now, and it would be able to fire on them easily.

As she'd done in the warehouse, Jelena thrust an image into the woman's mind, one of a ferocious lion springing to attack her. Claws slashed toward her throat, and a huge fanged maw snapped for her face. Jelena could feel the woman's surprise and fear, sensed the way she jerked to the side in her seat, her hands falling away from the controls for a few seconds.

Jelena had reached the ledge, and she hoped her distraction was enough. Even if all that happened was that the pursuing ship ended up flying past without firing, that would help.

As she sailed straight for the open cargo hatch, she saw Erick still standing outside of the *Snapper*, his helmet tilted toward the ship. Was he, too, trying to affect the pilot? Or, knowing him, some mechanical part of the ship?

Something dropped down in front of Jelena before she reached the hatch, and she jerked back, veering at the last second. It was someone in a spacesuit—the cyborg. She'd jumped all the way down from the ledge above, landing on her feet.

Instead of springing after Jelena, she leaped the other way and slammed into Erick.

Growling, Jelena hurried to get the bike and the pod into the airlock, reversing the thrusters at the last moment so she wouldn't crash into the interior hatch. She bounced off it anyway, the jolt almost pitching her off the bike. She half leaped, half fell off it, grabbing her staff as she landed. She squeezed past the pod and ran out to help Erick.

The cyborg flew past the hatch as Jelena stepped out. Erick was in a crouch, his staff held out with one hand, but he gripped his side with the other, and she could feel his pain. Had he been punched? Shot? The cyborg tumbled toward the ledge and would have gone over, but somehow, she twisted in the air and caught the edge as she fell.

Jelena ran over, not sure whether she meant to knock the woman the rest of the way off or just make sure she couldn't get up. It was more than a hundred feet to the bottom. She had no idea if that would be a killing fall in this kind of gravity, but they couldn't let the woman keep attacking them or board the *Snapper*, not when their pursuer—

Jelena jerked her gaze up, abruptly remembering the other ship. Had her mental attack caused the pilot to divert?

No. She stumbled back from the ledge. The ship was coming straight toward them, as if it meant to kamikaze crash into the *Snapper*. But it was coming in too low. It slammed into the ledge, right below the cyborg dangling from her fingertips.

The ground quaked, and Jelena wobbled, feeling like she was riding a wave. She envisioned the entire ledge collapsing, taking her, Erick, and the *Snapper* down into the canyon with it. She started to spin toward the ship, wanting to hurry in and pilot them away, but somehow, the cyborg had managed to hang on. She pulled herself up, one knee finding the top of the crumbling ledge as rocks fell away to either side of her.

Jelena ran toward her, raising her staff. She hated the idea of attacking someone trying to get her feet under her, but the cyborg had hurt Erick, and Jelena had no doubt she would kill both of them if she could. She rammed the tip of her staff toward the chest of the spacesuit.

Even off-balance, the cyborg snapped a hand out, catching the staff in her gloved palm. As hard as Jelena had thrust, the other woman barely moved. If it had been a normal staff, the cyborg might have ripped it from her hands, flung it over the side, and leaped at Jelena, but the Starseer weapon crackled with energy at the contact. Lightning raced up the cyborg's arm, and her helmet jerked back. Unlike the androids, she could feel pain. Jelena couldn't hear her scream, but she saw her foe's contorted features— her agony—through her faceplate.

While the cyborg stood there, her body locked in pain, the rest of the ledge crumbled. She disappeared from sight, and Jelena almost tumbled into the canyon, too, as rocks shifted beneath her feet.

She threw herself into an awkward backward roll, angling toward the hatch. Erick grabbed her with one hand, helping her to her feet. As they raced into the airlock, the image of that cyborg—that *woman*—screaming behind her faceplate filled Jelena's mind. Other people might have died, but she hadn't seen their faces, their pain.

The lock cycled, and Erick pushed her bike and the pod into the hold where his already waited. With air and atmosphere inside the ship, she could hear the alarmed cries of the animals again. She needed to tend to them, and she needed to get the *Snapper* out of here before Stellacor sent more pursuers, but she struggled to move her feet, to get that woman's face out of her mind.

"Jelena." Erick grabbed her arm and pulled her toward NavCom. "Time to fly. I'll unload everything. Try to get us out of here through the canyon. If there's any chance that they haven't identified our ship yet…well, it would be good to keep it that way."

"Yes," she said, his words sinking in. "I will. I am, but Erick? Can you take your bike and go out and check on that woman while I get us ready?"

"What? The cyborg?" He gaped at her, still gripping his side with one hand.

"Yes, and if that ship is down there, and there are people alive there, too…we should help them. At least drop them off where they can get medical help. We didn't—this wasn't supposed to go like this." She swallowed, shaking her head, willing him to understand.

He groaned, but turned back toward his bike. "Fine, but get up there and get the engine powered up. And then save me if I get myself in trouble doing this."

"I will."

"I mean it," he said, slinging his leg over his bike and flying into the airlock again. "I want *major* saving. Guns, blazer fire, explosions."

"Definitely." She managed a quick smile and raced across the crowded cargo hold deck toward NavCom.

The deck quaked, the rest of the ledge threatening to crumble under them, and she lost that smile. She banged her shoulder on the hatchway as she jumped into NavCom. She slid into the pilot's seat, made sure Erick had gotten out and wasn't near the thrusters, then powered everything up. He was flying over the ledge and down into the canyon to investigate.

As Jelena lifted off, she checked the sensors, expecting to see the wrecked ship lying down in the canyon under tons of rock. But it hadn't been completely destroyed. It was flying out of the canyon a mile away, only one of its thrusters working. She thought it might turn back toward them for another attack, but it limped away, toward the facility.

Jelena flew away from the ledge, hovering in the canyon while she waited for Erick. Rocks continued to crumble away from what remained of their landing spot, bouncing down to the boulder-littered floor. She shifted the *Snapper's* cameras and spotted Erick on his bike and also the cyborg woman. She lay on the ground, a boulder pinning her legs. She wasn't moving.

Jelena grimaced, fearing they were too late.

"She'd try to kill us if she was alive and we brought her on board," she muttered, trying to tell herself that it was for the best if the cyborg was dead or if they left her there, but she didn't truly want someone's death on her hands. On her conscience.

Erick flew low over the woman and stopped his bike beside her. Jelena hadn't removed her helmet yet, and his voice crackled over its comm.

"I think she's alive, but her faceplate is broken. If she's losing oxygen, she'll die in minutes if we leave her here."

"Bring her on board," Jelena said.

"She's not going to be grateful like your animals and lick your hand and let you rub her ears."

"Bring her anyway."

Erick grumbled under his breath and used his staff to lever the boulder off the cyborg. In regular gravity, he would have struggled, but the big rock tumbled away. He hefted the woman onto the back of his bike.

"I really think I deserve more than a sheet-cape for all my efforts," he said.

"You're probably right. I'll throw in a blanket too."

Jelena checked the sensors again as he flew his bike toward the *Snapper*. The damaged ship had landed and didn't look like it could fly back to bother them, but she wouldn't be surprised if the facility sent another round of pursuers out.

"I'm in," Erick said as soon as the outer hatch shut. "Let's get out of here before repercussions catch up with us."

"Gladly," Jelena said, and took the *Snapper* through the canyon, as Erick had suggested. She, too, doubted there was any way the Stellacor facility hadn't identified them yet, but maybe they would get lucky, and those repercussions he spoke of would never find them.

She removed her helmet and pushed a hand through her sweaty hair, fearing that was highly unlikely.

CHAPTER FOUR

A couple of workers in overalls drove forklifts through the *Snapper's* wide cargo hatch, angling toward the shipping containers that held their goods. One of them cast curious looks toward the dogs and pigs that Jelena was erecting pens around.

She wanted to let the animals wander freely after the imprisonment they had suffered, but after Erick had shooed monkeys out of engineering, she had reluctantly agreed that some manner of containing them would be wise. The monkeys now had large netted enclosures, though they seemed disappointed by the lack of branches and things to swing from. Once these men had their cargo unloaded, Jelena could fly the animals somewhere nice, maybe a shelter that would help find homes for the domesticated ones, and perhaps the monkeys could be left on a tropical island somewhere. From her mental interactions with them, she'd gotten the impression that they'd originally been captured rather than bred in captivity.

The first dog she had freed was trundling around after her, leaning against Jelena's leg whenever she paused, and looking up at her with soulful brown eyes. Her soft brown and white fur was matted with blood and grime, but she would be a cutie once she healed and had a bath. She seemed quite certain that the dog pen was not for her.

Most of the animals, monkeys aside, were too exhausted to care about being fenced in. They'd had water and a meal, both of which had delighted them, but now, copious napping was going on. The flexible fencing wouldn't keep any of the animals in if they were truly determined to escape, but she believed she'd conveyed to them that it was their new safe place and that they should stay in it for now.

Erick alternated between pacing and helping the men unload their cargo. He'd changed into his black Starseer robe, which should have made him look mysterious and wise, but his agitation came through. She knew he was worried that they had only flown a couple of hours and were just on the other side of the moon from the research facility. Not far, if pursuit had been sent. She didn't know if Erick still intended to go out and meet his friends that night. Jelena would prefer to get off the moon—and not visit again for a long, long time.

"We could unload our cyborg guest here," Erick said.

He'd gotten her broken helmet off and anesthetized her while Jelena had been flying them over here, the latter more so she wouldn't wake up and attack them than because she'd seemed to be in great pain. Jelena had gone down to check on her once she'd been able to turn on the autopilot, and the medical scanner hadn't reported any damage to her internal organs. She did have a fracture in her skull and two broken leg bones.

If she'd had more time and less to worry about, Jelena could have mended the bones with her powers, but she'd opted for programming the nanobots in the med kit to do the job instead. Thanks to Leonidas's insistence, both Erick and Jelena had received some mundane medical training as well as their Starseer training. One had to be self-sufficient when out on a freighter, far between planets.

"Is there a hospital here?" Jelena asked.

Even though she believed their patient would survive, she didn't like the idea of dumping her out in some alley. Gizmoshi was a series of connected domes and stations built into the light side of the moon, and though the Alliance had a government presence, she'd heard the mafia families were quite active, and that it wasn't a good place to be penniless and down on one's luck.

"Uhm, there must be something," Erick said. "We'd probably have to pay to drop her off at one though."

And neither of them was rolling in riches. Right.

"Maybe we should wait until she wakes up and ask her what she wants," Jelena said.

"I'd have to stop drugging her then."

"That might be the polite thing to do."

"She could try to kill me if she wakes up."

"I can go in and talk to her," Jelena said.

"Oh, she'll definitely try to kill you."

"Me?" Jelena touched her chest.

"You're the one who jabbed her in the chest and knocked her off that ledge."

"Actually, that's not what happened at all." Jelena remembered the way the cyborg had caught her staff, how she'd *easily* caught the staff. Even though the tool's power had surprised the woman, Jelena doubted it would have caused her to fall if the rocks hadn't crumbled away under her feet.

"I'm sure you'll have fun explaining it to her," Erick said. "While her hand is wrapped around your neck."

Hm, maybe they could foist her off on Xing's people. A bonus delivery along with their cargo. If the woman lost her job at the medical facility, she could stay and work for them. Surely a cyborg could heft boxes as well as a forklift.

A beep came from a panel, and Jelena froze, dread filling her. It was just a comm alert, but what if it was the head of security from Stellacor? Or what if the corporation had contacted the law enforcement agency in Gizmoshi, and troops were surrounding the *Snapper* even now?

That possibility seemed so likely that Jelena ran to the panel and called up the exterior camera displays before looking to see who was contacting them.

"Trouble?" Erick asked, frowning over at her.

The two workers simply continued with their forklifts, removing their cargo. A couple more men from their outfit were on the loading dock outside, but she didn't see anyone in uniform and nobody with guns. Good.

"I'm not sure yet." Jelena checked the comm message. When she saw who it was, the dread didn't disappear. It just turned to a different kind of dread. "It's Mom," she told Erick.

"Definitely trouble, then." He smirked. *He* looked relieved.

Sure, because he hadn't concocted the plan and wasn't the reason there were animals roaming the deck, animals she had to find homes for before she rendezvoused with the *Nomad*. Either that, or she had to explain to her parents what she had done. Was it possible they had already found out, and that was why Mom was calling? If they *hadn't* found out, was it possible Jelena could avoid telling them about it? Ever?

"Maybe Leonidas can come deal with our cyborg problem," Erick said.

"I don't think people automatically get along with each other, just because they're cyborgs," Jelena said. "Besides, a woman cyborg has to have come out of the Alliance program. And you know how all of the empire hasn't quite rubbed off Leonidas yet."

They hadn't had a reason to discuss Prince Thorian, the only surviving heir of the defunct Sarellian Empire, that often of late, but Leonidas got a wistful look in his eyes whenever his name came up, as if he still hoped that the empire might be reestablished somehow. As if the Alliance would disappear after ten years of unopposed rule.

Jelena barely remembered life under the empire, but to hear Mom talk, it had only been good for those in positions of power. Most of the rest of the system had either lived in fear, afraid to talk freely, or had buried their heads, immersing themselves in the various entertainment options provided and not worrying much about politics. It wasn't unusual to still run into disturbingly vacant-eyed people who'd had their memories and thought processes "improved" after sharing their unflattering opinions of the empire in the wrong crowds.

"At the least, his neck is sturdy enough to withstand having cyborg fingers wrapped around it," Erick said.

"The way you keep talking about that, I'm wondering if it happened when I wasn't looking."

"Not to my neck specifically." Erick hiked up his robe enough to show his underwear and his bare torso where a dark purple bruise spread across his abdomen. "That's from where she barely grazed me with a punch. It's too bad Stellacor is going to put me on their dead-to-us list, because I could probably use a few new organs."

"She fell off a cliff, and you're whining about a punch? I may downgrade you from superhero to useful-helper status."

"Do I still get to wear a sheet like a cape?"

"If it makes you feel important."

One of the forklift men whistled, and Erick lowered his robe, blushing. Apparently, he'd forgotten they weren't alone in the cargo hold.

"I always figured the Starseer community shunned us because of my grandfather," Jelena said, "but it's possible they just don't consider us suitable representatives."

"Why, because I showed my bare legs to some dock workers?"

"And they liked it." Jelena patted the dog, who was once again leaning against her leg, then turned toward NavCom. She had better find out what her mother wanted. If she didn't answer right away, and if the *Nomad* had already dropped off its own cargo, the ship might head to Alpha 17 to check up. "I'll see what Mom wants."

"Are you going to tell her about this?" Erick waved toward the half-built animal pen.

"It depends on whether she already knows."

"That would not be good. It would mean we'd been reported to some local news outfit and that Stellacor has definitely identified our ship. I bet they can afford to hire bounty hunters."

Jelena gave him an exasperated look. She was definitely downgrading him from superhero.

"And what do you mean we're shunned?" he asked, following her into the corridor. "Who told you that?"

"Haven't you ever wondered why Abelardus and Young-hee are the only Starseers that have talked to us since we started training with Grandpa Stan?"

"That's not true. I don't think." He scratched his head.

"No? Who do you chat with that's part of the community?"

"Well, no one, but I haven't really tried."

Jelena slid into her seat in NavCom and peered into her stallion mug. Empty. She grabbed one of her drink mixes from the pouch by her seat, dumped it in, and took it to the water dispenser in the mess hall. She told herself she wasn't dawdling. She was making sure she was suitably hydrated for a talk with her parents.

"When we were kids," she said, raising her voice to continue the conversation since Erick had stayed in NavCom, "remember how many Starseers were interested in us?"

"They were interested in *you.* Because of your supposedly superior genes. They wanted to breed you with Prince Thorian, who is also supposed to be from Saint Alcyone's line, so you two could make powerful Starseer babies." Judging by the noise Erick made, he found the idea disgusting.

"So I've been told," Jelena said, "but nobody has suggested anything of the sort lately. If my genes are so great, wouldn't you think I'd get some other offers for, uhm, breeding?"

She didn't particularly want those offers, especially if someone was only interested in her for baby-making purposes, but she often wished to meet other Starseers. Not to date, marry, or *breed* with them, but because she'd like to talk to more people like her, more people who understood what it was like to be different. She loved Mom and Leonidas very much, but neither of them had Starseer powers, so neither could truly understand her world. Her real dad, Jonah, had been the one to have them, though he'd kept it a secret from Mom the whole time they had been married. Mom carried the gene mutations, but she'd never developed the powers, something that was true for most people with the altered genes. Grandpa understood, but he was a little weird. She loved him, but she couldn't imagine having a chat about fitting in with a man who wore chaps and a cowboy hat on a spaceship. She longed for more Starseer friends around her own age.

"I'm concerned that you sound sad about that," Erick said.

"I'm just suggesting that we've been marked as *personae non gratae.*"

"Are eighteen-year-olds supposed to use words like that? Am I going to have to start consulting my earstar to understand what you're saying?"

"You barely wear your earstar, so that would be tough."

"Because Roxy nags me and won't let me download a less motherly AI."

"You *can* just use the voice commands without activating the AI, you know." With her caffeinated berry drink mixed, Jelena slid into the pilot's seat again. She couldn't think of any more legitimate reasons to delay chatting with Mom. "But you probably like being nagged by her, since your real mom is on the other side of the system and can't do it."

"Uh huh. Speaking of nagging, don't you need to talk to *your* mom?"

"I'm working on it."

"You just push that button there." He plopped down into the co-pilot's seat. His expression made it clear he intended to ensure she made the call. Now, who was nagging?

"Shouldn't you be down in the cargo hold, making sure those dock workers don't take anything that doesn't belong to them?"

"There's nothing else down there except for malnourished animals. *Most* people wouldn't steal those."

"I didn't steal them. I liberated them." Jelena pushed the button he'd sarcastically indicated, and the *Star Nomad's* information popped up on the holodisplay. She frowned over at him as she tapped the floating call button. "Don't say anything about it to them, please."

"Mm," he said neutrally. Or was that disagreeably?

Jelena looked toward the display, pretending she wouldn't make more pleas, but with her mind, she reached out to the cargo hold, to some of the more vocal animals down there. She made a few bargains with the monkeys in particular, promising she would find them some bananas if they assisted her. Unlike the dogs, cats, and pigs, they hadn't been impressed by the meat-flavored ration bars or the pet treats. Surely, somewhere in Gizmoshi, someone grew fruit in a hydroponic garden. There might even be some greenhouses. This side of the moon got plenty of sun, after all.

As the comm attempted to get through to the *Nomad*—Jelena was surprised it was taking this long since the freighter shouldn't be far away, just on another of Aldrin's moons—boisterous hoots and howls arose from the cargo hold.

Jelena frowned over her shoulder, then looked at Erick. "Will you check on that?"

His eyes narrowed suspiciously.

"Please?" She smiled and attempted to make her eyes look wholesome and without guile or deceit. Oddly, she always found that a challenge.

He grumbled and walked out. She locked the hatch after he disappeared. It was a symbolic gesture only, since he could thwart the lock with a flick of his mind, but she felt justified. She ought to be able to talk to her parents in private.

Another long minute passed, and Jelena started to wonder what could have happened in the ten minutes since Mom first commed. Maybe she had gone down to the moon, and the call was being routed to her.

Finally, her mother, Captain Alisa Marchenko, appeared on the display, the familiar drab gray of the *Nomad's* NavCom cabin behind her. Her auburn hair, several shades lighter than Jelena's, was pulled back in a braid. If there was any gray in it, Mom hid it with dye or hair mods. For some reason, she looked a little older than usual, though, with the slight lines at the corners of her eyes noticeable today.

"Hi, Mom," Jelena said, smiling brightly, hoping she wasn't the cause for the concerned look. She tried to portray that there wasn't anything out of the ordinary here, nope. Fortunately, the closed hatch muffled the sounds of the monkeys. When she got a moment, she would let them know that they had earned their bananas and need not continue.

"Hi, sweetie." Mom also smiled, but it appeared forced.

Jelena braced herself to answer questions about the trip.

"I have some…news," Mom said. "Leonidas is fine right now, so don't worry. I mean, he's stable."

"Uh?" Jelena asked, for the first time grasping that this might not be about her.

Mom took a deep breath. "He had a heart attack. We're heading to Arkadius where he'll have the best treatment at the best facility there. Dr. Tiang pointed us to a colleague of his, someone with experience with aging cyborgs. Dr. Horvald worked with the imperial cyborg program for years and reported directly to the emperor. He was one of their best until he defected from the empire during the war. Leonidas will be in good hands." She nodded, as if to reassure herself.

"Treatment?" Jelena mouthed, barely registering the information about the doctor. "Heart attack? But Dad's not old. And he's…" She groped in the air with her hands, feeling too stunned to articulate her thoughts. How could Leonidas have a heart attack? He was fifty. That wasn't that old. Grandpa was older than that. And Leonidas was so fit. He didn't have any fat on him, and his arms were bigger than most people's thighs.

"I know," Mom said, that forced smile coming out again. She was trying to be encouraging, motherly, but there were tears standing in her eyes now. "It surprised us all. We're lucky your grandfather was here."

"Yes, Grandpa can heal, right? He's the one who taught me the basics. Can't he fix it?"

"He's the reason Leonidas is in a stable condition right now, but he can't...It's not like a broken bone. The empire fu—" Anger flashed in Mom's eyes, and Jelena doubted the next words were the first ones that had come to her mind. "They dithered around a lot with his insides when they were turning him into a super soldier. He always knew, but...well, this isn't the end. We'll get him a new heart. A new everything if we have to. Screw the empire." The last words came out savagely, and she looked away, dashing her sleeve across her eyes before turning back to the camera.

Jelena felt moisture gathering in her own eyes, both because of her mother's distress and because she was worried about Leonidas. He might not be her real father, but he'd been one in all but blood for the last ten years, and she couldn't have asked for a better man to be there for her mother. And her.

She wished she were talking to Mom in person. Then she could have read her thoughts, her emotions. She wouldn't be relying on a picture on a holodisplay for cues. Was Leonidas *really* stable? Or was Mom trying to protect her? To keep her from worrying?

"Can I see him?" Jelena asked.

"He's resting now, but I'll have him send you a message later, or you can talk live if we're still close enough. Like I said, we're heading to Arkadius right away, and depending on what Dr. Horvald says during the tests, we may need to schedule a surgery for as soon as possible. Please meet us there once you've delivered your cargo. I know Leonidas will want you there. Erick too."

As soon as possible. That sounded ominous, and Jelena wondered again if Mom was telling her everything. She wiped her eyes. "We'll be there."

The animals could always stay aboard until after they made sure Leonidas would be fine. Her gut lurched as she thought of them. Of them and of her attack against Stellacor, a company that made—or stole—organs for people who needed them. What if Leonidas needed one of their hearts and because of her actions, there would be a shortage? No, it shouldn't work that way. Besides, she hadn't damaged anything except that animal warehouse. And some ships. Still, she couldn't help but wonder if this was some karmic retribution for her mission. But surely, the gods or the stars or whatever was out there couldn't want to back such an evil corporation.

"Thank you, sweetie," Mom said. "Is everything all right there? Delivery going smoothly?"

"Xing's people are picking up the cargo now." A monkey hooted, the sound muffled by the hatch. Jelena kept her face neutral and hoped it wasn't audible over the pickup. "Everything's fine here," she said, glad she'd lured Erick away from NavCom. This wasn't the time to give her mother something else to worry about.

"Good." Mom looked over her shoulder and lifted a hand toward someone out in the corridor. "I better go back to check on him. Take care of yourself, and please hurry along. Leonidas gets cranky without Erick to yell at, you know."

"He doesn't yell. He just looks sternly at Erick, and Erick melts into an apologetic puddle, feeling guilty for every sinful thought he's ever had."

"Leonidas's stern look has caused a lot of people to turn into puddles. Or leave them." For the first time, Mom's smile held a trace of her usual irreverent humor.

"Ew, are you being gross?"

"I wouldn't think of it." Mom reached for the comm, and Jelena expected a *goodbye*, but her hand paused. "Oh, Jelena? Have you heard from Thorian lately?"

"Thor?" she asked, puzzled by the topic shift. "He hasn't written or commed for years. The last time was when he was sixteen, and he said he was super busy with his training."

Jelena shrugged, as if the lack of communication didn't bother her. It *shouldn't*. Just because they had been friends when they had been eight and ten didn't mean they were supposed to stay friends into adulthood. They hadn't even spent time together in person since she'd been eleven, his instructors had given him a week-long break, and they'd been able to arrange a horse-riding trip on Upsilon Seven. He'd never been as enamored with the animals as she had, and he'd been talking about annoyingly grownup stuff the whole time, military strategy and the politics of the system. She'd suspected he'd been bored by hanging out with someone who still preferred talking about kid stuff.

Even if that hadn't been true, she'd wondered a few times if Thor had been told by the other Starseers, those training him and any others he'd met, that Jelena and Erick were to be shunned, and if that might have more to do with his silence than differing interests. He'd seemed a little grumpy and distant even during those last couple of years that he *had* been keeping in touch.

"All right, good," Mom said.

"Good?" Jelena asked, still puzzled. Or maybe more puzzled.

"If he does get in touch, let us know, please. Let *me* know. Leonidas doesn't need to get wrapped up in anything…political right now." Her lips pressed together, but Jelena wasn't sure why. Oh, she knew that Mom and Leonidas had never seen eye-to-eye about the fall of the empire and the emergence of the Alliance, but that was all so long ago now. What could be going on that would bring the old tensions out again? Something to do with Thor? He would be twenty now. He wasn't out there trying to raise a fleet to challenge the Alliance, was he?

"I doubt he'll get in touch," was all Jelena said, not wanting to make a promise she might not keep. She didn't know enough about the situation— whatever the situation was—yet.

Mom's eyes closed to thoughtful slits. She might not have Starseer talents, but she was good at sensing evasion.

"If he does," Mom said, "don't let yourself get drawn into anything. I trust I don't have to remind you that the *Snapper* belongs to the family business and that you're on a trial period captaining it."

"I know that."

A monkey hooted again. Jelena really needed to go down there and check on everything. And tell Erick about Leonidas. Now she wished she'd let him stay in NavCom with her, so he could have gotten the news from Mom, and she wouldn't have to explain it. She was certain she'd break down into sobs if she spoke about it and not be able to articulate her concerns—not be able to articulate anything. Maybe she would just play the recording of the call for him.

"Good." Mom's face softened. "Take care of yourself, Jelena. Meet us as soon as possible."

"I will."

Jelena bit her lip, dropped her face into her hand, and closed her eyes. Tears leaked through her lashes as her mind spun of its own accord, imagining scenarios of what had happened to Leonidas. Had he been working out in his gym? Or resting in bed? Or playing with the twins? More tears streamed from her eyes as she imagined him horsing around with the girls, and Nika and Maya having to see him clutch his chest and drop to the deck. They would have been terrified. They were only nine. Too young to lose their father. Jelena knew all too well how that felt. And damn it, she didn't want to lose *another* father.

The comm beeped. She ignored it.

A few seconds later, Erick spoke into her mind. *Jelena?*

She didn't want to answer that call, either, but he needed to know about Leonidas. After ten years aboard the *Nomad*, he surely considered Leonidas a father figure too.

Can you come up to NavCom when you get a chance? At least with telepathy, her "voice" couldn't break in the middle of a sentence.

Yes, in a minute. I'm helping Xing's people get the last of their cargo so I can lock up. But, uh, have you heard about anything going on with Thorian?

Did Mom comm you too?

What? No. The workers were talking about some interesting news that's apparently all over the system, for those who actually pay attention to such things. His words had a teasing quality to them. He definitely hadn't spoken to Mom yet. He didn't know.

Even though Thor wasn't high on her list of priorities right now, Jelena found it odd that his name had come up twice in ten minutes from two different sources. *What is it?*

According to the news, he's been assassinating people.

He's what?

I'll be up in a few minutes. We can look it up.

Jelena rubbed her eyes. This day was turning more and more surreal. Was there any chance she would wake up and find out she'd dreamed all of it?

She pinched her arm a little savagely to test the dream hypothesis. Nothing happened.

While she waited for Erick, she plugged Thor's name into a sys-net search. A year or two ago, she'd looked him up out of curiosity, but there hadn't been much. Not surprising, since he'd been lying low, pursuing his Starseer training for the last ten years. She was fairly certain the imperial loyalists handling it had wanted to spring him on the system as a surprise, the rightful heir to the empire returning to lead the rightful government to rule the system.

This time was different. Dozens and dozens of headlines for text and video reports sprang up on the holodisplay.

Former Prince Assassinates Another

Prince Thorian Sarellian Suspected in Chain of Assassinations

Vengeful Prince Springs out of the Shadows

Dux Bondarenko dead—Prince Thorian Responsible?

Retired Admiral and Mining Mogul Andrew Ruud Dead in Bed—Rogue Prince Suspected

Thorian Slays Men and Women Pivotal in Fall of Empire

"Slays?" Jelena asked, gaping at the headlines. "Assassinates? *Thor?*"

Feeling numb, she started one of the videos, as her mind played the memory of that horse-back riding trip again. Yes, Thor had been talking politics, and yes, she'd always known he wanted to fulfill the destiny his father had given him, to bring back the empire—after all, that was why he'd chosen to go with Dr. Dominguez and the imperial loyalist Starseers instead of staying aboard the *Star Nomad* and becoming a part of the family—but she couldn't imagine him as an assassin. A military leader, yes, or something otherwise honorable, but could these stories be true? How would he gather the men he needed for a coup if he was known as some murdering criminal?

The hatch opened behind her as she was watching the fourth video.

"You're not supposed to invite someone up for a chat and then lock the door on him," Erick said.

"It didn't seem to stop you," she mumbled, having forgotten she locked it.

"I can thwart any lock."

Jelena didn't look at him as he slid into the co-pilot's seat. Her gaze was riveted by a news reporter. So far, none of the videos had shown any footage of Thor, nor had they mentioned any statements he'd made or letters he might have left explaining his actions. She wasn't sure how he'd been identified as the person responsible for the deaths. Murders. The twelve men and women who had thus far fallen had either been poisoned with a dart or had their throats cut with a knife. Blessings of the Suns Trinity, could Thor have truly dragged a knife across someone's throat?

"You found something?" Erick waved to the news video.

"A lot of somethings," she said at the same time as Thor's picture came up, an old picture that stirred nostalgia within her.

It was the blond, ten-year-old Thor she remembered from their time together, on the run from assassins who'd wanted him dead and would-be tyrants who'd wanted to use both of them. Those hadn't exactly been good days worth remembering with fondness, but she and Thor had been close then. He'd protected her and helped her understand what it meant to have Starseer powers—she'd barely started developing her own then, and with her father newly dead, she'd been a mess. She wasn't sure why he'd helped her when the other kids had ignored her or teased her, but she'd often looked back and felt she owed him something for that. His face was sad in the picture, and she remembered how he'd lost his parents right before they met, too, how they'd had that in common.

"Doesn't look like the face of someone who's been killing people," Erick said.

"No, but they seem certain he's responsible. I haven't seen any of them talk about evidence or eyewitness sightings."

Erick scratched the back of his head. "Then how can they know?"

Jelena shrugged and pulled up some of the articles and ran a search for the words *evidence* and *proof.* After a few minutes of scanning, she gathered that nobody could prove Thor was behind the murders, but that some former imperial loyalist had detailed Thor's training to the media. Soon after, that man had been killed.

The list of people who had been assassinated added further clues to the culprit. The first five to fall had been men and women who had been behind the betrayal of the emperor's family, giving up the location of the hidden base where Markus had taken his wife and son near the end. Dux Bondarenko—then Senator Bondarenko—was the man who'd gone on to round up the remnants of the empire and take control of the planet Perun, and he'd been the first man to be killed. Perun was reportedly in chaos now, trying to decide if their next ruler should be elected from the people or if they should follow another of the selected-by-Emperor-Markus, lifetime politicians from the time of the empire.

"How did we miss hearing about all this?" Jelena asked, checking the dates. Things *had* been unraveling quickly, with the first assassination only five weeks prior, but she was surprised her parents, who followed the news so they knew spots to avoid when scheduling freight runs, hadn't mentioned any of this to her.

Her parents. She swallowed. She had to tell Erick about Leonidas.

"You were too busy planning ways to steal animals to check the mainstream news?" Erick suggested.

"Ways to *liberate* animals," she said reflexively, even as she groped for a segue. "That may be, but why didn't *you* hear about any of this? Were you too busy playing your game to watch the news?"

"I'd be too busy to watch the news even if all I had to do was pick lint out of my bellybutton hole."

"If only we could figure out *why* you have trouble attracting women."

"It is a mystery. My bellybutton is particularly fine, you know. And free of lint."

"Lovely." She took a deep breath. "Erick…"

The humor on his face vanished, and she could only imagine the look on her own that made him realize so quickly that something else had happened.

"I…here." She couldn't say it. She pulled up Mom's call and played back the recording.

He watched in silence, a grimace deepening on his face. At the end, he smoothed his features and looked over at her with what was probably supposed to be a heartening expression. "That's not good, but it sounds like he's stable, and your mom has a good doctor lined up."

"Yeah." Jelena tried not to think about how it was a journey of almost a week to get to Arkadius. Would Grandpa be able to keep Leonidas stable that whole time? And when they got there, would the new doctor be able to easily fix the problem? A heart transplant, Mom had said. That was major.

"It'll be fine. *He'll* be fine." Erick leaned over and wrapped an arm around her shoulder. Hugs weren't usually her favorite thing, but she accepted it, glad for the support. "Assuming Thorian doesn't assassinate his doctor," Erick added.

Jelena pulled back, horrified.

He winced, realizing his mistake right away, and lifted his hands in apology. "Sorry, it was a joke. I was just trying to make you feel better, but—no, it was a bad joke. I'm sorry."

It had *better* be a joke. Jelena stared at the holodisplay, where Mom's image still hovered. On the second play, Jelena had registered the information about the doctor. A former imperial subject who'd worked for the emperor himself and helped with the cyborg program. The news articles *had* emphasized that people who'd been key in the empire's fall were being targeted by the assassin—she refused to think of Thor as the assassin. There wasn't any damned proof. And wasn't it possible someone might be framing him? Still, what if whoever was responsible considered that doctor as someone who should be targeted? What if the assassin struck right before Leonidas went into surgery?

"I'm sure it's not a possibility," Erick said, wincing again. He must have been able to guess exactly what she was thinking. "At the least, it would be extremely unlikely."

"I...think we need to talk to Thor."

"Your mom said *not* to do that."

Jelena looked back to the articles about him, afraid for multiple reasons now. "We need to know if he's truly responsible for these assassinations, and if he's not, if he has any ideas as to who might be and where they might strike next. Of all people, Thor should be most aware of what the imperial loyalists out there are doing."

"Fine. Send him a note then."

"I don't know how to get in touch with him. He deleted his old sys-net address some time ago."

"Then it wasn't meant to be."

"Erick," she said slowly, thoughts percolating through her mind.

"Oh no." He lifted his hands.

"What?"

"I know that tone. You're about to ask me to help you with something dubious. Something *else* dubious."

"No, I was just thinking…"

"Always a dangerous occurrence."

"Do you still keep in touch with Admiral Tomich?" she asked. The Alliance pilot was one of her mother's friends, and Jelena had met him numerous times, but she couldn't ask her mom for help looking up information on Thor, not after that admonition to avoid him. "You once said he played that game, too, right?"

"*Striker Odyssey,*" Erick said, as if it were a crime to refer to it as "that game." "And yes, he's in my crew." His tone grew wary at that last.

Jelena's mind boggled at the idea of a military admiral, a real-life pilot and high-ranking officer, playing a game where one pretended to be a pilot exploring the galaxy and fighting aliens. Granted, aliens and galaxies might be more interesting than the limited offerings of their own system, but still.

"So you talk to him all the time?"

"He's not on *all* the time. He's a busy man. But he does get invited to beta test when the devs add new ships." Erick sighed wistfully.

"Can you get in touch with him?"

"Now? Do you want to confess your sins to him?"

"From the stories Mom has told, he has more sins of his own than I'll ever have." Jelena hoped that was true as she thought again of the people who had been injured—or maybe worse—in her escapade. "I'd like to know if he knows about this Thor stuff and especially if he has a list of people who might be targets for future assassinations. He's high up in the Alliance military. He might also know if Thor is truly behind this or if it's someone else." It occurred to her that the *Alliance* might be framing Thor, but that didn't make sense. Why would they be killing the people who'd helped them overthrow the empire and take power?

"I'm not sure a pilot would be that knowledgeable on the doings of an assassin. Senator Hawk might be the one to ask. He's been in office for years and probably plays golf and has tea with the president."

"Yes, but he doesn't play your game and know you. I assume."

Senator Hawk was another of her parents' acquaintances, but she knew his two eight-year-old sons much better than she knew him. She'd babysat for them at a few family-and-friends gatherings on Arkadius. She doubted it would be easy to get through to Hawk, and even if she could, news of the message might get back to Mom. Since Tomich had a non-Mom connection to Erick, he seemed a far more viable contact.

"You're determined to get me involved in this, aren't you?" Erick asked.

"We're not getting involved in anything. We're just gathering information."

"Uh huh. Can I point out that it's been less than twenty-four hours since the last thing you got me involved in?"

"Just comm him, please?"

"Fine, but you better go check on—"

"The animals, yes. I will. I hear the monkeys howling."

"I was going to say the cyborg," Erick said. "She's awake. And she's going to be trouble."

"Oh. You're sure?"

"Trust me. I can recognize trouble when I see it." He gave her a pointed look.

"Ha ha." Jelena headed for the hatch. If the woman was awake, she could already be planning some mischief. Or an escape. Which would be fine if she was medically fit enough to walk away. Maybe Jelena would go hold the door open for her.

"Take your staff," Erick warned as she headed out, his hand straying to that impressive bruise on his stomach again. "And maybe some grenades."

CHAPTER FIVE

Jelena passed through the cargo hold before heading to sickbay, in part to check on the animals, and in part to grab her staff. She grimaced at the idea of battling the cyborg woman again and hoped it wouldn't be necessary. She was perfectly willing to let her go. But what if the woman felt compelled to try and arrest them—or kill them—on her employer's behalf?

The forklift workers had finished unloading their cargo and closed the hatch behind them. The *Snapper* could take off any time. Even though Erick was supposed to meet friends, Jelena hoped he would forgive her if she left early. Those Stellacor people might have located her ship by now, and she didn't need to get into a battle here. No, she needed to head to Arkadius to meet Mom and Leonidas.

The hatch to sickbay was closed and locked—symbolically, Jelena supposed. A cyborg wouldn't have any more trouble thwarting a lock than Erick had. She'd probably just rip the entire hatch off the hinges.

Jelena pressed her palm to the control panel beside the hatch, and it thunked and swung open. The woman lying on one of the two exam tables lifted her head and glared at her, nothing welcoming in her gaze, certainly nothing thankful. Did she know they'd gone back for her when they could have left her? When she could have died, exposed to the vacuum of space?

"Hello," Jelena said, forcing cheer. She lifted a hand in greeting. "How are you feeling? You've got some nanobots working on your skull and leg bones." She waved toward a monitor attached to the side of the woman's head and the injector on the counter behind her. Dare she get closer to check on the progress?

The woman continued to glare at her. She had dark brown eyes, brown skin, and curly black hair clipped close to her scalp. Erick had only removed her helmet, and Jelena hadn't wanted to try to wrestle her out of the spacesuit, so she couldn't see much of the rest of her figure. She definitely had a thickly muscled neck, so Jelena imagined burly arms and legs, the female version of Leonidas.

Jelena wondered how she had become a cyborg, if that was indeed the reason for her strength and speed. The imperial army had only ever created male cyborg soldiers, but this woman wouldn't have been old enough to have been a soldier back then anyway. She appeared to be in her mid- to late-twenties. She could have been a part of the new Alliance cyborg program, though Jelena couldn't remember hearing about any women going through that yet.

"My name is Jelena," Jelena said. "What's yours?"

The stony glare continued. Jelena would have wondered if she understood, but it was hard to find people in the system who didn't speak Solis Lingua, the amalgam that had become common once the various colonies regained spaceflight and united.

"This isn't an interrogation, by the way," Jelena said. "And you're not a prisoner." She waved toward the open hatch. "You can go any time. We just picked you up because your helmet was cracked, and we didn't think your people would get to you in time to save you."

The cyborg's gaze shifted, not toward the hatch but toward Jelena's staff and the runes etched in the side.

"What *are* you?" she asked, her voice deep for a woman but not masculine.

"Me? I'm just Jelena." She smiled, reluctant to divulge her Starseer abilities if the woman hadn't figured that out yet. She was wearing normal clothes, brown trousers and a purple horse shirt with a few sparkles, rather than her black robe. Had she been in the robe, the puzzle pieces probably would have clicked into place for the woman. That was the image of Starseers that most of the system had, but sightings were rare, Jelena had always heard. Most of the Starseers were reclusive, keeping to their communities rather than mingling with the grubs, as they sometimes called normal people. "I'm a pilot," she offered, as if that might assuage the woman's suspicions.

"Do you work for Regen Sciences?" the cyborg asked.

"Uh, who?"

She squinted at Jelena. "They attacked the labs last month, destroying millions of tindarks worth of equipment. Stellacor responded decisively. We have been expecting another counterattack."

"From…a competitor?" Jelena could only assume Regen Sciences was another corporation. Did corporations regularly make war on each other? She couldn't imagine that being legal in the Alliance. But then, the Stellacor facility had been on the dark side of the moon, the non-Alliance side.

"They may have hired outsiders." The squint deepened. "But you are practically a child."

Jelena decided to agree instead of being affronted—hopefully, the cyborg wouldn't strangle a child. "Yes, yes, I am."

The woman grunted, possibly in disgust, then flopped back on the exam table with an exhalation that was almost a groan.

"Are you in pain? I can get you something for that. We don't have a doctor on board, but I've had some medical training."

"You don't look old enough to have had *potty* training."

Ah, she was going to be a grouchy guest. Jelena wished again that Leonidas were here, so he could deal with her. Also, if he were here, that would mean he was fine and in good health.

The comm panel dinged. "Jelena?" Erick asked.

"Yes?"

"Company is coming."

The cyborg lifted her head, squinting again as she watched Jelena. She no doubt wanted the cavalry to come and rescue her. Or maybe just mow Jelena and Erick down and cut them into a thousand pieces.

"I'll be right there." Jelena pointed to the counter again. "There's Painpro in the injector back there if you need it. And you can go any time."

She left the hatch open when she walked out, willing the woman to disappear. Jelena hoped she wasn't being naive—what if the cyborg decided to sabotage her ship instead of leaving? But even if Jelena locked the hatch, her guest could still get out and do that. Alas, she didn't have any chains strong enough to hold a cyborg, nor had the freighter come with a brig. Maybe freighter operators weren't supposed to take prisoners.

Her new dog friend joined her as Jelena was walking back into NavCom, wagging her tail and bumping against her leg.

"I'm quite sure you're supposed to be safely in that pen," Jelena said, pausing to ruffle her floppy ears. They might have to fly out of here quickly, and things could get rough if armed spaceships waited for them.

"I hope you're not talking to me," Erick said. He was standing in NavCom, eyeing the various holodisplays.

"*Your* pen is hardly safe with all that junk on the deck." She waved in the direction of his cabin as she joined him.

"That's not junk. That's my clothing."

"Some people store their clothing in closets and cabinets."

"Short people. My clothing is too long for that tiny *closet*." He made quotation marks in the air as he said the word.

"Some people also employ an obscure, little-known clothing storage technique called folding."

"You can't *fold* a Starseer robe. It misdirects the nap."

"What does leaving it in a heap on the deck do?" Not waiting for an answer, Jelena pointed at the sensor display, which showed the same ships that had been parked at the freight docks for the last two hours. She didn't see any new ones hovering in the air, weapons hot. "Where's our company?"

"Here." Erick stepped aside, revealing not a view of the sky above them but the display from the external camera next to the cargo hatch. No less than ten hulking men with blazer rifles were striding toward the *Snapper*. Men and women in overalls and mechanics' smocks scurried out of their way. "They stopped to discuss things at the head of the dock there," Erick said, pointing at the promenade behind the men. "It looks like they're done."

"I don't suppose there's any chance those are your gaming buddies coming to get you for that drink."

"I'm fairly certain those people are coming for *you*. And not for breeding purposes."

"No? How distressing."

Jelena commed space traffic control. Technically, the *Snapper* could leave any time—she noticed that Erick had already detached the clamps and water and oxygen resupply hoses—but the dock authorities tended to get huffy if pilots didn't make arrangements first. They would also need someone to open the dome gate so the ship could fly out.

"If I were you, I'd be *concerned* if they wanted to breed," Erick said. "That one is missing an ear."

"I doubt it's a genetic mutation. It looks like someone chewed it off."

"Well, that's all right then. Uh oh."

"What now?" Jelena, drumming her fingers as she waited for space traffic control to respond, looked where he was looking.

Erick had all six of the ship's exterior cameras up, as well as several of the interior ones. He pointed at the one that monitored sickbay. Their cyborg had rolled off the exam table and was poking through drawers. Jelena couldn't believe she was already walking. The nanobots shouldn't have been able to heal her broken leg bones that quickly.

"I thought we should monitor her," Erick said.

"That is most distinctly *not* where I told her the painkillers were."

"She's probably looking for things to help with an escape."

"I left the hatch open and told her she could go any time." Jelena might have to rescind that offer, though. The thugs had reached the *Snapper's* cargo hatch. One was pointing at the control panel that would allow them to comm her. Another was waving a large tool that looked disturbingly like Erick's plasmite torch.

"Maybe she's looking for some valuables to steal, so she has something to barter for a ride back out to that lab."

"Stealing from the people who saved your life seems rude."

"Even if they were the people who endangered your life in the first place?"

"Semantics." Space traffic control finally answered, and Jelena jumped on the comm. "This is the *Snapper* requesting permission to depart," she said, not waiting for a greeting.

"Pull us away from the dock," Erick whispered, nodding toward the thug with the torch, "so we can raise the shields."

"*Snapper*, this is space traffic control." No kidding. "The authorities have asked us to detain you until your ship can be searched. A prominent Alpha 17 resident has accused you of theft."

Authorities? So much for the dark side of the moon not having ties to the law.

"Will the authorities who visit us be in uniform? Or is the brute squad knocking on my door part of an independent outfit?" Jelena powered up the thrusters and eased the freighter away from the dock.

The men drew back, some of them waving their weapons. One fired at the *Snapper's* hatch. An alarm pinged on the console, letting Jelena know about it. She doubted the hand weapon would do anything to her heavily armored hull, but as soon as they had the clearance, she raised the shields.

"…in appropriate attire and will display identification," the control officer was saying, not that Jelena was paying attention anymore. "If you do not cooperate, your future visitation privileges will be withdrawn."

"I'm more worried about my exit privileges," she muttered, noticing that the dog had curled up next to her feet under the console. She would have to name her at some point.

Erick sat down next to her, resting his palms on the control panel, and closed his eyes. "I'll try to convince someone in space traffic control to lower the dome gate for us." One eye opened to give her a pointed look. "Even though I haven't received my deck of *Striker Odyssey* cards for the last time I helped you."

"It could be worse. You could be a monkey waiting for bananas."

"I don't know what that means, but sometimes, I'm concerned for you." His eye closed again.

"Only sometimes?"

Jelena flew them low over the towers and refineries of the sprawling industry hub that was Gizmoshi. Even though citizens could leave their buildings and walk outside, under the dome's protective influence, few seemed inclined to do so. All of the streets and trains were covered by tunnels that connected the buildings to each other in a sprawling complex dominated by metal. If there were any trees or parks anywhere, she hadn't noticed them. Her hopes for a greenhouse may have been idealistic.

I'll get you fruit at the next stop, she silently promised the monkeys, and shared a few less defined assurances with the rest of the animals.

The *Snapper* rounded a tower, and the opaque forcefield that blocked the exit from the dome came into view up ahead.

"How are your Starseer charms working on the person controlling the gate?" Jelena asked, swooping around the tower for another loop, relieved the sensors didn't show anyone pursing them. Not yet.

"Excellent. Unfortunately, that person was in the lavatory and is taking her time heading back."

"We'll have to ask Grandpa, but there may be a rule against speaking telepathically to people while they're using the facilities."

"I'm trying to find the button myself," he said, ignoring the other comment.

Jelena kept an eye on the sensor display. Still no pursuit. But she couldn't read what was happening on the outer side of the dome.

"Got it."

The opaque field faded, revealing a rectangle of starry sky. Jelena zipped the *Snapper* straight toward it, hoping for an easy escape, but with the gate open, the sensors could get a read on the sky above the dome. And the three ships occupying it.

Grimacing, Jelena took them out of the dome and down to the ground rather than straight toward orbit. It was possible those ships had nothing to do with them, but she would hope to slip out undetected by blending in with the terrain.

One of the ships, a hulking mining vessel probably there to deliver ore to the refinery, ignored her. The other two were smaller civilian yachts and started moving toward the *Snapper* within seconds of its exit.

"Why do I have the feeling they were waiting for us?" Jelena asked, pushing the thrusters to top speed as they flew away from the dome.

"They may not be our only problem." Erick was looking at the interior cameras again.

Their cyborg had moved from sickbay to the cargo hold. She stood with her fists on her hips, looking at the control panel that controlled the airlock hatch.

"She looks like someone who wants to leave," he said.

"Then she shouldn't have spent so much time rooting in our drawers. Keep an eye on her, please. I think I'm about to have all my eyes occupied." She nodded to the holodisplays. Both the sensors and the rear camera showed their pursuers closing on them.

The *Snapper* wasn't slow and pondering—for a freighter it had a lot of power—but those yachts were modern, streamlined, and fast. And armed. She kept most of her focus on the terrain ahead of them, seeking some inspiration, but had time to pick out e-cannons and blazers among their weaponry.

"Wonder if they have a grab beam," she muttered. And if so, would they use it? Would they want to try to get their animals back? Or would they simply pulverize Jelena and her ship for her audacity?

"I don't know, but the pilots on both are androids, so I can't manipulate them." Erick's lips thinned into a line. "They seem to have learned from their last encounter with us."

"You better get up in the weapons turret," Jelena said reluctantly. "Unless you can find something important to break on their ship, we'll have to do this the old-fashioned way."

She hated the idea of firing on and possibly killing people—just because those ships had android pilots didn't mean there weren't human beings among the crew—especially when she had started all this.

"I'm not familiar with those models," Erick said. "Without schematics, it would take me a long time to study them and figure out where the important, breakable parts are."

"That's what I was afraid of." The sensors beeped a warning, and their enemies fired the first shot. A blazer beam splashed off the aft shields, and an alert flashed, the shield integrity graphs joining the other displays floating in the air. "Weapons," she said, jerking her head toward the hatch.

Erick was already on his feet, but he hesitated. "What about the cyborg? I won't be able to fire at our enemies and watch her at the same time."

"We'll hope she'll be logical and won't try to sabotage the ship she's a passenger on."

Erick grunted dubiously but jogged out of sight. Jelena could fire most of the ship's weapons from NavCom, but the turret and the big star cannon had been a recent upgrade, made a couple of years earlier by the previous owner. It was possible they could blast through those yachts' shields with it in only a few direct hits.

But the yachts had plenty of big weapons too. Jelena searched the landscape ahead, seeking something to give them an advantage. The yachts were breaking away from each other now and increasing speed. They meant to flank her.

There weren't any canyons ahead, based on the map, and the moon was lacking in mountains and hills. Gizmoshi's big orbital shipyard came up on her sensors. Jelena raised the *Snapper's* nose, taking them toward it. If nothing else, it could be an obstacle to hide behind.

Angling upward exposed the top of the *Snapper*, and their pursuers unleashed their fire. Alarms flashed as the shields unhappily endured the attack. The bar showing the shields' power started to dip. Jelena shifted them sideways, so their narrower side would be toward their pursuers.

Her hand slipped, her palm sweaty. She grimaced and dashed it against her trousers.

She'd been in battles on the *Nomad* before, but never when she was the pilot. The practice maneuvers her mother had made her cycle through hadn't prepared her for this. But she found herself employing them now, fingers flying to take the *Snapper* through the evasive maneuvers that Jelena had balked at repeating over and over. They came automatically, and she was glad for Mom's insistence on practice. The shipyard was still several minutes away, however, and she started to doubt her decision to head for it.

A *thwump* reverberated through the freighter as Erick fired at one of their pursuers. Visible on one of the cameras, a burst of blue energy launched from the turret cannon, lighting up the night sky. It took one of the yachts in the nose. The energy struck its shield and dispersed, but that had to have hurt.

"Good shot," Jelena said.

Erick did not respond. A round of blazer beams struck the *Snapper's* shields, and Jelena tried to coax more power from the thrusters. If the ship started taking real damage, Erick would have to leave the cannon and head to engineering.

"Need a bigger crew," she muttered. If her grandfather were there, he could have waved his hand and made these ships crash—or simply leave them alone. Androids might not be affected by attempts at mental manipulation, but if there were any humans on the ship…"Erick, any chance the captains over there are human and susceptible to your charms?"

For the first time, Jelena wished she'd spent more time studying the art of telepathic manipulation than that of communicating with animals. The suns knew Grandpa had tried to give her a broad education. But there wouldn't have been time now anyway. Handling the controls, trying to keep those ships from lining up the *Snapper* for a straight-on blast, wasn't leaving her the bandwidth to concentrate on anything else.

The shipyard came into sight on the view screen, a huge framework orbiting the moon, numerous bays attached to its long struts and beams, a small station for housing personnel at the core. She was too far away to see if people in spacesuits were out, repairing or assembling ships, but numerous large projects were in the works. Even though she needed something to use for cover, she cringed at the idea of taking a battle into the middle of all that. Sane people wouldn't fire into a bunch of civilian techs, but could she be certain her pursuers were sane?

"Got him," Erick said.

Jelena had barely noticed him firing several more times.

"I think his shields are down," he went on. "He ought to give up… maybe."

The camera showed both yachts still in pursuit, weaving and banking as they kept the *Snapper* between them. A jolt went through the freighter as an e-cannon blast slammed into the shields. The flashing alarm on the console started beeping, warning her that power had dropped below fifty percent.

"To answer your question," Erick said, sounding irritated as he fired again, "I don't sense any people aboard those yachts."

"Then we can blow them out of the sky without worrying about more than financial damages."

"I *am* trying."

Jelena adjusted her course, intending to weave between some of the beams on the shipyard where it didn't look like ships were being worked on, but a huge vessel sailed out from behind the station, and her comm light went on. The heavily armored civilian cruiser sported enough weapons to blow up the moon below—and definitely any ships heading its way.

"Unidentified freighter," a male voice said over the comm, "you will fly away from the shipyard at once, or we will open fire."

"Any chance you can open fire on the yachts harassing us first?" Jelena asked, veering away from the cruiser, though she didn't immediately head out into space. There wasn't a damned thing out there to hide behind.

"You will not involve us with your squabbles," the voice said sternly.

Jelena glowered, both at him and at the cheeky yacht flying so close it could have picked her nose. She flung the *Snapper* into a loop, certain that the android would fire soon. She was right. Despite her attempt to evade the attack, another e-cannon blast slammed into them at close range. The freighter rattled, and Jelena would have been thrown from her seat if not for her harness.

She spun the *Snapper* before it came out of its loop and veered sharply to the port side, a hint of nausea plaguing her stomach as the artificial gravity struggled to compensate for her wild flying. The yacht, still close enough to shave her legs, drew back as she smashed into it. Energy sparked and flashed as her shield bumped against its unshielded hull, and her big freighter knocked the yacht away. Jelena didn't know if she had done any real damage, but seeing it spinning away, at least for the moment, gave her some satisfaction.

That satisfaction was short-lived as she glimpsed the shipyard's cruiser flying toward them. Toward *her*. He must have pegged her as the trouble-maker. Or maybe he'd heard from the authorities below that she had stolen goods aboard.

"Erick!" she blurted, a thought surging into her mind. "That cruiser has people aboard it." She knew that from her brief conversation with the man, not because she'd had time to stretch out with her senses and check. She had no idea if the pilot was human, but if the captain was...

"Yes, I hear they're often found aboard spaceships," Erick said, managing a dry tone, though his voice sounded strained. He fired again, shooting at the ship she'd bumped, the ship now recovering and heading back in.

"Stop firing for a minute and see if you can convince him to join in against these yachts."

For a moment, Erick didn't answer, and she was about to repeat herself.

"I'll try," he finally said. "You know you may be starting a war between that corporation and whatever corporation owns the shipyard."

"If we survive this, I'll stay awake nights fretting about it, I promise."

It was hard to hear Erick's sigh over the alarms beeping in NavCom. Shield power was down to twenty-five percent. Flying one-handed, Jelena reached over and took a few shots using the weapons controls on the console. The second yacht was right behind them, matching her every move, peppering their butts with blazer bolts. If nothing else, it was an easy target. She sent a barrage of her own bolts into its nose. It veered up, but only far enough to get out of the line of her weapons fire. It came back in right away, firing from above this time. Jelena dipped the *Snapper's* nose, trying to line him up with her blazers again.

White light flashed on the rear camera, coming from somewhere off to the side.

"Is that the cruiser firing?" she asked, fear surging through her. If Erick hadn't had a chance to manipulate anyone over there yet, the cruiser would be targeting her, not one of the yachts.

An explosion lit the starry sky behind her. The *Snapper's* shield alarm flashed a dozen times as its defenses were struck. Not by weapons, this time. Shrapnel. The cruiser hadn't just fired on the yacht; it had utterly destroyed it. Thousands of tiny pieces of wreckage were all that remained.

Another surge of energy lanced out, and the second yacht, the one that hadn't been shielded any longer, blew up even more spectacularly.

"Get us out of here," Erick said tightly.

Jelena did not hesitate. Whoever had done the firing would realize he had been manipulated somehow, especially when the rest of the crew started questioning him. Jelena turned the *Snapper* away from the moon and the shipyard. They could do repairs once they were at a safe distance. The dozen-odd alarms flashing on the console promised they would need to do at least some. She felt pity for the animals down in the hold—they would have been terrified during that fight. She'd meant to give them a better life, not a scarier one.

"I'll make it up to you," she whispered.

"What?" Erick asked, his voice more distant now. He'd probably left the turret to head to engineering.

"I'm sorry you won't be able to meet with your friends," she said, realizing he was losing out too. The *Snapper* wouldn't be allowed to visit Alpha

17 again. She knew there were a few ports where the *Star Nomad* couldn't go, but that was after years and years of flying. What would her mother think when she learned Jelena had gotten their new freighter blacklisted after less than two weeks of flying it?

"Just get us far away from here," Erick muttered.

CHAPTER SIX

Jelena found their cyborg guest in the cargo hold, leaning against the hatch and looking surly. She had removed her spacesuit and wore gray military fatigues underneath, but they contained neither name nor rank. Jelena didn't know if they indicated the woman had been in the Alliance army before becoming a guard, or if her employers simply favored the style. The cargo pockets on the trousers bulged, perhaps with items taken from sickbay, but she wasn't holding a weapon, nothing obvious at least. She could be hiding a laser scalpel—or a real one—under her palm.

Jelena stopped several feet away, resting the butt of her staff on the deck. Behind her, the animals whined and crooned and snorted. A monkey hooted—she was fairly certain that was the one she owed the fruit to.

Judging by the sneer the woman offered, Jelena figured she looked like some odd shepherd.

"You said I could leave," she said.

"Yes," Jelena said, "but something came up—your colleagues specifically—and we had to depart. You probably shouldn't have loitered so long before deciding to try the hatch. Albeit, I can see why you wouldn't be in a hurry to leave the luxurious accommodations of our fine ship."

The sneer deepened, one side of the woman's upper lip curling nearly to her nose. "The gray-green puke on the walls is hideous. Who painted it? A depressed convict from a military prison?"

"The previous owner was a smuggler. We didn't ask to see his work history."

"It feels like a cave in here. A coat of eggshell white with an accent wall over there would make it airier and brighter."

"Er." Jelena didn't know what to say. She hadn't expected their surly cyborg guest to offer interior design tips. "I'll take it into consideration." Assuming she was ever allowed to fly it again. "Anyway, I meant what I said before, even if events conspired against us. We can drop you off at our next stop, and you can get a ride back to your duty station." She decided not to mention Arkadius—it would be better to drop the woman off at a space station along the way so she couldn't tell her employers where the *Snapper* had ultimately gone.

"Oh, good. Because intra-system travel is so inexpensive."

Jelena was once again tempted to point out that they had saved the woman's life, but as Erick had mentioned, she still might not be grateful.

"Maybe your employers can reimburse you," she offered. "Since you were wounded in the line of duty."

"I was *kidnapped* in the line of duty." The cyborg eyed the animals. "And I'm not the only one."

"Yes, but the animals were happy to be kidnapped."

The woman snorted. "How do you know?"

"All you have to do is ask them." Jelena turned toward the animals, lifting her staff and smiling as she sent feelings of warmth toward them. The dogs wagged their tails, and the monkeys jumped up and down and hooted. One of the pigs rolled on his back, as if in a wallow. She supposed Erick would object if she suggested he build a big muddy pool for the cargo hold.

"Ask, right."

"If you saw the conditions they were in before," Jelena said, letting her voice grow stern as she turned back, "then you shouldn't doubt it."

For the first time, the surliness faded in something akin to enlightenment. Or maybe that was incredulity. "Did you break into Stellacor's high-security facility to steal the *animals*?"

"Of course. What did you think we were doing?"

"Stealing research secrets for Regen Sciences. That's what my boss said." The woman shrugged. "I just follow orders. I don't know everything, but who would risk their lives to steal animals?"

"We *liberated* them."

"You're spaced."

"Possibly so. Will you give me your word that you won't cause any trouble until we reach someplace where we can drop you off?"

The woman's expression grew doubtful, but she didn't object outright. She looked back and forth from Jelena to the animals. Jelena lowered her mental shields to try to get a sense for her feelings and whether she was planning duplicity. Just because she preferred not to use telepathy on strangers didn't mean she couldn't. It was just unpleasant. So different from interacting with animals.

"You'll drop me off at the next stop?" the woman finally asked.

Jelena sensed defeat rather than duplicity, but also sensed that the cyborg didn't want to give her word to be good. Who knew when an opportunity might arise?

Jelena caught an image flashing through the woman's thoughts, of her leading Jelena and Erick in chains back to some man in a white lab coat. Wishful thinking, or was she truly planning that?

"If you don't cause any trouble in the meantime." Jelena nodded firmly.

"And if I do? What then? You'll keep me aboard? That sounds like a punishment for all of us." She sneered at the green bulkheads again.

"Which is why I'm hoping for a lack of trouble."

"I bet you'll get yourself into trouble whether I do anything or not."

"In that case, there's no reason for you to cause it, right?"

"Whatever."

Such enthusiastic agreement.

The comm beeped. "I've got some information for you, Jelena," Erick said.

"Be right there." Jelena turned toward NavCom, but paused. "Do you want a cabin?"

"Huh?"

"It'll be three or four days to…" She paused to do a few mental calculations, thinking of stations on the way to Arkadius where the cyborg could find transport. "Starfall Station. Four days, yes. You're welcome to sleep with the animals, but if you want more privacy, we have a couple of guest cabins."

"Being nice to me isn't going to change anything. Stellacor is going to catch up with you and make you pay for thieving from them."

"Liberating."

"What?"

"I liberated living beings from them. You can't own living beings. Thus, I wasn't stealing."

"What kind of idiotic argument is that? There's slavery in half the system. You can own people, animals, bacteria, whatever you want."

"Not in the Alliance. You can keep animals if you provide for their needs in a suitable environment, but you can't own them. The government can take them away if you're mistreating them."

"We weren't *in* the Alliance."

"We are now." Jelena smiled a tad cheekily. "Take a right in the corridor up here. You can have the cabin that's the second hatch on the left." She waved and jogged off, not certain the woman wouldn't hurl a throwing knife—or perhaps a scalpel—between her shoulder blades. Maybe she should point out that she was the only pilot on board. Technically, Erick could fly, but he showed an alarming disregard for ship—and public—safety when he did. Freighters were not thrust bikes to be raced along a course at breakneck speed.

"I've given our cyborg a cabin," Jelena said as she plopped down in her seat in NavCom.

Erick looked at her from the co-pilot's seat. "Are we locking her in?"

"We're going to feed her and give her some freedom in the hope that she'll think twice about making trouble."

"So, similar plan as with the animals?"

"Exactly."

"Did you also offer her bananas?"

"Maybe I should. Leonidas eats a lot and likes his sweets. Cyborgs have fast metabolisms."

"Are we sure that's what she is?" Erick asked.

"That was *your* hypothesis."

"Yes, but I'm not a scientist. Or a cyborg expert."

"I suppose I could ask her what she is, but she hasn't even told me her name yet. Asking her to roll up her sleeves and show me the scars seemed personal at this stage in our relationship. What's your information?" Jelena tilted her chin toward the console, but the only holodisplay dangling in the air was the general navigation one, showing their position in relation to the stars and nearby planets.

"Admiral Tomich responded to my message."

"Oh?" Jelena sat up straight. She hadn't been certain Erick had actually sent a message. "What did he say?"

"The Alliance is aware of the assassinations, of course, and they do believe Thorian is responsible for them."

"Even though there's no evidence?"

"Just because the news reports don't have evidence doesn't mean Alliance intel doesn't."

"Did you ask if Tomich knew who else might be on the list?" Jelena thought of the doctor—Horvald—who would be performing Leonidas's tests and maybe his surgery, one of the few medical people left with expertise on imperial cyborg soldiers. What if the assassin got to him before the surgery? For that matter, could their family friend Doctor Tiang, formerly Admiral Tiang, be in danger too? He was another imperial officer who'd defected during the war. Tiang was quirky and fun and not at all like most high-ranking officers she'd met. Her throat tightened at the idea of him being some assassin's target.

"I did ask, and he said the Alliance could only make guesses. Thorian—"

"We still don't know it's him."

"Tomich seemed certain. And since Thorian has been targeting some high-ranking Alliance officers as well as retired imperial curmudgeons, they're implementing measures to stop him."

"What does *that* mean?" Jelena asked.

"He didn't say explicitly, but I read between the lines that they're sending assassins after the assassin. It was discussed at the highest level, and Senator Hawk and Senator Chen signed off on it. Apparently, Hawk let Thorian live once when he had the chance to get rid of him, so he's taking this personally."

"Assassins? Isn't that premature? I'd sure like to know what proof they have that Thorian is responsible. Isn't it possible some group is framing him to take the heat off themselves?"

Erick hitched a shoulder. "Tomich is out by Umbra, so I couldn't have a real-time conversation with him."

"How do you people game together when you're spread out all over the system?"

"Most people are on the core worlds, so there's not much lag. You have to be close to real time for the player-versus-player stuff, but with the quests, the game just catches you up when you're in proximity to satellites, and you can always chat with those local to you."

Jelena rubbed her face, not caring about the game and not sure why she'd asked.

"I'm sorry," Erick said quietly. "I know he was a good friend when you were kids."

"He was *your* friend too."

Erick made a wavering motion with his hand, neither confirming nor denying. They had been competitors, always testing their talents against each other, but Jelena had thought they liked each other under all that, even if there was a four-year age gap.

"And let's not talk about him in past tense as if he's dead," she said. "He's *still* our friend."

"We haven't heard from him in years."

"So?"

"If he's behind the assassinations, the Alliance is going to catch up with him."

"Please, the Alliance couldn't even catch up with him when he was ten. Now he's—"

"A murderer, apparently," Erick said.

"We don't know that for sure. We should talk to him first, get his side of things."

"Didn't your mother forbid that?"

"Not exactly."

"Uh huh. Look, we don't even know where he is."

"We know where he was doing his training. Leonidas kept in touch with Dr. Dominguez throughout the years and even assisted him a few times. He was out at some base in the middle of a wild forest on Halite Moon."

"But we've never been there," Erick said. "You don't know the location, do you?"

"It might be in the files." Jelena waved toward the navigation computer. "Mom transferred the flight history and all the business's records from the *Nomad* when we first got the *Snapper*. Besides, if I got close to Thor, I think I could sense him. We used to have a pretty strong bond."

"I highly doubt he's there now. Dominguez never would have endorsed assassinations. He takes his religion seriously, and the Xerikesh has rules about that."

"Why are you so sure Thor is doing it and isn't being framed?"

"Because he was a bitter, sullen kid, and people have been telling him about how he has to reform the empire for the last ten years. They've probably made everyone associated with the Alliance out to be a villain to him."

"He wasn't bitter; he was sad. Look, even if Thor isn't there, Dr. Dominguez may know where he went or how to get in touch with him. I just want to talk to him and warn him that the Alliance has people after him." And make sure Dr. Horvald isn't on his list, she added silently.

"I don't think Tomich gave me that information so you could pass it on to their target."

"Target? Erick, he's a human being. And he's one of *us*. You can't truly want him to get killed."

"I don't, but if he's chosen this path of death and destruction, we can't stop the inevitable. You would be better off concerning yourself with your own path. He's not the only one who has repercussions to worry about here."

"Our situation is nothing compared to his," Jelena said, not liking the direction the conversation was going. She didn't want to think any repercussions were inevitable, either for Thor *or* for her.

"Yeah, and what about Leonidas's situation?" Erick arched his eyebrows.

"Trust me, I'm thinking of him. I know you were joking when you said Dr. Horvald could be a target, but he *could* be, right? Going by the history Mom gave us on him and by who's been targeted so far."

Erick frowned. "Even if he is on someone's list, what are the odds of Thor—or whoever the assassin is—getting to him before he can operate on Leonidas?"

"I have no idea, but having him killed *after* the operation wouldn't be great, either. Oh, say, Leonidas, did you want to go see your doctor for a checkup? Too bad. Someone dragged a dagger across his throat last night."

Erick's frown deepened.

"Listen, Erick. I'm worried about Leonidas, and I definitely want to be there for him, but I think we can check up on Thor and still make it for the surgery. Mom said there would be tests first. And we don't have the full story on Thor. He may be in trouble. If the Alliance is sending assassins after him, I don't see how he couldn't be. He may need help."

"Right, as if he'd need us. He was more powerful than I was when he was just a kid. After all the training he's received, he's probably as strong as your grandfather. Maybe stronger."

"This wouldn't take long, Erick," she said earnestly. She was the pilot, and she could take them to Halite Moon whether he wished it or not, but it would be much easier to have his support. Or at least his acquiescence. If he commed Mom and told her about her latest antics...Jelena hated the idea of defying her mother, especially now. "From where we are now, Teravia isn't that far out of the way," she added, naming the planet that Halite Moon orbited.

A quick stop, and they could be on their way again. They would make it to Arkadius in time, she was sure of it.

Of course, if she was wrong, and if Mom had been underreporting how bad Leonidas was, Jelena could arrive too late. What if something happened to Leonidas during the tests or before he reached Arkadius? What if she never saw him alive again? Tears formed in her eyes, and she bit her lip.

Erick lolled his head back, shaking it as he looked at the ceiling, and Jelena began to doubt her resolve. Maybe they should go to Arkadius first, see Leonidas and make sure he made it through all right, and *then* go look for Thor. But if there were assassins after Thor, experts who had been hand-selected and knew exactly how to deal with his powers—what if the Alliance had chosen a cyborg who had dealt with Starseers before, someone exactly like a young Leonidas?—and Thor didn't have any warning, he would be in just as much danger of dying.

"He would want you to check in on Thorian, wouldn't he?" Erick asked.

"Who?" Jelena blinked, surprised by the turnabout. "Leonidas?"

"Leonidas." Erick sighed.

Jelena almost blurted a "*Yes*," because it supported her own desires, but she paused to consider the question.

Leonidas also had a relationship with Thor. Emperor Markus had ordered him to get Thor away from the hidden asteroid palace when it was being pulverized by Alliance ships, and he and Leonidas had spent a week cooped up in a tiny ship together, heading to a handoff point on Dustor.

Jelena couldn't know what had happened on that ship, but Thor had always seemed drawn to Leonidas after that, spending time with him in the weeks they had all been together after defeating Grandpa's crazy brother. Jelena had heard from Mom that Thor had asked Leonidas to go off with him when he'd rejoined the imperial loyalists, to be his supporter and military advisor. Of course, Leonidas had fallen in love with Mom by then, and he had chosen to stay on the *Nomad* and marry her, but Jelena knew Leonidas had checked in on Thor numerous times over the years—that had probably been his main reason for keeping in touch with Dr. Dominguez. Back when they had first parted ways, she remembered Leonidas telling Thor that he would come help him if he ever needed it.

"I think so," Jelena said. "He's known Thor longer than he's known me or you, after all."

Erick's lips twisted wryly. "You think he's always considered Thor the Starseer engineer he *wished* he had?"

Thor had also had a knack for manipulating mechanical things. Jelena remembered how he'd dragged his Zizblocks kit around everywhere they'd been taken when they were kids, and how he'd always been building spaceships or stations with them. He should have been an engineer rather than some prince destined to retake his empire—and certainly rather than an assassin.

"Leonidas likes his *current* Starseer engineer just fine," Jelena said, swatting him on the shoulder. "Though I'm not sure about the temporary engineer you found to take your place on the *Nomad* while we're on our trial run here, especially since he's not a Starseer and doesn't have a university education."

"What Austin lacks in knowledge and experience, he makes up for in enthusiasm," Erick said, naming his little brother. Seventeen-year-old Austin had cheerfully accepted the short-term job to help pay for his upcoming university costs. He *did* have a talent for building and fixing things, at least according to Erick.

"I'm sure that's why Mom and Leonidas were bandying around Mica's name when we left, wondering if she was done designing mega space stations and wanted to come back."

"Yes, the prestige of working aboard an eighty-year-old freighter is far greater than that of building stations that rival planets in population and complexity."

"How much prestige does a person need in a lifetime? She already got that fancy award."

Erick waved to the navigation console. "Plug in Halite Moon. You're right. It shouldn't take long to comm Dominguez and ask where Thor is. We might not even have to go down to the surface."

"What, you don't want to see the salt mines and lumber mills?" Jelena vaguely remembered picking up cargo there once five or six years ago. As she recalled, there wasn't much in the way of civilization. Just lots of loggers and miners living in caves or temporary huts and eating ration bars.

"I don't want to see you explain to the cyborg why we're still not able to let her go."

"Ah." Jelena had forgotten about working the woman into her equations. "I did promise that we'd drop her off at Starfall Station, and I did imply that would be our next stop. I'll think of something to tell her."

"Maybe she'd like to switch jobs and locations. She's burly enough to shove over some trees with her bare arms."

"I hadn't realized you'd seen her bare arms."

"Just a little wrist when she was taking off her spacesuit in sickbay."

"I'd forgotten you were peeping at her then."

"I was *monitoring* her to make sure she didn't run down to engineering to blow up the ship."

"Uh huh, and how was that wrist?" Jelena asked. "Shapely and appealing?"

"Burly. She'll make an excellent logger if you can convince her to change careers."

Jelena wished she had the charisma to do that, but even a Starseer with above average telepathy and mental manipulation skills couldn't change someone's long-term desires. She supposed it was uncharitable to fantasize about leaving the woman on Halite in a spot without off-moon communications so she couldn't report back to her employers.

"I'll think of something," she repeated sturdily.

CHAPTER SEVEN

"No answer yet?" Erick asked, walking in and joining Jelena in NavCom.

He was in his socks and pajamas, but since he was two hours early for his shift, Jelena couldn't fault him for a lack of professional dress. Usually, they let the autopilot keep an eye on things while they slept on the same shift, but with their surly guest skulking around the ship, they'd decided that one of them should be awake all the time.

"No answer," she confirmed, closing the comm. She'd been trying to reach Dominguez for most of the trip, at first leaving messages and then, as they'd drawn closer, hoping to catch him for a live discussion. Now, the verdant green moon was on the view screen, and they would be close enough to land in the next hour. "We'll have to go down and take a look. I have the coordinates for the base."

She'd been glad to find them in the system-wide locations database Mom had copied to the *Snapper*, because she wouldn't have otherwise had specifics. She might have had to comm Mom, which would have then involved explaining why she was disobeying orders. Or requests. Mom hadn't specifically *ordered* her to avoid Thor, after all. She'd simply been pleased that he hadn't contacted her.

"Go down?" Erick frowned. "I'd been imagining us having a quick chat while we simply flew past on our way to Arkadius."

"The chatting opportunities have been meager thus far. None of the loggers have even sent a welcome vid."

"No? You'd think they'd be quick to proposition visiting women for breeding."

Jelena rolled her eyes at him. "I'm regretting that I shared that with you. And used that word."

His eyes glinted. "Good. I shouldn't be the only one full of regrets around here."

"There's a nice tropical rainforest zone around the equator of the moon. If we go down, and the predators aren't too crazy, we could drop off the monkeys. From the contact I've had with them, I think they were originally wild rather than being bred for labs."

"Oh." Erick perked up. "That would quiet down the cargo hold significantly. Are there bananas down there?"

"I'd have to look it up. Halite wasn't terraformed. It came all tree-covered with breathable air. But I'm sure we humans introduced some of our favorite crops."

Jelena set a course toward the base's coordinates, a middle-latitude spot nestled under a mountain range and, as far as she could tell from the sky, deep within the wilderness. The coasts had been logged, but dense greenery carpeted their destination, and she wondered where she would be able to land. The base was supposed to be small, with only twenty or thirty inhabitants, but surely supplies had to be delivered now and then.

"That doesn't look like Starfall Station," came a cool voice from behind them.

Erick didn't seem surprised by the cyborg's arrival. He merely glanced over and gave Jelena an I-told-you-so look.

"Yes, I've been meaning to talk to you about that," Jelena said, turning in her seat now that the course was set. "But you've been scarce, not showing up for meals or to help feed the animals."

"Why would I feed the animals you stole from my employer?"

"Because they like it, and they're appreciative." Jelena pointed to where Alfie, as she'd decided to call her new furry friend, was curled up in her now-usual spot under the console. Jelena had folded up a blanket down there for her. "It's not something your employer *did* often."

The woman's brow wrinkled, and Jelena had the feeling she hadn't known much about the animals, perhaps not even that they had been in the facility.

"As you can see," Jelena said, "we've been forced to make another detour."

"*Forced,*" the woman said flatly.

"Indeed, and I would happily let you off here if you wish, but I have an alternative proposition."

"This should prove interesting," Erick said, resting his elbow on the console and his chin on his fist as he gazed over at her.

The woman looked toward the view screen for a long moment. Considering whether she could find a way home from here if she took Jelena up on her first offer?

"What proposition?" she finally asked.

"We'd like to hire you," Jelena said.

Erick's eyebrows shot up. The woman's eyebrows arched almost as high.

What are you doing? Erick asked telepathically.

Trying to suborn her to our side, she replied silently, all the while smiling at the cyborg.

You need money to hire people.

I have my allowance.

A substantial amount, I'm sure. You balked at buying me a pack of cards.

No, I balked at buying you a cape. We'll get the cards as soon as we're back on a civilized planet or station.

She's going to expect more than a pack of cards for a salary.

Mom pays you. Maybe you can loan me some money to pay her with.

Oh, wouldn't that be fun for me?

I should think so.

Anyway, I'm sure Mom would approve of taking her on as an employee. She's a cyborg. Mom loves *cyborgs.*

I thought she just loved the one.

Leonidas is a fabulous representative of his kind.

The woman's eyes closed to slits, and she looked back and forth between Jelena and Erick. Had they been exchanging some knowing eye contact? Surely, she couldn't have a clue about the telepathy. Unless she'd figured out what their staffs meant. Since Erick had been roaming the ship in sweatpants and pajamas instead of his Starseer robe, Jelena didn't think that any other clues had been given yet.

"I'd find you two suspicious and shifty even if you hadn't stolen right in front of my eyes," she said.

"Me?" Erick splayed his fingers across his chest, then nodded toward Jelena. "That's the mastermind over there."

"I believe you."

"I'm not sure if I should feel smug or alarmed about that," Jelena said. "And I told you already, we didn't steal, we liberated. Look how much better Alfie is looking after just a few days. Her sores have healed, and her fur is shiny. I've been giving the dogs and cats sardines."

"Aren't those our emergency rations?" Erick asked.

"Yes, but I think we'd both rather just starve if the emergency was ever so dire that we had to dip into the canned sardines. I'm pretty sure Leonidas got those from one of the original colony ships."

The woman rubbed her temples with the thumb and fingers of one hand. "I'm not looking for a new job unless my employer comms me and says I'm fired for failing to catch his thieves." She lowered her hand, regarding Jelena through slitted eyes again. "I don't suppose you'd like to let me comm him and find out."

"Not at this time, no." Jelena was surprised the woman hadn't tried to attack one of them when they'd been alone so she could use the comm. It wasn't as if Jelena had managed to extract a parole from her. Maybe she *had* figured out they were Starseers and was biding her time. "But I have no problem with you moonlighting on the side."

"How generous of you."

"My family has always offered fair and fine work conditions. Just ask Erick."

"I really stayed more for the educational opportunities," Erick said dryly.

Jelena kicked him under the console. He bared his teeth at her.

The woman muttered something under her breath. *Idiots*, perhaps. She looked around NavCom, as if contemplating her options.

"The paint is just as ugly in here, isn't it?" she asked.

"Uh, it's the same all over the ship, I think," Jelena said. "We haven't had time to decorate."

"Consider yourself fortunate," Erick said. "Jelena's cabin back home is covered from floor to ceiling with pictures of ponies."

"Better than decorating with dirty laundry," Jelena shot back.

"Her mom kept waiting for her to grow up and show an interest in boys—normal teenage girls put pictures of boys on their walls, I understand. Her only concession to puberty was to add a picture of a boy *on* a pony."

"Gerard Jacquet is a famous forceball player, not a *boy*. And he's on a stallion in that picture."

"What girl wouldn't dream of those things together?"

"*Exactly.*"

"You two are siblings?" the woman asked, her eyes narrowed again as she watched the exchange.

"Not by blood," Jelena said. "But more or less."

"It was either that or an old, married couple. Given that you're still in diapers, that seemed unlikely."

"*Diapers.*" Erick stood up, almost clunking his head on the ceiling. "I'm twenty-four."

"Extremely venerable," the woman said.

"How old are you?" Jelena asked. She hadn't thought the woman was much older than Erick.

The woman hesitated, as if answering the question would be giving up some top-secret intel. Finally, she shrugged and said, "Twenty-nine."

"I'm surprised you don't need a cane," Erick grumbled, sitting down now that he had made the point that he was taller than she.

"We're definitely not a married couple," Jelena said before he could further insult the woman she was trying to hire. "In fact, Erick is available if you're interested."

Erick managed to make a gagging sound and send her a betrayed look at the same time.

"Wonderful," the woman said, her tone almost as dry as Leonidas's when he got dry. Maybe something about cyborg surgery turned people sarcastic. Or maybe it just took that kind of person to want cyborg surgery.

"Jelena is also available," Erick said. "But her step-dad is a cyborg. That dissuades some suitors."

The woman's eyebrows rose again, and Jelena thought she might ask for more information. About Leonidas, not about her availability. But all the woman said was, "I'll consider your offer."

Then she walked out.

"She meant my offer of *employment*, right?" Jelena whispered. "Because I'm not as into her bare wrists as you are."

"Just get us down there so we can drop off monkeys, find the doctor, find Thorian, and get to Arkadius where we belong."

"Yes, my chief engineer."

"I'm your *mom's* chief engineer."

"What are you to me?"

"I used to be the babysitter. I probably still should be."

His heckling dwindled as Jelena flew them into the moon's atmosphere. Unlike Alpha 17, it had a gravity similar to that of Perun and Arkadius, the most populated planets in the system. As they flew onto the daylight side of the moon, soaring over the lush green forests and glittering blue lakes, Jelena found it surprising that it hadn't been colonized by anyone but itinerant workers.

"Why doesn't anyone live here, Erick?" she asked, too busy flying to look up the moon for herself. They were encountering some turbulence. She should have orbited for longer and come in more directly.

"Uh." He muttered a couple of commands to his netdisc and skimmed a readout. "There are a lot of scary predators, but mostly, it looks like the first groups of colonists got killed off by some brutal parasites and infectious diseases. Some vaccines have been developed for the diseases. The parasites, hm. Don't drink the water while we're here. Or eat the food. Or get a cut."

"Sounds like a lovely place for a Starseer training facility." Jelena tapped the sensors, trying to get more information about the area around the coordinates. Now that they were close, she could see that it was more open than she'd thought with several big gaps in the trees.

"One you want to keep secret, I imagine so."

As Jelena flew closer, she realized those gaps were very irregular and appeared to have been made recently. Dark gray smoke wafted from one spot.

She guided the *Snapper* over the area for a better look, then sucked in a startled breath as she spotted a wrecked ship in a small clearing surrounded by downed trees. Those trees looked like they'd been downed by blazer fire, not an axe or robo-logger. The ship itself, one of the new Alliance Striker-21s, had smashed into one of the thicker logs, and its entire front end was crumpled in, including the cockpit. Jelena doubted the pilot had survived.

"Huh," Erick said, gazing at the view screen.

"Not what I was expecting from a secret base, either." Jelena pointed as she spotted another crashed Alliance fighter among more downed trees. The ejector seat had been fired on this one, the cockpit blown open, but she didn't see anyone walking around. "Looks like this happened a day or two ago."

A one-story rectangular building stood at the edge of the combat zone, moss and grass growing from its living roof, vines twining along the sides. A satellite dish perched on one end, the only thing suggesting it had modern amenities and access to the rest of the system. If not for the downed trees, Jelena never would have spotted the building while flying by from above. A third Striker had smashed into one end of the structure, and rubble lay all around it. Smoke still wafted from its thruster housings.

Jelena did not see any non-Alliance ships crashed on the battlefield. If this had truly been a small training facility, and nothing more, the Starseers living there might not have had ships of their own. A shuttle could have brought in supplies now and then.

"I guess this place wasn't a secret from the Alliance, after all," Erick said. "If Thorian was here…they may have already gotten him."

"I don't know. It looks like the Alliance lost the battle."

"I don't sense anyone inside there." Erick waved at the structure.

The sensors didn't show any energy readings coming from the building. Had it been abandoned? Or what if everyone inside had been killed?

"They could have shielded it," Jelena said. "Both from Starseers and from anyone flying by in a ship."

"*These* people found it." He pointed at one of the wrecked ships.

"And regretted that, I wager. See any place we can land that won't involve balancing across two logs?"

"If you prefer three logs, there's a spot."

"Funny."

Jelena flew over the structure, looking with her eyes for signs of life. There weren't any. Unease settled in the pit of her stomach, along with the fear that they were too late. "I could try landing on the roof."

The big freighter might fit. Mostly.

"I wouldn't. The whole roof could crumble under your weight."

"Didn't your father ever teach you that it's not nice to comment on a woman's weight?"

"No, but I haven't seen him much since I started my Starseer training. Tommy was the one who chatted about women with me when I was a teenager," he said, naming the man Jelena had called "Uncle Tommy" growing up. He'd been the *Nomad's* security officer and chef for years before finally making it big with his line of barbecue sauces. He and his wife had settled on Arkadius, and he catered for some important people now. Maybe *he* would have been a good person to comm for information on government happenings. "His advice leaned toward culinary techniques to make a woman happy," Erick added.

"I wouldn't mind having a cook on this ship," Jelena said, deciding to find a less tenuous landing spot. "I miss Uncle Tommy's offerings."

"We *all* do. Leonidas and your mom are...good business owners."

"Who have zero interest in cooking unless sweets are involved, I know. At least they can afford decent quick-meals these days."

"We should have brought more of those along. They're disappearing at an alarming rate now that we have a third person on board."

"Since we essentially kidnapped her, I don't think we can complain that she's eating while she's here."

"*You* kidnapped her."

"You flew down and got her."

"Because you ordered me to. Actually, since you're not officially in charge, it was more begging and pleading."

"That's cute." Jelena flew toward a spot on the edge of what she was thinking of as the combat zone. Hoping the ground was solid, she gingerly set them down in a flat, muddy area between a pond and a few logs.

"What is?" Erick asked warily.

"That you think I'm not in charge."

Mom had named her the captain, after all. Of course, Leonidas had also told Erick to watch out for her and that he had the power to veto her decisions if necessary.

The landing legs sank into the mud a couple of inches, and Jelena held her breath. But the ground did not give further. In the center of the view screen, the remains of a warped piece of hull stuck up out of the pond like a charred metal flag.

"I'll ready the thrust bikes," Erick said, standing up.

"We're only a half mile from the building. I bet we can make the epic journey on foot." Jelena powered down the freighter and locked the console, just in case their passenger turned out to be a pilot—or to *not* be a pilot—and tried to take off while they were gone.

"It's muddy out there. Planets and moons are so messy."

"So is your cabin, but that doesn't keep you from venturing in on foot. You—" Jelena broke off with a startled squawk when something large flew past the view screen. It blurred by so fast, she couldn't tell if it was a ship, a bird, or a leaping animal. "What was that?"

"Another reason not to go on foot."

"That looked more like a reason not to go without combat armor."

Jelena brought up the sensor display, scanning for life forms. The forest was full of them, animals, birds, and reptiles of all sizes. Some of those *sizes* were quite substantial. Most of the creatures were under the forest canopy, not out here on the battlefield, but a pack of animals—something akin to wolves?—was circling the area. She wasn't sure what had leaped or flown past the view screen. A couple of the bigger animals were near one of the wrecks. They appeared to have greater mass than humans.

"Unfortunately, my salary isn't large enough to encourage me to go shopping for combat armor," Erick said. "Also, engineers aren't supposed to need it. Engineers stay in engineering, puttering with machines and not going out on messy moons."

"And pilots are supposed to stay in NavCom, but since there are only two of us on the ship, we have to do double duty." Jelena headed for the hatchway.

"We could send out the cyborg."

"She hasn't accepted my scintillating job offer yet."

"I was thinking more as bait than as an employee."

Jelena headed for her cabin to grab a blazer pistol as well as her staff. "Superheroes aren't supposed to hide behind other people. I'm going to confiscate your cape."

"You mean my sheet? Darn."

Despite his grousing, Erick also grabbed his staff and a pistol. They found the cyborg woman in the cargo hold, petting a couple of the dogs. Most of them were being quite frisky. Maybe they knew they were on solid ground and wanted to go out to explore. Unfortunately, this didn't look like a good place for exploratory romps.

Erick trotted to the back of the hold and unclasped the two thrust bikes from their stands. Jelena checked the exterior camera display next to the rear cargo hatch. She didn't see any of the large animals poised to charge the ship. If they had been drawn to the area because of post-battle carnage—a grisly thought, that—then they should go for the easier meat rather than attacking people.

"Sounds like a reasonable argument," she muttered to herself.

"Where are you going, pilot?" the cyborg asked, walking up behind her.

"Jelena," Jelena corrected. "And your name is?"

"None of your business."

"Then where we're going is none of your business, but if you'd keep an eye on the animals while we're gone, I'd appreciate it."

Erick flew over on his bike, leading Jelena's behind him. Ignoring the cyborg's glower, Jelena checked for predators one more time, then opened the hatch. This was the larger exit opposite the airlock hatch, and a ramp extended downward and settled in the mud.

A clang sounded above them.

"Animal up there," Erick said.

"What *kind* of animal?" the cyborg asked. "That's thirty feet up."

Jelena reached out to get a sense of it and found a shaggy, two-legged, fanged creature crouching up there. It was larger than a person, and when she brushed its mind, she founds its thoughts surprisingly disorganized and chaotic. It seemed afraid but belligerent as well, and she glimpsed images of it planning to attack them by leaping down.

She tried to soothe it, to share the idea that they were friends, or at least not an appropriate dinner. Usually, animals listened to her suggestions, but this one only grew more belligerent, and something between a roar and a howl floated down from the roof.

"That's problematic," Jelena said.

"What?" Erick asked.

"It doesn't seem to like me."

His eyebrows rose. "I thought all animals liked you. Once you manipulate them into doing so."

The cyborg frowned in confusion.

"This one has a strange mind, almost as if—"

The roar came again, louder this time. The dark, shaggy shape dropped onto the ramp with a thud and whirled toward them. It loomed ten feet tall, with great muscled thighs under its shaggy fur, those thighs bunching to spring. The monkeys in the hold hooted in alarm, and dog barks echoed off the bulkheads.

Keeping her gaze on the creature, Jelena lifted her staff, but Erick reacted first. A wave of energy struck it in the chest as it leaped toward them, its long fangs bared. It was hurled backward, landing hard at the bottom of the ramp. It roared and jumped to its feet again, raising its furry arms in anger, sharp, black claws catching the sunlight. It raced up the ramp, and Erick flung another wave of energy at it. This time, the animal proved smart and dropped to the ramp, claws gripping the sides as handholds. Erick's power battered it, but it wasn't hurled backward.

Jelena kept her staff ready, but she focused on the creature's mind instead of attacking. *Flee!* she commanded it, sharing images of a wildfire roaring through the trees and catching and engulfing the animal.

Instead of fear and compliance, she got frenzied anger. The shaggy animal sprang to its feet again and leaped straight toward her.

Jelena, startled that her mental compulsion had done nothing, was slow to get her staff up. The cyborg snatched the blazer pistol from her holster and fired.

The blast took the creature between the eyes, but its momentum brought it toward them, claws still slashing. Jelena leaped to the side as the animal barreled through the air at her. She was fast, but not fast enough, and one of those shaggy arms clipped her shoulder, spinning her away.

She crashed into the bulkhead, but managed to keep her feet underneath her. This time, she didn't hesitate to raise her staff and use it to channel power at the creature. Like a typhoon, a wave of power swept through the hold, ruffling her hair as it struck their furry attacker, knocking it not only to the end of the ramp but twenty feet out into the clearing. It slammed against a log and dropped to the ground, not moving.

Belatedly, she decided that much power hadn't been necessary. The cyborg's attack should have killed it. Jelena had reacted with fear and frustration. Why had the animal forced her to do that? Why had it been so impossible to get through to it, to warn it to leave them alone?

Erick cleared his throat, and Jelena wrenched her gaze from the fallen creature.

The cyborg still had Jelena's pistol, and she was eyeing Erick, who was eyeing her back, his staff pointed toward her. She wasn't pointing the weapon at him, but she had a good grip on it, the barrel toward the deck. Given how quickly and accurately she'd shot the creature, she might think she could take him out before he could bring his mind powers to bear. She might be right.

Jelena took a step toward her, lifting a hand. "Thanks for the help. I'll take that back now, if you don't mind. I might need it out there. Apparently, this landing spot hasn't been approved by local space traffic control."

The cyborg pinned her with her gaze, not looking like she wanted to return the weapon. But then she flipped it in her hand and tossed it butt-first toward Jelena.

"Masika," she said.

Jelena caught the pistol and returned it to her holster. "Is that your name?"

"Masika Ghazali. If you're going to hire me, temporarily, to watch your asses, you might need to know. For your accounting. Do thieves do accounting?"

"Freighter operators do." Jelena looked at Erick and silently asked, *Are you manipulating her? Or did she return the blazer of her own volition?*

I didn't do anything.

Huh.

"We're not thieves," Jelena added.

"Oh, right. You're liberators. We can discuss how much my salary should be when you get done roaming out there. I'll watch the ship." She—Masika—waved toward the animals. The monkeys were still hooting, eyeing the fallen creature outside as if wondering if it had been some distant relative. If so, it had been a crazy relative.

"Sounds good," Jelena said.

She started toward her bike but decided to toss the pistol back to Masika before hopping on. Jelena doubted she could use it on an animal, even a crazy one. Her staff would be enough.

"In case any more predators show up," Jelena said.

"I was planning on shutting the hatch," Masika said dryly.

"Just as long as you open it back up when we're ready to board," Erick said.

Masika squinted at him. "Somehow, I don't think you two would have trouble opening hatches, whether they were locked or not. What are you? Starseers?"

"We've had some training," Jelena said. "What are *you*?"

"Someone who's likely going to be in as much trouble as you when my employers catch up with this ship." Masika sighed and walked toward the animal pen.

Jelena didn't like the way she seemed so certain that Stellacor would continue to hunt for the *Snapper*. Erick drove his thrust bike down the ramp, reminding Jelena that they had a more immediate problem. Searching the base and hoping to find someone alive who could tell them where Thor was.

CHAPTER EIGHT

Jelena cast a last puzzled look at the dead animal as she and Erick rode their thrust bikes over the logs and toward the stone building.

"It may have been affected by the parasites the sys-net entry mentioned," Erick said. "I didn't do in-depth research, but there are plenty of instances of parasites that can change the temperament of the host."

"Like rabies back on Old Earth?"

Erick shrugged. "As you said, there must be some good reasons that this place doesn't have any serious settlements on it. The miners might not have as much trouble if they spend most of their time deep underground. And the logging would be mostly robot-driven."

"Just so long as we don't find Dr. Dominguez and the Starseers, and they're all crazy too."

"Maybe that would explain Thorian's new assassination hobby." Erick grinned at her.

She didn't find the comment funny. She hit the accelerator, taking the lead as they flew over and around fallen logs and charred craters in the ground. The greenery around the structure was undisturbed, except for the spot where the ship had crashed into the corner of the building.

Two wolf-like animals leaped away from the wreckage as Jelena and Erick approached. They raced into the trees, where similar animals greeted them with mournful howls. Another of the shaggy, two-legged creatures hunkered in the shadow of one of the wrecks farther out, and Jelena tensed, afraid it would attack. It glowered balefully at them, a bone in its mouth.

A human bone, she realized, her stomach twisting. These animals were out here feeding on the pilots that hadn't made it. It was part of nature, the circle of life and all that, but she couldn't help but feel unsettled.

"That one going to be trouble?" Erick nodded to the bipedal creature as they slowed the bikes in front of two closed double doors made from the same stone as the rest of the structure.

Jelena took a breath, willing her queasy stomach to calm, and mentally reached out to the creature, assuring it that they would not take its meal. This one's mind was more reasonable, more what she expected from an animal. It kept its eyes on them as it hunkered lower, returning to eating, but she didn't get the sense that it would attack as long as they kept their distance.

"No," she said.

Erick stepped off the bike and onto a stone patio in front of the door, lush moss growing between the pavers. The entire place looked like it had been there far longer than the ten years that Thor had been with the loyalists, training to be a Starseer and a leader and whatever else. He'd never talked much about what his education involved back when they'd still communicated from time to time.

Jelena also parked her bike and contemplated knocking on the door, though she doubted her knuckles would make much noise against the solid stone. She let her senses trickle outward, wondering if they should force their way in. Was anyone left alive to answer the doorbell?

"I don't sense anyone," Erick said, "but I also don't sense *anything* inside the walls. I think the entire structure is shielded from probing minds—probing sensor equipment, too, most likely."

"I didn't read anything from the ship," Jelena agreed.

She tapped on the stone with her staff. Nothing happened.

Erick didn't wait for long before lifting his staff and applying some of his telekinetic power. One of the doors groaned open, scraping on the stone floor. Jelena was on the verge of saying it looked like it hadn't been opened in years when she spotted someone's leg, the brown snagor-hide boot surreally highlighted by the slash of sunlight beaming inside, dust motes visible in the air around it.

Erick led the way in, pausing to examine the leg—and the rest of the body. It had been a woman, her hair still tidily bound in a bun, though her cap had fallen off, and her rifle had fallen from her hands. She wore a gray Alliance uniform, her rank marking her a sergeant.

There wasn't any blood, at least that Jelena could make out in the shadowy interior, and she couldn't tell what had killed the woman. A Starseer attack? There were stories of Starseers who could stop people's hearts with their minds, though Grandpa had never taught her and Erick anything like that. He'd always been almost painfully careful to not teach them morally questionable talents, but even the most basic talents could be used to hurt people if the users were thoughtless. Or naive and shortsighted, Jelena amended silently, wincing at the memory of the people she'd hurt while retrieving those animals.

"This didn't happen that long ago," Erick said. "Yesterday, maybe even last night or this morning."

Jelena thought of the smoke still wafting from some of those wrecks. "I agree."

There was another body on the other side of the room, in front of a door on the back wall. This soldier, also wearing an Alliance uniform, had been male.

Other than the bodies, the room itself was surprisingly empty, a flagstone floor stretching from wall to wall with a few pieces of stone or wood furniture here and there. At the far end, sunlight trickled through holes in the ceiling where it had crumbled after the ship struck it.

"This is the whole building," Jelena realized, looking up and down the room's length.

"Basement?" Erick guessed, nodding toward the back door.

They headed toward it, not stopping to examine the male soldier's body. Jelena hadn't dealt with death much in her life, and she found it easier not to look. She resolutely told herself that if these people had come to kill Thor, they'd gotten what they deserved. But was that true? If Thor was assassinating people...

"There's a hall back here." Erick had pushed open the back door, this one made from wood, and stuck his head through. "And a stairway." He lowered his voice. "I can sense people now. A few of them."

Jelena followed him into the hall, letting her own senses trickle outward. She detected two—no, three—people down the stairs somewhere. One of the minds she brushed reacted, almost like a stallion rearing up.

Who are you? the male voice demanded. There seemed to be a warning in the words, and she imagined the man—a Starseer—preparing a mental attack.

Jelena Marchenko, she replied. Then, realizing that wouldn't mean anything to him, she added, *An old friend of Thor's. We came to check on him.*

A long pause followed. Erick had stopped at the top of the stairs, his hand on the wall, and Jelena wondered if someone had also contacted him.

Thorian isn't old enough to have old *friends,* the man finally said. Fortunately, his tone sounded more dry than dangerous now.

He was ten when I met him. Is he here?

Not any longer, no. The voice turned bitter. *Too bad. This is his mess.*

Jelena frowned. It sounded like her guess had been right, that the Alliance had attacked because they thought they were taking out Thor.

Erick looked back at her. "I'm not sure if we're invited down," he whispered.

"I'm not, either." She shrugged back at him, then asked the Starseer, *Is Dr. Dominguez here?*

Yes.

Can we come down?

Might as well. Don't let any of the animals in.

Erick must have heard that last part, because he looked back the way they had come, his eyes growing distant. The scraping of stone on stone sounded again, followed by a thud.

"I doubt that crumbling roof would keep those bipedal animals out if they decided to come in," Jelena whispered.

"Probably not, but they have food enough out there." Erick grimaced.

They continued down the steps into a more modern area, the walls made of some black metal instead of stone, and the floor switching to tile. Up ahead, artificial light came from an open doorway, one of several in the hall. A robed figure stepped out into the hallway and turned toward them. Gray-haired, stocky, and bearded, he wore a gray robe instead of a black Starseer one, the waist tied with a simple rope belt. The light glinted on a silver necklace hanging around his neck, three suns clustered at the bottom.

"Dr. Dominguez?" Jelena asked, stepping in front of Erick.

The man hadn't visited the *Nomad* since he'd left with Thor ten years earlier, but Jelena had seen him on the comm several times since then, talking with Leonidas about Thor's progress and about politics that she'd found extremely boring at the time.

"Good afternoon, Jelena," he said gravely, then nodded at Erick. "Ostberg." He smiled faintly, though he appeared weary, with bags under his eyes and deep lines etched at the corners. "No chickens following you around anymore?"

"No, sir. Jelena usurped most of the chickens when she came on board. Also, Yumi left a few years ago, so we haven't had as much fowl. There are cats now though. Jelena finds one to rescue at almost every stop."

"The cats are handy," Jelena said. "Leonidas said so. They eat the rats."

"I think he put those rats there so the cats would have something to do."

"I hardly think that's true."

Jelena closed her mouth on further comments. The conversation seemed inane, especially when there were bodies upstairs, and was that blood on Dominguez's robe?

Dominguez must have had similar thoughts because he nodded toward the doorway next to him and said, "You might as well come in."

Jelena and Erick trailed him into a room full of tables, with large holo-displays floating in front of one wall, showing news from around the system. Were the people here monitoring the Thorian gossip? Or just the news as a whole?

Someone moaned softly, and Jelena looked toward a couple of sofas near the far wall. Two men in Starseer robes, one bald and one with white hair, lay there. A medical kit sat open on the floor next to one of them, and she realized they'd interrupted the doctor while he'd been working on them.

"Injuries from the attack?" Jelena pointed toward the ceiling, toward the wrecked ships.

"Yes." Dominguez started toward the man who had groaned. "These two will survive, but we lost three others when the ceiling caved in over there." He pointed toward some deeper basement room that she couldn't see. "We're fortunate that half of our team had gone off looking for Thor, but at the same time, it would have been easier to repel the Alliance strike team if they had been here to help."

"Put away your bag and let her attend us, Alejandro," the man on the couch said, the one with white hair. Though he appeared to be in his sixties, one of his voluminous sleeves had fallen back, revealing a thick, muscular arm. He was clearly fit under that robe. When he turned his bruised face toward her, she noticed old scars on his jaw and across his nose. His brown eyes were pained but faintly amused too. Was he the one who'd spoken to her on the stairs?

Dominguez frowned. "I think her specialty is horses."

"Actually, Grandpa has taught me to heal bones and seal cuts," Jelena offered, though she was less certain that she could fix internal injuries. With his face an unhealthy blend of purple and yellow bruises, he looked like he had been caught in a rock fall.

"I don't care if her specialty is paramecium. She's *far* prettier than you, Doctor."

"I don't think you're supposed to leer at women young enough to be your grandchildren, Vlad. The Alliance has laws about that kind of thing."

"That's why we're trying to overthrow them, right?"

"The empire had laws about it too."

"Ah, how unfortunate." The man—Vlad—settled his head back on the cushion. "Perhaps we should be fighting for anarchy then."

"That seems to be the tactic Thorian has chosen," Dominguez said darkly.

"What happened to him?" Jelena asked. "Is he really…is what the news is reporting true?"

"Who knows?" Dominguez grumbled. "He sneaked away when the supply shuttle departed and didn't leave so much as a note."

"His fight with Huan surely precipitated it," Vlad murmured. "I suppose that was a long time coming. We just chose not to read the signs."

"What signs?" Jelena knew the men had things on their minds other than answering her questions, but she felt impatient and wanted to pull Dominguez aside for an interrogation. These people had the answers to everything she wanted to know.

Vlad opened his mouth to answer, but Dominguez spoke first, frowning at Jelena. "Did Leonidas send you? Or your mother?"

Jelena hadn't prepared an answer for questions as to why they had come, and she stared back at him, not sure which way would be best to answer. If he found out she had come of her own volition, without permission from either parent, would he refuse to respond to her questions?

He's suspicious of you, Erick whispered into her mind. *Of us.*

What? Why? Jelena kept herself from looking at him, not wanting to alert Dominguez to their silent conversation.

Your mother is loyal to the Alliance, and he's not sure if you're with them or not.

"I came because Thor was—he *is*—my friend," Jelena said, afraid Dominguez would find her long pause even more suspicious, "and when we saw the news, we figured he was in trouble."

Vlad snorted. "Him and everyone around him, thanks to his premature impetuousness."

"Is there ever a time when impetuousness is mature?" Dominguez asked with a sigh.

"When your allies are prepared for it. And your enemies aren't."

"I'm not sure he considers us allies, despite all we've done for him. We've driven him too hard. But we had to, didn't we, Vlad? It was what Markus wanted."

"It was what he wanted," Vlad agreed quietly. "But Markus has been dead more than ten years. Perhaps we should have adjusted our expectations and been more realistic about what is possible these days. Much to our chagrin, the Alliance has grown balls and a prick and figured out what to do with them." He waved a couple of fingers toward Jelena. "Pardon my language, my lady."

Dominguez grunted. "That's far milder language than you use with Thorian."

"Now now, I called him your imperial highness every time I discussed balls and pricks with him. I know how to be respectful."

Do you know where Thor went? Jelena silently asked Vlad, thinking he might be more open with her than Dominguez. *We want to warn him that the Alliance is after him.*

He knows. There's no way he cannot.

Then we want to help him.

Vlad turned his head toward her again. *You have not grown up with a promise to serve the old empire, to see it reborn. It would be foolish of you to get involved in a battle that isn't yours. Besides, Thorian has made it clear that he wishes no help.* Vlad winced. *He has turned his back on those who would be allies.*

Why?

Who can know the minds of young men? He has been guarding his thoughts from us since he was a boy.

Do you at least know how to contact him? He no longer responds to his old sys-net address.

He has been off the grid for years. We've wished it that way.

Aware of Dominguez's gaze on her, Jelena met his eyes. "Doctor, my parents don't know that I'm here. I came to see Thor because I was worried about him. And I dragged Erick along because—"

"Because he made the mistake of saying yes when Leonidas asked him to be the engineer for Jelena's maiden voyage," Erick grumbled. "A maiden voyage that was only supposed to be a simple freight run, mind you."

"Yes, and he's very much enjoying his time with me. I knew it was unlikely that Thor would still be here, but I thought you might tell me where he went."

"We don't know. Our people are looking for him, hoping to find him and stop him before he destroys everything we've worked for. If it's not already too late."

Jelena looked at Vlad, and he nodded once. Dominguez frowned, as if irritated by the conversations he must sense were going on around him. If he'd been working with Starseers for the last ten years, he ought to be used to that.

"You should also know that Leonidas is on the way to Arkadius," Jelena told Dominguez. "Something happened to him. Mom said it was a heart attack, and that he may need a replacement heart."

Dominguez blinked.

"I know you're friends, so I thought you should know," Jelena said. "We're on our way there ourselves." Especially if she couldn't find out where Thor was, she thought glumly. Diverting here had been a waste of time.

"I see. I'll check in on him as soon as I'm able." Dominguez looked down at the blood dried on his hands, and Jelena regretted bringing him more bad news.

"We should go," Erick murmured, "unless there's something we can do to help." He lifted his brows toward Dominguez.

"No. We'll be as well as can be expected. But tell Leonidas I'll come visit him soon." Dominguez scowled. "And tell him not to die. He's survived too many people trying to kill him to die on some surgeon's table."

"Maybe you should come do the surgery," Erick said.

Dominguez grunted. "Maybe I should. But no, I'm out of practice. Marchenko will find someone good on Arkadius, I'm sure." His mouth twisted with bitterness. "She knows enough Alliance people with sway to make certain of it."

The bitterness surprised Jelena. After all these years, was he still angry that the empire had fallen and that people had moved on with their lives? Or was it just that her mom had been one of those who fought to topple the empire?

Erick touched her elbow. "We should go."

"Yeah," Jelena said, but she didn't move. They had come all the way down here. To leave with nothing would be so fruitless, and if the people who had worked with Thor these last years didn't know where he was, how would she ever find him? "Wait." She lifted her hand, a thought coming to mind. "Can we see his room? Did he leave any of his things here?"

"Yes, but he didn't have much," Dominguez said. "We've all lived simply here."

How sad that Thor had grown up in this gloomy, spartan place. Had he even been allowed to play with those Zizblocks he'd enjoyed as a kid?

"I'd like to take a look if it's all right," Jelena said. Maybe he had left behind some clue, something they could use to figure out where he'd gone.

"The room was damaged in the bombing," Dominguez said, "and we've already looked through his things."

"Oh, let her look, Alejandro." Vlad waved a weak hand. "You shouldn't be so crotchety with pretty women."

"She's not going to tend to your wounds no matter how often you call her that," Dominguez told him.

Vlad winked at her. "You never know. Don't give up on hope, old friend."

Dominguez sighed again and headed for the door. "Don't die while I'm gone," he called over his shoulder.

"I wouldn't dream of it."

Jelena followed him out of the room, pleased by the small victory. She hoped it would lead somewhere. Even though she couldn't truly claim to know Thor anymore, she believed she might see something the old men had missed, some hint that might be clearer to someone who'd once fled from planet to station to moon with Thor. Or maybe her younger eyes would just be better at spotting clues.

Dominguez led them down the hall and around a corner. Up ahead, the ceiling had caved in, and rubble blocked the route. He turned before they reached it, pushing open an unadorned wood door.

Even though the stark room they entered held a narrow bed, Jelena wouldn't have thought of it as someone's bedroom. More like a guest room that rarely saw use. A dresser and a desk, both empty on top, were the only other furnishings. Rubble littered the floor, and uneven cracks marred all the walls, proof of the damage Dominguez had mentioned.

Jelena walked to the only wall with something on it. It held a massive map of the system, the three suns, the dozens of planets and moons, and even the major stations. It was made entirely of puzzle pieces that had been glued together and mounted to the wall. There must have been five or ten thousand pieces. Several had fallen out and lay on the ground among dirt and rocks.

While Erick moved around the room, poking in drawers, Jelena picked up one of the dusty pieces. It was from one of the planets, with a small skyscraper on it to represent one of the major cities. Perun Central, she decided, when she spotted the matching hole on the map. It seemed a shame to have the puzzle, which must have taken hours upon hours to complete, in disarray, so she plunked the piece back into its slot.

"I need to get back to my patients," Dominguez said.

Jelena nodded and lifted a hand. She would prefer to investigate without anyone watching over them. After she finished fixing the puzzle. She bent down to poke through the rubble for more pieces and found one under a rock. She paused. Was that strange? That the pieces would have shaken loose first? It seemed more likely that they would have fallen as the rocks were falling or would have been knocked from the wall because rocks had struck them. In that case, shouldn't most of the pieces be on top of the rubble?

"Underwear, socks with holes, and a few black and gray T-shirts," Erick said, pushing drawers shut. "No clues there, other than that he didn't have room in his bag to pack everything."

Jelena stood up with the second puzzle piece in hand. It had a dark sphere with lights on it to represent a space station. She eyed the map, looking for the spot it had come out of. There. Labels were integrated into the puzzle, and the one below the missing piece read Primus 7.

"Doesn't look like he left any papers or anything in his desk drawers," Erick said. "No diary full of his plans to take over the system. No to-do list with assassination targets on it, either."

Barely hearing him, Jelena let her gaze roam over the rest of the map. There were about twenty-five pieces missing, and interestingly, they were all locations. Space stations or cities on moons or planets. With ninety percent of the puzzle taken up by empty space and stars, what were the odds that the only pieces that had fallen out were from the other ten percent? From *places*.

"Jelena?" Erick stepped up beside her and poked her in the arm. "Is this map more interesting than it looks, or are you in deep contemplation over the socks and underwear?"

She shook her head. "No."

He gave her a confused look, and she realized that hadn't answered his question.

"If you *are* contemplating the underwear, I assure you, it was boring," he said. "You'd expect an assassin to have statement pieces. Blood red briefs. Midnight black. That kind of thing."

"You think you can judge a person's occupation by his or her underwear choices?" Jelena pulled out her netdisc, only half-heartedly responding to his jokes.

"Well, their personality, anyway."

Jelena tapped into the satellite on the roof and from there into the sys-net. She searched for a full list of the assassinations that had been attributed to Thor.

"Like your ponies speak volumes about you," he added.

"They're unicorns."

"Unicorns are just as chatty as ponies."

"This is interesting," Jelena said, scanning the list.

"I assume you're referring to something other than this conversation."

"That's a given. Look." She turned her netdisc toward him, the list of names floating in the holodisplay. And the list of locations where those people had died. Primus 7 was on the list. So was Perun Central. "By the Suns Trinity, Erick. I think we found his to-do list."

He squinted at the map, then at her netdisc, then back at the map. "Hm, you've got twenty-three missing pieces—"

"Twenty-four." Jelena pulled Perun Central back out. "I just stuck that in."

"All right, twenty-four missing pieces, and twelve people killed, twelve locations. I see what you mean about them matching up."

"So, maybe those other twelve are the locations of the next targets." A chill went through Jelena as she considered the rest of the map, at how premeditated this had all been.

"Ah." Erick's face wrinkled with distaste. Similar thoughts? "If that's true, then we know where he's going next. Or I guess we know the twelve spots he's going next. But not in which order."

"Maybe we can narrow it down." Jelena tapped her search results, reorganizing them to organize the list by dates. The Perun Central one—Dux Bondarenko—had been first. From there, she went down the list, checking the locations on the map and nodding to herself.

"Something enlightening?" Erick asked.

"Just that he started on Perun and then went to Draco, one of Perun's moons, then here, here, here, and here." She tapped the locations on the map as she spoke. They weren't precisely linear, since space wasn't overly linear, but he had chosen them in an order designed to make the travel time between destinations as short as possible. "Still on the to-do list, it looks like we've got..." Her gut clenched as she stared at a familiar planet with two missing puzzle pieces in that location. "Arkadius."

She met Erick's eyes.

"A lot of people live on Arkadius," he said. "Odds are against Dr. Horvald being one of his targets."

"But how many of the people living there were important people who defected during the war?"

"Probably a lot more than we know about. But look, Arkadius wouldn't be his next logical stop. It would be the one after this one." He pointed to another planet. "Blue Armadillo, a city on Upsilon Seven."

Jelena grimaced. "He's going to kill someone on the planet where we used to ride horses? That's disturbing."

"It's all disturbing." Erick grabbed her netdisc and shut it down.

"What are you doing?"

"Look, Jelena. It was one thing when we weren't sure if he was responsible, when you thought someone might be framing him. But that's not the case." He tapped the map with his forefinger. "He had this all planned out weeks ago, if not months ago. *Years* ago. Who knows?"

"I get that."

"Do you?" Erick raised his eyebrows frankly. "This isn't the boy you played Zizblocks with as a kid. He's all grown up and he's turned into a psychopath."

"That's not necessarily true. He's going after the people who wronged his family, who were responsible for killing his parents and maybe for the fall of the empire. Clearly he *cares*. He's not randomly—"

"It doesn't *matter*. You don't kill people because they helped the side you weren't rooting for in a war. Especially not after ten *years*. There has to be a statute of limitations on this kind of thing."

"Really?" This time, she gave him the frank look. "If someone killed your parents, you'd just forget about it because X number of years had passed?"

"I wouldn't *assassinate* the people who did it. I'd let the law handle it."

"Yeah, and what if the people who made the laws were protecting the people who did it because those people happened to be on their side?"

"You sound like you're *condoning* his actions."

"I'm *not*," she snarled, then took a deep breath and lifted her hands. "I'm not," she said more quietly. "I'm just not ready to condemn him."

"*I* am."

Erick walked out of the room.

CHAPTER NINE

The comm beeped, and Jelena reached to answer it, but hesitated when she saw the caller's identity. Mom.

The *Snapper* had left Halite Moon two days earlier, and Jelena had set a course for Arkadius, but she kept thinking about how they were still at a point where they could easily veer off toward Upsilon Seven. Back on the moon, they had found a large island near the equator, one without any giant, crazy predators stomping about, and she had dropped off the monkeys there.

The dogs, pigs, and cats, all very domesticated, would need to go somewhere with homes where people would take them in. Somewhere like Upsilon Seven perhaps. With all the open spaces there, it should be an animal paradise, and she had already looked up a few shelters that could help with placement. She'd almost talked herself into making the course correction, and here was a message from Mom coming in, a reminder that she and Leonidas and the rest of the family were waiting on Arkadius.

Jelena needed to see them first. Erick didn't think she should go see Thor at all, at any point. *Ever.* He hadn't been subtle about stating that multiple times, and he'd also pointed out that the Upsilon Seven assassination hadn't happened yet, or at least that nothing had been reported by the news. The *Snapper* should reach Arkadius before Thor could, and they could report to the Alliance that Thor was coming to that planet. If Dr. Horvald *was* a target, the Alliance could protect him if they had warning.

It made sense, and Jelena didn't disagree with the notion, but...

She couldn't help but feel she would be abandoning Thor if she didn't go and warn him about the Alliance assassins. And she hated the idea of giving them tips on where he planned to go next. Oh, she wanted the assassinations stopped, especially if someone important to her family might be a target, but what if, in tipping off the Alliance, she set Thor up to be captured? Or killed.

If she could find him first and talk to him, maybe she could somehow convince him that what he was doing was wrong. Erick might not be right about everything, but he was right about that. She didn't disagree, even if she could understand what was motivating Thor. There ought to be some other, better way for him to fulfill his father's wishes. Had his father truly wanted this? Revenge assassinations?

The beep came again. Jelena answered it, though she feared it would be bad news. Even if it wasn't, Mom would be wondering where she was. She felt guilty that she was glad they were too far away for real-time communications. This would be a recorded message reaching her.

Mom's face came up on the display. She smiled, but that weary tenseness still marked her face, the worry lines framing her eyes. Seeing that brought tears to Jelena's own eyes and made her regret her side trip.

"Hello, sweetie," Mom said. "We haven't heard from you for a few days, so I wanted to check in. Are you on your way to Arkadius? We've arrived, and we're taking Leonidas to see Dr. Horvald now to find out what option is best. How far out are you? Let me know when you're close. He's been asking what you're up to. He has that suspicious squint to his eyes when he asks, like he thinks you're off finding trouble somewhere." She smiled at what she must have thought was a joke.

Jelena swallowed, more guilt swelling in her throat.

"It's that same look he used to get when he suspected you'd stuck more than the agreed upon four stickers on his armor case," Mom added. She paused, her own throat sounding like it was tight. After taking a breath, she went on. "Anyway, we hope to see you soon. Update us as soon as you get this, please. Yumi and Mica and Beck—Uncle Tommy—are coming to visit, and I think Abelardus and Young-hee may even be coming. You know nothing will force Leonidas to get better more quickly than Abelardus making smug comments about his physical condition." She glanced toward the spot where the chronometer was on the *Nomad*. "I better go. They'll be ready for him now. Oh, but one more thing." Mom's expression shifted to wry and knowing, and Jelena suddenly worried that she had heard about everything, or at least about the animal rescue. "I don't have time to record a message for Erick, but do let him know that he left something off Little Ostberg's résumé."

Jelena blinked. Erick's brother was seventeen—how much was he supposed to have on his résumé? It was impressive as it was that he was so good with machines and engines. Clearly, he got that from his older brother, even if he hadn't developed Starseer talents.

"Erick didn't mention that Austin is afraid of ghosts," Mom said.

"Er," Jelena said and almost answered further, forgetting this wasn't a live message.

"He's decided that since the *Star Nomad* is eight decades old, tons of people must have died on it." Mom's eyes tightened, and Jelena remembered that her own mother had passed away on the ship when a mechanical failure had stranded her without life support. "He's set up what he calls a ghostometer in engineering," Mom continued, "and now, he's got the twins certain that they're seeing ghosts. They're alternating between being afraid to go to bed, because ghosts will leap out of the cabinets, and wanting to go ghost hunting in the middle of the night with Austin." Mom shook her head, somewhere between bemused and exasperated. "If there *are* ghosts on my ship, not that we believe in such things, I don't want him stirring them up. We may have to do an engineer trade when you get to Arkadius. Take care of yourself, sweetie. See you soon." Mom lifted her hand, and the display darkened in closing.

"Sorry, Thor," Jelena whispered, and removed her hands from the console, all thoughts of changing their course leaving her mind.

Since she knew he planned to go to Arkadius after Upsilon Seven, maybe she could catch up with him there. The idea of standing by and letting him kill someone else was distasteful, but she also couldn't imagine contacting the authorities on Upsilon Seven and warning them about his plans. She didn't want him to keep killing people, but she also didn't want him to be caught. Did that make her some kind of accomplice? Was she doing the wrong thing?

"How is this even my battle?" she muttered. Just because she'd stuck her nose in and gathered some information…

But she didn't truly know that much, right? She knew the destinations, but not the names of the people he would target at each place. Admittedly, with some research she could make some likely guesses. But was it her job to do this research? So she could turn in an old friend? An old friend who'd turned to murder.

She groaned, her head starting to hurt.

Under the console, the heretofore silent Alfie flapped her tail against the deck.

"Don't worry, girl," Jelena said. "We're still going to find you a nice home."

Alfie nuzzled her hand. She might have been offering comfort or she might have been looking for a dog treat. Jelena fished one out of her pocket and gave it to her.

"We still heading to Arkadius?" Erick asked, shooting her a suspicious look as he walked into NavCom. He'd asked that question and given her similar looks every time he'd passed through in the last two days. Even though Grandpa had promised she'd gotten to the point where she could protect her thoughts from other Starseers, Jelena suspected something might be leaking out. Or Erick just knew her too well.

"Of course," Jelena said, as if it would be silly to think anything else.

Erick leaned over her shoulder to verify their course. She gave him a dour look.

"What?" he asked. "You told the cyborg that she was going to Starfall Station, and the next thing she knew, she was looking out the porthole at a big, green, forested moon."

"She has a name now."

"Yes, and she has a hobby too." Erick's expression grew bemused.

"What do you mean?"

"Follow me." He crooked one finger and walked out of NavCom.

Curious, Jelena trailed after him, with Alfie rising to her feet and trailing after *her*. He turned down the corridor toward their guest cabins. The hatch was shut on the one Jelena had given Masika. Erick knocked on it.

"What?" came the surly reply.

"Landlord," Erick called cheerfully. "Room inspection."

Jelena lifted her eyebrows, wondering if Masika would actually open the hatch. She hadn't yet tried pestering the woman when she was in her cabin.

A long moment passed, but eventually, the hatch opened. Masika stood uninvitingly in the hatchway.

"What?" she repeated.

"I wanted to show the boss's daughter your upgrades, so she can decide if they're allowed," Erick said.

"I am improving your ship for you. Don't be ungrateful, thief."

Having no idea what they were talking about, Jelena stood on tiptoes and tried to peer past Masika's shoulder. Masika lifted her chin and stepped aside. An invitation to enter?

Erick extended his arm, letting Jelena go first. Alfie bypassed them both and sauntered in. Jelena stepped through the hatchway and almost tripped as she realized what had changed. She hadn't spent much time in the guest cabins, but as far as she'd known, all the cabins on the ship were painted the same drab gray-and-green color as everything else on the interior. She'd assumed the former owner had been going along with the turtle shape of the ship and attempting something akin to turtle skin.

But this cabin was no longer gray and green, and the air smelled of paint. The bulkheads were an appealing sky blue with one dark blue accent wall behind the bunk. A mural of stars, clouds, and images of the sun gods stretched above the blanket and pillows. A *good* mural. It was as if a professional artist had done it.

"You painted?" Jelena asked. Then, realizing she was stating the obvious, changed her question to, "I mean, where did you get paints? We haven't gone anywhere with shops or anything."

"Tell me about it," Masika said.

The words reminded Jelena that their cyborg guest didn't want to be here, murals notwithstanding, and might try to turn them over to the authorities if given a chance. She remembered wanting to drop Masika off at Starfall Station so she couldn't let her employers know the *Snapper's* final destination. Thanks to their diversion, Starfall Station was no longer on the way. Should she change course and go there regardless? Or maybe she should have Erick pay their painting security guard so she would feel less inclined to turn them in.

Alfie must not have minded the paint smell because she hopped up on the bed. Masika propped a fist on her hip and eyed the dog.

"Where *did* you get the paint?" Erick asked, peering around the cabin. "And multiple colors at that."

"Two colors. Blue and white. I mixed them when needed. But there are actually quite a few cans of paint in that storage closet in the cargo hold. Some were gift wrapped with cards pleading the recipient to make use of them."

Erick snorted. "You're lying."

"*I'm* not the criminal here. I can show you the cards if you don't believe me. I assume Alberto was the previous owner of the ship?"

Erick looked at Jelena.

"Alberto Ramírez, I think, yes." Jelena considered the walls again. "Uhm, you could paint more of the ship if you wanted."

"Lucky me."

"I assume you enjoy it," Jelena said. Anyone who could paint like that had to have done a lot of it.

"I just couldn't stand being further depressed by four storm-puke-colored walls leering down at me while I slept."

"They are drab," Jelena agreed. "I hung some posters in my cabin."

"I didn't find any posters gift-wrapped in the storage closet."

"We'll pay you for it," Jelena said, growing enthused as she imagined the entire ship redone. "The painting, that is. Maybe we could get some more colors. Oh, can you do animals? What if, down in the cargo hold, we did a whole aquatic mural with turtles?"

"Turtles." Masika stared at her as if turtles were floating out of her nostrils right now.

"Haven't you noticed the ship has a somewhat terrapinian shape?" Erick asked.

"It's hard to tell unless you're on another ship and looking at it," Jelena said.

"Jelena actually *liked* that feature. I thought it was abysmal. I told her parents to get the ship shaped like a pterodactyl if she had to have an animal. It was fierce."

"A fierce freighter. That's completely normal."

"It's better than—"

An alarm beeped, the high-pitched noise echoing through the corridor.

"A discussion for later," Jelena said as she waved a goodbye and jogged to NavCom. That was the proximity alert. They shouldn't be close to anything on their current route. They were still two days out from Arkadius.

Erick followed, saying, "It's a ship," as she popped into NavCom and saw it on the view screen.

A winged civilian craft, it looked vaguely like the avian dinosaur Erick had been describing, with a pointed head, a neck, and a tail. Various e-cannons protruded from the front edge of the outstretched wings.

"It came up on us fast," he said. "I didn't sense anything until the alarm went off."

"Maybe you were being lulled into placidity by Masika's serene mural."

Jelena silenced the alarm as she slid into her seat and slowed down the *Snapper*. The ship had planted itself directly in their path. No chance it was just passing through.

The comm light flashed. Jelena considered ignoring it and setting a course that would take them around the ship, but she wagered it was faster than the *Snapper* and would catch up.

"This is Captain Marchenko," she answered the hail. Even though her parents had dubbed her acting captain, she felt presumptuous claiming the rank and also using her mom's title.

"Prepare to be boarded, Turtle," a disdainful male voice said.

At least they didn't seem to be dealing with another android. But how had this ship found her out here? She hadn't filed a flight plan with anyone, and surely her detour to Halite Moon couldn't have been anticipated by anyone.

"See," Erick said, looking over his shoulder. "It's clearly a turtle if you're looking at it from a distance."

Masika stood in the hatchway. She only grunted at his comment, her gaze toward the view screen.

"We're an independent civilian freighter," Jelena responded over the comm. "Who are you, and why would we let you board us?"

"This is Captain Zhu of the *Falcon*, working for Stellacor Incorporated. You have something that belongs to my employers."

"I can't read him," Erick whispered, touching his temple.

Jelena frowned at him. Were they dealing with androids, after all?

"Sorry, Captain," Jelena said. "We already dropped off the animals. We found a better home for them than your employers provided." Well, they had dropped off *some* of the animals.

"That is unfortunate for you. If your stolen cargo can't be reacquired, there will be unpleasant repercussions."

"I'm wagering your employers ordered you to unpleasantly repercuss whether you get the cargo back or not, but we don't have time for that now. You'll have to pardon us if we don't invite you to board." Jelena raised their shields and tapped the controls, setting a course to go around. She didn't expect the ship to let them go around—not without a fight—but the less time she gave the captain to think about options, the better. She muted their end of the comm. "I need you to study that ship as quickly as possible and find something to break, Erick."

"I'm not familiar with pterodactyls at all."

"Better find a sys-net entry."

"Yes, we're aware that you're trying to reach Arkadius," Zhu said. "If you somehow evade us, be assured that *many* more ships will be waiting for you there. Stellacor's reach is long, and they have offices on Arkadius, as well as ships. Powerful ships to ensure they're not trifled with. You won't be able to get anywhere near the planet to sell your stolen cargo."

Jelena's first thought was indignation—did they truly think she meant to sell the animals?—but then a chill went through her. Arkadius, he'd said. How could Stellacor possibly know her destination? Had they looked up the *Snapper*, learned it belonged to her parents, and then looked *them* up? Had her communications been monitored somehow? Or had someone figured out that Leonidas was in trouble and assumed Jelena would be going to visit? Or—Jelena glanced at Masika, who was observing with a stony, unreadable expression—was it possible their guest had figured out where they were going and gotten to the comm at some point to send a message? Jelena and Erick had been splitting the shifts, so that shouldn't have been possible, but—

No, she realized with a silent groan. That wasn't true. Masika had been alone on the ship when they'd been in the Starseer base. Why hadn't Jelena thought to lock down the comm?

"We're not going to sell anything," she said. "I told you: we dropped off the animals."

"We have sensors," Zhu said, as if he were speaking to a dense toddler. "We can tell there are more than two life forms aboard."

"Damned inconvenient when your enemies can count," Erick muttered, then pointed at the screen. "He's angling to cut you off."

"I see it."

Jelena sent full power to the thrusters, hoping she might surprise the captain and get by with a burst of speed. It might be a vain hope, since she was certain he could catch her again. They needed to disable that ship somehow, ideally putting Zhu out of commission for a couple of days.

Masika took a step into NavCom, and Jelena spun in her seat, pinning her with a glare. She sensed unfriendly intent from the woman, like she was thinking of attacking while they were distracted. Or at least doing enough to keep them from escaping the other ship.

"Don't," Jelena said, trying to put a dangerous chill in her voice. "Erick, will you escort our guest to her—"

Masika lunged with incredible speed, throwing an elbow into Erick's chest as he started to stand. He gasped and was flung backward, falling out of his seat on the other side. Without pausing, Masika punched Jelena.

Instinctively, Jelena threw up a block, deflecting what would have been a fist to the face. Even though she succeeded, a jolt of pain ran up her arm from the power of the blow. She tried to stand so she could have room to maneuver, but Masika was already punching again, with the same lightning speed of Leonidas.

Jelena ducked, the fist tearing out some of her hair as it grazed her scalp. She twisted in her seat, kicking out, trying to force Masika back. Her foot connected with Masika's stomach, but it was like kicking a metal wall. It didn't give, and Masika didn't so much as grunt in pain. She lifted her arm to deliver what would surely be a chop hard enough to break Jelena's skull.

Jelena flung herself out of her seat, rolling awkwardly across the deck and bumping into the co-pilot's seat as she tried to jump up. Masika's blow landed, not on her skull but on the console. Her fist sank into the navigation control panel, leaving a dent like a crater. An alarm wailed in protest. Masika whirled, springing toward Jelena, and Jelena flung a desperate attack with her mind. At the same time, a wave of power whooshed past her like a tornado, almost knocking her back to her knees even though she wasn't the target.

Masika flew over the pilot's seat and struck the bulkhead, her skull cracking against the metal, her face contorting with pain. Erick grabbed Jelena and helped her to her feet.

"We have to knock her out," Jelena blurted. Already, Masika was shaking her head, snarling away the pain as she recovered from the crash.

"I was thinking of *shooting* her," Erick growled, even though he didn't have a pistol.

"Keep her busy," Jelena blurted and ran through the hatchway, spun around the corner, and sprinted down the corridor toward sickbay.

A crash and a thud came from NavCom, and Erick cried out. Damn it. Jelena ran faster, skidding as she grabbed the hatchway and spun herself into sickbay. She lunged for the drawers, hoping Masika hadn't thought to remove the sedatives when she'd been rummaging. There *were* some sharp objects missing, but Jelena found the drawer with the drugs in it unbothered. She snatched out a sedative and jammed it into an empty injector, almost firing the dosage into her hand in the process.

She sprinted back to NavCom, jumping through the hatchway and crashing into someone who was tumbling back out of it. Erick. Masika snarled and leaped after him, her hands wrapping around his throat. Jelena squirmed under both of their arms, yanked up Masika's shirt, and jammed the injector against her skin. An elbow came out of nowhere and slammed into the side of her head so hard that stars exploded behind her eyes. She was aware of her body flying across NavCom, but she couldn't move her arms, couldn't do anything to soften her fall. As she crashed into the bulkhead, much as Masika had done seconds earlier, she heard the tinkle of the injector landing on the deck.

Had she managed to inject enough of the drug to do anything? She blinked, trying to clear the dark spots swimming before her eyes and trying to ignore the stabbing pain in her skull.

A dark shape loomed above her, and Jelena lifted a hand in a feeble attempt to protect herself. But it was Erick. Masika lay crumpled on the deck behind him.

"We have trouble," he said, not looking at her but toward the view screen.

"What?" Jelena croaked. Then a white light flashed on the screen, followed by a shudder reverberating through the ship. "Never mind," she rasped.

Grab beam. The other ship had captured them.

CHAPTER TEN

"We shouldn't have bought a freighter that didn't come with chains strong enough to restrain a cyborg," Erick growled as he and Jelena hefted their unconscious guest onto an exam table in sickbay.

"Maybe you could check the storage closet and see if any were gifted to Alberto," Jelena said, wincing. Speaking hurt her head. *Everything* hurt her head. She glanced toward the drug drawer, figuring she better take some Painpro. If they had time. Any second, the pterodactyl ship would be close enough to clamp onto them, extend an airlock tube for boarding, and invade the *Snapper.* "I can't believe she painted our cabin and then turned on us."

"I can," Erick said. "We kidnapped her, after all."

"We *rescued* her."

"After you knocked her off a cliff." Erick poked through the cabinets and pulled out some cable ties.

"Her *own* people knocked her off the cliff. I don't think that's going to restrain her. Did you see what she did to my control panel? And almost to my head?" Jelena headed for a drawer. They needed to keep Masika out while they dealt with the boarding party that came over. Jelena, envisioning troops in combat armor, did not yet know how she and Erick would do that, especially if they were androids and wouldn't be affected by mind attacks.

"I saw. It looked like you got a glancing blow. You're lucky your brains aren't splattered all over the deck in NavCom now."

"A cheery thought." Jelena dragged out a collapsible IV stand and tubing. "I'm going to set her up with a continuous drip, keep her knocked out."

"Does that mean you're not willing to entertain my suggestion of shooting her?" Erick, apparently not satisfied that drugging her would be enough, tied her ankle to the bar under the exam table.

"Not until we convince her to paint the rest of the ship."

An ominous clang reverberated through the *Snapper*.

"If they steal the ship and kill us, we won't be around to appreciate the paint," Erick said.

"That would be unfortunate. Are you figuring out how to disable their grab beam as we speak?"

He gave her an exasperated look as he tied Masika's other ankle. "When would I have had time to do that?"

"As a superhero, doing two things at once should be within your skill set." Jelena finished setting up the IV and went fishing for a vein in Masika's arm, glad for the computerized guide on the needle tip, since Masika wasn't in a position to make a fist for her.

"Now I'm back up to superhero status? I thought you took my cape away."

"Just temporarily."

"I'll try to figure out where their grab beam generator is, but—"

Another clang reverberated through the *Snapper*. Jelena didn't need to stretch out with her senses to know the enemy ship was fully clamped on now.

"We're going to have to figure out a way to deal with the boarding party. Ideally, *you* will, so I can sit in here and concentrate on doing incredibly dastardly Starseer things to their ship."

"I'd settle for quasi dastardly things." Jelena slid the needle into the vein, slapped a patchtab to hold it down, and tapped the computerized IV bag to provide a steady drip. She risked giving Masika a little more than her weight would have suggested, thinking of the way Leonidas metabolized things quickly.

"I'm serious, Jelena. Do you think you can keep them busy for a few minutes? If I just have some time…" He finished tying Masika's wrists and backed up, resting a hand on the bulkhead and closing his eyes.

"I'll do my best." Jelena reached out with her mind's eye, hoping to gauge how many people were on that ship and how many were coming over. She had no idea how she would delay a pack of androids, but to her surprise, she sensed four armored men standing next to the airlock on the enemy ship, one of them manipulating the tube and the clamps, another gripping a space-rated plasmite torch for a forced boarding. There were four more people on the ship, two men and two women, and they were split between the bridge and engineering. "Erick, you said you couldn't sense any humans over there?" she asked, surprised that he would have missed them.

"Oh, I sensed them, but try touching their minds," he said without opening his eyes. "I think they've taken some Qui-gorn or another anti-mind-manipulation drug."

"Ah." She saw now. She couldn't get any sense for the emotions or thoughts of the men near the airlock. Not that their intent wasn't perfectly clear.

"All right. I'll try to give you your time." Jelena grabbed one of the pain-killers before leaving, going straight for the injectable drugs rather than the pills. After growing up with Leonidas, she should have known better than to get into a fistfight with a cyborg.

Soft scrapes came from the hull as the airlock tube was attached. Jelena jogged to her cabin and grabbed her staff, struggling for calm and focus. Four strong men in combat armor was a daunting thing, but she didn't have to utterly defeat them, just delay them long enough for Erick to sabotage their ship.

"You can do this," she whispered, jogging into the cargo hold.

Meows, whimpers, whines, grunts, and nervously wagging tails greeted her. If the men hadn't been armored, she might have unleashed her animal army on them, but no, they would only get hurt if she tried something like that. Better to keep a fight from breaking out in here. She did a quick mental check on Alfie and found her still in Masika's cabin. The hatch had shut, leaving her inside. Probably as good a place for her as any.

Jelena stretched out with her mind again, this time studying the airlock tube. Telekinesis wasn't her strength, but it was a simple device. Maybe she could tear a little hole or disengage it somehow.

The men opened the exterior hatch on their ship. She didn't have much time. She prodded at the spot where the tube connected to her ship's O-ring.

If she didn't mind damaging her own ship temporarily, and making it so they couldn't dock until they fixed it, maybe she could—

"Hah," she whispered as she broke the seal with a soft tearing from her mind. She imagined the hiss as air flowed out into space. She made another tear in it, and the tube, with three of the men walking across, unfastened and swung away from the hatch.

The men inside, protected by their self-contained combat armor, weren't in danger from the vacuum, but she imagined their alarm as the tube whipped about. The man still inside the ship hit the button to withdraw the tube, pulling his comrades back into their airlock as he did so. Jelena sensed them standing in their chamber, looking across the gap to her ship. Discussing their options.

She walked to the camera display and turned it on. Watching them with her eyes would save her brain some effort, especially since the painkiller hadn't kicked in yet, and her head was still throbbing.

One of the men pointed across, seemingly right at her. The camera was beside the hatch. He squatted and pushed off, maneuvering across the gap with a jet pack built into his armor.

"Well, that didn't delay them for long," Jelena muttered as the others followed suit.

Soon, all four men, clad in gleaming silver armor that looked brand new and state-of-the-art, gripped the *Snapper's* exterior, their magnetic boots helping them latch on like ticks.

Jelena resisted the urge to check in with Erick, knowing he was doing the best he could.

What else could she do to delay them? She could stand toe-to-toe in a fight with someone in combat armor, as long as she could deflect blazer bolts and keep him out of arm's reach with her staff, but with multiple opponents, her odds got a lot dicier.

As the man with the torch climbed toward the hatch, Jelena tried to hurl a blast of energy at him to knock him off her hull. But these people knew what they were dealing with. As if he expected it, the man found a handhold and clamped down. His legs flew away, but he quickly brought them back to the ship, and his comrade gripped his shoulder to help support him.

Jelena focused on the torch for her next blast of energy, but the man kept a solid grip on that too. Perhaps her attacks weren't as effective out in space—it wasn't as if there was any air to channel and throw like a spear. Erick might have peered into the works of the torch and known which little switch or mechanism to break, but Jelena only saw a confusing mess.

The torch came on, the red glow of its tip contorting oddly in space, but not so oddly that it wouldn't be effective. The man lifted it toward the hatch, and Jelena grimaced. She didn't want to see her ship damaged—it was bad enough that they might have to do some repairs in NavCom before they could fly away. Using her mind, she pressed the button to open the exterior hatch.

The man who'd been about to cut a hole twitched in surprise and almost dropped the torch. Jelena snorted. Sure, *now* he loosened his grip.

He and his cohorts gathered around the airlock chamber and peered in. They hesitated, seeming to expect a trap.

"If only I knew how to make one." Jelena imagined gouts of fire shooting out from the walls as her foes entered, followed by spikes coming out of the deck and the ceiling to stab and macerate them to death. A shame the previous owner hadn't installed any such features.

The men talked for a couple of minutes before entering the airlock chamber. If Jelena hadn't been worried about what they would do once they got in, she might have laughed that opening the door and inviting them in was giving Erick more time than if she'd let them cut through the hatch. They debated for another minute, judging by their gestures, about whether to try to get the lock to cycle and fill with air or if they should apply the torch and barge their way in.

Jelena pressed another button with her mind. The outer hatch closed, locking them in. If they hadn't had tools, she would have happily left them there, but they would only destroy her inner hatch if she did. Instead, she cycled the lock. They seemed content to wait. That provided another two minutes.

"Hope you're making use of this time, Erick," she muttered. "I'm expecting something genius."

Jelena created a barrier in front of her as the inner hatch finally opened. She tried to appear casual, gripping her staff in one hand, the butt resting on the deck. She'd seen men in combat armor before, plenty of times. Nothing to get worried about. Just because Leonidas was resourceful enough to beat Starseers in battle didn't mean they would be.

The four big men stomped in, all pointing rifles in her direction.

Not being able to get any sense of their intent left her uneasy, and she double-checked her barrier, wrapping it completely around herself. The leader looked at her through a tinted faceplate, so she couldn't even gauge him by his eyes. His helmet turned toward the pens.

A couple of the dogs barked, but most of the animals hunkered fearfully along the back wall. Jelena debated whether she needed to extend her barrier to protect them—the larger and more complicated she tried to make it, the more difficult it was to keep her concentration.

"Where is she?" the leader asked.

She?

Did he mean Masika? Jelena couldn't imagine who else they would be referring to, unless one of the female monkeys had been somehow significant, but had the corporation truly sent all these people and all those ships after them just for a security guard? Jelena had a hard time picturing them caring about their employees that much. They certainly hadn't cared about the animals. She was surprised there had been pursuit at all, at least after the *Snapper* escaped that canyon.

"The cyborg?" Jelena asked for clarification and to further stall.

The leader looked back at one of his men, not answering right away. Or maybe speaking on his comm to someone. Jelena couldn't hear their communications through their helmets.

"Masika Ghazali," the leader said.

"You're more than welcome to her." Jelena almost pointed to sickbay, but remembered Erick was in there too. "I've been trying to find a place to drop her off since we inadvertently acquired her."

"You will return her now." The leader looked over his shoulder again. "Graf, go hack into the comm, and make sure they didn't send any medical information off to anyone. Noh, check sickbay. See if they took any samples. Byun, find the man. She wasn't alone."

"Yes, sir," came out of three mouths, and the men jogged toward the corridor that led to the cabins, sickbay, the mess, and NavCom. Another identical hatch in the back led to engineering and the machine shop. Interestingly, they didn't hesitate with their choices. Had somebody looked up the model of her ship and its layout? These men definitely weren't amateurs. If only she could say the same about herself and Erick.

Erick? she spoke silently into his mind. *You're about to have company. They want our cyborg. And they seem to think we've been taking scans of her or blood samples or something, so they're going to rifle through all our stuff.*

Jelena shifted from foot to foot as the sole remaining soldier walked toward her, that unreadable faceplate pointed in her direction. He held his rifle casually, but his fingertip was wrapped around the trigger, and something about the way he seemed to be trying to make her think he wasn't aiming at her made her believe he intended to take her by surprise, to shoot. Or to get close enough to yank her staff away. Her barrier would block such an attempt, unless he led with something that startled the concentration out of her.

I think they may have orders to kill us, Jelena added, gripping her staff to help with focus.

You can read them?

Just a hunch. I—

The rifle whipped up, and a crimson blazer bolt streaked at her from only a few feet away. It bounced off her barrier.

She sprang at the man, hoping to startle him, and thrust her staff toward his armored chest. To her surprise, he didn't try to dodge or block the blow. Did he think this was a plain stick?

It cracked against the chest piece, his armor not giving at all, and a jolt ran up her arm, but she let her mental energy flow into her staff. The tool enhanced and altered that energy, sending lightning against his chest and out to his limbs.

He jerked, stumbling back, the power seeping through his armor in a way normal weapons did not. She attacked again, feinting toward his faceplate. This time, he reacted, jerking his head back. But she hadn't expected that attack to hit and followed up immediately with a more committed one, jamming the tip of her staff into his solar plexus.

He brought his rifle up again, even as her energy poured into him, sizzling and scorching him through his armor. She knocked the rifle aside, and spun with the movement, lifting her leg for a side kick. She slammed it into his armored groin, throwing her mental energy behind her physical power, adding far more strength to the blow than she would have had otherwise. She doubted it hurt him, but she had the slight satisfaction of seeing him stumble back.

"Sergeant?" came a surprised bark from the direction the rest of the men had gone.

Jelena cursed. She'd been dealing with one, but how was she supposed to handle two?

Expecting the attack, she erected her barrier again. It wasn't for naught. The man in the hatchway fired at Jelena without warning. The blaster bolt struck her barrier, bouncing off. She gritted her teeth and focused, knowing she couldn't let annoyance at his appearance affect her concentration. But she couldn't attack the first man and defend against this newcomer at the same time. And the first man was recovering, raising his rifle toward her again.

She backed away, so they couldn't flank her.

Several dark shapes streaked past her, and she almost lost her concentration at a fatal moment. The dogs. They'd leaped out of their pen and were racing toward the man in the hatchway, their jaws snapping. To her surprise, the pigs followed, bowling through their fence as if it were no more obstacle than a spider web. They moved surprisingly fast, catching up with the dogs and hurling their substantial masses at the man.

The animals wouldn't have been able to bite him through his armor, but he snarled and aimed at one of the dogs, regardless.

"No!" Jelena cried, and with fear, horror, and anger mingling, she hurled all of her mental energy at him.

Her foe flew backward, his boots leaving the deck as he crashed into the bulkhead behind him. Out of the corner of her eye, she saw the closer man trying to take advantage, lunging toward her. She attempted to fling a second attack at him, but he closed too quickly.

A gauntleted hand wrapped around her shoulder, a vise clamping on and crunching. Pain surged up her neck and down her arm, and she flailed at him with the staff, batting ineffectively. Without her mind's power behind it, the weapon thwacked uselessly against his armor.

The ship lurched wildly, the deck tilting under them. Startled, the man loosened his grip.

Though she was afraid the *Snapper* had been damaged, Jelena took the split second to gather herself. She clenched her staff with both hands, and this time, she threw her mental power into her thrust, aiming it squarely at her attacker's chest. As it struck, lightning flared so brightly that she winced and looked away. The man *flew* away as if she'd struck him with a battering ram. His rifle fell out of his hands and clattered across the deck.

She started after him, but paused, glancing toward the second man. He hadn't regained his feet. He sat against the wall, his helmet slumped forward, his weapon fallen at his side. The dogs were growling and barking at him, while the pigs butted their heads against his armor, but he seemed oblivious.

Jelena was surprised she'd struck him hard enough to cause that, but she did not object to the result. She picked up the rifle on the deck, tossed it into one of the animal pens, and ran toward the man she'd just struck, having a notion of battering him into unconsciousness with her staff.

But he sprang to his feet, yelled something over his comm, and ran toward the airlock hatch. Jelena stopped, staring after him. He ran into the airlock chamber and waved toward the corridor as two men came out of it, dragging the unconscious one. One of those men looked like he'd been caught in a fire, with his armor charred and soot-covered. The other one's helmet was dented, and he ran crookedly.

"You forgot your cyborg," Jelena called as they ran by, confused by their behavior.

She kept her staff up and ready, anticipating parting shots. But they charged into the airlock chamber and closed the inner hatch. The panel beside it flashed, indicating that they'd forced their way out without waiting for the lock to cycle.

She strode up to peer at the camera display in time to see them jetting back to their ship. An open hatch waited for them, the same as before, but the ship was tilted to one side, and she gaped when she spotted a ragged hole in the hull. The *Snapper* hadn't fired. Something on their ship must have exploded.

Erick appeared in the hatchway, leaning heavily on the jamb, his face white. The dogs had scattered as the armored troops ran out, and now, they simply sat back on their haunches or milled, as if their work was done and they were waiting for treats.

"What did you do?" Jelena asked. "Are you all right?"

"I think I overexerted myself." One of his eyes squinted shut. "Can brains cramp?"

"Maybe you need some potassium." Jelena walked toward him, patting a few dog heads on the way by. She wanted to slump against a bulkhead and recover, but whatever had happened to that ship, she was sure they would find a way to fix it. The *Snapper* needed to get out of its sensor range while it could. "There are still some bananas from that island on Halite where we dropped the monkeys." They had, indeed, found some favorite human fruits growing in the tropical zone.

"We should have some time," Erick said, stepping aside as she passed. "An important part of their engine had a pressure failing."

"Does that mean it exploded?"

"Yes. Handily taking out the grab beam generator at the same time."

"That was handy. If you could learn to do that to every enemy ship we meet within the first thirty seconds of them threatening us, it would keep me from having to dent my staff on combat armor."

"I'd have to be intimately familiar with all the possible designs and specs of every potential enemy ship in the system for that."

"Yes, and? You're an engineer. Aren't you supposed to memorize all the ships out there?"

"I don't think so. I wouldn't have any time to play *Striker Odyssey*, then."

"I'm not sure you're committed enough to your career, Erick."

He stopped in the corridor as she stepped into NavCom and looked toward sickbay. "Are you going to leave her sedated?"

"I'd like to put her back in her spacesuit and leave her out there for her friends to pick up."

"You'd have to give her your spacesuit, since her helmet is still cracked. Are you saying I should have let them have her?"

"You should have *thrown* her at them. Apparently, she's the reason Stellacor is still after us."

"Oh? That's surprising."

"I thought so too." Jelena grimaced at the dent in her console and verified that the grab beam no longer held them. Fortunately, she was able to put the *Snapper* back into motion. The pterodactyl ship hadn't moved. It remained in place, its wings tilted at an angle that made the ship look broken. "I'm now rather curious about her and thinking that tissue samples and gene scans would be interesting if we had the equipment to do either."

"Technically, I think we could take a tissue sample with a paring knife."

"True, but we wouldn't have any way to analyze it. It doesn't matter. I'm *definitely* dropping her off at the next stop. Had I known she was what Stellacor was after, I would have left her on that island with the monkeys."

"We can leave her on Arkadius."

Jelena leaned back in her seat, making sure the enemy ship was still receding on the camera before turning to meet Erick's eyes. "Actually, I don't think we can."

"What?"

"You heard that captain when he commed. Stellacor knows we're going to Arkadius, and they've got people—probably *ships*—watching out for us there."

"We can't *not* go," Erick said. "What about Leonidas and his surgery?"

What, indeed?

The idea of not being there when Leonidas—her *dad*—underwent a potentially deadly surgery horrified her. What if he didn't make it through? What if they couldn't cure his problem? What if she never saw him again? Never got to make any more jokes about his tree-trunk arms? Never again got to help the twins pick out stickers to put on his armor? Never got to lean on him when the Starseer training was too hard and Grandpa didn't understand? Never got to show him that even though she'd decided not to go to a university right away, as he'd thought she should, that she could do something important with her life? Be someone who added value to the universe. She wanted him to know that just as much as she wanted her mother to know it. If he was gone from the universe too soon, it just wouldn't be fair.

"Jelena?" Erick prompted softly.

She sniffed and looked away, wiping her eyes. "We're going to get to Arkadius, and we're going to get there in time, but I don't want to lead trouble into Mom's lap. Normally, I'd be happy to take these bastards straight to the *Nomad* so Leonidas and Grandpa could deal with them, but Leonidas can't deal with anybody right now, and I don't want them—it concerns me that Stellacor knows our heading. They may know all about the family business. And the family."

"Stanislav can protect the family if they try something," Erick said. "And he can help us too." He smiled faintly. "Maybe now that you've been in combat, you'll let him train you more seriously in telekinesis, so you have more weapons to use against thugs in combat armor."

"I did all right when I had to," Jelena said, though she knew she'd feel more comfortable battling multiple enemies if she could hurl them all across the room with the barest thought. She was still surprised she'd managed to throw the one man hard enough to knock him out—knocking out someone in shock-absorbing combat armor wasn't easily done with anything short of an e-cannon blast. Seeing the dogs in danger must have given her more strength and fear to pour into her attack.

"Yes, and I'm glad you handled a couple of them, but you could be truly powerful. Not that leading a dog army isn't wonderful, but you have potential to do a lot more than that. Stanislav has said so. You share his blood, after all, and he can do amazing things."

"So could Tymoteusz," she said, naming her crazy uncle who had kidnapped Thor and been responsible for the deaths of hundreds, if not thousands, of people when he'd created an earthquake on Arkadius. And then he'd concocted a plan to make himself ruler over the entire system. If not for Mom and Leonidas taking down his ship and killing him, that might have actually happened. Jelena had never spoken with Tymoteusz, but she'd heard about him from Thor and the others, and had confirmation that he'd been spaced in the head. And super powerful. A dangerous combination.

"What do you mean?" Erick's brow furrowed. "So what?"

"I share his blood, too, right? I don't want to turn crazy and become… and stop caring about people. And animals."

"Stanislav isn't like that. And he doesn't seem in danger of going crazy. Granted, he's *quirky*."

"Yes, and so is Mom."

"That does seem to run in your family." He bumped her arm with his fist.

"You're quirky, too, so you can't judge. Look, let's not talk about this now. What's important is getting to Arkadius, like you said, but I think if we show up in the *Snapper*, we might never get to land."

"We're not the legal owners, so we'd have trouble trading it in for another ship."

"What if we docked it somewhere else for a couple of weeks and took public transport to Arkadius? Stellacor wouldn't be looking at transport ships with hundreds of passengers aboard."

"Maybe not, but who's going to pay for the docking fees? Even if we parked at Starfall Station, which is pretty close, we'd have to pay a premium to leave the ship there for multiple days."

"It would be cheaper to go to a planet and pay some farmer a few tindarks to park in a field. Or—" She straightened as the thought of fields launched a new idea into her mind. "What if we go to Upsilon Seven and park there? We could look up Thor, and maybe he'd help us. Maybe *he* has a ship that we could use."

Erick groaned. "Not him again."

"He's powerful, too, if you want a Starseer ally that's more comfortable with hurling people around."

"I don't want an *assassin* ally. And I highly doubt that we'd have a trouble-free landing if we showed up in Arkadius's orbit in an assassin's ship. Do you think the Alliance doesn't know what he's flying? Can Thorian even fly?"

"He probably can by now. Part of his uber training and all. Oh." Jelena thumped her hand on her thigh as the idea further solidified in her mind. "This is good. We'll find him and ask him for help—even if he doesn't think he owes us anything, he *definitely* owes Leonidas. He should feel obligated to join us, at least for the time it takes to get to Arkadius, and then if he's flying with us, he won't be assassinating people. Maybe we can even talk him out of finishing that morbid list he's got in his head."

"*We?*" Erick slapped his palm to his forehead. "Jelena, we're not a *we* when it comes to talking to Thorian. Or anything crazy you plan. And I don't want to ask him for help. He's just a little kid."

"He's twenty now." Jelena didn't point out that she was even younger, just in case Erick had forgotten.

"He's arrogant."

"You barely remember him."

"I remember him being arrogant."

"You just thought that because he was younger than you and could do things you couldn't." Jelena had never found Thor to be arrogant, but she also hadn't been competition for him. She'd barely been able to scratch an itch with her mind back then, so she'd been playing catch-up to all of them. "Even if we don't ask Thor for help, or if we don't even find him, if we go to Upsilon Seven, it'll be a less expensive place to temporarily store the *Snapper*. And we can get transport from there."

"Probably in the back of a cargo hauler full of cattle," Erick grumbled. "Or in a refrigerated hold full of steaks."

"That's perfect. Why would Stellacor look for us in a meat locker?"

Erick shook his head at her. "I don't know why you're worried about power making you crazy. You're already spaced."

Ignoring his ongoing frown, Jelena plugged in the coordinates for Upsilon Seven. They could drop their passenger off there—oh, how she wished Erick hadn't been so efficient in defending sickbay, so those thugs could have simply taken Masika—and find Thor. Then, finally then, they could rejoin the rest of the family.

CHAPTER ELEVEN

The *Snapper* flew over lush prairies thick with blue and green grass, with cattle grazing, strung out around watering holes. Jelena guided the ship toward Blue Armadillo, one of the few major population centers on the continent and the city denoted by a missing puzzle piece on Thor's map.

Unlike most of the skyscraper-filled galactic cities, this one sprawled across the rolling hills, most buildings made from wood and stone, and rising only two or three stories. Here and there, stadiums for sporting events and rodeos took up prominent spots in the city. A river flowed by on the southern end with a space base perched along its bank. The base was a modern facility in the shape of an open-walled cylinder with six levels of ship docks sticking out like spokes on bicycle wheels. Several roads and a half dozen sets of train tracks went to the base.

"Paying for storage there will cost more than leaving the *Snapper* in a farmer's field," Erick said, walking into NavCom.

"We won't stay long. I want to see if Thor has arrived and also take the animals to the shelter here. I already talked to the lady who runs it, and she agreed to help. I'll be sad to let them go, but we wouldn't be able to take them on a transport, not easily."

Erick snorted. "Yes, Stellacor may indeed find us in a refrigerated meat locker if we're buying tickets for a hundred dogs, cats, and pigs as well as two people."

"Is Masika awake?"

"I heard a few thumps coming from her cabin."

"You didn't knock on the door?"

"You just told me to check and see if she was alive."

They hadn't seen her during the four-day trip to Upsilon Seven, not since taking her out of sickbay. Jelena had been afraid there might be complications if she tried to keep the woman sedated the whole trip, so they'd removed the IV and her bonds and left her in her cabin with food and water.

Jelena had considered locking the hatch, since the guest cabin had a fold-down sink and toilet, but had assumed Masika could break out if determined. Instead, she'd locked her *own* hatch at night when she slept and had set a few alarms so they would know if Masika started roaming the ship. She'd kept to herself. Maybe after her escape attempt had failed, she'd figured there wasn't much point to fighting them, not when she would find herself stranded in space without a pilot if she won.

"Here," Jelena said, waving Erick to her seat. "We're in a holding pattern. I'm waiting for space traffic control to approve our request to dock. I think we're waiting for those people to load their cargo and for that slot to open up." She pointed to the view screen, which showed a mix of drones and cowboys on horses funneling hundreds of steer up a ramp toward a big freighter. "Let me know when we get an approval. I'm going to talk to Masika."

"Take your staff. And maybe an injector full of drugs."

Jelena didn't make the sickbay stop for the drugs, but she *did* pause in her cabin to grab her meager collection of physical currency and also her staff. The first couple of days after the encounter with the Stellacor ship, she'd carried it everywhere with her, even into the lav, but since Masika hadn't left her cabin, she'd become less vigilant.

She knocked on Masika's hatch and stepped back, concerned the woman would greet her with a punch.

But the Masika who opened the hatch did not look like fighting. Her brown skin was paler than usual, and she looked rumpled and weary, as if she hadn't been sleeping.

"Are you all right?" Jelena asked, trying to remember if she'd done any flying that might have affected someone prone to airsickness. No, not since escaping the other ship.

"What do you care?" Masika grumbled, looking toward the wall beside Jelena instead of into her eyes. Odd, she usually had a challenging and direct gaze.

Maybe she felt bad about leaping on Jelena and Erick in NavCom when they hadn't done anything to her.

Jelena snorted softly. Sure. Besides, she could understand wanting to escape if she were being held prisoner somewhere.

"Well, I want you to be healthy enough to leave my ship," Jelena said. "And preferably return to your Stellacor employers so they'll stop chasing after me."

"Have we reached Starfall Station?"

"Not exactly." Jelena glanced toward the hull but remembered that none of the guest cabins had portholes. Masika wouldn't be able to see the grassy prairies stretching away from the city. "Upsilon Seven."

Masika groaned, stepped back, and sat on her bunk. "Why don't you ever take me where you say you're going to?"

"I like being unpredictable. But look, you can arrange transport from here, right? We're landing at the Blue Armadillo space base."

Masika stared glumly at the deck. Jelena didn't understand. Didn't she want to escape and go back? She'd certainly seemed to want to when she'd attacked them in NavCom.

"That's a long way from Alpha 17," Masika said. "An expensive trip."

"I figure you can comm your people, and they'll come get you, as they seem oddly attached to you, but even if that's not true, here." Jelena held out a few bills. "This should be enough to buy a ticket home."

Masika stared at her hand and didn't reach for the bills. "You're giving me money? I didn't agree to work for you."

"No you didn't, and you've been a pain in the ass since we brought you aboard. This is for painting the cabin." Jelena nodded to the mural. If Stellacor hadn't been after the woman, Jelena would have tried to get her to stay and finish the rest of the ship. She was tempted to make a pitch anyway.

Masika slowly reached out and accepted the money, though she stared at it as if she didn't understand what it was. Then she looked toward the bulkhead, or perhaps toward the mural painted on it.

"Is it beautiful out there?" she asked.

"Pardon?"

"Upsilon Seven. I've heard it's beautiful when the suns set over the prairies. There are supposed to be areas where the grass grows in a rainbow of colors, all dotted with wildflowers. And then the suns set over it, highlighting everything red and orange like burnished copper. A challenge to an artist's palette to capture it. And once you get away from the cities, they say you can walk for miles without seeing another human being. A person could disappear in a place like that. Off the grid. Off the radar. Maybe have a little ranch house and just come into town now and then to sell her art for cash."

Jelena stuck her free hand in her pocket while she puzzled out the comments. And the fact that their burly combat cyborg—or whatever she was—used words like *burnished* and *rainbow*.

"Masika…do you not *want* to go back?" Jelena asked, though that hardly seemed possible. She'd fought hard to be reunited with those Stellacor people.

"It doesn't matter what I want."

"Why not? You're not a prisoner, are you?" Indignation arose in Jelena as she imagined Masika being the equivalent of one of the lab animals locked up in a cage.

"If I am, it's because I knowingly walked into the trap." She still wasn't meeting Jelena's eyes, instead continuing to gaze toward the wall, as if she could see through it to the grasses and sunsets outside that she ached to experience.

"Why would you do that?"

Masika's mouth twisted with bitterness. "The bait was right."

"Well, you're not in a cage now. Why don't you just walk away and go where they can't find you? Like you said, Upsilon Seven might be an ideal place to go off the radar."

"I can't. I gave them my word. Not to try to return would be breaking that word." Masika took a deep breath and pulled her gaze from the wall. "It's not forever. Ten years was what they asked for, and it's what I agreed to. We made a deal. They expect…" There was that twist of the mouth again. Did she truly care what they expected? Or maybe she'd realized she'd made a deal with people who weren't good people.

"Thor once said that the expectations of others are a cage we build around ourselves, and it's the hardest kind of cage to break out of."

"Thor?"

"Prince Thorian." Jelena wondered if she would have to clarify further, since the empire was gone, and there weren't technically any princes anymore, at least according to the Alliance.

"Hm. He's been in hiding since the fall of the empire, hasn't he? When did you hear him say that?"

"When he was ten."

"He said that when he was ten?" Masika asked dryly.

"I think when you're a prince, the expectations of others are a problem you deal with from birth."

Masika grunted. "Probably. What's worse, do you think? People having expectations for you to live up to? Or nobody caring enough about you to have expectations?"

"I...don't know." Jelena wasn't sure what to make of this conversation. All she'd planned to do was hand Masika the money and open the hatch for her to leave.

The comm beeped.

"We've got permission to dock," Erick said. "Unless you want me to try to do it, you better come back up here."

"As I recall, landing spaceships isn't one of your superhero powers," Jelena said and stepped out of the cabin. Alfie waited out there and wagged her tail. Maybe she wanted to see the grasses too. It would be hard giving her up to a family here, but that would probably be better for her than keeping her indefinitely on a ship.

She caught Masika still looking at her. Feeling she should say something more, to impart some words of wisdom, Jelena added, "There are some situations where keeping your word isn't the honorable thing to do."

Anger flashed in Masika's dark eyes. "I'm sure you know all about honor, thief."

Maybe speaking again hadn't been a good idea. Still, Jelena felt compelled to defend herself. "History doesn't call those who helped free slaves thieves. It condemns those who kept slaves in the first place."

"Animals aren't slaves."

"No? Look up the definition and expand your preconceptions of the word *person*." Jelena walked up to NavCom, sat down when Erick vacated the seat, and took them toward the docking spot flashing on the holomap.

"She going to be trouble?" he asked.

"Maybe to her employers someday, but not to us. I don't think. I gave her some money so she can leave."

"That seems safest for us."

"Yes." Jelena took a steadying breath and glanced at him as the freighter descended. "I'd like to take a day and look for Thor. We also need to arrange a way to transport the animals to the shelter. It's in the country outside of town, and they don't have any way to come pick up a hundred dogs, cats, and pigs."

"You're not mentioning the part of the plan where we seek transport to Arkadius."

"That happens after the other two things. Can you do me a favor and find a rickety vehicle of some kind that we can use to get around town? Something inconspicuous? In case it's not legal to transport animals onto the planet without inspections or licenses or who knows what?" Jelena imagined gate guards raising a lot of eyebrows over thrust bikes pulling escape pods full of dogs and cats and pigs. "Something like you cobbled together back on Inner Trason and Dustor maybe."

"You want another of my junkyard specials?"

"They're fine and inexpensive modes of transportation. Your skilled hands haven't failed us yet."

"Sure, put an extra scoop on my Asteroid Icy. Have you commed your mother and explained everything yet?"

"Not yet. I've been debating on *how* to explain everything."

"I hear starting at the beginning and saying everything that's happened works."

"I will."

"Before you go looking for Thorian."

"But if we find him quickly and—"

"*Before*," Erick said. "If you don't tell her, I will. She deserves to know where her daughter is and why she's delayed."

Nothing in his tone brooked argument, and Jelena had a feeling she couldn't talk him out of making that comm call this time. How could she give lectures about honor and doing the right thing to Masika when she couldn't find the courage to tell her mother about her exploits?

Jelena sighed. "I'll comm her before I go out."

"Good. I want to see a record of that comm in the log when I check later."

"You're a nag, Erick. I'd say you'd make a good parent someday, but you'd probably have to find a woman first."

"Not necessarily. They can grow babies in labs, you know. I could even have myself cloned. Isn't science wonderful?"

"Wonderfully disturbing."

Erick headed out of NavCom, hopefully to grab his netdisc and start researching junkyards, but he paused in the hatchway.

"How exactly do you think you'll find Thorian?" he asked. "Blue Armadillo isn't huge by system standards, but it's still got hundreds of thousands of people, and I doubt Thorian is advertising his presence anywhere these days."

"When we were kids, I could sense him from quite a ways away. I'm hoping I still can."

Erick raised a skeptical eyebrow. "Can you sense *me* from a ways away?"

"I don't know. You'd have to go away and stop pestering me so I could check."

"Being grown and birthed in a lab might have improved your personality."

Jelena looked around for something to throw at him, but her stallion mug was not expendable. He left before she found a substitute.

She finished the docking procedure and braced herself to send a message to Mom.

CHAPTER TWELVE

Erick whistled cheerfully as he tinkered on an engine, the framework of a ground truck in the packed dirt next to him, heaps of junk forming a mountain range behind him. Jelena hadn't seen him this happy in days. She handed him tools now and then, but mostly poked at her netdisc's holodisplay while he worked.

Despite her claim that she would *feel* Thor if they were close, she didn't feel anything yet, so she was doing sys-net research. She'd feared that Thor would strike at his Upsilon Seven target before they arrived, but the news hadn't reported any such thing yet. In fact, the headlines featuring him had died down since there hadn't been any new assassinations in over a week. Her first thought was to consider that a good thing, but then she wondered if he'd been detained somewhere along the way. Had the Alliance caught up with him? Or what if he'd decided to skip Upsilon Seven and was already on Arkadius, hunting for his targets there?

Shaking the thoughts away, Jelena focused on her research, looking up the prominent citizens in the area. A lot of cattle barons came up on the list, but she couldn't imagine Thor would have a grudge against a rancher, unless that rancher had fought for the Alliance. Even that probably wouldn't be enough of a crime. So far, he'd focused on those who had betrayed the empire. Especially the *emperor*. His family.

"Here's someone who used to be an imperial senator," she murmured. "He retired on a five-thousand-acre ranch to the north of town. Hm." She ran a few searches to see if he had done anything openly nefarious, at least from the imperial point of view.

The clanks and clangs coming from under the truck frame were her only answer. Erick's work ethic was admirable, especially with two warm suns beating down on them. It was summer here, the air muggy and thick with blood-sucking bugs buzzing cheerfully as they flew over from the wetlands near the junkyard.

"We got a real treasure trove of parts for only forty tindarks," Erick commented, ignoring her Thor topic in favor of a subject of which he approved.

Jelena eyed the rusted engine parts, the dented oil cans, and the tire he'd patched three times before he could inflate it. "A treasure trove, yes."

The vehicle might be worth more than forty tindarks once he had it working, but she remembered what Erick had done the last couple of times he'd turned wrecks into operating conveyances, and she didn't count on them earning any money to put toward their tickets to Arkadius. Besides, it was likely Mom would send some money once she heard Jelena's message. Reluctantly, but feeling she had to come clean since there was a possibility the family could be in trouble because of Jelena's entanglement with Stellacor, she'd explained everything. The only thing she had left out was that she was looking for Thor. Unless she actually *found* him, there seemed to be little point in mentioning it.

"This Senator Albrecht is going to be my guess," Jelena said. "There's nobody else listed as a prominent resident here that I could imagine Thor targeting. Albrecht's sys-net entry doesn't mention any betrayal of the imperial government, just that he retired and came here after the fall. But considering he was a modest school teacher before lobbying for and being appointed to a position in the Senate, and considering that the senators weren't paid a huge salary, well, five thousand acres is a lot of land, especially this close to a major city."

A thump sounded, followed by a rumble as an old combustion engine started up. "Hah," Erick said.

Jelena figured that was the closest thing to a response she would get and started looking up information on Albrecht's ranch.

"Those senators were all taking money under the table," Erick surprised her by saying. "We studied this in school, in recent history classes. How do you think a school teacher made enough money to campaign for an appointment? He made promises to someone, someone whom he no doubt paid back once he was in office."

"Are you saying he could have gotten rich enough to buy a big ranch without betraying the emperor?"

"I am saying that, yes."

"*But*," Jelena reasoned, "even if those senators all got rich when they were serving, they got rich in imperial morats, money that lost ninety-nine percent of its value after the fall. There are a lot of ex-senators and other career politicians that are broke now because they had their money in imperial banks and their stocks in the imperial market. The ones who made it out of the war rich…well, it kind of presupposes that they had some knowledge of what was coming, doesn't it? They were able to prepare, to protect their wealth."

"I doubt it took a genius in the end to see what was coming."

"I don't know. A lot of people didn't. Mom said the empire and most of its loyal citizens always thought it was too big, too powerful, to fall." Jelena waved her netdisc. "I want to go out to Albrecht's ranch and see if I can sense Thor. If Albrecht *is* his target, he might be sniffing him out right now."

"Is that before or after we deliver the animals?"

"Once you have this fine vehicle running, we can do both at the same time. Maybe Senator Albrecht would like to adopt a dog."

Erick's response might have been a grunt or a groan. It was hard to tell when he was under the frame of the truck again.

• • • • •

Jelena was glad to find the animals were being good when she and Erick returned to the *Snapper*, driving the rust-covered truck up the ramp that spiraled up to their third-level docking spot. She was less glad to find Masika sitting on a crate outside of the ship, wearing a pensive expression as she gazed out over the river and the city.

Masika had walked out of the ship with her and Erick when they'd headed to the junkyard, and Jelena had locked the hatch behind her. She hadn't wanted to tempt Masika to enact some sabotage or other mischief before she left. Even if Jelena had paid her and they were letting her go, she might still feel some loyalty to recover the stolen animals for her employer—or to see Jelena and Erick punished by her employer, since she was determined to think of them as thieves. Jelena did not like the way her gaze shifted skyward as she and Erick drove up. She wasn't expecting Stellacor to show up here, was she? For that matter, how had they found the *Snapper* in the empty space between Halite Moon and Arkadius?

"If you're going to brood, could you do it elsewhere?" Jelena asked, making a shooing motion with her hand as she stepped out of the truck.

"I've looked up the transports, and there's nothing leaving today that's going anywhere that will get me home with the money I have."

"Well, your invitation to remain on the *Snapper* has been revoked, on account of surly, armored people looking for you."

"*And* on account of her attacking us in NavCom," Erick grumbled, heading for the cargo hatch.

"Ah." Masika smiled faintly—disappointedly?

What had she expected? She didn't want to stay. She'd made that clear.

Masika rose to her feet as Erick opened the hatch. He drove the truck into the hold to make loading easier.

"You're taking the animals somewhere?" Masika asked.

"To find a shelter that will find homes for them."

"Do you need help?"

Jelena eyed her suspiciously.

Masika shrugged. "You paid me too much for that small amount of painting I did. And my work was poor and clumsy."

"It looked good to me."

Masika's small smile took on a wistful aspect, but Jelena sensed a hint of condescension from her too. She probably thought Jelena didn't know anything about art. And unless one counted the hours Jelena had spent tracing horse pictures as a girl, she would be right.

"I've thought about it, and I can't accept this much money for so little work. I considered whether it was fair to take it because you kidnapped me—"

"*Rescued* you. Didn't you see that crack in your faceplate? You were going to die."

"Because you pushed her off a cliff," Erick called from the cargo hold, where he was trying to coax the pigs up a makeshift ramp and into the back of the truck. He would definitely need help. But because of that comment, Jelena decided to let him struggle for a couple more minutes.

"Weren't you the one to disable the ship that crashed into the cliff and truly caused her to fall?" she called back.

"You helped with that."

"Listen, Masika," Jelena said, turning back to her. "If you decide you want to snub your awful employers and you need a place to stay, we can talk—I'm sure we truly could employ you." As the words came out of her mouth, Jelena realized that maybe she shouldn't have said them. She didn't expect Masika to take her up on the offer, but what if she did? Then she'd be stuck with someone that Stellacor was willing to go to great lengths to get back. "But I sense that you don't feel you can leave them. And also that you don't like us much."

"This is true," Masika said, not fazed by Jelena's bluntness.

"Thank you so much for your honesty."

"You're thieves." Masika shrugged. "But very well. I shall leave your threshold."

"Good luck with your life."

Hearing meows and grunts of protest, Jelena jogged into the cargo hold. A pig zoomed past at top speed, chasing three dogs. Or maybe teaming up with the three dogs to avoid being rounded up. Cats meowed from up on the small catwalk that surrounded the hold. Erick was trying to telekinetically wrestle a couple of dogs into the truck's cargo bed, but they were barking, alarmed at floating through the air. The animals jumped down as soon as they landed in the truck.

"I used to be better at this," Erick said, giving her a plaintive look. "At least with chickens."

"You haven't spent much time bonding with these animals." Jelena sent out a wave of comfort, trying to calm them all down. She gave the promise of food and cozy pens and cat or dog beds. Maybe a forever home one day soon. Alfie trotted up and sat next to her, leaning on her leg. "This is a nice planet, girl," she said, bending to pat her head. "You'll have a nice life here, better than you would on a spaceship."

An unexpected lump formed in her throat, even though she hadn't been caring for the dog for long. Mom had always said no to dogs aboard the *Nomad*. It had taken Jelena years to argue and plead her way to her first cat. She wondered if Missie, Alex, Primp, and River would mind sharing their cabin on the *Nomad* with Alfie.

"Jelena, a little help?" Erick asked from where he was trying to coax the cats down. "I know you're good at this. You can always get your cats out of Leonidas's armor case with a chin jerk."

"Yes, and if I could get the cat *hair* out of his armor case, he'd be even more pleased. He usually keeps the lid closed, but when he opens it to don his armor, it's fair game. He grumbles a lot at the fact that all four of them magically know when they can jump in and curl up in the leg pieces. I believe the sanitizing process leaves everything in his armor case slightly warm and thus attractive to a cat." A twinge of homesickness washed over her at the memories the words stirred.

"I'm amazed he lets you have cats."

"He complains about them, but I've caught him reading on his bunk with cats lying on his chest. He doesn't seem to object to their presence then."

Jelena reached out to the animals, coaxing all of them from their perches. Almost as if they were a singular entity, the dogs, cats, and four pigs trundled to the truck. She would have to keep a mental touch on them since the cargo bed was open, and they could jump out if they were so inclined.

Erick scratched his head, looking stunned as they jumped into the truck. He had to help up the pigs and some of the dogs. The cats, being independent sorts with legs like springs, refused help.

Alfie looked up at her, ears perked, head tilted sideways, as if to ask if they were going to do something fun. She also didn't seem to think she was included in the gentle command to jump into the cargo bed. Hm.

"I wonder how Leonidas would feel about dog fur in his armor case," Jelena said.

"I doubt it's what he wants to see when he returns from his surgery."

Reminded of his predicament, Jelena let the subject drop. Erick closed the tailgate of the truck. Several faces peered over it and out to the open air beyond the *Snapper* and the space base.

"Should we bathe them before taking them to the shelter?" Jelena wondered, eyeing the matted fur on one dog's head.

Since leaving Alpha 17, the dogs and cats had bathed themselves and each other in the usual tongue-washing manner, and they no longer had that antiseptic laboratory smell, but she thought they could be cuter and fluffier. Surely that would help people feel more inclined to adopt them.

"I'm not trying to bathe any cats," Erick said. "You should be more worried about whether or not they've had shots and about how we don't have any record of that. We may get questioned by port authorities as we try to drive out of the base with a bunch of animals from off-world. Saying they're from some mad scientist's lab might not help."

"I wasn't planning to say anything. I'll convince them to lie low back there, and if necessary, maybe you can convince whoever questions us that there's nothing of interest in the cargo bed."

"You know Stanislav frowns upon us using our talents to diddle with the minds of people, unless it's a drastic situation and we're facing enemies."

"The port authorities could become enemies to our mission if they learn about the animals."

"*Your* mission. Not *our* mission. Your mission that you made up for yourself."

"That's how the universe runs. Some people make up missions and some people follow them. Let's get going." Jelena waved to the front of the truck. "Do you want me to drive?"

"Absolutely not." Erick jumped into the driver's seat while Jelena and Alfie climbed in on the other side.

"Because you don't trust my piloting skills or because you want to see how fast your rusty truck can race away from trouble?"

"Oh, we'll see how fast it can go at some point, whether there's trouble or not." He smirked at her, looking for a moment like the gangly fourteen-year-old boy he'd been when she first met him.

Alfie tilted her head.

"Yes, we should have had him install harnesses, girl," Jelena said.

Erick drove down the winding ramp, and Jelena did her best to convince the animals to settle low in the back. The men in the port authority guard shack hadn't batted an eye when she and Erick had driven in, but empty trucks going to pick up cargo were commonplace. It was the ride out where people were typically questioned.

To Jelena's surprise, the security men—four of them—were already out questioning someone. Masika.

She stood with her fists on her hips and her chin up, wearing the same gray military fatigues she'd had since Alpha 17—it wasn't as if she'd had other clothing options along. She didn't have any obvious weapons, but with fists like battering rams, maybe that didn't matter. One man was standing in front of her, talking and pointing a finger at her face. Three others stood uncomfortably close, their rifles pointed at her.

"Looks like we can slide by without the port authorities noticing us," Erick said.

Jelena frowned. "You don't think we should help her?"

Granted, Masika was more enemy than ally, but it seemed strange to abandon her to whatever trouble she'd found after they'd traveled together for several days.

"Do you think she would help us?" Erick asked.

"That's a horrible attitude for a superhero to take."

"I'm a practical superhero. We're driving a truck full of contraband, remember?"

"How can you talk about the animals like that?"

Alfie put a paw on Erick's thigh and gazed up at him.

He groaned. "You made her do that, didn't you?"

"She's a very intuitive dog. Just drive up beside the guards, so we can get the gist of what's happening."

"I can get the gist from here." He continued forward, despite the words. "They think she's a wanted criminal."

"Oh? Is she?" Jelena would find it ironic if, after calling her a thief all week, Masika turned out to have a criminal past. It seemed unlikely though. Stellacor would surely hire people who could pass background checks to be their security guards. Of course, they had already determined that Masika was something other than a simple guard.

"I doubt it. She's surprised and indignant."

Erick pulled the truck to a stop beside the group. Those rifles were still being pointed at Masika. Judging by the way her knees were bent, hands no longer on her hips but up in a boxer's pose, she was ready to spring into action at any second.

"Problem here?" Erick drawled, and Jelena sensed him trying to soothe the men with his mind, the same way she soothed animals.

"You can go through the checkpoint," one said, jerking the muzzle of his blazer rifle toward the exit as he barely glanced at the truck.

"Excellent. Mind if we bring her too?"

The guard who had spoken scrutinized Erick more closely. "There's a system-wide warrant out for her arrest."

Jelena was tempted to ask if there was a warrant out for *their* arrest. "What's her crime?" she asked instead.

Erick shot her a don't-talk-to-them-while-I'm-trying-to-diddle-their-minds look.

"The warrant doesn't say, but it's been issued by the Alliance, so we are obligated to enforce it." His eyes narrowed. "You're not *with* her, are you?" He looked over the truck.

"The Alliance?" Masika mouthed, and Jelena sensed her surprise. Not comforting to know that Stellacor had favors it could call upon with the Alliance law enforcers, but if they were known for delivering organs and saving lives, why wouldn't they have people who would support them? People who didn't know about the scummy things they did in their labs.

"Do we look like criminals?" Erick asked affably, leaning his arm on the door.

The man squinted past him and looked at Jelena. She sat with her staff between her knees, looking perfectly normal, she thought.

"All right, she's a little shifty, but I'm just an engineer," Erick said.

I don't think you're doing this right, Jelena told him telepathically. *They look more suspicious rather than less.*

Because you're clearly shifty.

I'm just sitting here.

Shiftily.

"She actually stole from us," Jelena said, trying to pour some of her mind's energy into making the words more persuasive. Just like herding cats into a truck, right? "It's fortunate that you caught her. I'd thought the money would be gone. There's two hundred tindarks in bills in one of her pockets.

It was mine. We're loyal Alliance citizens heading to the capital on Arkadius next. We could take her with us to save you some trouble."

Masika sent her a scathing look rather than an appreciative one.

"Search her for physical currency," one security officer said.

Masika bristled like a cactus, and looked like she would object, but Erick widened his eyes at her, perhaps saying something into her mind. She stood still and allowed the search.

The officer extracted a wad of bills. "Huh, two hundred. Just like she said."

"We're doing a few errands here and then taking off," Jelena went on, again trying to pour that persuasive element into her voice. *Believe me*, she thought, holding the man's gaze. "If you let us take her, we'll see to it that she's turned in, and you won't have to do any paperwork."

The officer looked at the other men, who shrugged back, their eyes appearing glassy. Maybe Erick was helping control them.

"It sounds like a good idea to let them take her," the speaker said, his voice wooden. None of his men objected. They lowered their rifles so the muzzles pointed at the ground.

The one that had counted the wad of bills walked it over to the truck. "Here's your money back, Miss."

Jelena reached across Erick to accept it, holding the man's gaze, willing him to continue to comply. She felt dirty using these tricks, manipulating people, but she doubted Masika deserved to be incarcerated. Maybe she would just end up back with Stellacor, but maybe not. Jelena didn't feel she had a grasp on their strange passenger. Ex-passenger, she reminded herself.

Their movements as wooden as their words, the security officers walked back into their guard station. Masika hesitated, but at Erick's finger flick, she climbed in, perching on a narrow bench behind the front seat. Erick drove off, his foot heavy on the pedal, and tires squealed as they rounded a corner.

"You think *I'm* shifty?" Jelena asked.

He grinned at her.

"That's the first thing you two have done that was what I expected," Masika said.

"Rescuing you from the grubby clutches of those guards?" Jelena asked, offering the bills to her over her shoulder.

"I didn't need to be rescued. I was about to shove their rifles up their favorite orifices. I'm talking about manipulating people's minds. I thought all Starseers did that, but I don't think you've tried on me or anyone else."

"Not *all* Starseers do that," Erick said.

"All the Starseers I know about do."

Jelena looked at her curiously. "You know Starseers?"

"No, I just know about them. The mind manipulation thing is always a level-one skill in the games."

"Games?" Jelena asked at the same time as Erick roared around another corner and glanced back at her.

"You're not talking about *Solar Age*, are you?" he asked. "The depiction of Starseers is totally nadir in that game. None of the games get it right. They clearly need me as a beta tester."

"Have you applied?" Jelena asked.

"*All* the time. I don't think they believe I'm a Starseer. Besides, all they worry about getting right is the tech specifications on ships. That's why Tomich gets invited to beta test everything." Erick looked back at Masika again. "Do you play games?" His tone suggested he would find that even more surprising than her hidden artistic abilities.

Masika hesitated, then shrugged. "I did some when I was at the university."

"*Solar Age*?"

"That and *Launch to Antares*."

"Huh. What about *Striker Odyssey*?"

"That wasn't out yet when I…quit school."

"You should try it," Erick said. "You'd level quickly if you've played *Solar Age*. We could use a few medics in our crew if you want to play on my server."

"Are you really trying to recruit her to play your game, Erick?" Jelena waved the wad of money at Masika. "If you don't take this back, we're going to spend it on dog food."

Masika took the bills and slipped them into her pocket again. "The Starseers in the games always wear robes while they're manipulating people. I thought that was a requirement."

"We have robes," Jelena said, "but Erick's is always rumpled because he never hangs it up."

"Wearing a robe is a good way to stick out," Erick said, careening around another corner, hitting a pothole, and eliciting yelps and barks from the back of the truck.

"So is driving a hundred miles an hour. Slow down, will you?"

Erick peeked at the mirror. "I guess. I saw a couple more security officers jogging out to that station. I thought we might be pursued. It won't take long for those men to realize their desire to avoid paperwork was uncharacteristically great."

"Getting back later may be a challenge." Something seemed to tickle the back of Jelena's mind, a memory brushing her senses along with something real, something from the present, the now.

"I'm sure those people will be off shift by the time we get all these animals off-loaded at the animal shelter. You said it's a ways outside of town, right?"

Jelena didn't answer. She was distracted by that faint tickle, that faint brushing of her mind. She leaned toward her window, peering up into the sky, as if she might see a ship flying overhead.

"Jelena?" Erick prompted.

"Yes, let's go to the shelter and get the animals taken care of."

"You all right? You look odd."

"I sense…I think Thor is here."

CHAPTER THIRTEEN

The bumpiness of the road out to Albrecht Ranch suggested people usually flew when they visited the area. The cityscape was still visible behind them, but grasslands had replaced houses and buildings, and it seemed like they were hundreds of miles from civilization instead of five or six. The rain-water-filled potholes in the road were large enough to qualify as ponds. Two suns burned low in the sky, shedding reddish light that reflected off the water.

Erick had a tendency to drive through the pools instead of around them. Unfortunate, since the window did not close on Jelena's side. She'd wiped mud from her cheeks more than once.

Masika still sat behind them, as she had since before they dropped off the animals. If she minded that Alfie had the more comfortable front seat spot between Jelena and Erick, she hadn't mentioned it. Of course, with the rusty spring thrusting through the ripped material and prodding Jelena in the butt, she wouldn't say the seat was that desirable.

"You still sense him?" Erick asked, nodding to the dirt road ahead.

A mesh electric fence and a wooden gate framed by peeled log posts had come into view. There hadn't been any turnoffs for a while, and Jelena didn't know what they would do when they reached that gate. Ring the bell and ask for an appointment with Albrecht? Did she want to warn him that Thor was coming for him? She'd prefer to find Thor and stop him herself.

"I do," Jelena said, though she didn't sense that he was ahead of them. More that he was above them somewhere.

"Can you tell if he's ten miles away? Or a hundred? Or if he landed or just flew over?" Erick didn't sound skeptical, not exactly, but he didn't seem to know what she was experiencing. "Because we're about to come to the end of the public road."

Jelena barely knew how to explain her connection with Thor, so all she said was, "I don't think he's landed yet. He seems to be up there somewhere." She waved toward the sky back in the direction of the city. "Closer than before, but…"

She frowned as the tickle at the back of her mind seemed to change. As she had long ago, when they'd been children on the run, and he'd been kidnapped by Tymoteusz, she got the sense that Thor was in trouble. She had no idea how she could tell or how they even shared a link after all this time.

Jelena leaned out the truck's window, peering toward the clear blue sky. Abruptly, his presence felt closer than it had for the last hour, much closer. He had to be flying in. Where would he land? At the ranch? Back at the space port? Albrecht must surely have security keeping an eye over his property.

A black, dart-shaped ship appeared on the horizon, exhaust streaming behind it as it sped toward the city at an alarming speed. It was an old imperial star clipper. Was Thor piloting it? He wasn't angling toward the space port. And he was coming in so fast. He'd have to do some fancy flying if he planned to land anywhere nearby.

"Wait," Jelena muttered. "That's not exhaust."

"What?" Erick asked.

"It's smoke. Someone hit him. Or he's having engine trouble."

A *lot* of engine trouble. Plumes of gray smoke streaked behind the clipper.

A second ship came into view, one not much larger than the clipper, but it wasn't damaged. Its hull gleamed gold under the suns' influence as it sped after its prey. An Alliance military craft. One of the new Strikers.

Jelena immediately thought of the ones downed back on Halite Moon. This one didn't look like it was in any danger of crashing. Its prey on the other hand…

Two crimson blazer blasts streaked toward the clipper. The damaged ship turned on its axis, as if its pilot—Thor—had known the attack was coming.

The blasts passed on either side, close enough to shave any lint off the roof and belly of the craft. The clipper righted itself and looked like it was trying to zigzag, to make a more difficult target, but its movements were jerky, and she imagined the pilot fighting the stick, not getting the response he needed.

Three more Alliance Strikers came into view, and Jelena groaned. No wonder Thor had been struck. How many were back there? How many were after him?

"He's losing altitude fast." Erick had stopped the truck and was peering out his own window.

"I think he's already lost control."

"That ship is definitely crashing," Masika said as it came into view through their windshield.

The clipper's wings wobbled again as more fire blazed through the sky after it, but this time, one of the blasts struck the craft. Fire spat from its port wing, and Jelena gasped as it was ripped off. More smoke poured from the craft. She reached out with her mind, not toward Thor but toward the ship following most closely. The pilot seemed to be human, a hulking man that barely fit in the cockpit.

Avert your mission, she ordered, trying to persuade him the same way she had the security officers. *You've already destroyed your target. He's crashing. You've won. Avert now.*

She didn't get any sense that the pilot was swayed or even heard her. In fact, she didn't get a sense of the man at all, beyond his physical presence in the cockpit.

"I think they're drugged," Erick said. Maybe he'd been trying to do the same thing. "More Qui-gorn."

Jelena slumped. Yes, that made sense. The Alliance knew it had sent its men after a Starseer assassin.

The one-winged clipper spiraled, completely out of control now. It streaked over the ranch gate as it descended, smoke billowing behind it. It disappeared from sight when it flew low over a wooded area to the left of the road and maybe two miles into the ranch, but there was little doubt as to its fate. Soon, black smoke billowed up from the woods.

Thor? Jelena tried to reach out to him. She hadn't wanted to distract him while he was fleeing, but now, she wanted to know if he was conscious and how badly injured he'd been. Had that clipper come with an ejector seat? Had he been able to use it?

She didn't receive a response to her telepathic inquiry. She could still sense Thor's aura, his life, but she had a feeling he might be unconscious.

"Here comes his buddy," Erick grumbled.

The Striker flew over the fence and toward the trees. A chill ran through Jelena as she imagined some heartless assassin striding up to the wreck to slice a dagger across Thor's throat before he woke up.

The three ships that had been following at a distance also zoomed over the fence toward the trees.

"*Buddies,*" Erick corrected as their noses dipped to land.

"Go." Jelena slapped his leg. "We have to help him."

"We can't drive through that fence or gate."

Jelena gripped her staff with one hand and the door handle with the other. "Get me as close as you can, and I'll go on foot."

Erick sighed but obeyed, and the truck surged forward. "*We'll* go."

Alfie barked.

Erick hit a pothole, and Masika's head cracked against the ceiling.

"Why do I have a feeling I should have let security arrest me?" she grumbled.

"That could still happen," Jelena said as Erick screeched to a stop inches from the wooden gate. She flung open the door and jumped out.

A security camera on an articulating arm shifted to record their vehicle. And them.

"Maybe you can take the truck off a ways and wait for us," Erick suggested. "You'd be the escape-vehicle driver. Those people hardly ever get arrested in the vids."

"Don't they usually get shot or blown up by the mafia?" Masika grumbled.

Erick jumped out. "We'll contact you when we need to be picked up."

"I don't have a comm unit."

"We'll contact you anyway." Erick touched his temple, pointed to her head, and winked.

She groaned. "You people are freaks."

Jelena jumped up to catch the top of the wooden gate—which was not electrified like the fence—and barely heard Erick's response of, "Someday, you'll have to tell us what *you* are, because we're fairly certain it's not a cyborg."

Jelena almost lost her staff as she pulled herself over the gate, but she managed to shove it over to the other side. It hit the ground, and she snatched it up as soon as she landed. The rutted and pockmarked road stretching deeper into the ranch was in no better condition than the one outside, so she took to the waist-high grass, figuring she could run through it just as quickly. The smoke was coming from deep within that wooded area, so she would have had to leave the road soon, regardless.

An engine rumbled behind them—Masika turning the vehicle around. Erick landed behind the gate and ran after Jelena, his longer legs allowing him to catch up easily.

Jelena grunted as she stumbled over the uneven ground. Navigating it and pushing through the waist-high grass wasn't as easy as she'd expected. The trees were also farther away than she'd judged. Soon, her breaths came in labored gasps, and she feared she would be forced to slow to a walk.

No, she couldn't. She could still sense Thor, his presence closer than ever, but who knew how much time he had? If he was injured, he might not be able to concentrate enough to use his powers. And if he was unconscious...

Jelena's foot found a hole—they were impossible to see under the heavy grass—and she gasped as pain shot up her ankle. She gritted her teeth and pushed on. Even though evening approached, the hot, muggy air had not abated, and her clothing soon stuck to her body. Sweat dripped down the side of her flushed face, adding further discomfort.

"Thor, you better...appreciate this," she growled through her labored breaths, urging her legs to keep going. She and Erick were almost to the trees. Hopefully, the groundcover would be easier to navigate in there.

"You're going through a lot of work for him. Especially since it looks like we won't be able to get a ride to Arkadius in his ship."

She glared at him, both for the insinuation that Thor wasn't worth the work and also because he wasn't breathing hard. The bastard. Was he using some Starseer trick she didn't know about? Or had he simply been spending more time training with Leonidas in the gym? All she wanted to do was bend over, grip her knees, and suck in deep breaths.

"Did you wink at her?" Jelena asked, trying to take her mind off her burning legs. How long had it been since the crash? Those Alliance pilots could have landed and slit Thor's throat multiple times by now.

"Masika?" Erick glanced at her. "I did."

"Was it…a flirtatious wink? Did you change your mind…about the appeal of her wrists…when you learned she'd played…some of your games?"

"I'm not sure. It wasn't a conscious wink. Do you think…she'll ever stop thinking of us…as thieves?" He finally sounded winded. Good.

"Don't know. She has…high standards…for someone the Alliance…is trying to arrest."

"I'll wager Stellacor just wants her back…and had the Alliance…put out an arrest warrant for them."

Jelena flicked her hand in acknowledgment. She couldn't manage speaking anymore. Fortunately, the grass grew shorter and less thick under the trees' canopy. They ran through mud and soggy leaf litter, while weaving around trunks and dodging low branches. Smoke tinged the damp air. It was darker in the woods, as if twilight had already come.

The trees blocked the view ahead, but Erick held up a hand.

"People up ahead," he whispered, slowing to a jog.

Though Jelena did not want to slow down, she forced herself to and tried to step lightly. If those Alliance men had been hand-selected to hunt down Thor, they would be good at their jobs. And they'd be very alert as they closed on him, not knowing what to expect.

Just be conscious, Thor, she thought, sending the words out for him, if he was listening. She sensed him, but still couldn't tell much about his status. She also couldn't pinpoint his location. It was as if he, too, was using some drug to muddle her attempts at reaching his mind.

I can't tell where he is, Erick said silently, glancing at her. *Can you lead us?*

Yes, but I'm struggling to get a bead on him too.

Jelena jogged ahead of him, her legs leaden after the long sprint, and kept her staff gripped tightly. She could sense life in the woods, animals hiding and birds staying silent in the aftermath of the crash, but also men. Four of them. They were working independently rather than in a group, so she and Erick would have to be doubly careful approaching the wreck. She could sense the downed ship up ahead, and two of the men were near it. Since she couldn't tell where Thor was, she and Erick would have to check the crash first.

She slowed to a walk, stepping carefully, glad the leaves were too wet to crunch. Even so, she suspected they'd already been detected. The two men farther from the wreck were circling it and coming toward them. Coincidence? Or were they coming to see who had barged into the forest?

Jelena bit her lip, torn between hiding from them and striding straight to the wreck, then using her power to protect herself if the men attacked. Imagining Thor lying broken and unconscious in his smashed cockpit, she decided on the latter.

They know we're out here, Erick told her, perhaps alarmed when she gave up stealth and strode forward with determined intent.

So? We're not assassins. They shouldn't shoot civilians.

What about civilians who are trespassing on a senator's ranch?

They're trespassing too. You think an old imperial senator would welcome Alliance soldiers onto his land?

If he wants to keep his land on this Alliance-run planet, yes.

Orange light flared ahead, and Jelena did not respond. Was that some weapon? There hadn't been an explosion.

She stepped behind a tree and peered deeper into the woods. Flames leaped into view, racing along the soggy leaves as if they were dryer than straw. Jelena stumbled back. A wall of fire soon charged through the trees, lighting them on fire as it leaped from trunk to trunk. It roared toward Jelena and Erick, and fear surged in her chest. The fire stole the shadows as it grew in intensity, and the air filled with smoke.

Fighting instincts to flee, Jelena forced herself to concentrate, to raise her staff and create a protective barrier around her and Erick.

Good, keep that up, he spoke into her mind. *I'll try to figure out who...Smell that? QuickFlame. I think the soldiers started it intentionally.*

Focused on keeping the barrier up, Jelena did not answer. The fire reached them, and she poured more energy than was required into protecting them. The flames burning all around them, licking at her invisible shield, daunted her even if they weren't touching her and she couldn't feel their heat. If her mind slipped for a second, they would be burned to crisps.

I bet they started it to flush him out, Erick added.

A crash sounded up ahead, and a silvery figure sprinted through the trees. Thor? No, the orange light of the flames reflected off combat armor.

Jelena groaned to herself. No wonder the soldiers wouldn't be worried about the fire. Their insulated, temperature-controlled armor would protect them from extreme conditions.

A dark shape stepped out from the burning tree beside her, and she almost shrieked and lost her concentration. Some of the heat seeped through her barrier when it waned, and fear clutched her again. She poured everything into her shield and could feel Erick channeling energy into it too.

The armored soldier, someone as tall as Erick but much brawnier, reached toward them. Jelena fought her instinct to jump back, trusting in her barrier. The man's silver gauntleted knuckles bumped against it. He stared at them, the flames all around reflected on his faceplate. She couldn't see his eyes, and if he said anything, she couldn't hear it over the roar of the fire.

His helmet shifted as he looked past them. Had he heard something?

He leaped over her barrier as if he were on a trampoline rather than solid ground, then sprinted in the direction he had been looking. The direction of the wreck.

Jelena's stomach twisted. *I'm going that way,* she warned Erick silently.

With you.

She wanted to run, but she walked, careful to keep the barrier extended around both of them. The core of the fire had swept past them, but individual trees continued to burn, and flames danced on fallen logs and branches on the ground.

Full night seemed to have fallen, or maybe the thick smoke was blocking out the fading light from the suns. Even with her barrier up, the scent of charring wood and leaf litter reached Jelena's nose, coming up from the ground they passed over. Heat rose from the ashes they walked across, and she did her best to extend her protection into the ground.

She stretched out, again trying to get a sense for where Thor was, but it was a struggle to maintain her barrier and read the area around them at the same time.

There's his crash site. Erick pointed past her shoulder.

A breeze cleared some of the smoke, and the mangled shape of the old imperial star clipper came into view, the nose smashed deep into the ground, the hull warped and contorted. The remaining wing had struck a tree, and the trunk lay across the back of the craft. A testament to the sturdiness of the hull, it hadn't been crushed, but Jelena couldn't get a good look at the cockpit from her position. It was possible the pilot had been pinned in there.

She quickened her pace, but before she'd gone more than a few steps toward the wreck, Erick gripped her shoulder. He pointed to something else.

One of the armored soldiers lay on his back on the ashes. Was it the one that had stared at them? He wasn't moving now, and when she reached out with her mind, she didn't sense any life.

Not sure she wanted to, she walked closer. His faceplate was broken. More than that, it looked like the liquid Glastica had been blown in or blown out, leaving a huge ragged hole. When she peered into his helmet, she jerked back, sucking in an alarmed breath. The man's face had been burned away, leaving nothing recognizable, nothing alive.

Thorian must be awake, Erick spoke grimly into her mind as she turned away, not able to look any longer. *And able to defend himself.*

You think he did that? Jelena asked, drawing back from the idea, preferring to think that the man's faceplate had broken in a fall and that he'd been a victim of his own fire.

Erick came up beside her and shook his head slowly, pointedly. *I'm sure it wasn't the retired eighty-year-old senator who lives here.*

Jelena had temporarily forgotten that they were on someone's property and not out in the wilderness. Would some of the senator's people be along to check on the fire and the ships soon?

She quickened her pace toward the wreck. It was hemmed in by other trees, some still dancing with flames, and they had to climb over the log atop it to reach the cockpit. Keeping the barrier up while they navigated the obstacle was difficult, but every time Jelena felt a hint of heat seeping through, she reinforced it.

To her relief, the cockpit wasn't smashed. The cracked canopy had been lifted, and there wasn't anyone inside. Good.

Jelena started to withdraw but paused. In the flickering orange light, she made out a dark spatter on the seat and more drops on the control panel. She hesitated, then touched her finger to the liquid. It had almost dried from the heat of the fire, but a smear came away on her finger. Blood.

He's injured. She showed her finger to Erick.

Anyone would be after that crash, but he's clearly got his faculties about him. He—

A wrenching sound came from behind them, and they both spun away from the wreck. A massive tree toppled, the draft it created stirring the smoke. A crunch echoed through the woods, and someone screamed.

Imagining Thor being crushed, Jelena ran toward the tree. Someone was pinned under the thick trunk, but it wasn't Thor. It was one of the men in armor, ash and soot dulling its silver sheen. He lay on his back fully under the tree, but he was still alive, and even as they watched, he gripped the charred trunk with both hands. He roared and hefted. Surprisingly, the trunk moved. He shoved it several feet into the air and rolled to the side with amazing speed, clearing the ground before the tree landed again.

Jelena stared, hardly believing the feat. Yes, the combat armor would increase his strength, but even with it, should he have been able to lift a massive tree? Especially from that position with so little leverage? Maybe he was one of the Alliance's cyborg soldiers. It made sense that the best would have been chosen to go after Thor.

Pain radiated from the man, but he jumped to his feet. He turned toward Jelena and Erick and jerked his arm up, the blazer weapons embedded in his armor popping up, ready to fire.

Jelena gripped her staff, letting more energy flow into maintaining her barrier. She was getting a headache from the ongoing effort required, but to let it down would be suicidal.

Though clearly prepared, the soldier did not shoot. He must know that neither of them was Thor. His target. But at the same time, he would find their presence here suspicious.

Jelena opened her mouth, but she wasn't sure what to say. *We're not your enemies?* Was that true? When they had come to help Thor? But even if she wanted to help him, she didn't want to pick a fight with the Alliance. It was already possible they would be linked to the death of the other man. And what then? She couldn't run freight for her family if she was wanted by the Alliance, not when their control extended over half the system now. The *desirable* half of the system.

Once again, the wrenching of roots being torn from their beds sounded behind them, along with thunderous snaps. Jelena turned toward the noise, afraid one of the trees would smash down on them. Seeing movement, she threw everything into her barrier and lifted her staff toward the sky.

But, though less than ten feet away, the tree did not fall in their direction. It smashed down between them and the wreck, the ground shivering as it struck.

It might be a good time to leave, Erick spoke into her mind.

I…am not sure I object. Yet Jelena did not truly entertain the notion. She didn't know if Thor was nearby and knocking over these trees, or if they were falling because of damage from the fire. He might very well be hunkered in hiding somewhere, his injury making it difficult for him to flee.

Erick looked gravely at her, and whether through his telepathic link or from her own thoughts, an image appeared in her mind of the man with the broken helmet and his face burned off.

She turned back toward the soldier, both because it wouldn't be a good idea to leave him at their backs and because she thought she might negotiate with him. With words if not mental power—she assumed the men's drugs hadn't worn off yet. Maybe she could offer to help them track Thor but then lead them away.

But the man wasn't standing anymore. She stepped back, horror lurching into her at the sight before her. His armored body lay in the ashes, and his helmet—his *head*—lay several feet away.

"What in all the suns' hells?" she blurted.

Even Erick seemed stunned. He gripped her shoulder, and she felt his horror through the tightness, his alarmed fingers squeezing her. She sensed that he wanted to get out of there, to throw her over his shoulder and carry her away if he had to.

What could have done that? She stared at the helmet, at the decapitated man, unable to tear her gaze away. A properly angled and sustained cut from a blazer beam might severe a man's head from his body, but not an *armored* man's head. Blazer fire usually pinged right off combat armor. Sustained fire might bore through it, but damn, Jelena hadn't been looking away for that long.

A pissed-off, surly teenage assassin. Erick's grimness came across far more than any sense of humor.

Using what? she demanded incredulously. She doubted even Grandpa could tear a head from an armored man's body with his mind. Not that he would try. This was more like something his crazy brother Tymoteusz might have done, but even then, she couldn't imagine how. And her mind shied away from making a connection between Thor and her dead uncle.

The squeal of blazer fire rose over the snaps and crackles of burning wood. It seemed to come from somewhere behind the wreck. Jelena walked in that direction, climbing over the fallen log again.

Are you sure we want to check that out? Erick asked.

Jelena paused in the shadow of the wreck, dreading the idea of coming upon another gruesomely killed soldier. *No,* she admitted honestly.

Then a snap came from the other direction, from where the beheaded soldier had fallen. Jelena had barely turned around when an armored figure leaped over the log toward them. A rifle hung on a strap slung across his torso, but the man did not grab it. He yelled in fury and sprang toward them, his gauntleted hands open, his fingers spread, as if he meant to grab them and tear them limb from limb.

"We didn't do it," Erick yelled.

Jelena reinforced her barrier one more time to make sure he did not reach them, but she stepped back as she did so, intimidated by the huge armored man. Her heel caught on something under the ashes, and she pitched backward, losing her balance. She flailed and caught herself on the scorching hull of the wreck.

Pain burst from her hand at the contact, and she yelped, clutching it to her chest, forgetting the soldier—and her barrier—for a second.

A second was all it took. The man bowled into Erick, slamming him against the wreck. Bone crunched, and Erick yelled in pain.

Jelena started to remake her barrier, but it was too late. She couldn't block out the soldier when he was grabbing Erick. Instead, she lunged at the man, channeling her power into her staff and thrusting it at his hip.

Lightning crackled all around his armor, but he kept yelling, too full of rage to feel the pain. Jelena struck him again, this time in the side of the neck. He roared, hurled Erick over his head, and whirled toward her. He grabbed for her staff as Erick flew over the log and landed out of sight on the other side. Jelena tried to yank her staff away before the man caught it, but he was too fast. Another cyborg?

For a moment, fear overrode her concentration as she remembered being a kid and watching Leonidas come out on top in sparring matches against a former Starseer crew member, Abelardus.

Her staff did not break and crack under the soldier's squeezing grip, but without her power flowing into it, it didn't crackle and do any damage to him or his armor. He yanked on it, almost pulling it from her grip. She hung on tenaciously and found herself flying through the air.

She twisted, trying to get her feet under her as she soared past the burning log, glimpsing Erick as she went. He'd regained his feet and faced the soldier while she twisted and landed in a crouch beside him, her staff striking the ground and flinging up ashes.

With her barrier down, heat and smoke railed at them, and Jelena couldn't keep from coughing. Ashes coated her mouth and throat. She forced herself to stand, certain the soldier would spring after them. She was right.

But as he leaped over the log, Erick thrust his own staff out. He struck the man with a telekinetic blast. This time, the soldier was the one to fly backward, his back striking against the hull hard enough to dent his armor. Even so, he landed on his feet and ran at them again.

His face grimy and grim in the flickering firelight, Erick hurled him backward again. "We are not your enemies!"

The soldier roared and didn't seem to understand—or maybe he couldn't believe Erick. He must believe they'd been the ones to decapitate his comrade.

Jelena stood next to Erick, ready to lend her power to his, but not sure how to stop the determined soldier. Instead of charging them again, the man yanked his rifle up. Jelena made her barrier faster than she ever had in her life.

Crimson blazer bolts streaked through the smoke, bouncing off their invisible protection. Even though he must have known he wasn't getting through, the man did not relent. He stalked forward, finger squeezing the trigger, one long sustained beam pointing at them, as if he could burn a hole through the barrier.

Maybe he could. Unlike before, Jelena's head ached, and she felt herself weaken at the power that was required to keep her barrier up under the onslaught. She had done too much. She was tired. It was almost as if she were the *Snapper*, and her shields were slowly being depleted.

"Erick," she whispered to let him know she needed help.

He growled in frustration, maybe already aware of the problem, and stepped forward, raising his staff. Once again, the soldier flew backward into the hull. The soldier cried out, but he kept his grip on the rifle, kept firing at them.

His face angry and tense and frustrated, Erick attacked again, making the man's helmet bash into the wreck over and over. Finally, the rifle dropped from the soldier's hands. The man slumped to the ground, his helmet dented in a dozen places. Jelena reached out with her senses, praying they'd only knocked him unconscious. Yes, he was still alive, but he would need medical attention soon.

"Damn it, Jelena," Erick snarled, whirling toward her.

Startled by his anger, she stepped back and lifted her hands, almost dropping her staff.

"Those are Alliance soldiers—the people who keep the shipping lanes safe for *us*. And you've got me out here helping a murderer to kill them."

"He's not dead, Erick," she said quietly, patting the air with her hands and tilting her head toward the unconscious soldier. "And we didn't help—"

"We might as well have," he roared, his voice thunderous even over the crackling of the dozens of surrounding fires. "We shouldn't *be* here. Even if we didn't kill anyone, someone will know we were here, and they'll blame us for being a part of this. And they won't be wrong. We've picked a fight with people who are on *our* side. You think he won't remember that?" He thrust his hand toward the soldier. "Remember *us*?" His voice turned less angry and more forlorn as he added, "What are we even *doing* here? We should be with your family, with Leonidas. He could already be—" His voice cracked, and he didn't finish. His shoulders slumped, and he stared at the ground between them.

Jelena opened her mouth, but she had no idea what to say. After ten years, Leonidas was as much a father to him as he was to Jelena. And could she truly say that he was wrong? She'd dragged him off on her foolhardy mission, and nothing had gone right since then. Maybe homes would be found for those animals, but was that worth the fact that she and Erick were now being hunted by Stellacor, and they might have just turned themselves into criminals in the eyes of the Alliance?

Erick's head lifted, and extreme wariness marked his eyes. Jelena started to ask what was wrong—was the fourth soldier coming?—but he turned to look up and to the side. She followed his gaze.

A dark, hooded figure stood atop the wreck, smoke curling about his lean form, ashes dusting his black attire. It wasn't a Starseer robe that he wore, though Jelena thought she spotted a few familiar runes from the old Kirian language along one hem. No, the clothes reminded her more of something out of Old Earth history, the flowing but fitted costume of a ninja. Or maybe it was the curving sword gripped in the man's hand that caused her to make that connection. Firelight gleamed orange on the bluish-silver blade, a blade stained with blood.

Jelena could feel his eyes upon them, even though she couldn't see them under the shadows of his hood. She licked her lips, recognizing his presence with her senses even as her mind informed her that there wasn't anyone else that this could be.

A joke formed in the back part of her mind, an irreverent thought to tease him about the sword and the outfit, but with the carnage around them, the *dead* people around them, she couldn't voice it. He seemed so cold and distant up there, and she couldn't get a feel for his thoughts. She definitely didn't get the sense that he was glad to see them. She wasn't even sure he *recognized* them.

Erick looked at her, as if to say this was her mission, and he was her project. She shook her head bleakly as she stared up at Thor. It was like looking at a stranger, and she had absolutely no idea what to say to the man before them.

CHAPTER FOURTEEN

Erick was the one to break the silence. While Jelena was still trying to figure out what to say to the stone-faced man looking down at them, the man who seemed nothing like the boy she'd ridden horses with years earlier, Erick lowered his staff and spoke.

"Nice sword, buddy. You make that out of Zizblocks?"

Jelena had dismissed a joke as an opening, as it seemed wholly inappropriate given the corpses nearby, but Thor grunted and jumped lightly to the ground. He pulled out a dusty kerchief, wiped the blood and ash off the sword, then flicked his wrist. The blade retracted into the hilt, as if it were some telescoping camera stand rather than a weapon. He attached it to his belt with some magnetic clasp. A blazer pistol and a multitool were attached similarly on his opposite hip.

"Finely honed cobalt ahridium actually," Thor said, his voice deeper than Jelena remembered. Cooler, too, almost disdainful. "With a few *teylenese* enhancements."

Teylenese? Jelena thought she remembered Stanislav using the word in regard to the Starseer tool-making techniques he'd been instructing Erick in, but she didn't know what it meant.

"Yeah, I can sense that," Erick said. "Stanislav makes a lot of tools, but it's definitely not his signature on it. Who made it?"

"I did."

Thor looked around the woods, where the fires had dwindled but continued to burn, then gazed off to the west. Wondering if someone else was coming, Jelena sent her own senses in that direction. The animals had fled from the woods as soon as the fire began, so there was little life nearby, but she could detect people in what she assumed was the senator's ranch home. A cluster of them stood together in an outbuilding—maybe a barn or a hangar?—but it was about three miles away, and she didn't sense any of them coming yet.

"Snazzy." Erick looked at Jelena, as if to say that he'd had as much of a conversation with Thor as he could manage, and it was her turn now.

Thor also looked at her, and Jelena made herself look back, though she didn't know what to say. She felt uneasier in his presence than she had expected she would, even knowing about the assassinations.

He pulled his hood back, and she could finally see his face. It was lean to the point that his features were sharp, his cheekbones and jaw pronounced. His hair fell to that jaw, straight and the same length all the way around, closer to brown now than the sandy blond it had been in his youth. Fresh gashes at his temple and in his cheek had smeared blood on one side of his face, but he didn't bring up the kerchief to wipe it or staunch the blood flow. Maybe that care was reserved for his sword.

His eyes, which Jelena remembered as blue, seemed more of a stormy gray tonight. They weren't friendly or welcoming, and that sent an unexpected pang of disappointment through her. After coming all this way, she'd hoped for...she wasn't sure what exactly, but more. More than this. More than a boy who had turned into a killer. More than to have been forgotten. Dismissed.

"You came to stop me?" he asked, sounding certain of it, and also not pleased by the idea. Eyes narrow, he looked from Jelena to Erick and back to her again.

The hairs rose on the back of Jelena's neck. Had he read those thoughts in her mind? One of her earliest lessons as a Starseer had been learning to keep her mental barriers up so that other Starseers weren't bothered by hearing her thoughts with their sensitive telepathic minds and also so that she could have privacy, even among her kind. He shouldn't be able to read her thoughts now, but he didn't sound like he was guessing. Maybe he was simply applying logic. Maybe he couldn't imagine any other reason they would have come. Or did he think they had been sent by someone? Perhaps the Alliance? If so, that could explain his wariness, his coolness.

LINDSAY BUROKER

Erick nudged her. "I think it's your turn to talk."

Jelena flushed, realizing she'd been staring at Thor as she tried to figure him out. "Originally, we came looking for you to warn you that the Alliance was after you. But I guess you know that already. We also got ourselves into a little trouble along the way, so then I thought we might ask you for help. We need to get to Arkadius, but there are some people waiting for us there, people who wouldn't mind killing us. Since our ship is known to them now, we thought we could leave it here and get a ride with you, if we could talk you into going that way. Leonidas is about to undergo surgery, if he hasn't already."

She thought he might express concern at hearing about Leonidas, but he said nothing, merely gazing at her with that cool wariness. Did he think this might be some kind of trap? As if she would ever use her family in some ploy. As if she would turn in an old friend, no matter what he was doing these days.

"But you also wish to stop me," he said.

Something about the way he held her gaze, his eyes cool, made her feel compelled to tell the truth. The whole truth.

"I did have the thought that we might talk you out of assassinating people while we were here," Jelena admitted, "because it's not very nice."

"What these people did to my family was not *very nice*." He sneered with those last two words, and bitterness hung in the air around him.

"No, it wasn't, but aren't you supposed to become some great leader? Isn't that what Dr. Dominguez and all those Starseers and people who were loyal to your father were grooming you for?"

"You don't think people will accept me as a leader if I kill a few old enemies first?"

She couldn't tell if he was being dry and sarcastic or genuinely wanted to know the answer to the question.

"Well, they might find it creepy to follow some broody kid dressed all in black with blood dripping off a sword."

"Broody?" His eyebrow twitched.

"Oh, yes. You're oozing broodiness. Look, I see my hope of having you fly us to Arkadius probably isn't going to happen now—" She glanced at the wrecked clipper, which never could have housed the three of them, if it was even capable of interplanetary flight. "But can you at least take a week out

174

of your schedule to come help us? I know Leonidas would like to see you, especially if…" She couldn't manage to finish the sentence with the words that came to mind, *especially if he was dying.* She didn't want to think that could be true, that it was a possibility.

Thor's already narrowed eyes narrowed further, and she thought she sensed his touch on her mind. Maybe he *was* reading her thoughts through her defenses. If so, that was rude. She folded her arms and glared at him.

"You *do* owe him," Erick said, drawing Thor's gaze toward him.

"Leonidas?"

"He got you out before everyone else in that hidden asteroid palace was killed, right? That's the story you told us."

Thor gazed into the darkening woods. "It might have been better for the system if he hadn't."

Add self-pity to brooding, Erick told Jelena silently, an exasperated tone to the words.

"He risked himself to keep you alive," Erick said aloud, "to obey your father's dying wishes. And then he and Captain Marchenko were the ones to come after you when Tymoteusz kidnapped you. And we all risked ourselves to help get you. And you know why? Because *Jelena* talked everyone into it. Even though you were a quiet, surly little kid, she liked you, and she cared what happened to you. You owe Leonidas, and you owe her."

Even if Thor accepted that, he didn't look like he appreciated the reminder. His face grew flinty as he turned back to Erick and Jelena.

"While I'm so pleased that you flew across the system to lecture me," Thor said, "this isn't the time for it. The senator's people are coming." He tilted his head in the direction of the ranch.

Jelena checked on the people in that barn again. Yes, they had climbed into a shuttle, and they were flying this way. It would only take them a minute or two to find the wreck—and the bodies. They would find her little group, too, if it didn't move.

Thor hopped up to the mangled cockpit, moved the seat back, and pulled out a duffel bag.

"Is there a reason you're losing your temper with everyone tonight?" Jelena murmured to Erick, not bothering to speak telepathically since she had a hunch Thor would hear them even if they did.

"Because Thor's assassinating people, not just people on his list, but anyone who comes after him. We're lucky he didn't drop trees on *our* heads. Though I suppose the night is young."

Thor jumped down, slinging his bag over his shoulder.

"Will you come with us?" Jelena asked, holding up a hand to hold off any further diatribes from Erick. "We have an escape vehicle waiting."

At least she hoped they did. She still wasn't sure whether Masika wanted to stay with them or turn them in to her employers. Sometimes, it seemed she wanted both.

"I haven't fulfilled my mission yet," Thor said.

"You'll have a hard time doing so with the entire ranch awake and alert right now."

A searchlight flashed through the smoke and the branches from above, as if to emphasize the truth of her words. Thor glowered toward it. He shook his head and turned in the opposite direction, toward the fence and the gate.

Jelena and Erick hurried after him as the light from the shuttle probed the remains of the torched woods. Running wouldn't be a bad idea, she thought, but the light shifted in another direction.

"They've spotted where the Alliance ships landed," Erick said.

"It won't take them long to find the wreck," Jelena said.

Thor, striding ahead of them, said nothing.

Is he coming with us, or are we all just walking in the same direction? Erick asked silently.

I'm not sure. He didn't seem to love your lecture. When did you turn into such a responsible grownup, Erick?

Don't tell me you're not having the same thoughts. He owes you and your family, and everything he's doing is selfish and self-centered. And illegal and horrendous.

He is…was…the prince and the heir to the empire. He grew up believing he'd rule over billions. The imperial loyalists probably treated him like that was still going to happen one day. It would be odd if he wasn't somewhat self-centered.

I can't believe you're defending him.

Thor glanced back. They had moved away from the burning area, and Jelena couldn't read his face or tell if he was looking at them or checking for pursuit. She also couldn't tell if he'd heard their conversation, but decided that talking about him behind his back—even telepathically—wouldn't be a good idea, especially if they wanted to regain his trust. She couldn't help but feel bleak at the thought that they should *have* to regain his trust. What had she ever done that could make him believe she would be against him?

"Is Masika out there?" she whispered to Erick as they came out of the trees and entered the waist-high grass. She picked up her pace, drawing even with Thor. It was still a long walk to the fence, and it would be much easier for that shuttle to spot them from above now that they were in the open.

"Yes," Erick said. "I've asked her to drive back to the gate."

The rumble of the shuttle's engine floated toward them. The craft might have paused to fly over the Alliance landing site a few times, but it was on the move again now. That searchlight flashed over the trees behind them. Jelena picked up her speed, transitioning to a jog. She expected Thor to start to run, too, but noticed he was limping.

"Do you need a hand?" she asked, though she didn't know what she could do other than lend a shoulder to lean on.

"No." He glanced darkly at her, as if he resented her noticing his weakness.

It wasn't as if it was much of a weakness. He'd still handled those soldiers. She just wanted to hurry and get over the fence in the hope that the shuttle wouldn't catch up with them. That could end up in more deaths, this time of innocent civilians, not soldiers on the hunt.

The craft cleared the trees behind them, their searchlight shining onto the field.

"That's going to be a problem," Erick said. "We better get down in the grass and hope it's thick enough to hide us."

"They won't see us," Thor said without looking back.

"What?"

"You heard me. Keep going."

Jelena exchanged a long look with Erick, but kept jogging, trusting that Thor had the power to influence those people and muddle their thoughts. The ranch workers wouldn't have expected Starseers on their doorstep and shouldn't be drugged the way the soldiers had been.

Still, her shoulder blades itched as the shuttle flew closer, the night turning noon-bright as the searchlight flared all around them. The beam landed squarely on them as the craft passed overhead, and she was certain there was no way the shuttle pilot could miss them, especially when she sensed five other people in the craft with him. Could Thor influence so many?

The shuttle passed by, then banked to search the field on the other side of the road. Thor kept going toward the fence, and Jelena let him lead, even though he wasn't angling toward the gate. They would have to go over the electrical part, or maybe he intended to cut that mesh with his sword.

"Masika is coming, but it'll be a few more minutes," Erick reported. "She saw the shuttle take to the air and hung back for a while. She's driving up now."

Thor said nothing.

"Good," Jelena said. "Tell her thanks, please."

Erick nodded curtly. He still seemed upset over the night's events.

They reached the fence, the mesh stretching from the ground to a line more than twelve feet high. The air close to it hummed with an electrical current.

"Can you get over?" Thor stopped and looked at them.

"Uhm?" Jelena pointed toward the gate, about a quarter of a mile away. "We came over that. It wasn't—" She broke off with an alarmed squeak as her feet left the ground.

Eyes intent upon her, Thor lifted her into the air with his mind. Before she could decide if she wanted to protest—given time, she could have figured her *own* way over the fence—she found herself in the grass on the other side. A couple of seconds later, Erick landed beside her. It was telekinesis, the same as they both used, but it felt utterly strange having it applied to *her,* as if she were a crate of cargo manipulated by a hand tractor beam.

Thor crouched and leaped over the fence as if it were three feet high instead of twelve, and as if he wasn't injured. Some of it was athleticism, but she also sensed him using his power, enhancing his jump. Jelena had never learned to do that.

She wondered if Erick would be offended if she shared the thought that came to her mind, that all of her life they had only been playing at being Starseers, like Masika playing that game where she had leveled up a Starseer character. Here was the real thing, someone whose training had been varied and intense, not simply part of a regular academic curriculum.

"Masika will be coming up the road," Erick said, angling in that direction after Thor landed.

"I'll go that way." Thor pointed straight ahead toward trees in the distance, trees that were not near the road.

It took Jelena a second to realize he didn't intend to come with them.

"Thor," she blurted, "we came here for you."

"Then that was a mistake."

Erick growled in his throat like a dog, probably thinking of Thor as being selfish again. Jelena didn't think that, but she certainly felt stung that he wouldn't take a week's vacation from his dire assassination plans to help them.

"We were friends once," she said, her voice coming out more hurt than she intended.

"That was a long time ago." He sighed, sounding less cool—less cruel—but no less unrelenting. "It's too dangerous for you to be anywhere near me. Why do you think I stopped writing?"

"You said you were busy."

"Busy being trained to be an enemy to the Alliance, to kill their leaders and to raise an army to reestablish the empire and take over the system again."

"Is that still what you intend to do?"

"Masika's here," Erick murmured, glancing to the road and then back through the fence.

The shuttle had landed near the trees, and its people had climbed out and were going to search around the wreck. Once they saw all those bodies, they might call in the local law enforcers. That would make it difficult to drive back along this road and into the city without being seen—especially if Thor didn't come with them to help camouflage the vehicle. Jelena knew all that, but she kept her focus on him, waiting for his answer. If he *did* answer.

"I haven't figured out *how* yet," Thor said softly, "but it's what my father expected me to do."

Expectations. The words she'd quoted to Masika floated through her mind again.

"It sounds suicidal," she said.

"I know. But it's my path." He looked toward the road, the rumble of the truck's engine floating over the grass. "You'll only get in trouble if you're seen with me." He pointed to the trees, to his own road. "This is for the best, trust me."

"We can get into trouble just fine without you."

"It's true," Erick said, surprising her since it was support of a sort, arguing for Thor to come with them. "She should be at her father's side right now, but she stole lab animals and kidnapped an apparently invaluable guard, and now we're being chased by a powerful corporation whose people are trying to kill us."

"The animals were *liberated*." Why couldn't anyone get that right? "And the guard was *rescued*."

Thor snorted, sounding faintly amused for the first time, but when he spoke, there wasn't any humor in his words. "Who's in charge of the corporation?"

"Uh." Jelena had no idea. "Some collection of board members?"

"Find out," Thor said. "Convince them to leave you alone."

"*Convince?*" Erick looked back the way they had come, perhaps thinking of the headless soldier.

"If someone wants to kill you, you either have to kill them first or convince them to leave you alone. Anything else is to spend the rest of your short life living in terror."

"Erick *did* blow up part of one of their ships."

"Good." Thor nodded, as if that was the end of the conversation, and started toward the trees.

"Thor," Jelena lunged after him and grabbed his arm, though she immediately felt presumptuous for doing so. "Come with us. Please. Just to Arkadius. Leonidas…"

She thought he would shake her arm off and keep walking. After all, they had already made all their arguments, and this was nothing new.

But he paused. "What happened exactly? Leonidas had a heart attack?"

Jelena knew she hadn't said that, but she would worry about his mind reading skills later. "That's what Mom said, yes. I haven't spoken to her real-time yet. And, uhm, I haven't asked her for as many details as I should have because I haven't wanted to admit to some of the trouble I've picked up, since—well, that's a long story and not important. I just know Leonidas is having a surgery, and it may involve a heart transplant, so it's a big deal, and I'd really like to be there with him, but now, I'm afraid we'll bring this trouble down upon the family, and even though Grandpa can handle just about anything, I'd rather not…I'd just rather not," she said, finishing quietly.

She was on the verge of admitting that she'd screwed up and didn't want her parents to be disappointed in her over that. She couldn't regret saving the animals, but she'd gotten in over her head, and she knew it. She didn't want to *have* to ask Thor for help, and she'd find a way to make it all work out on her own if she had to, but it would be good to have him along. Not just for her sake. Leonidas had always cared about him, and he would want to see him.

Erick stirred. "I think some law vehicles are coming, either up the road or in shuttles. We may want to have this chat somewhere else."

That would be hard to do if Thor insisted on going in a different direction. Jelena groped for something else she could say to sway him. But he spoke first.

"All right. I'll come."

"Good." She had an urge to hug him, but thought of the bloody sword and the dead men, and instead, only squeezed his arm and stepped back. He wasn't her childhood friend anymore. That saddened her, but she lifted her chin, telling herself to accept what he had offered. It would have to be enough. "Thank you."

CHAPTER FIFTEEN

Jelena was relieved when the truck came into view, already turned around to head back to the city. Once they reached Blue Armadillo, they ought to be able to disappear into the anonymity of its population. Alfie's woofs and Masika's subsequent *sssshh* came from the vehicle as they approached.

When Thor gripped the handle to the passenger door of the truck, it fell off.

"This is your escape vehicle?" He eyed the rusted hulk. He hadn't even sat on the springs thrusting through the seat yet, and he already sounded disappointed.

"I can fix that," Erick said, picking up the latch and fiddling in the dark at the door.

Masika peered through the open window at them. "You really found him?" she asked, sounding surprised.

On the way out here, after she'd admitted to sensing his presence, Jelena had explained they were hoping to find Prince Thorian and keep him from assassinating more people.

Thor had pulled his hood over his head again, so he might have been anyone, as far as Masika knew, but she seemed to assume they'd acquired their target.

"Starseers are good at finding people," Jelena said.

Thor looked at her, but she couldn't read him in the dark—she wished she could get a sense for his thoughts as easily as he seemed able to decipher hers. Was he irritated that she'd told a near stranger about him and where he was?

Sirens sounded in the distance, and red lights flashed in the sky over the road leading to the ranch.

Jelena nudged Erick. "You can do that later. Let's go."

"Already done." Erick lifted his hands with a triumphant noise, then jogged to the driver's side. "Scoot over, not-a-cyborg. I'll drive us back to the space base."

"You sure? I noticed the truck hit a lot fewer potholes when I was driving."

"Then why was the handle falling off over there?"

"Because of your subpar workmanship."

"*Really.*" He shooed her out of his seat. "Scoot, scoot."

Grumbling under her breath, Masika crawled into the back again. Jelena, worried that the law enforcement shuttles were heading straight toward them, accepted a quick lick from Alfie, then urged her to get into the back too. The sooner they got off the senator's doorstep, the better.

Thor sucked in a soft, pained breath as he climbed into the truck, and she remembered his injuries. She would have to talk him into letting her give him some painkillers—and maybe a few repair nanobots—in sickbay when they returned. She slid in beside him, her shoulder and hip pressed against his. There was barely room for three, and she almost clunked him in the head with her staff when she shut the door.

The vehicle surged forward, Erick not hesitating. They hit three potholes in the first five seconds, and Thor almost ended up in Erick's lap. Alfie crooned a protest. Or maybe that was Masika. There wasn't any padding on that bench behind the seats.

After the next pothole, Thor gripped the dashboard with his hand. "I'm already regretting the loss of my ship."

"This isn't a thrust-bike race, Erick," Jelena said. "I think you can slow it down a tad."

"I don't want to be right up the nose of the ranch when the law enforcement shuttles fly overhead. Wasn't there a turnoff up here a ways?" Erick leaned forward, eyeing the red lights of the approaching shuttle. *Shuttles.* There were two, and they were almost on top of them.

"Slow down," Thor said. "I'll make sure they don't see us."

Erick frowned over at him. "How can you do that to so many people at once?"

"The same way Jelena can lead herds of chickens at once, I suspect."

Jelena started to smile, pleased that he remembered, but her smile faltered. Did he think of those law officers—of human *beings*—as being as simple-minded and easily manipulated as chickens? The notion made her uncomfortable, and once again, she had the thought that she was riding shoulder-to-shoulder with a stranger, and she didn't know how she felt about being pressed so close together, of being aware of the heat of his lean form against hers.

The shuttles passed over the truck without slowing down. None of them turned back as Erick drove in the opposite direction. Jelena let out a relieved breath when they reached the city limits, and the roads turned into broader streets, all paved and pothole free.

After a few minutes of navigating traffic, the river and the space base came into view, the latter lit up for the night, its ramps and tiers of docks outlined by the lights. Unfortunately, it wasn't that late, and there were a lot of people out in the city as well as on the main road leading into the base. When Erick drove past the guard station, not committing to turning down the road leading to it until they investigated, they spotted twice the people that had been there earlier.

"Busier than before," he noted, cruising past and turning down a side street in the opposite direction.

Jelena reached out with her mind toward the *Snapper*, hoping to find the area around the ship empty. Her stomach sank when she encountered people. Not simple passersby, but a group of men and women in combat armor loitering outside the cargo hatch.

"Someone's waiting for us," she reported glumly. She couldn't tell if they were Alliance soldiers or if this was another group sent by Stellacor.

"Yes," Thor said, his voice distant, distracted. "That's your ship now? The big turtle-shaped freighter?"

"The *Snapper*, yes," Jelena said. "We talked Mom and Leonidas into expanding the fleet and letting me start to run freight on my own."

"*We?*" Erick protested. "That was all your plan."

"You agreed to be my engineer."

"I agreed to come along and keep an eye on you and your engine for your first run. That's not quite the same thing."

"You also found a replacement engineer for the *Star Nomad*," Jelena said. "That suggests you were planning to stay for a while."

"A replacement? I talked my brother into coming to work for a few weeks so he could save some money for school. I fully plan to return to learning from Stanislav while working for your mom."

"I'm wounded that you want to leave me already."

"Did you actually complete a cargo run?" Thor asked.

"We absolutely did," Jelena said, as if that outcome had never been in question.

"So long as Xing was willing to make a full payment when he saw how much monkey and dog hair was sticking to his cargo." Erick turned down a dark alley and slowed to a stop. "We better wait until closer to midnight to attempt to get up to the ship. In the meantime, I need to find someone to give the truck to."

"Give?" Masika asked.

"We're not going to keep this one?" Jelena added, though she'd seen Erick refurbish a vehicle before and knew what to expect.

"No need. We have our bikes on the now animal-free ship."

Alfie whined. It might have been because she wanted to get out of the truck, or it might have been a response to Erick.

"Mostly animal-free," he amended. "I'd like to find something for us to eat too. I'm starving, and I'm deathly sick of ration bars. Why don't you schemers and skulkers go study the base and figure out a way in while I run my errands?"

Jelena opened the door and climbed out. Thor said nothing as Alfie clambered over the back of the seat beside him and also hopped out. He hesitated, then followed suit.

"Schemers and skulkers?" Masika asked. "Am I in that group too?"

"Unless you want to come on a dinner date with me and spend some of that big money Jelena gave you."

Masika clambered over the seat back and out of the truck.

"Yup," Erick said. "I've still got my touch with women."

"If there are people waiting at the ship, they probably have to do with me." Masika looked in the direction of the base and then deeper into the city. "I should go. I drove your escape vehicle. I believe that's a fair trade-off for the help you gave me."

"Erick, have you noticed that nobody truly wants to come with us on our adventures?" Jelena asked.

"Because they know you're trouble."

"Just me?"

"Definitely just you. I'm a simple engineer."

"If I turn myself in to the local enforcer station," Masika said, still gazing toward the city and not acknowledging their conversation, "they may withdraw the troops guarding your ship."

"We're not even sure those troops are there for you. They could be Alliance soldiers looking for Thor. Or for *all* of us, I suppose." Jelena thought of the camera that had been at Albrecht's gate, the one that would have footage of her and Erick climbing over the gate. "If you want to go, Masika, that's fine, but if you don't want to…" She shrugged, not sure why she was hinting that Masika could stay. The road ahead would be easier if she went back to her corporation, and Stellacor no longer had a big reason to chase after the *Snapper*. Jelena didn't know if they would completely forget the stolen animals and the damage done to their facility and ships, but they might be less motivated to hunt her down if they had Masika back.

"I'll go." Masika started to walk away, but paused and peered into the truck. "What did you mean when you said you'd give your vehicle away?"

"We don't need it anymore," Erick said, "so I'll find someone who can use it and give it to them."

"He's done it before," Jelena said. "Even though he complains a lot and drives like a maniac, he has a good heart."

"I like to be useful. Helpful." He smiled at Masika. By the suns, he wasn't trying to flirt, was he? "Not everybody has my exquisite tool-handling skills and can go into a junkyard and fix up an old truck from scratch."

"He's also arrogant," Jelena said. "And doesn't know he shouldn't brag to women about handling his tool."

"I said *tools*." He glared at her. "Screwdrivers. Wrenches. Nothing dirty."

"Huh," was all Masika said. She lifted a hand in parting, crossed the street, and headed into the alley on the other side.

"I'll catch up with you soon, Jelena," Erick said, but he hesitated to drive off. He frowned slightly at Thor, then gave her a concerned look. He wasn't worried about letting her go off alone with him, was he?

She almost snorted in dismissal at the idea, but maybe his concern wasn't unfounded. Neither of them truly knew Thor anymore, did they?

"Good," she said, nodding firmly, hoping he wouldn't worry. He ought to know she could take care of herself. "We'll see you soon."

Besides, she wouldn't be alone. She had Alfie, who was currently sniffing behind a dumpster a few feet away. Not that she looked like a fearsome protector. Oh well. Jelena also had a Starseer staff and experience kneeing men in the groin when necessary.

Thor looked at her, his expression inscrutable.

She walked toward the end of the alley, and he followed her, as did Alfie—though at a much slower pace. The dumpsters here were *extremely* interesting.

Jelena turned one corner and then another, and they came out back on the main street. She thought to stand there, in the mouth of the alley, studying the space base from afar, but she spotted a trail along the river. That would allow them to observe from even closer.

"Let's go over there," she said, nodding toward the trail.

Thor offered another look she couldn't decipher, but this time, she had a sense that he found this skulking about bemusing. He would probably stride straight in and deal with those men in combat armor, as he'd done in the woods. But even for him, facing so many must surely be a challenge. He might be powerful, but if he were invincible, his ship wouldn't have been shot down in the first place.

"It was sabotaged," he said dryly, as they crossed the street.

Jelena stumbled. "What?"

"My ship. Somewhere along the way, probably while it was getting maintenance at Triton Station, someone planted an explosive. I made it all the way here without trouble, but I believe it was capable of being remotely detonated. As I was descending into the atmosphere, it blew. I managed to react quickly, and partially contain the explosion, otherwise I'd be dead alrcady. But those Alliance ships appeared out of nowhere seconds afterward, before I could even think about attempting repairs." His dryness had turned cool as he spoke, and he sounded vengeful when he added, "I won't make the mistake of leaving a ship with a mechanic without staying to supervise again."

"You *are* reading my thoughts," Jelena said, hurrying to finish crossing the street, since ground vehicles were roaring toward them.

"Yes." They strode down dimly lit stairs that led to the river trail. "Why are you surprised?" *When you're also a Starseer,* his tone seemed to add.

"Because I guard my thoughts. All Starseers do."

She winced in anticipation of a comment that would suggest she and Erick weren't *real* Starseers since they weren't a part of the community and had only trained with Grandpa.

"I know back doors," was all he said, looking toward the space base.

Since they'd descended to reach the riverside, the space base wasn't as visible as Jelena had hoped. The upper tiers were, so maybe if they walked farther, they would be able to see the *Snapper* in dock. Maybe the people standing outside of it would be visible too. She guided them through the shadows between the lampposts as much as possible, lamenting that the Blue Armadillo kept its trail lit at night. A jogger passed them, his forehead gleaming with sweat in the warm night air, and Alfie woofed and eyed his ankles. Jelena gave her a mental nudge to ensure good behavior.

"Don't you think it's rude to open back doors to other people's houses, when you haven't been invited?" Jelena asked, though she'd slipped into the minds of non-Starseers on occasion. And she knew that some Starseers made a regular habit of it when dealing with mundanes. But Grandpa had always emphasized the importance of respecting people's boundaries, mundane or not.

"Better rude than dead," Thor said.

"I don't see how that's an excuse for monitoring *me*. Do you really think your life is in danger based on what you've read in my mind in the last hour?"

"Perhaps." He didn't have the good grace to look sheepish at his eavesdropping. "You might push me into the river to save an animal."

"Please. I wouldn't risk your life for fewer than *two* animals." Jelena pointed to a bench in the shadows between two lampposts, one that looked up the hill toward the *Snapper*. "Care to share a romantic interlude?"

"A what?"

"Sit on the bench with me and pretend we're lovers gazing at the river together while we surreptitiously spy on the base."

He contemplated the bench for a moment, then shook his head. "I can tell you what you want to know from here."

Apparently, he wasn't interested in romantic interludes. She thought about mentioning how Zhou, the boy she'd dated on Arkadius when she had been there practicing for her flight exams, would have sat with her, but quashed the idea. What did that have to do with anything? They were here for a mission, not romance, pretend or otherwise.

Another jogger headed their way, and Jelena sat on the bench. She would feel conspicuous standing on the path and staring at the base. Alfie was content to sniff bushes beside the trail.

Jelena reached out to see if all those troops were still there and grimaced because they were. If anything, there were one or two more. The base was lit up brightly, too, with few shadows.

There wasn't as much activity on the roads and ramps and lifts as there had been earlier, but there was still plenty. Cowboys and drones prodded along a herd of cattle, taking them from a train to a big freighter two levels below the *Snapper*. The way was well lit for them. Jelena's hopes of climbing to the *Snapper* from above or below and sneaking in through the airlock hatch dwindled. She scowled toward the ramp that held the armored men, willing them to go away.

"They want the woman who was driving the truck," Thor said. "Masika Ghazali."

"If she's turning herself in, maybe they'll leave."

"They have orders to kill you and Ostberg too. And destroy your ship. They don't feel they can do the latter while it's in dock here, but—ah. They've planted an explosive." His tone turned bitter. "Must be the trendy thing to do to enemies this year."

"Is it on the inside or outside of the ship?"

"Outside. I can point it out to Ostberg when we all get back up there." He looked at her.

"Are you wondering why I don't suggest we—or you—simply kill them all?"

"I was wondering how you managed to get people hating you as much as the Alliance hates me right now." He looked down at Alfie.

"Masika, the woman we rescued so she wouldn't die, is more than the security guard we thought she was. I'm not sure if she's part of some experiment they did or what, but she's very strong. And fast. Erick and I assumed she had cyborg implants for a long time. And maybe she does, but there seems to be something proprietary or otherwise valuable about her because Stellacor wants her back, and they were also super concerned that we might have taken tissue samples or scans or something, and shared the information." Jelena was starting to wish she'd shared the footage she'd taken of those men unpacking corpses. Maybe to a news outlet. If they'd reported on it, maybe it would have distracted Stellacor from chasing down Masika.

"Stellacor?" Thor asked. "I didn't cross that name in any of their thoughts."

"Maybe these were bounty hunters or paid thugs and they weren't sure who had hired them."

"Possibly." Thor sounded doubtful. "Either way, you'll have an easier time convincing the corporation to leave you alone if Ghazali isn't with you."

"That's a given. But she hasn't been very eager to go back to them, even though she told me she gave her word that she'd stay with them. Ten years. Bet she regrets that. A lot."

"Well, let's go get rid of your ship's unwanted patio decorations." Thor nodded toward the armored men, as if it would be a simple matter.

"And how will we be doing that?" She didn't want to leave piles of dead men behind. Even if Stellacor had decided that she should be killed, she still had a hope of getting that death warrant revoked, especially if she could prove that she hadn't shared any information on Masika—she didn't *have* any information on Masika. Maybe she could even blackmail them to leave her alone by using the footage she'd taken.

"We'll think of something," Thor said, leaving the path and walking up the grassy hill rising from the river.

They had barely reached the top of it when a clanging came from the direction of the security office. Lights flashed near the road. Up on the *Snapper's* ramp, Jelena sensed the troops stirring and looking down at the commotion.

"Is that your something?" Jelena whispered.

"It's not."

A gate that had been closed was opened, and an armored truck drove in. A law enforcement vehicle.

Four of the men guarding the *Snapper* jogged down the ramp toward the main level. Jelena started to get an inkling of what might be in that truck. It stopped on the main level of the base, at a dock where a recent-model civilian cruiser perched, lights on behind its portholes. The back doors of the truck opened as the four armored men strode up. Several uniformed enforcers hopped out. They weren't in armor, but they all carried blazers, and they pointed them warily into the back of the truck.

Jelena was too far away to hear what anyone was saying, but she used her mind to check on the occupant in the truck. Masika.

She jumped out, her wrists bound with intellicuffs. The enforcers stepped aside as the armored men strode up. One pointed toward the cruiser. Masika turned in that direction, her head down, her shoulders slumped.

Why are they taking you away like you're a prisoner? Jelena asked, speaking into her mind for the first time. Thor, standing at her side in the shadows, didn't react to any of this. Jelena knew she shouldn't do anything, should let Masika go without another word, but she worried that she was being taken back to some fate worse than being a security guard. *Didn't you voluntarily give yourself up?*

Masika lifted her head and started to look around, but seemed to think better of it. *I made a mistake,* she replied in her mind. *These aren't Stellacor people, and I don't think Stellacor was the one to bribe the Alliance to put a bounty on my head, either.*

Whose people are they?

Regen Sciences. That rival corporation I told you about. They have a lot of reasons to want to strike a blow against Stellacor, but I think they just happened upon the information that I was on the loose. They want to cut me open and examine me, see what Stellacor has been making.

Cut you open? Jelena gaped at the horrid picture that came to mind.

That's the impression I get, but I don't know for sure. These are just local enforcers and hired thugs, not their scientists. I'm not sure I want to meet their scientists. Masika gritted her teeth and flexed her shoulders, looking around, as if weighing her options for escape. As fast and strong as she was, what could she do against so many? What could she do *alone* against so many?

Any chance you'd like to stay with us and paint the rest of the Snapper? Jelena looked around, wondering how she might facilitate that.

Even if I got away, I should go back to Stellacor. But…

You don't want to.

No.

Masika was almost to the ship. If Jelena was going to do anything, it would have to be soon.

You are better people than they are, Masika thought.

That's a given. We're wonderful *people.*

Thor looked over at her, and she sensed disapproval, though she wasn't sure if it was for the comment or the fact that she was contemplating rescuing Masika again.

I would stay long enough to paint your ship, Masika offered. *After that, it wouldn't be a good idea. Stellacor will keep coming for me.*

We'll see about that.

Masika paused to look up at the stars. Wistfully? She stood before the threshold of the cruiser.

The armored guards gathered behind her. Someone in a white lab coat came to the open hatch and looked down at her. Was that an injector in his hand? Maybe one of the scientists *had* come along.

"We have to get her back," Jelena whispered.

"She's the source of your troubles."

"Not entirely." Jelena looked down at Alfie.

A guard prodded Masika and pointed to the open hatch. For the first time, Masika looked toward the grassy hill where Jelena and Thor stood. She didn't form the words, "Help me" in her mind, but Jelena read the plea in her gaze. That was enough.

Jelena looked across the base to where the first of the cattle had almost reached their own open cargo hatch. They were hot, she sensed, from their ride in the train and the muggy night.

Water, she announced, flooding their minds with imagery of the nearby river. *Delightful, cold water!* The next image she sent was of cattle standing chest deep in the water, feeling refreshingly cool and drinking deeply.

Don't get in, Jelena whispered into Masika's mind, seeing that she'd started forward again.

The excited moos of the creatures rang out, echoing across the base and bouncing from the hulls of the ships docked there. It sounded like thousands of cattle instead of a couple hundred. The guards, having doubtless been aware of them before, did not bother looking over, not at first. But Masika paused, her foot in the air as she'd been about to step up into the ship.

Then the stampede began.

The noise of hooves thundering over the pavement drowned out the startled yells from their tenders. Alfie whined and hid behind Jelena's legs.

The armored men spun toward the cattle, realizing they were in the creatures' paths. The big animals charged toward them, the river the only thing in their minds. The men lifted their rifles, but must have known they couldn't fire on someone else's cargo. Instead, they jumped into the cruiser to get out of the way.

One man grabbed for Masika to take her aboard, too, but she dodged, throwing herself to the ground and rolling out of reach. The guard jumped back out of the ship to try to get her. She sprang to her feet, not overly hindered by having her wrists cuffed. In combat armor, the man might catch her even if she sprinted away.

The cattle were almost upon them, though, and the man hesitated. Masika hesitated, too, not sure which way to run. She glanced toward the roof of the cruiser, but with her hands bound, couldn't have climbed up to it.

Jelena nudged the lead cattle, promising them an easier way down to the water if they didn't pass close to that ship. But it was hard to adjust their intent now that they were excited.

The guard lunged for Masika, but something struck him from the side, hurling him against the hull of his ship. A second later, Masika was lifted into the air, as Jelena had been when Thor levitated her over the fence. She squawked and kicked, not knowing what was happening. The cattle raced by below her.

The armored man tried to recover and get to his feet, but the steers had reached him. Massive, furred shoulders rammed into him as the creatures stampeded past. Even though his armor insulated him, it must have been terrifying to have all those big animals running past, bumping against him. He slipped and went down, and the cattle kept running past.

Masika landed in a crouch on the top of the cruiser, but she didn't stay there. She ran across the ship and jumped down on the opposite side.

"Come on," Thor said, grabbing Jelena's arm.

He led her away from the cattle's path and around ships on the outskirts of the base, heading in the same direction as Masika. Alfie followed right behind them. Masika must have spotted them, because she angled toward them, running amazingly quickly, especially considering she couldn't pump her arms.

They reunited, and Jelena started to speak, but Thor kept running. He circled around the cowboys chasing vainly after their cattle and to the back side of the freighter waiting forlornly for its cow cargo. Thor leaped, another amazingly high jump—it was almost like following Leonidas through an obstacle course—and landed thirty feet up on the roof of the freighter. Jelena reached the hull and was contemplating how to adjust her staff so she could climb up, but stiff air came up below her like an elevator platform. It lifted her, Alfie, and Masika from the ground.

Masika cursed, lowering into a crouch, but she didn't otherwise question the unorthodox travel method. Jelena soothed the alarmed Alfie with her mind.

They landed next to Thor on the roof, and he took off without a word. He ran to the end and leaped up, catching the lip of one of the ramps that led to the level above. He pulled himself up, again lifting Masika, Alfie, and Jelena after him.

"I could do this without help if my hands were free," Masika grumbled.

Jelena doubted she could break intellicuffs easily, especially while running and climbing, so she did not reply.

There are still six men in front of the Snapper, she warned Thor, though she doubted he had forgotten.

Yes, and the bomb to remove, he responded, running up the ramp without looking back.

Jelena raced after him, trusting he had some ideas. As far as she knew, Erick wasn't anywhere near the base at the moment, so they would have to remove the bomb themselves if they wanted to take off.

Thor found the ramp that led up to the *Snapper* and charged up without slowing down. Jelena thought he might camouflage himself from the troops standing outside the cargo hold, but he didn't bother. They saw him coming and raised their rifles. But they hesitated to fire, probably not recognizing him. Then they spotted Jelena, Masika, and Alfie coming up the ramp from behind. Their hesitation vanished. Since Thor was in the lead, they fired at him.

The crimson and orange blazer bolts bounced off a barrier he'd erected across the ramp ahead of him. He kept running. There was a pause as the men gaped at him uncertainly, not firing. In that split second, Thor lowered his barrier and hurled a wave—no, a tsunami—of energy at them. Jelena couldn't see it, but she could *feel* it, feel the immense power.

All six men flew away from the ramp. They hurtled through the air all the way to the edge of the space base before dropping to the ground.

"Open," Jelena ordered the cargo hatch as soon as they were close enough.

It lifted, and the ramp descended for them. Masika and Alfie ran inside without hesitating.

"The bomb?" Jelena stopped at the base of the ramp, sucking in deep breaths after the wild run. She looked toward the river below them and off to the side, where cowboys shouted and tried to round up their charges. The cattle mooed happily from the water.

Thor stopped beside Jelena, and an image flashed into her mind. A dark, compact disk attached to the side of the *Snapper* in front of one of the thruster housings. It was nestled into a spot without camera coverage, and it was almost invisible against the dark green paint of the hull.

"I think it'll explode if we try to move it," Thor said.

"Where's Erick when you need him?" Jelena looked toward the city, wishing they hadn't split up. She tried to reach out to him and call for him to come, but she wasn't sure if the mental cry reached him—there were hundreds of thousands of people in the city, making it hard to pick out one.

"We can handle it. I'll detonate it, and you make a shield around it to contain the explosion."

That sounded daunting, especially when the *Snapper* would be severely damaged—if not outright destroyed—if she wasn't able to contain it. And then what? They wouldn't be able to take off. Down below, the men were collecting themselves in the aftermath of the stampede. The ones Thor had hurled across the base had survived, thanks to their armor, and were racing back.

"How about you make the shield, and I'll detonate it?" Jelena asked.

"Fine, but you should have more faith in your abilities."

"I'll have plenty of faith when the bomb is attached to someone *else's* ship."

Thor looked toward the thruster housing, though they couldn't see the bomb from their position. "I've got it shielded."

Jelena sought the device with her own senses and might have missed it, so nicely camouflaged was it, if not for feeling Thor's power around it. At first, she couldn't figure out how to manipulate the bomb at all through his barrier, but he sent a tendril of energy toward her, a guide of sorts, leading her and showing her what to do.

It was a strange experience, the mingling of their mental energies, and she had no words to describe it, but decided it wasn't unpleasant. It reminded her of the way he'd taught her some things when they'd been kids. He'd always been the more experienced, the more powerful, and nothing had changed. She wondered if Grandpa would be disappointed at how little she seemed to have progressed, at least in comparison to Thor.

I couldn't have stampeded the cattle, he thought into her mind, sounding a touch wry. *Not all at once.*

It isn't hard. You just have to get the leaders going in the right direction.

I imagine so, but that's not what you did. I was watching. You touched all of their minds at once. It's odd to me that you marveled that I could touch a handful of human minds at once when you just manipulated hundreds. He pointed a mental finger at the inner workings of the bomb. *Just push that to there, and it'll blow.*

All I did was throw an image of the river and delightful bathing into their minds. That's not really manipulating. They're so much happier now, and they knew they would be.

That's all manipulation is, making someone believe they'll gain something if they do what you want. I'm ready. Go. The soldiers are running up here again, this time with reinforcements.

Now that Thor had shown her the spot, Jelena had no trouble closing the connection within the wiring and igniting the bomb. She winced as it flared in her mind's eye and expected a massive explosion that would make the ramp tremble. But Thor's barrier enclosed it like an ahridium strongbox. She barely heard the explosion, and she didn't feel a thing. The ship's hull, though right next to the bomb, wasn't damaged. The spent casing tumbled to the ground below.

Before she could thank him for the help, Thor spun away from her, running several steps and yanking out his sword. He flicked his wrist, and the blade sprang to its full length, glowing a faint blue in the night.

Eight armored men were charging up the ramp toward them, rifles in their hands, determination in their steps and their minds. Their steps seemed a touch odd, almost sticky, and she realized they'd activated the magnetic feature in the soles of their boots. That was meant for spacewalks on the hulls of ships, but maybe they hoped they'd be able to stay on the ramp if Thor hurled power at them again.

Jelena doubted that would be the case, but she started after him with her staff in hand in case he needed help. Masika, too, came back out, though she had no weapons to use, and her wrists were still bound.

Ready the ship, Thor spoke into Jelena's mind without looking back. He stood in a fighting stance, his sword raised over his head like the old-fashioned ninjas he seemed to be emulating with his black clothing. *I'll take care of them.*

Can you knock them over the side again? Jelena glanced to the pavement below, grimacing as she spotted several armored vehicles charging onto the base and enforcers jumping out. It seemed Regen Sciences had called for the backup.

Yes, but that won't stop them forever, he replied as the first blazer fire streaked toward him. It bounced off the invisible barrier he'd erected around himself. *Ready the ship, and yell to Ostberg to get his ass up here, so we can take off. We can pick him up if we have to.*

Jelena hesitated as the first men reached Thor's barrier. Three bounced off, but surprisingly, one made it inside. Thor lunged at him, his sword a blur as it swept toward the man's neck. His foe whipped his blazer up in a clumsy block, and the blade sliced through the barrel like a laser cutter slicing through butter. The follow-up attack came so fast, the blade snapping up like a bullwhip, that Jelena didn't register what happened until the man's helmet toppled to the ramp and bounced off. The helmet *and* the man's head.

"Thor," Jelena blurted, gripping her staff hard, feeling the need for the support. Logically, she understood that the men wanted to kill *them* and destroy the *Snapper,* but she couldn't wrap her mind around the choice to kill people—and the ramifications and retribution that would come from doing so. "Can't you just—"

Ready the ship, Thor snarled into her mind as he leaped for the remaining troops, men who'd faltered, staring at their decapitated comrade. *Now!*

Jelena wasn't sure if the order contained some mental compulsion, or if she was just reacting to the urgency in his tone, but she whirled and ran into the ship. As she pounded through the hold and toward NavCom, she decided there might be a third reason that she'd moved to obey so quickly. She didn't want to see Thor killing people.

Masika followed Jelena, racing into NavCom right behind her. Alfie was already inside, hiding under the control console.

"Can I do anything to help?" Masika asked, gripping the hatch jamb as Jelena flung herself into the pilot's seat.

"There's a blazer rifle in my cabin if you want to go shoot at people," Jelena said, fingers flying over the control panel. "At anyone who gets past Thor."

"Blazer fire won't do much against combat armor." Despite the words, Masika jogged down the corridor to the cabin.

"Swords shouldn't, either," Jelena muttered, amazed and horrified at the weapon Thor had created.

Jelena! Erick barked into her mind.

There you are—good.

I'm coming as fast as I can. Do you need help? Are you all right?

"Cameras." Jelena looked at the exterior displays when they popped up. Between Thor's barrier, his sword, and the rest of his powers, none of the troops had made it past him yet, but a squad of enforcers was charging up to reinforce the hired men. A couple of them carried grenade launchers. No, those were *rocket* launchers, huge ones. Would they think to attack the ship and not just Thor? He wouldn't be able to shield the entire *Snapper* from attacks.

For the moment, Jelena replied, *but you should definitely hurry. We need to take off as soon as possible.*

I had no idea you planned to move from scheming and skulking to a frontal assault so quickly.

Neither did I, but Thor wasn't interested in lingering romantically on park benches. She would explain Masika later, once they were safely away from the planet.

I hope that's a joke. I don't think your mom wants an assassin for a son-in-law.

Jelena glanced at the camera display again, at three downed men at Thor's feet and at the blood dripping from his eerie sword. *It's a joke. Hurry, Erick.*

The squeal of blazer fire reached her ears, the clang of metal against metal, and the enraged shouts of men. She eyed the enforcers in the back, the ones with the rocket launchers. There were more than twenty men on the ramp outside the *Snapper* now, laying siege to Thor and the cargo hatch. Was he aware of the men with the rocket launchers? He seemed too focused on fighting the ones at the front, of alternately deflecting their blazer fire and attacking, to notice someone in the back.

"Ship's ready," Jelena muttered, thumping her fist on the console. "What do you want me to do now, Thor?" She didn't ask it telepathically, not wanting to distract him. But those men with the rocket launchers made her nervous. If they targeted the ship…well, she couldn't raise the shields while the hatch was open and they were attached to the dock.

Be there in two minutes, Erick informed her, his words sounding breathless, even though they rang only in her mind.

An idea jumped into her head.

Don't come up the ramp, she told Erick, leaping from her seat and running to the cargo hold.

Yes, I can see from here that it's a cluster of chaos. Any suggestions for an alternative route?

We jumped on that cattle freighter, then climbed up from below.

Erick's tone turned wry. *I'm carrying pizza boxes.*

Dinner isn't our top priority right now. A stray blazer bolt streaked through the hold and bounced off the side wall as Jelena ran toward the ladder that led up to the gun turret. Despite still being cuffed, Masika stood at the hatch, returning fire, and she shouted a curse at whoever had shot.

Speak for yourself. I'm tired of ration bars and quick meals.

Climbing the ladder and hoping not to be shot, Jelena did not answer. She flung open the roof hatch and pulled herself into the compact space. She yanked down the pullout chair and grabbed the cannon control grips, swinging the rotating gun toward the ramp and hoping she'd have line of sight to the enforcers. The turret provided a three-hundred-and-sixty-degree view around the top of the ship, and could be angled upward or downward, but the roof of the *Snapper* cut off the possibility of firing at anything under it.

She spun in the seat to face the ramp. Thor and the men closest to him were out of sight, but she could make out the enforcers setting up their big rocket launchers on tripods. The broad muzzle of one pointed at the ship, not at Thor.

"I knew it," Jelena growled, powering up the star cannon and aiming it. Seeing them trying to take out the *Snapper* stole her compunctions against possibly killing any of them. She would just have to deal with the ramifications later.

For such a close shot, she didn't turn on the targeting computer. As the soldiers finished setting up their rocket launcher and one reached for the trigger, she told Thor, *Brace yourself,* and fired.

The star cannon, intended to fire at ships across hundreds of miles, slammed into the ramp like a meteor.

The explosion of white made Jelena fling up her hand to protect her eyes. Clatters and cracks echoed in her ears, along with the terrified and pained screams of people. Armored men flew away from the *Snapper* like toy soldiers. Her weapon left a gaping hole in the ramp—and the level below it. Then the entire ramp buckled and collapsed.

Thor! Jelena blurted, afraid he'd been knocked off—or worse.

She didn't get a response, and she dropped out of the seat, jumping instead of climbing down the ladder. She landed on the cargo-hold deck and sprinted for the hatch. Masika still stood there, her rifle lowered, her mouth dangling open as she stared out into the night. As Jelena ran to look for Thor, a thunderous snap came from below them, and the deck shifted. She lurched, almost toppling. An ominous groan followed the snap, not from the frame of the *Snapper*, she trusted, but the entire docking structure sounded like it would give out below them.

She sprinted faster. The ship was ready to take off, but she needed Thor and Erick before she could leave.

"Thor?" she called, running out onto the cargo hatch's ramp. Before, it had rested on the ramp leading to their dock, but now, it simply extended out over open air like a diving board. The armored men were all gone. But so was Thor.

"Thor!"

Yes? came his dry reply in her mind.

A single hand came up and gripped the end of the ship's ramp.

She ran forward to help him up, but his other hand came up before she reached him, and he pulled himself up, landing in an easy crouch. He'd folded his sword up and returned it to his belt. He glanced over the side at something, and she feared some of the troops had managed to hang on and were also climbing up. Another hand appeared, clasping the lip of the ramp. But the hand wasn't armored, and Thor knelt down, offering help.

Two pizza boxes came up from below to rest on the ramp. Jelena would have laughed at a sight that seemed so ludicrous amid all this, but the cries of hurt men drifted up from below. She did not laugh.

Thor helped Erick, who had a bag of drinks and other snacks dangling from his wrist, the treats decidedly battered, but he'd refused to leave them behind. Jelena, not feeling that useful, grabbed the pizza boxes, and the three of them jogged inside again.

Another snap came from below, and the deck quaked underfoot. Jelena thrust the boxes at Masika and raced for NavCom, trusting the others to pull in the ramp and close the hatch. It was more than time to get out of there.

CHAPTER SIXTEEN

Jelena ignored the piece of pizza balanced on her stallion mug—the ravenous Erick hadn't deemed plates important enough to hunt down when he'd been distributing shares of his pies—in favor of coaxing as much power from the engines as she could.

The grasses and trees of Upsilon Seven were receding in the *Snapper's* rear cameras as they arrowed through the thinning atmosphere, but she worried the Alliance would have orbital ships monitoring the planet and that there might be pursuit. For the most part, they'd been squabbling with some corporation's hired guns down there, but the enforcers were another matter. And then there was the portion of the space base they'd blown up in order to escape. The Alliance government probably owned and operated that base. What kind of repercussions could she expect? A bill for damages? An arrest warrant? And did the Alliance know that Thor had flown away in the *Snapper* with her?

Thor had warned her about being seen with him, and she'd talked him into coming anyway. Just as she'd prodded Masika into wanting to come with her.

"You're a suicidal maniac, Marchenko," she muttered. What had her mother been thinking in allowing her to captain a ship? Jelena wasn't nearly mature enough to be in charge of anything. Maybe by the time she was seventy or eighty, she'd be able to plan a mission to liberate some animals without getting everyone she knew in trouble.

"Giving yourself a pep talk?" Masika asked, walking into NavCom.

"I could certainly use one."

Masika sat down with a groan in the co-pilot's seat. She must have stopped at sickbay, because a bandage was wrapped around her hand. A large purple lump darkened her temple. At least she'd found a way to cut off the intellicuffs.

Jelena was surprised she had managed to get through the night unscathed, aside from weariness. Her legs ached from that top-speed race through the grasses to help a man who didn't need any help.

"Was Thor in sickbay when you popped in?" Jelena asked, remembering he had been wounded *before* they got to the space base and he fought off all those troops. And had a ramp blown out from underneath him.

"No, but he looked like he should be. He's helping Ostberg scan the entire ship to make sure there weren't any more explosives or booby traps planted while you were gone."

"I'll have to intercept him and divert him to sickbay once we're clear of the planet." Jelena eyed the sensors again, expecting ships to veer in their direction at any moment. "And we're certain nobody's following us."

Masika gazed glumly at the various holodisplays and the view screen showing the stars ahead. "I'm afraid they'll keep following to get me back. If not Regen Sciences, then Stellacor. Maybe I should have just let them have me."

"Uh huh, you're welcome for the rescue."

"I shouldn't have *needed* to be rescued. I thought I was turning myself in to Stellacor, so you people could get away and wouldn't be harassed anymore." Masika slanted her an indecipherable look. "I was *trying* to be selfless."

"Do you want me to take you back?" Jelena reached for the controls, as if to turn the ship around.

"No." Masika grimaced and looked away. Her voice lowered to a whisper. "I don't want to go back. To either corporation. I want…I don't know what I should want anymore."

"How about a job as a security officer and painter on a freighter?"

"You have low standards when it comes to hiring."

"In hiring security officers? Since we don't have one, or anyone lining up to apply, there's not much competition for the job."

Masika snorted. "Painters."

"Why do you say that? The mural is beautiful."

Masika shook her head. "With a broad brush and a huge canvas that forgives flaws, I'm all right, but it's nothing compared to what I used to be able to do. To create." She spread her palm and looked down at it. "I once carved an intricate mural on a grain of rice. And I painted…I was considered one of the best young artists coming through the program at Giotto di Bondone University. It came easily for me. Whether I was looking at anything or not, I could see what I wanted to paint in my mind, knew exactly which brush strokes would result in what picture."

Jelena expected to see a tremor or something that would indicate some disease, something that would be affecting her fine motor skills. "What happened?"

"This." Masika gestured at her torso, herself.

"Your, ah, not-a-cyborg surgery?" Jelena guessed. She had yet to see Masika in anything except the unrevealing military fatigues, but there was no doubt that she had enhanced muscles. Still, she wasn't ridiculously brawny, not like so many of the male cyborgs Jelena had seen.

"My not-a-cyborg surgery, yes."

"What happened? How did you end up working for Stellacor? Or was it being worked *on* by Stellacor?" Jelena hadn't pried that much thus far, and she wouldn't now, but in addition to being curious, she felt she had a right to know why Stellacor—and Regen Sciences—wanted her passenger so badly.

"Both." Masika leaned her head back and closed her eyes.

Would she answer further? Jelena was tempted to poke into her thoughts, especially since the answers were probably near the surface of her mind now, but if Masika did not want to share, it wasn't within her right to steal the information.

"Five years ago I guess it was now, I was looking into how much it costs to get cyborg implants. They're out there, available for civilians, but they're expensive. You can get them off the black market, but they're still expensive, and then you have to find a surgeon willing to implant them, and only the sketchy, disreputable ones will do it if they know they were illegally obtained. Either way, it was far more than I had as a student attending school on a scholarship. Then I found an ad on the sys-net, a medical research facility looking for volunteers for genetic manipulation that could give a person cyborg-like strength, among other traits. Faster healing. Greater speed and agility." She shrugged.

Jelena made an encouraging noise, hoping she would continue.

"Genetic engineering for humans is nothing new, but usually, as far as I was told, altering the DNA has to be done to embryos. If the military wanted genetically engineered soldiers, it would have to fund the project for eighteen to twenty years before getting its super men and women. Stellacor has been tweaking living people, using a retrovirus to alter their DNA and, in my case, they took away a gene that limits the development of muscle mass and strength. Among other things. I've also had numerous injections of who knows what property compounds, and now, they're monitoring me to see if everything sticks, or if I revert back. Or if there are other complications." She grimaced. "I gathered they wanted to make super soldiers without having to breed them from scratch or spend huge amounts of money on state-of-the-art implants. The cyborg surgeries for the military are extremely extensive, and apparently, there are some dangers. That part doesn't get mentioned in the recruiting posters, but people can die or their bodies can reject the implants, causing all kinds of health problems."

Jelena thought of Leonidas's heart and its problems. She didn't know the cause, but would not be surprised if it had to do with all the surgeries he had undergone in his youth.

"So I volunteered," Masika said. "I was determined to be…strong. Strong enough to take care of myself against anyone that wanted to bother me."

"Did someone? Bother you?" Jelena had a hard time imagining someone who was drawn to the arts caring that much about being *strong* without a good reason.

"Yes. Many someones. A group of men. Students." Her mouth twisted bitterly. "Drunken idiots, but that didn't justify them being assholes. Criminal assholes. They were punished later and kicked out of the university—I always thought there should have been a worse punishment, but it wasn't as if I could afford to hire a lawyer. I came from…Let's just say that if there hadn't been a scholarship, I never could have afforded school." She lifted a shoulder in an indifferent shrug, but pain rather than indifference came through in her voice. "I tried to get over it, to move on. The logical part of my brain kept telling me that it wouldn't happen again, that the odds were against that. But I jumped at every noise. I was scared at every interaction with strangers. I snapped at anyone who flirted with me or looked at me with what I was sure was sexual intent. I started carrying a blazer pistol in my purse, and I took classes in self-defense, but I just couldn't get past it. I finally started thinking that if I was super strong, like a cyborg soldier, nobody would be able to hurt me, no man, not anyone. So, Stellacor.

"They offered to do it all for free, but they wanted something in exchange. They wanted you to stay there for years, so they could watch you and keep tinkering. I wasn't sure about that, but the modifications sounded so perfect...I signed up. Maybe if I'd had more time, I wouldn't have done it, but I can be impulsive. And they said they'd train me to fight, too, and I longed to make sure nobody could hurt me again..." Another shrug. "So I became their guinea pig. They experimented on me, even more than they did on those animals you rescued. There were others, but they all left the program. Later, I learned that some had died instead of leaving. I'd signed a contract to stay, otherwise, I might have left, too, but I was also afraid of what might happen if I left and...something happened. I'm still afraid. I don't want to die. All I ever wanted was to be able to take care of myself." Masika opened her eyes and stared morosely at the view screen. "Though now that I've had some time away, some time to think about it, that seems selfish, doesn't it? To want to care only for yourself? Especially when you're stronger than those around you. If you're given extra power, do you then have this duty to protect others?" She squinted at Jelena, as if she would know the answer.

Maybe she should.

"Some people feel the call of that duty, whether they're stronger than others or not. I haven't noticed that Starseers are any more likely to be humanitarians than mundane people. A flaw, perhaps."

"Hm." Not sounding satisfied, Masika turned back toward the view screen, as if her answers lay out there among the stars.

"Are you on any drugs?" Jelena asked, glancing at her hands again. "Anything we have to worry about getting for you?"

"Just a supplement blend that provides the building blocks for Human Growth Hormone—part of their tinkering ensured I produce a lot of it. I know the blend, and I can find it. I suppose I should if I want to keep my muscles." The wry twist to her mouth made it clear she wasn't sure she did.

"If you didn't take it, would everything return to normal?"

"No. I'll never be normal again." Masika studied her palm once more. This time, her fingers wavered slightly. The tremor Jelena had expected before. "They're not as steady as they were when I was an artist. And the strength makes things hard too. I've unintentionally snapped brushes just picking them up."

"Ah, you should talk to my father about that. Maybe he'd have some advice."

"Your father the cyborg?" Masika raised her eyebrows, and Jelena remembered she'd mentioned Leonidas before.

"Yes, he's my stepfather, technically. He was in the imperial military. Apparently, they made their young cyborg soldiers practice crafts to learn how to control their new strength. He's made my mother several needlepoint pictures for the cabin. Most are of battlefields, but he did a space scene with the *Star Nomad*—our ship—in it for a wedding present, and she got him to do some kittens as a gift for me once."

"Needlepoint isn't *quite* where my interests were."

"Still, he may have some tips on learning gentleness."

Assuming he was still alive and up to seeing visitors. Jelena closed her eyes, a wave of homesickness and worry washing over her.

She cleared her throat and looked at the sensor display again. Nothing was after them. Thank the three suns for small favors. She guided them into deep space and laid in a course for Arkadius. Most likely, they would have to deal with Stellacor when they drew close, but they had a few days to figure out how they would do that. She just hoped Regen Sciences wouldn't show up again too.

"I'm going to go check on Thor and Erick," she said, standing up.

"Jelena?" Masika asked, stopping her in the hatchway.

Jelena was fairly certain it was the first time Masika had used her name instead of calling her thief. "Yes?"

"They can track me." Masika's eyes were hooded, wary. "I'm not sure how deep it is, but there's a tracking chip in my arm." She tapped her sleeve near her biceps.

Jelena nodded, not surprised. Stellacor had been uncannily good at catching up with the *Snapper*, so this explained that. Maybe Regen Sciences had learned the frequency too. "We'll come up with a plan for dealing with them, and if—*when*—we get to Arkadius, we can find someone to remove it."

She stepped into the corridor, but Masika spoke again, softly.

"Jelena?"

"Yes?"

"Thank you."

"You're welcome."

• • • • •

Jelena found Thor and Erick in sickbay, Erick with his shirt off as he sprayed QuickSkin—or maybe that was an antiseptic—on scratches all over his pale abdomen. He was gangly and lean—she charitably did not use the word scrawny—despite his cheerful willingness to shovel slices of pizza into his mouth. Maybe Starseer robes had intentionally been designed to hide weaknesses of flesh and bone.

Thor sat cross-legged on an exam table, but he didn't appear to have gotten out any drugs or bandages. He'd removed his hood but nothing else, so Jelena did not get to gauge the weaknesses—or lack thereof—that a shirtless state might reveal. His chin was tilted toward his chest, his light brown hair flopping about his face. The soft, loose hair seemed at odds with his lean, hard features, and Jelena was surprised he didn't favor some harsh, military buzz cut. Especially considering that hair currently had blood crusted in it. Dried blood smeared his face, too, and the gouges from the crash looked deep and painful. Would he object to some nursing? His eyes were closed at the moment.

Erick hissed and grumbled under his breath.

"The climbing didn't go well?" Jelena waved to his scratches.

"*No.* Scrambling up fifty feet of ships and ramps and struts while carrying pizza boxes and FizzPops is *not* recommended. Did I mention that a bunch of crazy people were shooting up the place while I was climbing? And that someone with a *sword* was the craziest of them all?"

Jelena lifted her eyebrows toward Thor, expecting a response.

"He's meditating." Erick sprayed his stomach again, then pointed at a bump. "Does that look like a bruise? Or something weirder? Like a growth?"

"A growth? Was it there yesterday?"

"No."

"Then it's a bruise." Seeing that he was using QuickSkin, she took it from him and handed him the antiseptic. "Those scratches aren't deep. Just clean them off, and you'll be fine."

"Are you *sure* that isn't a growth?" Erick's spine bent impressively in his effort to get his eyes close enough to the bump for a good look.

Jelena sighed. She'd forgotten about Erick's hypochondriac streak.

"Thor, do you need anything?" Her nursing instincts prompted her to reach out to touch his shoulder, but she hesitated, not wanting to disturb him. Also, it was hard not to think of how he had been out there hurling soldiers a hundred yards and cleaving heads from their bodies.

Logically, she knew Leonidas had killed a lot of people—he'd been an elite cyborg soldier, and it had been his job—but the violence seemed more distant from him, something he'd mostly done in a past life. Aside from a few encounters with pirates that Grandpa hadn't been able to trick into leaving the *Nomad* alone, Leonidas hadn't had any reasons to go on killing sprees in recent years. With Thor…everything was very current, and the violence clung to him, as if he welcomed it. Maybe he did. It seemed that he could have hurled those soldiers off the ramp a few more times, events they would have survived because of their armor, but he'd strode forward to challenge them, as if he'd wanted an excuse to fight. To kill. Did he reserve his violence for his enemies, or, given the right circumstance, would he become dangerous to those standing beside him? For that matter, *should* she be standing beside him?

"Have you looked up the majority shareholders or board members for Stellacor yet?" Thor asked without looking up.

Jelena blinked and stepped back. Had he truly been meditating, or was he surfing in her thoughts again?

"Not yet. I was making sure nobody was pursuing us."

"Do the research. We need knowledge to come up with a plan to get through them on Arkadius and to get them to leave you alone, especially since you've stolen their prize again."

Jelena bristled at what came out sounding like a command. She'd grown up obeying her mom and Leonidas—taking orders from superiors was part of life on a ship—but Thor was her peer, not her captain. Still, he had a point. It was silly that she hadn't yet thought to look up any information on Stellacor. She'd been reacting rather than acting, thinking completely defensively.

"I will," she said. "I'll look up Regen Sciences, too, in case they want to continue to be a problem as well. Can I wash your face? You look like a ghoul."

Erick looked up. "I don't get an offer to be washed?"

"I think you can handle washing yourself."

"As can I." Thor shifted his legs to the side and started to slide off the exam table, but Erick stopped him with an outstretched hand.

"Thorian, buddy, if a woman offers to wash you, you let her wash you. It's a rule."

"Oh?"

"Especially if it's a pretty woman." Erick smiled winningly at Jelena, and for a second, she thought he was flirting, but then he added, "A pretty woman with expertise in healing. Come look at this weird bump, will you? Just for a second? I'm fond of my abdomen, especially this lower right side. I don't want any pieces to fall off." He flung himself atop the other exam table, his legs dangling off.

"Healing expertise?" Thor asked, watching as Jelena sighed and walked over to look at Erick's belly.

"Some," she said. "A few years ago, I was certain I wanted to become a veterinarian, and I started learning how to do a few things, mostly for animals. But after I threw up when I watched an actual operation, I decided I'd stick to Starseer methods of healing. Erick, that's a blood blister."

"I *knew* it was something weird." He sounded triumphant, but his eyes got big and round. "Is it serious?"

"No. Leave it alone, and it will heal. All of your owies will. Do you want me to see if the previous owner left any bandages with cartoon figures on them?"

He squinted at her and grabbed his shirt. "I hope animals appreciate your bedside manner more than people do."

"Animals aren't moonpuffs the way people are."

"On second thought, Thorian," Erick said, "you should definitely not let this woman touch you." He hopped off the exam table. "I shall conclude the bomb hunt."

"There aren't any bombs," Thor said. "We already checked."

"*You* checked, but you're not an engineer. You may have missed something."

"I did not," Thor said stiffly.

"I'll double-check." Erick walked out.

Jelena shook her head, reminded of the competitive nature of their relationship from when they'd been kids. Erick, at fourteen, should have been more mature than a ten-year-old prince, but that hadn't ever kept him from engaging in silly arguments with Thor.

Thor pushed himself to his feet and walked slowly and stiffly to a counter where Erick had left out bandages, sani-sponges, and numerous tubes and spray cans. Thor picked up one of the fresh sponges and bent over a mirror to clean his face. Jelena winced in sympathy, knowing the disinfectant agent washed but also stung. She wanted to hook up a scanner to make sure he didn't need help greater than the counter offerings.

"You're familiar with *dreysu*?" he asked, cleaning his face.

"The healing meditation? Yes, Grandpa spent some time teaching us. Erick didn't pay much attention. He was more interested in tinkering with tools than learning about his own body."

"I wasn't that interested, either, but I didn't have the option to not pay attention."

Yes, how had it been for him? Growing up in places like that bunker they'd visited on Halite Moon? Surrounded by men who wanted to turn him into some great Starseer general and future emperor. Had he ever been allowed to simply be a boy? To play?

"I'm sufficient at it," he said, not commenting on her thoughts if he was reading them. "If you have a cabin I can use, I'll rest there. I can heal my injuries, given time. Which I'll have while you research your enemies." He gave her a pointed look.

"Are you *nagging* me, Thor?" she asked lightly, though she had a feeling he was trying to get rid of her. Because he didn't want her to see him dealing with his injuries? Or just because he didn't care for the company? "I wouldn't have thought they'd teach you that at your intensive Starseer war leader academy."

"No? Dominguez is very good at it."

"You can take the cabin right here." She pointed into the corridor to one of the side hatches adjacent to sickbay, then stepped out. If he wanted to be alone, she wouldn't inflict herself on him.

"Thank you," he said, then met her eyes. "Using the turret gun on the ramp was inspired."

She paused in her retreat, warmed by the praise. "Technically, I was just trying to hit the men setting up a rocket launcher aimed at my ship. It, uhm, escaped my notice until later that there was a ramp under the men."

"Ah. Nonetheless, it made short work of their siege." He nodded at her.

Though pleased with the compliment, she said, "Unfortunately, it probably means none of us will ever be invited back to Upsilon Seven again. I'll miss riding horses there."

"I *will* return," he said, his voice growing cool and determined.

"To assassinate Senator Albrecht?"

"To avenge my parents' deaths."

"By assassinating an old man?"

His eyes narrowed. "An old man who sold out the empire because the Alliance promised him wealth and land if he did so, and oh, if he could just give a few intelligence tips about my father's hidden bases…He should have died ten years ago. He's been living on borrowed time."

Jelena didn't know what to say, not in the face of his bitterness. He hadn't been like that when they'd been kids, but he had been very sad. She supposed that could have changed to feelings of revenge once he'd learned enough to realize he actually could avenge his family. What would she do, she wondered, if she was able to find out the specific people who had bombed her apartment building and killed her father?

Realizing the silence had grown uncomfortable, at least for her, Jelena said, "Well, thanks for taking a break from it all to come help us."

He was glaring down at the counter, lost in who knew what thoughts, and she didn't know if he heard her.

She took another step back into the corridor but paused, a new chilling thought coming to her.

"Who's on Arkadius?" she asked, remembering that one of her main reasons in seeking him out had been to make sure he didn't plan to assassinate Dr. Horvald. It occurred to her that she was transporting Thor to Arkadius, which could facilitate his efforts to kill two more people.

"What?" He frowned over at her.

"You had two puzzle pieces pulled from Arkadius."

"You went to Halite? That's how you found me?"

"Yes."

"Why did you bother?"

"I told you. We—I—wanted to warn you the Alliance was after you. At the time, I didn't know if you knew, and I imagined them sending some fearsome assassin after you."

His lips thinned. "They did. Before the cyborgs. I don't know what they'll send next."

"Yet you'll keep going down your list?"

"Until those who wronged my family are all dead, yes."

"Who's on Arkadius?" Jelena asked again, some inkling of a feeling making her certain she wanted to know. Or maybe she didn't want to know.

"Vichet Sok, the owner and decision maker for the munitions company that conspired with the Alliance to send us malfunctioning ammunition and explosives. My brother was training with the 11th Infantry Brigade and was in the building when a shipment blew up." His eyes grew even stormier, his mouth tense, almost anguished. "*He* was originally my father's heir, the one who should have been...It doesn't matter now. The other man is Chima Onwudiwe—Admiral Hawk, when he was in the military."

Jelena reeled back. She'd been bracing herself to hear the name Dr. Horvald. She hadn't truly expected to hear the name of someone she'd known for years. "Senator Hawk?"

"Yes."

"But he's..." Jelena almost said a friend of the family, but how would that sway Thor? "I know he switched sides during the war, but he didn't act dishonorably, did he? He is—he's always seemed like an honorable man.

He and Leonidas and Mom worked together to stop Tymoteusz. He's the reason the fleet was there, fighting Tymoteusz so we could get to *you*."

"I am aware, but he was also one of my father's most trusted and relied upon military leaders. When he left, he took countless troops and several ships with him—he *stole* from the empire. And then my father was forced to rely upon Admiral Antonescu, a man who lied to his face, who was only worried about appearing to be obeying orders, but who never actually showed up at the end, to defend the asteroid base where my father's men were outnumbered and outmatched."

"Thor," Jelena said slowly, horrified at the idea of Hawk being one of his targets, "some of this is just war and how it is. People defect. The empire was a scary authoritarian place for most of its subjects. Of course it would have been fine for you, but there's a *reason* people fled to the other side. It wasn't personal."

His expression turned scathing. "How wonderfully knowledgeable about it you are, considering you were eight at the end and barely born when the war started."

"You weren't much older. Are you *sure* these people you're killing were all greedy and disloyal and without justification in what they did? How could you possibly know when you were still playing with Zizblocks during your father's meetings?"

"I've had plenty of time to do research since then."

"But Hawk—"

"*Leave* me," he said, almost shouted, raising a hand as if he would slam the hatch shut in her face.

She stared defiantly back at him, not caring for the imperious order. This was her family's ship, and he wasn't a prince of anything anymore. It was time for him to get over that and get on with his life.

Thor lowered his hand, the anger in his gaze fading to something more anguished. Almost...betrayal?

What, had he expected that she would fully understand his choices to kill people? Maybe she could understand some of it, but she couldn't condone it. *Especially* for Senator Hawk. He'd helped Thor once, back after Mom and Leonidas had recovered him from Tymoteusz. Hawk's people had come over to the *Nomad*, and Hawk could have ordered a search for Thor, but he hadn't. He'd known the Alliance would have killed or imprisoned Thor so he would never grow into a threat, and he hadn't wanted to hand a ten-year-old boy over to that fate.

"Please, leave," Thor said, quietly this time, and flicked a finger.

The hatch shut, not with a slam but with a soft clink.

CHAPTER SEVENTEEN

"How's the research going?" Erick asked, walking into NavCom. He moved to sit down in the co-pilot's seat, but Alfie was curled up there, snoozing contentedly. "Hm."

"It's daunting." Jelena waved at the various displays floating over the console, displaying pictures of people, walls of text, and rolling stock market pundits' analyses that highlighted Stellacor. The *Snapper* was only about twelve hours out from Arkadius. She'd wanted to have a solid plan in mind by now, beyond flying in and hoping they wouldn't be intercepted before they could land in Laikagrad, the city where Leonidas had been taken for his surgery.

"Can't find information on the board members?"

"Oh, I've found the owners." She flicked at one of the holodisplays to enlarge pictures of a man and woman in their sixties. "The founders and majority shareholders are a brother and sister that live on Arkadius—above it, actually—with their extended family. Their names are Luca and Ida Vogel. They're semi-retired, but from stock reports, it sounds like they're still aware of the goings on in the business. They visit the facility on Arkadius often and annually address the stockholders and employees."

"Do they visit the facility on Alpha 17?"

"It's not in the reports, but who knows? Maybe. They can certainly afford interplanetary travel if they wish." Jelena enlarged another picture, this one of a stone castle that looked like something out of an Old Earth history book, except it was floating on a very modern island flying through the sky above Arkadius. "This is their home. It's called Sunset Island because it originally flew around the planet at ten thousand feet, following the setting suns. Now it seems that they float it over whatever continent or tropical island is appealing at the time."

Erick leaned in to read a description. "The castle is real, not a reproduction, one of the early fortifications the colonists made to protect them from the fearsome wildlife that occupied the Mindarian continent at the time. They bought it and stuck it on their hover island."

"So it seems. Kind of interesting, but I don't see how their eccentric domicile tastes help us. What are we going to do? Fly down, land in their courtyard, knock at the door, and ask them to stop pestering us? I sincerely doubt that the owners are even aware of us—or the fact that their company wants to kill us to keep us from sharing secrets about Masika."

"Probably not, but if we *made* them aware…isn't it possible that could change things?"

"I don't know. It would depend on if they were good people—and considered *us* good people. People worth helping." Jelena thought of the way Masika had called her a thief and assumed that about her for a long time. "That's debatable. There are articles showing charitable contributions they've made to various organizations, but the events were all highly publicized, as if they did it more for the press than because they cared." She hitched a shoulder. "I know Thor said to confront them, to convince them to leave us alone, but I'm not sure how."

"I assumed he meant to kill them. That seems to be his answer for dealing with those who oppose him." Erick prodded Alfie. "Do you want to share that chair?"

The dog's tail flapped, but she didn't get up or otherwise move.

"If you had more furnishings available," Erick said, "you could invite Thorian in to help with the planning."

Jelena hadn't seen much of Thor since he'd closed the sickbay hatch on her. He'd found his cabin and had been staying in it. The few chance meetings they'd had in the corridor had been uncomfortable, as they'd both stepped to the side to let the other pass, and stared awkwardly at each other when neither went first.

"She's mellow." Jelena waved to Alfie. "She'd let you pick her up if you set her in your lap afterward. Just like with the cats back home."

Home. The *Nomad*. Jelena was beyond ready to see her family again. She even missed the clunky old freighter. With its two levels, it seemed more spacious than the *Snapper*, and the mess hall was larger with a huge table for everyone to sit around.

"What's she weigh? Forty pounds? That's heavy for a lap dog."

"It's not any more weight than when you have all four cats in your lap on the *Nomad*."

"Yes, but that's difficult. My lap isn't very big. I have slim hips."

"Keep bringing pizzas aboard, and that won't be a problem for long."

"Ha ha. I—" Erick looked toward the hatchway.

Thor stood there. Alfie flapped her tail against the seat, but again made no move to get up. She looked comfortable. The greeting, however lazy, surprised Jelena, since she didn't think Thor had interacted much with the dog. Of course, Alfie was easy. Always wanting to be petted, she wagged her tail for anyone.

"We're trying to figure out how to storm the castle," Jelena said, waving at the holodisplay. She figured Thor would be more comfortable jumping right into their problem rather than mentioning things from their previous conversation.

"Storming isn't the problem," Erick said. "We can fly over the wall."

"Assuming there isn't a forcefield," Thor said. "Which I wouldn't assume." He didn't seem surprised by the castle fortress, and he didn't step in to read the text about it. Maybe he had independently researched the corporation and its founders.

"Given some time, I imagine I can get a forcefield down."

"While being fired at?" Thor reached past Jelena's shoulder to touch the holodisplay and zoom in to the castle walls. "MH-7500s. Those artillery guns are very modern and effective. Interesting that these people feel the need for such armament on a residence within Alliance borders. They could blow a small hole in the planet. Even heavily shielded warships would hesitate to approach."

"What about heavily shielded freighters full of fearsome Starseer warriors?" Erick asked.

"Fearsome?" Jelena lifted her brows at him.

"I'm tall and magnificent in my black robe and staff."

"So long as you don't get a blood blister?"

"That thing was *weird*. It's still discolored. Look." Erick pulled up his shirt, again bending his spine impressively to inspect the grievous injury. It had flattened out and faded and looked to be healing fine, but he prodded it uncertainly.

"Very fearsome," Thor murmured, then nodded toward the holodisplay. "Despite their weaponry and defenses, a direct approach, forcing your way in if necessary, seems most likely to net results. Visit them and convince them to call off their attack dogs."

"By killing them?" Erick lowered his shirt and grimaced. "Wouldn't others step up and fill their roles in the company? And then maybe want revenge on us even more?"

"I did not say you had to *kill* them. Convince them. Use guile, deceit, diplomacy, whatever your strengths are. I will point out that very few people in the system have a clue when it comes to what Starseers can and can't do, and most are uneasy around us. Maybe you can use that. Or perhaps they would like to meet one of their company's creations." Thor flicked a hand toward the corridor that held Masika's cabin. "Perhaps she would like to meet *them*."

"I think that might end with killing," Jelena said, though Masika was wielding a paintbrush now instead of a blazer. During their trip, she had started a mural out in the corridor while lamenting several times an hour the lack of color options.

"Scientists being killed by their own creations is not without historical precedent." Thor's eyes gleamed at the prospect, and Jelena wondered if he truly believed they could convince the Vogels to stop hunting them without bloodshed. A lot of bloodshed.

The comm beeped.

Erick groaned. "Are Stellacor ships already coming out to see us?"

"Not exactly." Jelena eyed the caller identification. "It's Mom. And it looks like we're close enough for real-time communication."

After all they'd been through and what they were contemplating, a message from her mother shouldn't make her nerves jangle, but Jelena licked her lips, dreading Mom's response to the vid she'd sent from Upsilon Seven. She was surprised there hadn't been one already. Had Mom been busy with

Leonidas? Or had she just been waiting until they could talk in real time and she could pepper Jelena with questions and get the answers she must want?

"What are we going to tell her?" she murmured.

"We?" Erick scooted toward the hatchway, shooing Thor aside. "She's *your* mom."

"You're not fearsome by any definition of the word, Erick Ostberg," Jelena shot over her shoulder.

"Wait until you see me in my robe with my sheet tied around my neck," he called back, already out of sight.

"Thor?" Jelena asked. "I bet Mom would like to see you." And maybe the sight of him would distract her from her daughter's exploits and antics over the last couple of weeks.

"When we arrive, perhaps," he murmured, and walked out.

"This freighter is absolutely *not* full of fearsome Starseer warriors." Reluctantly, Jelena answered the comm, which had been beeping quite insistently.

She braced herself for Mom's face to fill the display. Instead, she got an image dominated by pigtails. Four of them to be precise. Two belonged to Nika and two to Maya, Jelena's little sisters. Half-sisters, technically, but they'd all lived together on the *Nomad* for the last ten years, so they were close. As close as one could be to overly exuberant girls nine years younger than oneself. Jelena felt bad, but she'd been secretly delighted to escape her babysitting duties when she'd left, though admittedly, those duties hadn't been that onerous lately. The girls were getting to the point where she could have logical conversations with them. Jelena hadn't thought they were to the point where they were using the comm on their own though, and she peered past their heads, expecting Mom in the background.

"*Jelena*," Nika said in a stern voice. "Where *are* you?"

Maya nodded solemnly. She'd never been as chatty as her twin sister, but Jelena had never been certain if that was because she was a natural introvert or if Nika spoke over her so often that she'd given up.

"On my way to Arkadius," Jelena said.

"*Still? It's been forever.*"

"We've had a few delays." Jelena did not know how much Mom had told the girls and didn't want to worry them.

"Mom said you were liberating animals," Maya blurted as Nika opened her mouth. Nika frowned at this interruption.

Liberating. At least someone had gotten it right.

"I was. And, uhm, we liberated a person too. And then we found some-one else too." Jelena couldn't claim that they had liberated Thor. Should she warn them that he was coming to visit? She didn't know if they remembered him. They'd only been three or four the last time the family met up with Thor in person.

"Are there any *bunnies*?" Maya asked. "Will you bring them back to the *Nomad*? Can I pet them?"

"Sorry, there weren't bunnies. There were dogs, cats, pigs, and monkeys."

"Monkeys!" Maya squealed. "Monkeys are smart. Are you bringing back a monkey?"

"I'm afraid we left the monkeys on a tropical island where they would be happy. And a shelter on Upsilon Seven is finding homes for the rest of the animals now. All except one." Jelena wanted to talk to Mom, but she took the time to adjust the display to take in Alfie. All of this chatter had caused the dog to sit up, and she tilted her head and perked her ears at the faces hovering over the comm panel.

"A dog!" Maya clapped.

Nika frowned sternly, and Jelena could imagine her fists propped on her hips, even though only her head and shoulders were visible. "Mom and Dad said you can't have a dog on the *Nomad*. Dogs are too big for spaceships."

"We're on the *Snapper*, not the *Nomad*. I don't believe there are rules about dogs on this ship yet."

Concern replaced the sternness. "Aren't you coming home? Back to the *Nomad*?"

A good question. Jelena had imagined her cargo delivery to Alpha 17 being the first of many missions, not the first and only one, but after all this, would Mom and Leonidas trust her to fly on her own again? Would it be safe for her to do so with the enemies she had made? Even the Alliance might be after her now.

"I'm not sure yet. Is Mom there?" Jelena tried to peer past the twins again. She recognized Mom and Leonidas's cabin in the background, but she didn't see either of them.

"She went to the hospital," Nika said.

The nerves that had been tangling in Jelena's stomach tightened for a reason that had nothing to do with worrying about reprimands. "Because of Dad?"

She usually thought of Leonidas by name, but she called him Dad when speaking to the rest of the family. He'd been pleased when she'd started doing so a couple of years after he and Mom married. She'd ended up liking him a lot, even if she'd originally been afraid of him, so she'd wanted to make him happy.

"He's having his surgery tomorrow," Nika said.

Maya nodded solemnly again, her eyes glinting with moisture this time.

"He's getting a new heart," Nika added. "Mom said everything's going to be fine, but...you should be here, Jelena. Dad needs all of us. Austin is taking us to the hospital in the morning."

"You need to come," Maya said. "Will you be here tomorrow?"

"I..." Technically, the *Snapper* should make Arkadius's atmosphere before then, but would she be able to fly straight down to the planet? Or would they meet opposition? "I'll try."

"Promise," Nika said. "Promise you'll be there for Dad. You can't *not* come."

"I can't promise, but I'll try my hardest."

"Uncle Tommy is meeting us there," Maya added. "With cookies and brownies and bread pudding, and all of Dad's favorites."

"I'm sure that'll be good for his new heart," Jelena murmured, though she knew those happened to be all of Maya's favorite goodies too. "I hope to see Uncle Tommy."

"Yumi and Mica are already there," Nika said, "And Mister Hawk and Admiral Tomich are coming too."

"Mister Hawk said he'd bring Wren and Jay to play!" Maya added.

Jelena, frozen in silent horror at the mention of Senator Hawk, couldn't manage a response. Blessings of the Suns Trinity, she couldn't bring Thor down if Hawk was going to be there. She envisioned him yanking out his sword and trying to kill the senator while standing over Leonidas's hospital bed.

A hatch clanged open behind the twins. Someone tall leaned down to peer over their heads and into the camera. Austin. He was similar in looks to Erick, though his face was full of pimples, and he had brown eyes instead of green.

"Hello, Austin," Jelena said. "Were you the one to tell the girls to comm me?"

"No, I believe this is an unsolicited and unauthorized comm call. In fact, ten minutes ago, Maya and Nika were helping me fine-tune the ghostometer down in engineering. I came to look for them to make sure they weren't burning anything down."

"This is *important*," Nika said, pointing at Jelena.

"So is gathering proof that the *Nomad* is haunted," Austin said, not looking like he was joking or pulling the twins' legs. "Once I have proof that there are malevolent spirits here, I can convince the captain that we need to have an official cleansing. It's not a good idea to fly on a ship full of ghosts with malicious intent."

"Maybe the ghosts are friendly," Maya said.

"I doubt it. I've been looking back through the logs." This time, Austin was the one to assume the stern expression, something even more out of place on his boyish face than it was on Nika's. Ghosts? Cleansings? Jelena couldn't believe Austin was the same age as she was. "Do you know how many times enemies boarded the *Nomad* while your parents were looking for you, Jelena? People were killed all *over* the place."

"Austin," Jelena said, frowning. He shouldn't say such things with nine-year-olds around.

Not that the girls appeared daunted. Maya turned wide, interested eyes toward him, and Nika said, "If any ghosts bother us, Dad will beat them back to the graveyard. When he gets better. Tomorrow." She looked at Jelena again. "You *have* to come, Jelena."

"I'll do my best," Jelena said, wishing she could promise to be there.

Austin shooed the girls out of the cabin and waved a goodbye to Jelena before turning off the comm.

She leaned back in her seat, wanting more than ever to be there for Leonidas and the rest of the family. Even if she had to make sure Thor and

Hawk never crossed paths. Was there any chance the *Snapper* could fly in, avoid all Stellacor ships, and head straight for the hospital?

A quiet clink sounded behind her, Masika moving a paint can. Jelena wished she had enough paint to do the *outside* of the ship. Not that a different-colored hull would keep enemies from identifying them. They would have to find a way to hack the ship's ident chip for that. She didn't know if Erick had the experience to do that but doubted it. Even if he did, Masika and her embedded tracking chip would remain a problem. They would need a doctor to remove that, and even then, who knew if Stellacor had booby-trapped it somehow to make it difficult to remove?

Jelena thought of Thor's suggestion, of convincing the corporation to leave them alone through—what had he said to use? Guile, deceit, or diplomacy. Whatever her strengths were. As if she knew. Was she supposed to be that self-aware already at eighteen? As far as she knew, her only strength was communicating with animals. That floating castle didn't look like it had a courtyard of cattle she could entice into stampeding.

"Maybe we could get an invitation," she mused, propping her heels on the control console and studying the ceiling thoughtfully. She grabbed her stallion mug and sipped the orange vitamin drink inside. "It's a foregone conclusion they're not going to invite me in...or Erick..." But what if Masika commed them and said she wanted to turn herself in? She could say she'd changed her mind and didn't want to be on the run anymore. "But even if they believed that, one of the ships in orbit would be sent to take her. We'd never get in to the owners' castle."

Unless they could get the direct comm contact information for the place and trick or manipulate whoever answered into inviting them down. With an invitation, they wouldn't have to worry about forcefields or artillery weapons mounted on the walls. Jelena didn't think she or Erick could manipulate someone at a great distance and over a comm channel, but maybe Thor would be able to reach out that far. Or maybe they could trick the person without using mental powers.

"Guile, huh?" she murmured.

"All that talking to yourself can't be healthy," Masika said from her painting spot around the corner.

"I'm talking to Alfie."

The dog had curled up in a ball with her nose under her tail and didn't seem to be listening.

"I doubt that's healthy, either."

"You're clearly not an animal person."

"I painted a portrait of a cat for a roommate once," Masika said.

"Did that experience convert you into a cat lover?"

"It mostly annoyed me because all those different colors of fur were a pain to get right. I suppose I could love a solid-colored cat."

"I'll put that on your adoption application for the Arkadius animal shelters."

Jelena sipped from her mug, thinking that maybe, just maybe, they could finagle an invitation to the castle. If Masika was willing to go along with her burgeoning plan. But then what? If they got in, how could they possibly change the Vogels' minds about them? Especially when Masika had no intention of truly turning herself in?

"One step at a time," she muttered.

"You sound like you're scheming," Masika said.

"How would you like to comm the Vogels, pretend you want to turn yourself in, and get the *Snapper* invited down to their hover castle?"

"You're *definitely* scheming." Masika did not sound pleased.

"It's a family tradition. I learned it from my mother." Jelena was surprised she'd needed Thor's prompting to get her mind into gear on this. And that he'd said the right thing to make her wheels turn. Maybe he was wiser than his surly demeanor and broody black clothing suggested. What else had he said? That few people knew what Starseers were and weren't capable of. And that they had a tendency to fear Starseers. Couldn't she use that somehow?

"Did you also learn to sit on your butt in a chair while someone else works on your ship for you?" Masika asked, clinking her paint can again.

"Technically, yes. My mother's a captain. The captain's job is to sit and scheme while the hired help does the physical work."

"I'm not quite sure that's the job description listed in the military officers' handbook."

"This is a civilian ship. Besides, if I helped you, your murals would be full of sparkles and glitter."

"That's appalling. How young *are* you?"

"Not that young, but I have nine-year-old sisters, and I have to teach them the ways of womanhood." Jelena decided not to mention that her favorite nailzazz color was the metallic blue with all the silver glitter. Sadly, she hadn't had time to think of sheening her nails lately. "Who do you think showed them how to properly affix stickers to their father's combat armor?" She gazed fondly toward the comm. The channel had closed, but she hadn't yet snapped off the last image, of Austin chauffeuring the girls away to study his ghostometer.

"That's the cyborg father? The one who needlepoints?"

"He's a special man. You'll enjoy meeting him." Tomorrow, Jelena added silently. How could they resolve all of this so they could be there for the surgery tomorrow? Maybe if they could get into the castle, she could wing it. Or maybe—

"Ghostometer," she said, dropping her feet to the deck as an idea popped into her mind.

"What?"

"I…think I'm ready to implement my schemes."

CHAPTER EIGHTEEN

"They're coming," Thor said, no hint of worry in his tone.

Jelena wished she could feel that calm. She waved a finger through the sensor display to show the ships he was talking about. There were dozens around, orbiting Arkadius or flying to or from the populous core planet, but two of them were heading toward the *Snapper*.

"Thus ends my hope that Stellacor wouldn't notice us and we could fly right down to meet my parents," Jelena said, not adjusting their course. She'd been looking for Sunset Island down there, and she kept doing so as they flew closer. They were close enough for the *Snapper's* sensors to scan the planet's surface—and objects floating ten thousand feet above it.

"Judging by the schemes bouncing around in your head, you didn't truly believe that would happen," Thor said.

He leaned against the hatch jamb. Masika was sitting in the co-pilot's seat, while Erick stood behind her, surfing the sys-net on his netdisc. His toolbox rested at his feet—Jelena had asked him to bring it up. Alfie had been lured to her blanket under the console with a piece of a ration bar. Oddly, she seemed to prefer those to the dog treats Jelena had purchased for the rescued animals.

"No, but I *hoped* it would." Jelena wrinkled her nose. NavCom smelled of paint. She looked forward to fresh air. Fresh air in a floating castle.

"At what point am I comming these people to turn myself in?" Masika asked.

"As soon as Erick finds their contact info."

"Their *unlisted* contact info," Erick said.

"If it were listed, I wouldn't need you to find it. Thor?" Jelena glanced back. "Can you convince those two ships that we're not here? Or not where they think we are? It would be ideal if we could get down to the planet without engaging in a dogfight along the way." She hoped the pilots were humans and not androids. The ships were still too far away for her to tell, though that wouldn't be true for long. They were coming fast. And the sensors showed a lot of weaponry on them. Cheeky of them to pick a fight in Arkadius's space with Alliance military vessels patrolling from orbit. Jelena might have commed them and asked for help, but she didn't want to draw the military's attention, not when she might be on some people-to-be-detained-for-damaging-space-bases list.

"I'll see what I can do," Thor said.

"Thank you. Have I mentioned that we appreciate you coming along to help?"

"Yes."

"Good."

"You *haven't* mentioned that you appreciate *me* coming along," Erick pointed out, swiping through lists with a finger.

"I haven't? Huh."

He squinted at her.

"What? My parents are paying you to be here. You're a salaried engineer."

"If you saw how little they pay me, you'd be more grateful. I stay for Stanislav's wisdom, not for the financial perks. You should see some of the job offers I got after I finished school. My engineering skills were in high demand. And here...well, I haven't even gotten my pack of *Striker Odyssey* cards yet. Or my cape."

"Cape?" Masika looked over her shoulder, a puzzled furrow to her brow.

"Yes, Jelena has likened me to a superhero and suggested I should have a cape that flaps majestically in the breeze."

Masika's puzzled gaze turned toward Jelena.

"I didn't say anything about majestic breezes." Jelena tapped the sensor panel. "Thor, they're going to be in firing range soon. Should I raise shields?" When he didn't answer right away, she peered back at him. His eyes were closed as he presumably concentrated on those ships. Normally, she wouldn't interrupt him, but she needed an answer. "Thor?" She tugged his sleeve.

"I'm sorry. I was distracted imagining Ostberg in a cape."

"It's an arresting image, isn't it?" Erick asked.

"Are you *only* wearing a cape?"

"Of course not. I'd be wearing my black Starseer robe and carrying my staff with the runes glowing impressively."

"Good," Jelena murmured, surprised that Thor was making a joke. Or maybe he was mocking Erick. That would be less surprising. "Nobody wants to see your blood blister."

Masika's wrinkled lip suggested agreement.

"Androids are piloting the ship," Thor said, the change of topic—or return to a relevant topic—startling Jelena.

"So you can't stop them?" She jabbed a button to raise the shields.

"I can destroy the ships or I can sabotage them. There are humans on board. I assume you don't want to kill them."

"I'd prefer not to give the Vogels more reasons to hate us right before we visit."

"I'll attempt non-explosive sabotage then."

"That's usually my job," Erick grumbled.

"You're looking up comm codes for me," Jelena said.

"Because I've been demoted to secretary."

"We'll still get you a cape." Jelena turned back to the console, certain that evasive maneuvers would be needed soon. "But only if you *find* that code before the androids blow us up."

"I'm a creative soul; I don't work well under deadlines."

"Tough."

Reluctantly, Jelena adjusted her course to orbit Arkadius instead of heading straight down. There was little point in flying toward Sunset Island before they talked to someone there. Besides, she no longer wanted to storm straight into the castle. If they were going to use Starseer guile, they would need to take a less direct approach. Even knowing that, it felt like a failure to head away from the island. Letting the oncoming ships flank her wouldn't be a good idea, either.

"Got it." Erick leaned forward and punched a code into the comm console.

Jelena took her hands off the flight controls long enough to point the holo camera at Masika. "You're on. You remember your lines?"

"Yes, it was thoughtful of you to write a script for me."

"You sound sarcastic."

"She's an artist," Erick said. "She may want the freedom to improvise."

A faint shiver ran through the *Snapper*, and Alfie whimpered from under the console. The first of the two ships had fired. It was a Teravian moon hawk, fast and maneuverable despite its weaponry and heavy armor.

"They're firing already?" Erick groused.

"Rude of them not to comm and give us terms first." Jelena pushed the engine to avoid the slight pull of Arkadius's gravity and looked for other non-Alliance ships they might hide behind. She thought of the way they'd convinced the shipyard guard vessel to fire on their pursuers back on Alpha 17 and wished they dared approach some of the military ships out there.

The comm showed the call connecting, and Erick shifted so he wouldn't be in the camera's view. "Shall I get in the turret?"

Jelena blew out a slow breath. Maybe they could slow down the moon hawks with a few shots fired across their noses. Or *up* their noses. But she hated to return fire before they'd given her plan a chance to work.

"Yes, but don't fire until we've talked to someone." Jelena tilted her head toward Masika.

A woman's face appeared in the holodisplay, and Erick only responded with a wave, then ducked into the corridor. Thor remained, his eyes closed again. Instead of scrunching up his face in concentration, the way Erick did when he called upon his mental powers, he looked peaceful. Serene. None of the anger that often lurked about him was visible on his face now.

"This is the Vogel residence," the woman said. "You're comming from an unlisted code. Please identify yourself."

"My name is Masika Ghazali. I'm an employee and...product of Stellacor Corporation. I'd like to speak with one of the founders."

The woman frowned deeply. "This number is for making landscaping and maintenance appointments."

Jelena would have sighed at Erick if he had been there—and if she hadn't been busy flying toward one of the civilian space stations orbiting above the southern hemisphere. She doubted she would find help there, but there would be a lot of traffic to weave around, and the androids might hesitate to shoot.

Another shiver ran through the *Snapper* as her pursuers picked up speed and both opened fire. Jelena grunted. Maybe they knew what she had in mind.

Blazer blasts peppered the freighter. Their shields were holding for now, especially since Jelena was zigzagging unpredictably as she flew, but that wouldn't last.

"Can you patch me through to the appropriate comm code then?" Masika asked with a forced smile. Smiles didn't seem to come naturally for her under any circumstances.

The woman was already murmuring to herself and tapping a silver ear-star. "One moment, please," she said to Masika.

Jelena grimaced, not wanting to wait for *moments.*

"I can sabotage the ships now if you want," Thor said quietly.

"Can you disable their engines without affecting life support?" Jelena asked, taking the *Snapper* closer to the space station. A difficult feat when those ships were looping and weaving all around the freighter's back side, trying to find a weakness in her shields. They had e-cannons, but hadn't powered them up yet. Maybe the androids had orders to board and collect Masika without destroying the ship—or without destroying it until *after* they had her.

Jelena had told Erick to wait, but she reached over and told the targeting computer to open up the rear blazers, hoping to convince their pursuers to back off.

Shudders wracked the *Snapper,* and the shield integrity indicator flashed a warning.

Thor opened one eyelid. "Their life support? Is that your primary concern when they're firing on us?"

"Not primary, but it's *a* concern. We are trying to find a peaceful solution here."

A man's face replaced the woman's on the comm. "Masika Ghazali, you are under contract and are ordered to surrender yourself at once."

"Ordered," Jelena mouthed. As if Masika was a soldier in the fleet. At least the man knew who she was.

"Yes, that's what I'd like to do," Masika said, that forced smile still on her face. "I realize I've made a mistake in not finding a way back as soon as possible. But I'll only surrender myself to Luca or Ida Vogel. I don't trust the thugs the corporation has been sending at me. They've shackled me and beaten me, as if I'm a prisoner, not an employee."

Jelena glanced at her. Beaten? When had that happened? Or was she adding that for flare? To make it more believable that she would want to deal with the Vogels instead of their minions?

"I've spoken to my employers, and they know who and what your situation is," the man said. He wore a suit and had an air of self-importance about him, but he hadn't yet given his name or position. Was this someone they could negotiate with? "You'll lower your shields and surrender yourself to the ships following you now."

"They're *firing* on us, not following us."

Another shudder went through the freighter. A couple of comm messages came in at the same time, both from the space station. Jelena had a feeling she was about to get warned not to bring her trouble over there.

Thor? Jelena was too busy flying to look back this time. *Is there any chance you can make the person Masika is talking to more…acquiescent?*

I can do that or stop these ships. And I can only guarantee the ships. It's almost impossible to affect someone over a comm.

He should be on Sunset Island. Can't you find the island and reach him in the usual way? There shouldn't be that *many people floating around on it.*

That island is on the other side of the planet from where we are now.

Is that far for you? Huh. Guess I'm expecting too much of you.

Jelena did not look back, but imagined she could feel his flat look upon her.

Deal with the ships, please, she added, glancing at the shield integrity again. She funneled more power into the rear shields, since their attackers were focusing on her backside. Typical.

I can tell you he's not in charge of anything important, unless being one of the senior staff for the homeowners counts. I think he's the sommelier.

The what?

The wine steward. He's thinking about that now because he was in the middle of making space in the cellars for a shipment coming in later.

How can a castle hovering in the clouds have cellars?

"You're on a ship known to have thieves and troublemakers aboard," the man—the sommelier—said. Faint clinks sounded behind him somewhere. Jelena imagined the Vogels sitting at some dining room table just out of view of the camera and relaying messages while sipping offerings from a flight of wine. "You will surrender to those pursuing you, or the company, deeming that ship a threat, will order that it be destroyed."

"This ship is owned by Alliance citizens, not rogue thieves," Masika said. "It would be a crime to destroy it and them, especially in Alliance space. If you'll let me come turn myself in, I'll happily explain it all. They're not to blame for my mistakes." Masika sounded sincere, and Jelena wanted to object, but she kept her mouth shut, knowing the man would hear her.

Ostberg is working on our pursuers, Thor told her silently. *I believe I can influence him now if you wish.*

That was good, but if the sommelier's bosses were nearby, he wasn't going to be able to amble out and lower the forcefield.

An idea popped into Jelena's mind. *Wait—both of you. Thor, can you tell where his expected shipment is coming from and when?*

Another round of blazer fire hammered the shields.

Jelena? That was Erick. *I can disable them, but we need to act soon if we don't want a lot of damage to repair. Or worse. I know I don't want that.*

"Then surrender yourself now," the man said after a long look to the side. Someone was definitely instructing him. "Halt that ship you're on and have the captain lower the shields."

"Sure," Jelena muttered, closing the comm, "that's going to happen." Silently, she said, *Give Thor a minute, Erick.*

He's expecting the shipment in approximately five hours, coming in a shuttle from Hierarchy Cellars, which is based on the mainland, about a hundred miles from their current location.

Excellent. Thank you, Thor.

The freighter lurched, throwing Jelena against her harness. An audible alarm wailed, and several lights flashed on the panel. Their pursuers had unloaded the e-cannons.

Jelena? Erick prompted her, his exasperation coming through the silent link.

I need you and Thor to work together on something. Jelena banked, wobbling the ship erratically and descending toward the planet. They had been up near the pole, so she angled her descent to take the *Snapper* toward the equator, closer to the castle. Or, more specifically, closer to that wine place. *We need to make it look like we're crashing, without actually crashing, preferably without doing any damage at all.*

How do you want us to do that? Erick demanded.

Androids won't be fooled by mind illusions, Thor said.

Our shields could protect us if we crashed into the ocean and disappeared. Jelena imagined the *Snapper* plunging into the water, staying submerged for long enough for the ships to assume they'd been destroyed and forget about them, and then coming up and flying off. *If our enemies believe we're all dead, they won't continue to hunt for us,* she added, starting to like the idea. *And if Erick and his toolbox can come up with an idea to muffle or interfere with the transmission of Masika's tracking device until we can have a doctor remove it, then she'll appear to be dead too.*

Just one problem with your scenario, Thor said.

Just one? Erick managed to sound impressively incredulous via the telepathic link.

We can't disappear into the ocean. The ship is full of air—it'll float. Even if we strike with significant velocity, we'll pop back up again. Our pursuers will see that we're not truly damaged. They'll probably be able to read the energy signature from our raised shields too.

"Marchenko, what *are* you doing?" Masika, not privy to any of the telepathic communication, gripped the console with both hands.

Jelena had added an uneven roll to their descent, hoping to convince their pursuers they were damaged, even though their shields were still up. Now that they had entered the planet's atmosphere, the ship's artificial gravity generator was groaning to compensate and keep them in their seats. Jelena wished she could vent some smoke from somewhere for more verisimilitude.

"Trying to figure out how to crash."

"Those are *not* words a passenger wants to hear from her captain."

Jelena? Thor prompted, sounding mildly alarmed. Probably because they were now hurtling toward an ocean. *Your plan won't work.*

What if we close off the cargo hold and let it fill with water? There's nothing in there now that we couldn't lose, aside from Alfie's dog food.

And our thrust bikes! Erick cried into her mind, as if she'd suggested sacrificing children.

Wouldn't they just get wet? You could fix them, I'm sure. We're running out of time. What do you two think?

That you're spaced, Erick promptly replied. *Thorian agrees.*

It would take ages for the cargo hold to fill up, Thor said. *Just...take us in. I'll figure out a way to make us heavier than the water we need to displace.*

How in all the suns' hells are you going to do that? Erick demanded. *You're spaced too!*

Thor did not respond, and Jelena imagined him cogitating hard as he tried to figure out a solution. She almost backed away from her plan, but the ocean was coming up fast, and those ships were on the *Snapper's* tail.

We need the shields up for this, right? she asked both of them. It seemed logical, but their pursuers might not believe they'd needed to crash if they dove into the ocean with their shields up.

Lower them, Thor said. *Erick will erect a Starseer barrier around the ship to protect it from the landing and the water pressure as we descend.*

A barrier around the entire ship? Erick asked. *Have I mentioned that you're both utterly and completely spaced?*

You can do it.

Masika gripped the console more tightly as the choppy, blue and white ocean waves filled the view screen. The two ships had been following relentlessly, albeit holding fire as their prey descended, and now they swept upward to avoid splashing down.

"We're going in," Jelena said, hoping Erick could do as Thor asked. She would do her best to lend her own power to the effort.

She toggled the shields on and off a few times, as if they were failing, then left them off. She took them into the water at a steep angle, having already checked the sensors to make sure nothing was hiding under the surface that they might crash into. There was an underwater canyon, so she took them toward that, hoping that having rock all around them might befuddle the enemy ships' sensor scans.

When the *Snapper* struck, Jelena expected a jolt and for splashes to spatter the camera lenses, but Erick had gotten his barrier up. The ship slipped under the surface, angling downward, like an experienced diver arrowing in without a splash.

"Thank you, Erick," she murmured, gaze locked to the view screen as they plunged into the canyon and the water rapidly grew darker and darker.

But their momentum soon slowed, and she grimaced. The ship would start rising soon.

Thor?

Working on it.

An ominous crack sounded, and Alfie whimpered under the console.

"Was that the *ship*?" Masika demanded, her knuckles white as she gripped her armrests.

"I don't think so." Jelena glanced at the indicators, then used her mind to check Erick's barrier. She sensed it wrapping fully around the ship, hugging the contours of the hull.

An alarm flashed and beeped, making her jump in her seat. The proximity alert.

Something's falling toward us, Erick blurted into her mind.

A second later, she sensed it herself. A huge slab of rock had sheered off one of the canyon cliffs. It tumbled toward them as the *Snapper* floated upward toward it.

Jelena lent her power to Erick's to reinforce the barrier around the ship. Abruptly, even more power flowed into it, Thor's contribution.

The massive slab of rock landed atop the *Snapper* with a thud, and the ship lurched, shifting downward. Alfie howled. Or maybe that was Masika.

A horrific scrape echoed through the canyon, and Jelena thought the slab was damaging the ship, despite their barrier, but that was the sound of it striking the rock walls outside, catching against them. The proximity alarm complained vehemently—the slab had missed hitting the turret and the star cannon by inches—but it slowly dawned on Jelena that the ship was no longer rising. They were pinned in the canyon.

Masika looked over at her with round eyes. Maybe Jelena should have shared more of her plan aloud before plunging them into the water.

Turn off the power so they believe we're dead in the water, Thor ordered.

Erick walked in as Jelena did so, hitting all except one switch in a line on the main power panel. The lights went out, and dim emergency lighting flickered on, the red glow creating strange shadows on people's faces. The constant hum of the engines disappeared, and it grew so silent that Jelena could hear everyone's breathing. Only a few small indicators remained on. It felt as dark and isolated as if they were in deep space.

She hoped the Stellacor ships would give them up for dead soon and fly away. Since the sensors were out, they would have to rely on their Starseer senses to gauge that.

"I'm confused," Masika said. "Does this mean I'm no longer trying to get invited up to the island to turn myself in?"

"Correct," Jelena said. "As soon as it's clear our pursuers have left, we'll float up, fly to Hierarchy Cellars, sneak aboard the wine shuttle going to the island, and get in without having to worry about forcefields or invitations."

"Hierarchy Cellars? I clearly missed something."

"Thor was reading the mind of the wine steward we were talking to and plucked some information out of his thoughts."

"That was the wine steward threatening me? He seemed rather self-important for that."

Jelena shrugged. "Maybe he's got a lot of seniority among the staff."

"Who gets to move this giant rock off us when it's time to leave?" Erick asked.

Thor looked blandly at him and did not respond. Instead, he nodded to Jelena. *Taking us into the canyon was an inspired idea.*

Jelena managed to respond with, *Thanks,* instead of a snort. It wasn't as if she had foreseen his plan.

"Erick," she said. "Before we take off, I need you to find a way to nullify or block Masika's tracking device so it can't transmit."

"If she doesn't know exactly where it is, that could be difficult. Unless you want me to turn the lav into a Faraday cage and lock her in there."

"I don't know what that is, but make sure to send the cleaning robot through there before locking anyone in."

Masika scowled at both of them. "It's in my arm." She pointed to a spot on her biceps.

"Oh, I can fix that then. Well, I can at least shield it a bit. Should help." Erick reached for his toolbox. "I was wondering why you had me bring this up here."

"The Stellacor ships are leaving," Thor said, his voice distant, his eyes closed.

Jelena let her senses trickle upward and spotted the enemy ships flying away from the area.

"Good," she said. "Let me know when you're ready to leave the ocean."

"Let me know, too," Masika grumbled. "I'm sensing that telepathy has been happening around here."

"Yes, among multiple parties," Jelena said.

"A level five skill. Impressive."

"Telepathy is level five when mind manipulation is level one?" Jelena asked. "Erick is right. The games get it all wrong. Those are two branches of the same art, and mind manipulation is a lot trickier than having a silent conversation with someone."

"Games?" Thor's eyes opened slightly.

"Yes, things children—and apparently many adults—engage in for fun," Jelena said. "Didn't they let you play games when you were in training on that moon?"

"Kai Chen, my combat trainer, let me go out and hunt daygboi with a spear. It was sort of a game."

"Daygboi? Those aren't the giant angry apes with the fangs, are they?"

"Yes. Dr. Dominguez wanted fewer of the ones infected by Ezer's Disease around the camp. They'd been making visits dangerous for the supply shuttle pilot. He assured me he could treat me if I became infected. I did my best to avoid being cut."

"Some game," Jelena muttered, wondering what all Thor had been put through by those imperial loyalists. After having his parents killed and enduring Tymoteusz's torture, he definitely should have been permitted to play games. No wonder a spring in his brain had snapped free, and he'd gone off on a killing spree.

Not all of us had the luxury of a cozy family life and a normal childhood, Thor spoke into her mind, his words somewhere between bitterness and wistfulness.

I had that after my mom *was gone for* years *and after my* dad *died,* she said, sympathetic but also annoyed that he seemed to think he'd been the only one whose life had been messed up by the war. *Besides, you could have had what I had after we found Mom again too. Leonidas invited you to stay on the* Nomad, *as I recall. You chose to go train with daygboi.* Daygbois? What was the appropriate plural for crazy apes?

I'd been hoping *Leonidas would come with me,* Thor replied. *I did ask.* There was the bitterness again, and this time, a hint of resentment.

He was rather attached to my mom by then, and I don't think my Alliance pilot mother was interested in helping reinstate the empire. Or skulking around in forests full of rabid predators.

I know. Men make foolish choices because of women. Thor sneered slightly, looking from her to the still-dark view screen, the hardness in his eyes suggesting the conversation was over. And also that he'd never let feelings for some mere woman interfere with his plans for the future.

That was fine with Jelena. Just so long as he knew she wasn't going to let him kill Senator Hawk while he was destroying his future by assassinating all the important people in the system. Admittedly, her own future was in a questionable place right now. At least he was self-destructing intentionally and for what he believed was a good reason.

"All done," Erick said cheerfully.

Masika had removed her fatigue jacket and wore a gray T-shirt underneath, revealing strong, sinewy arms, along with…

"Please tell me that's more than aluminum foil wrapped around her arm," Jelena said.

"Of course it's more than aluminum foil. I'm not an amateur."

Jelena eyed the crinkly metallic armband dubiously. "Is aluminum foil a *component*?"

"Aluminum foil is electrically conductive and can reflect and absorb radio waves. It's a perfectly legitimate substance for an engineer to have in his toolbox."

LINDSAY BUROKER

"If you say so. Can I ignite the thrusters and get us out from under this rock?" Jelena looked at both Thor and Erick.

"Erick, maintain the barrier while I move the boulder." Thor closed his eyes again, and Jelena sensed the lessening of the barrier as he shifted his attention elsewhere.

The huge slab of rock floated off the *Snapper* without so much as a scrape or clink. Jelena couldn't believe Thor's telekinetic skills were strong enough to move so much mass.

The slab levitated to the side of the freighter, and Thor let go. Thuds and clacks reverberated through the water as the rock banged and bumped down to the bottom of the canyon. With the weight no longer atop it, the ship rose toward the surface.

Jelena powered up the *Snapper* and was surprised by how dark the water remained when the view screen came on.

"Night fell," Erick said. "Hope we're not going to be too late to catch that wine shuttle."

"Me too," Jelena said quietly.

The ship broke the surface with a bob that startled her. Soon, they floated on the waves, still cocooned by Erick's barrier.

"It's safe to take off," Thor said.

As soon as they rose above the surface and Erick could lower his shield, he headed for the corridor. "I'm heading down to engineering to see what got shaken loose in that mad flight if anyone wants to join me and hold my wrenches."

Jelena suspected the offer was for Masika, but Alfie rose to her feet and trotted through the hatchway after him, nails clacking on the deck.

"Alfie is coming to help," Jelena called after him.

"How is she at holding wrenches?"

"I don't think that's her area of expertise. If you need a stray bird flushed out of the machinery in engineering, she'd be a good ally."

"We should have kept one of the monkeys."

"How long will it take us to reach this wine cellar?" Masika asked, ignoring the exchange and pointing at the view screen. Darkness had indeed fallen, and stars gleamed in the sky over the ocean. Land wasn't visible from their current location.

240

"Not long," Jelena said. "How are you at stealthily sneaking aboard wine shuttles?"

"My stealth is excellent." Masika prodded her metallic armband. "Assuming this doesn't rustle every time I move my arm. What are we going to do if we successfully reach the island?"

"Be sneaky." Jelena glanced at Thor. "And then use guile."

CHAPTER NINETEEN

The town of Nueva Cartagena, where a map told them Hierarchy Cellars lay, sprawled for miles up and down the Tarangan Coast. There wasn't a space base listed, not that Jelena had any intention of looking for a legal place to dock the *Snapper*. Ships that had been utterly destroyed by enemy fire did not amble into public docking areas, not if they didn't want word to get out of their survival. Thus, she set the freighter down in some tall grass above a pebbly beach in a cove fifteen miles south of town. A few sleepy houses looked out from the hills, but most of their lights were off, and the beach itself was dark. As long as they returned by dawn, she doubted anyone would notice the ship.

"A long walk," Thor observed.

Judging by the clanks emanating from the rear of the ship, Erick was still working on repairs. Masika had muttered something about getting weapons and left a few minutes earlier. Maybe she hadn't wanted to be in NavCom for Jelena's next unorthodox landing. This one went smoothly, however, with no need for Starseer protection.

"Erick and I have thrust bikes," Jelena said. "It won't take much time to ride up the beach."

"So only Masika and I will walk?"

"Flirt with Erick a little, and I bet he'll let you ride behind him." She cut the power to the ship and rose from her seat, smiling at Thor.

He did not smile back. Maybe imagining Erick in his cape earlier hadn't excited him. Not that she'd caught him smiling often for any reason. Even as a kid, he'd been somber. No, *especially* as a kid. She had been, too, back then, but her dad's death seemed a long time ago now. Too long ago to hold a grudge against whoever had dropped that bomb.

"Are you sure?" Thor asked softly, his eyes intent.

"That Erick shares his bike with those who flirt with him? Absolutely."

"That you wouldn't do something if you knew who dropped that bomb."

Uncomfortable with him reading her thoughts, she started to shake her head. But was it the truth? She wasn't sure. She just knew she didn't feel compelled to go on a killing rampage over it, not anymore.

"I don't know." She looked away from his intent gaze.

"Do we have to worry about people finding and reporting the ship?" Masika asked, walking back into NavCom carrying a rifle and wearing a dagger at her belt. She'd put her jacket back on so her metallic armband wasn't visible now.

"I'll add some camouflage to it." Thor's expression grew distant for a moment, then he nodded to himself.

Masika eyed him up and down. "Level Ten is when Starseers really get creepy."

Jelena decided not to make suggestions as to what Thor's level might be. Higher than hers. She was glad he was here and for his help. She should get him a cape too. A nice one with some glittering sequins along the hem.

Thor squinted, whether for her thoughts or Masika's comments, Jelena did not know.

She tapped the comm. "Erick? How much longer do you need?"

"Just a few minutes."

"We don't want to miss the wine shuttle. You can stay here if you need to."

"I'll be ready. I want to make sure we can take off in a hurry if we need to."

"Good idea. When you're done, put on your robe, please. Just in case we run into people and need to look powerful." Jelena glanced at Masika. "And creepy."

"Just my robe? No cape?"

"You don't have a cape yet. We haven't had time for shopping."

"I have a sheet."

"One of the rumpled sheets from the bed you never make is not going to make you look powerful and creepy."

"That's disappointing."

Jelena started toward her cabin for a quick change of her own, but paused in the hatchway to tell Thor to dress his most powerful and creepiest too. One glance at his sword hilt and black clothes made her decide the admonition was unnecessary.

Thor looked wryly at her, probably monitoring her thoughts again.

After donning her robe and grabbing her staff, Jelena headed for the cargo hold. Masika and Thor waited near the cargo hatch, but Erick hadn't arrived yet. Jelena unclamped their thrust bikes from the storage rack and turned them on. They sputtered a few times, then rumbled and rose to hover a few inches above the deck.

"There's nobody nearby on the beach," Thor reported.

Masika gave him that wary look, perhaps thinking about levels again.

Erick trotted into the cargo hold, his robe thankfully unwrinkled, his hood up and his staff in hand. Thor had his hood up also, along with a head wrap that left only the top of his nose and his eyes visible.

"We look fearsome, right?" Jelena asked Masika, who wore her only clothes, the gray fatigues. Jelena was tempted to tell her to leave the rifle behind, since force wasn't what she intended to use up there, but she could envision her plans falling apart and the group running into trouble at the winery or, more likely, when they arrived at the castle.

"I'd be alarmed if I saw you three coming."

"Good." Jelena planned to use illusions rather than showing themselves when they reached the castle, but if that didn't work, she would negotiate with the Vogels in person. In which case, she would prefer to come across as a mature and dangerous Starseer rather than an eighteen-year-old girl in over her head. "Anything we can do to add to the fearsome effect?"

"Don't tell anyone if you're wearing your ponies underwear," Erick suggested.

Thor's eyebrows twitched upward.

"They're unicorns, and I'm not. You better not be wearing your asteroids pajamas under that robe."

"They're asteroids *and* spaceships, and I'm not."

Thor pulled out his sword, flicked his wrist to extend the blade, and pointed it at the hatch. "With my cavalry at my back, I charge," he murmured, as if quoting some general of old.

The hatch hissed as the seal broke, and it swung open. The ramp lowered, and the scent of salty sea air wafted in, along with the roar of ocean waves breaking beyond their cove.

Jelena slung a leg over her thrust bike and waved to the back of her seat for someone to join her. "Whoever's riding with me better not jab me in the back with a sword."

"You'd be safer with Masika then," Erick said, "for multiple reasons."

Thor flicked his wrist to draw in his telescoping blade, giving Erick a flat look. Jelena suspected he enjoyed flicking that sword in and out just because.

"But," Erick added, "the bikes do have weight limits. Probably better for Thorian to ride with you and Masika with me." He smiled brightly at her.

At least he didn't wink. Given the past she had alluded to, Masika might not appreciate winks. But she climbed on behind him without comment.

Thor considered the empty spot behind Jelena, and she had the distinct impression that he would prefer to drive. Too bad. It was her bike.

She didn't know if he heard the thought, but he climbed on. At first, he was careful not to touch her, perhaps because of her sword comment. Or because he thought girls had cooties. But there weren't grips or handles back there, so he would have to hang on to her. Or use his special Starseer skills to keep him from tumbling off.

"My balance is quite good," he murmured, as Jelena accelerated the bike down the ramp and into the grass.

"What?" Jelena wasn't sure she'd heard him correctly over the rumble of the engine.

"I do a lot of stretches and exercises for flexibility and balance."

"Well, if you don't want to hang on, that's your choice. But if you fall off, I'm not coming back for you."

She wondered if she should be offended or disgruntled that he didn't want to get close. Weren't young men supposed to take every opportunity to squeeze female flesh? Granted, she didn't have as much personal experience with that as someone her age should—a byproduct of usually having a hulking and muscular stepfather around when the family visited a space station or city. Leonidas wasn't exactly overprotective, but all he had to do was look at a man who was looking at Jelena, and the interested prospect tended to find something else to occupy his eyes—some of them outright fled.

Erick zoomed past Jelena, calling, "Race you!" over the roar of the ocean.

His thrusters flared red as his bike shot through the grass and out onto the beach.

Jelena grumbled and followed, but didn't roar into top speed, not wanting to intentionally buck Thor off—or crash into a log she didn't see in the dark. She did bank hard as she turned onto the beach and zoomed after Erick, less because she wanted to race and more because she felt the press of time. That shuttle would be leaving soon.

Perhaps aware of her thoughts of crashing into logs, Thor scooted a little closer and rested his hands on her waist. His grip was light, and there was definitely no squeezing going on, but she could feel the heat of his palms through her shirt. *He* probably wouldn't be scared away by a cyborg glowering at him.

We're falling behind, Thor commented in her mind.

Erick is a maniac. It's impossible to keep up with him.

Oh? There was a challenge in that single word.

The thrum of the engine grew more pronounced, and the wind whipped into Jelena's eyes, bringing tears. Why hadn't she grabbed her goggles? Her ponytail whipped behind her, probably pummeling Thor in the face. She smirked slightly, deciding he deserved that, but the thought soon faltered. No, he didn't deserve any extra torment. He'd had enough go wrong in his life.

Thor lifted a hand to her shoulder and rested it there for a moment before returning it to her waist. The simple gesture seemed to be an acknowledgment or maybe even appreciation, and she was tempted to say something, to invite him to tell her about how the last ten years had been, but he would volunteer such information if he wanted to share it. Besides, the glow of Erick's thrusters had grown closer, and they had a race to win.

She leaned into the handlebars, urging the engine to its full speed, ignoring the tears in her eyes. The beach was empty and there were few obstacles.

Soon, the lights of the city came into view. Even with her engine roaring at full power, she couldn't catch up to Erick. He had too much of a lead.

But then the glow of his thrusters lessened, and she thought she smelled smoke. His engine faltered, a choking sound audible over the waves. His bike stuttered and slowed to a stop.

Do you need help? Jelena asked, slowing her own bike.

It was too dark to read the look he sent them, but she sensed suspicion. *No. I can fix it.*

All right, meet you at the winery.

They'd both looked at the map, and she knew he could find it. She didn't want to risk missing that shuttle.

It's a simple obstruction in his exhaust pipe, Thor informed her. *He'll be along shortly. After we win the race.*

Odd that you know so much about it.

I have an aptitude for mechanical constructs, as you may recall.

Handy.

Indeed.

Jelena took the first path that headed to a street running perpendicular to the beach. The winery was on the far side of town from the ocean. Fortunately, Nueva Cartagena wasn't a large town. Jelena zipped down the street, hugging the shadows and avoiding the circles of light cast from the lampposts as much as possible. A few ground cars and hover trucks rumbled around the town, but nobody paid attention to her thrust bike.

After a few more miles and turns, she reached an adobe wall that stretched along the street fronting the vineyard. She drove them past a well-lit iron gate with a couple of guards reading or watching vids in a kiosk next to it. One glanced up as she passed.

Going in the front doesn't look feasible, she commented silently. *Not unless they're open to late night vineyard tours.*

Drive around the corner. We'll go over the wall. Have you scanned the interior yet?

No. I will. Jelena blushed a little, feeling she already should have, but she was concentrating on driving, following the long front wall that went on and on. Did they have their whole property walled in? Including acres of vineyards?

There are a lot of shuttles back there where the warehouse and loading facilities are.

Jelena let her senses drift past the wall as she turned the corner and headed down a darker street. This one wasn't well-lit, and she slowed down, thinking to simply park by the wall. She couldn't sense much beyond a house up near the gate, where a few people were awake, congregating by a fire pit on a patio.

Go farther. Toward the warehouse in the back.

Jelena tried to get a feel for that warehouse, but as usual, she had a much easier time sensing people and animals than buildings and inanimate objects. She noticed rodents out in the fields—vineyards—behind the house. A coyote. A bramisar, one of the native animals that pre-dated the Earth colonists. A couple of big dogs lounged on the patio with the fire watchers.

I see you're taking note of the important things, Thor thought, and shared a very sharp and very detailed vision of a warehouse with over a dozen shuttles lined up along a loading dock.

Why aren't there any people at the warehouse? she grumbled silently. *If they're getting shipments ready…*

Looks like robots are handling it. You can pull over here.

Thank you for giving me your permission, your majesty.

Your majesty? You're thinking of kings. I was to be an emperor.

Oh? What's the proper butt-kissing honorific for an emperor?

Your imperial highness.

I'll try to remember that. Should genuflecting be involved? Jelena pulled the bike into the shadows and stopped it on a clump of weeds.

In the old days, you were supposed to drop to your hands and knees and press your forehead to the floor. Thor hopped off the bike.

Sounds unsanitary.

Thor jumped to the top of the ten-foot wall, landing lightly in a crouch atop it, his sword in his hand. Jelena rolled her eyes, regretting slightly that she hadn't taken a few of the turns harder and made him fall off the bike.

She pulled her staff out of its holder, debating how to jump up there, grab on, and pull herself up while gripping it. She supposed she could simply toss it over to the other side and hope it didn't clatter on pavement.

Thor leaned back and held out his hand, the gesture barely visible in the starlight. It took her a second to realize he was offering to hold it for her.

She tossed it up to him and decided not to have any more snide thoughts. At least not for the next five minutes.

Not as gracefully as Thor, she leaped, caught the edge, and pulled herself up. She was glad she didn't need help, and also somewhat pleased that he didn't assume she would and offer it. He handed back her staff once she crouched beside him atop the wide wall.

Lights brightened the area around a warehouse that looked exactly like the image Thor had shared with her. On a wide expanse of pavement, fourteen identical shuttles with grapes and glasses of wine painted on the side lined a long loading dock. Judging by the lights, six of them were powered up and ready to go somewhere. Their rear hatches were open, and wheeled cargo robots rolled back and forth from the warehouse to the shuttles, carrying boxes or pallets of wine. Jelena let her senses trickle over the area, but like Thor, she didn't spot any people around. It was all automated.

"So, which one is heading up to our castle?" she murmured.

"I don't know."

"Can you pluck the information out of one of their computerized brains?"

"No."

"I thought you had an aptitude for mechanical constructs."

"If you want me to override one's programming and send it dancing through the vineyards, I can do that. Reading orders—I don't think it's possible. They don't even have monitors to display information." Thor pointed at one of the robots rolling across the loading dock on its wide wheels. "You'd have to walk up and ask them who the order is for, and I'm sure they don't tell just anyone."

Jelena thought about saying that they weren't "just anyone." They were fearsome Starseers. But she had yet to meet a robot or android that was afraid of her fearsomeness. Or anything else.

"Maybe there's a clipboard on a wall down there," she mused. "Or, if I could get to their navigation controls, it's likely the routes are already programmed in, especially if autopilots will be doing the flying." That seemed a likely assumption since nobody was around, and the people in the house seemed to be done working for the day. "I might be able to see where they're heading without any special clearance." Most of the autopilot systems she was familiar with displayed maps of the surrounding area and routes, in case a human pilot needed to override the computer and take over.

Thor nodded. "I don't see any clipboards, so we'll have to get you down there. That was the plan anyway, right?"

"Right. Think those robots will sound an alarm if they detect someone unauthorized snooping around the shuttles?" Jelena didn't like how well lit the area around the warehouse was. The robots probably had sensors rather than optics and wouldn't need lights to see, regardless. Still, one liked some nice, thick shadows for skulking around.

"Maybe not, but we should assume that's the case."

The rumble of a thrust bike sounded in the street below them. Erick and Masika pulled to the side of the road and parked under Thor and Jelena.

Jelena filled them in on the situation—Masika shifted uneasily at the telepathic communication—then added, *Thor and I are going in to snoop.*

She waited to see if Thor would object to being volunteered, especially when he had only come along to see Leonidas, but he nodded and jumped down, landing soundlessly.

Jelena dropped down, landing less soundlessly. The house was a couple hundred meters away, but she sensed one of the dogs lifting his head, ears perked. She sent a silent assurance to it and pointed out that some of the rodents in the vineyard were particularly active right now.

She trotted after Thor, but kept a mental eye on the dog, who was now debating a nocturnal hunt. They stopped at the front door to the first powered-up shuttle, using the wings to hide them from the rear of the craft and the robots loading it. The shuttles, designed for local deliveries rather than interplanetary travels, looked more like large flying cargo trucks than spacecraft. A small two-person cab was at the front, with the storage area in the rear and a small door allowing access between them.

Jelena tried the handle, but it was locked. She glanced toward the dock, hearing the faint whir of one of the robots approaching.

Thor took her spot and rested his fingers on the handle for a couple of seconds. It clicked, and he opened it, nodding for Jelena to go in.

I'll stand guard.

Jelena handed him her staff and slithered up and across the seat.

Do you want us to follow you down there and start checking the other shuttles? Erick asked. He and Masika were crouched atop the wall now.

Can you unlock doors with your mind?

Of course. I'm not an amateur.

Then yes. We may not have much time. An indicator in the cab showed the rear compartment loaded to ninety percent of its capacity. That made Jelena suspect this wasn't the shuttle going to Sunset Island—how much wine could one family need?—but she still scanned the controls. She waved her hand over the navigation console, hoping a holodisplay would pop up. It did. And she was right. Her craft was heading toward a city on the northern continent.

I'm coming out, she warned Thor before scooting toward the door.

Wait.

She froze, her butt dangling out of the cab.

One of the dogs heard Ostberg jumping down. It's coming over.

Far more worried about robots than animals, Jelena slid to the ground. She located the dog—it was the same overly alert one—and made him believe rodents were scurrying up and down the rows of the vineyard, cavorting under the starlight. The dog veered in that direction.

Jelena always felt bad about fooling animals, but there *were* rodents out there. Maybe the dog would catch something.

Next cab, Jelena told Thor while checking on Erick and Masika's location.

A clang came from a few meters away. One of the rear cargo hatches shutting.

Thor led the way, skipping past two shuttles and stopping at a third. *This one's fully loaded and will likely leave soon.*

Jelena ran for it, glancing toward the house, aware that the two hundred meters between it and them was quite open, with only a few shrubs in the backyard partially blocking the view.

Another clang sounded indicating another shuttle fully stocked and ready for takeoff.

Check that one, she told Erick as Thor unlocked the door to the first one. Its engine already hummed, preparing to leave. *Nice of you to pick locks for me, Thor.* She scooted across the seat. *If you ever want to engage in a life of crime—of lesser crimes than assassination—you may have a calling for it.*

What's the route for that one? he asked, ignoring her comment.

The cargo hold was only fifty percent full, and it was heading to a town up the coast.

This isn't it. As Jelena attempted to back up, the door she had entered through closed. She turned around and tried to open it. It was locked. *Thor?*

One moment.

A clunk sounded, followed by a couple of beeps. Damn it, the shuttle was taking off. With her in it.

I may not have *a moment.* Jelena gripped the handle and examined the locking mechanism with her mind. She wasn't an amateur, either, but she also lacked an aptitude for the mechanical. She had no idea which part of the assembly inside the door moved that bolt.

Her shuttle lifted into the air. She tried to roll down the window, but that was locked too.

Thor, this isn't the trip I was planning to take. She lunged across the seat to the other side and tried that door. It was also locked. She reached for the navigation controls. Overriding them would surely alert someone somewhere, but she didn't have a choice. The shuttle was five feet off the ground already, and it would pick up speed as soon as it cleared the warehouse.

Just as she was going to fiddle with the controls, the door opened. She flung herself across the seat, paused only long enough to make sure the shuttle hadn't risen abruptly to thirty feet, then jumped out. She landed on the pavement next to Thor, and a robot tipped on its side a few feet away. It wasn't moving.

He handed her staff to her. *I had to deal with a problem.*

So I see. Do you think it reported our presence?

He gazed toward the house. *I don't think so.*

An engine roared, another shuttle starting up.

Over here, Jelena, Erick barked into her mind. *This is the one. And it's leaving now.* Right *now.*

Jelena and Thor raced around the fronts of three other shuttles on the way, and barking started up. She winced, thinking the dog had ignored her promises of rodents and was sounding the alarm. But the barking was coming from out in the vineyard. Ah, he'd found his rodents. And he was letting everyone know about it.

Two of the people by the fire pit stood up, and Jelena grimaced, hoping her plan hadn't backfired. For now, they were looking out toward the vineyards, but if they peered toward the warehouse and saw people running around and robots tipped over…

Hurry, Erick urged, flinging a door open as their shuttle lifted off.

Cursing to herself, Jelena sprinted the last few meters. Erick leaned out, extending his hand. She jumped up and caught it, her ribs slamming against the frame of the shuttle. She bit back a groan as Erick pulled her into the cab and scooted in to make room. Thor, making another of his athletic—and no doubt mentally enhanced—jumps, almost landed atop her. He pulled the door shut, and all four of them—Masika was sitting in the pilot's spot—squeezed together in a space meant for two people.

"This is cozy," Erick remarked, as more lights came on below.

Jelena shifted out from under someone's hip and peered through the windshield. More lights were on around the house and also along a road heading out into the vineyard. She thought she glimpsed a dog racing along that road, but then the shuttle banked and tilted its nose upward. Stars replaced the view of the ground.

"Any chance we got out of there before they figured out stowaways were jumping into one of their shuttles?" Masika asked.

Jelena thought of the robot Thor had incapacitated. At the least, the vineyard owners would know someone had been there. She hoped they didn't have a way to monitor interior cameras of this shuttle and let the Sunset Island people know that intruders were riding along.

"Let's scoot into the back." Jelena nodded at the door behind the seat, though she wasn't quite sure how to turn around and open it when she was pinned between Erick and Thor. "Where I'm hoping it's dark. Just in case there are cameras in here."

"Good idea," Erick said, then shrugged his shoulders. He was just as packed in as she was. "Who's going first?"

"Whoever doesn't mind having everyone looking at his or her butt while he or she wriggles over the seat." Jelena twisted, bracing herself for the attempt.

"That can't be me then," Erick said. "I'm shy about my butt."

"I'll warn your future lovers." Jelena turned sideways, reached over the seat, and shoved at the door. Fortunately, this one wasn't locked.

"Is it important that they be aware of his modesty?" Masika asked.

"If they're fans of flamboyant displays of immodesty, yes." Jelena pulled herself over the top of the seat, groaning again, and into the cargo hold. She promptly cracked her head on a pallet of boxes. "This is going to be a fun flight," she muttered, deciding they would be just as squished in the rear.

"Let's just hope the Vogels don't already know we're coming," Erick said.

CHAPTER TWENTY

"What's the plan once we land?" Masika asked.

She and Erick hunkered by the door, while Jelena and Thor had ended up wedged between stacks of boxes a few feet away. It was darker than a coffin in the cargo hold, and Jelena had no idea where they were in their trip. When she reached out with her senses, all she detected was the ocean below and the sky above.

"Sneak out of the shuttle without being discovered," Jelena said, hoping the winery workers hadn't commed a warning ahead to the Vogels—or their sommelier.

"And then?"

"Yes, and then?" Erick repeated. "You've been oddly close-mouthed about your plan. You're not usually close-mouthed about anything."

"Only because the plan has been in flux. We're going to sneak out, visit the Vogels in their bedrooms after they've fallen asleep, and convince them that our now-dead spirits are going to haunt them and do dire things to them if they don't amend their ways by leading a nicer corporation that doesn't experiment on people or animals or do whatever they were doing with those illegally acquired corpses."

"Haunt?" Erick asked skeptically.

"Yes, haunt. And maybe we'll hint that there are all manner of unsettled ghosts in this centuries-old castle that would help us in the endeavor. My plan was inspired by your brother and his ghostometer."

"Inspired by Austin?" His skepticism turned to incredulity. "That can't possibly work then."

"My backup plan is to convince them by more forceful means if necessary, but that would involve revealing that we're alive and didn't crash after all. No matter what happens here, I'd prefer that they and the long arms of their corporation believe we're dead. There's no point in going after dead people for revenge."

In truth, she'd started wondering if they needed to continue on to the castle at all. If the Vogels believed them dead, including Masika, then they shouldn't have a reason to continue to hunt for them. But if they left a bounty out there for them, just in case, Jelena would never be able to travel without worrying about being found. It was also possible that some chance crossing in the future would result in the Vogels learning that they were still alive.

Jelena looked toward Thor, though she couldn't see him in the dark. His shoulder was pressed against hers. He hadn't commented on the wisdom—or ludicrousness—of her plan, but she doubted this was coming as a surprise to him. Did his silence on the matter mean he accepted it? That he thought it could work?

"We're approaching their forcefield," he said. Too busy sensing the route ahead to comment? If so, his silence might not represent an endorsement. "And..." he added, then paused thoughtfully.

Jelena tried to extend her senses, but he spoke again before she caught up with him.

"There are three ships in the air outside of the forcefield," Thor said. "The two that pursued us down and one other one, a large one."

"Is there a *battle* going on?" Jelena reached out with her own senses. No, the ships were flying around the castle on its island, as if on some kind of patrol. All three of them. "They're not there because of *us*, are they?"

"I don't know. It's an android and robot crew on the larger ship. The humans on the smaller ships...They're sleeping."

"Sleeping? Well, that implies they're not expecting trouble. I assume. Could this be the standard patrol that guards the castle?" Maybe the Vogels had irked more than just animal lovers over the years, and had so many enemies, they couldn't relax fully even in their own lofty home.

"It could be." Thor didn't sound that convinced.

"Let's hope so," Eric said, "because if something is up, they may not open the gates for wine shuttle deliveries."

"The sommelier would be disappointed by that, I'm sure." Jelena shifted to her feet in case they needed to take action soon, but she didn't know how much action she could manage while wedged in the back of the cargo hold.

"The forcefield is lowering," Thor said.

"Good." Jelena tried to get a sense of the castle itself as the shuttle sailed toward it.

They were heading toward a landing pad in a courtyard behind tall, thick walls, the stones worn by wind and time. The castle was made of the same stone, at least on the exterior, and did indeed feel like something out of the Early Colonial Era—or even medieval times on Old Earth. It had turrets and towers that looked out over the walls, along with several interconnected buildings accessible behind a portcullis blocking the way to an inner courtyard. In the outer courtyard, a barn and a fenced area rose to the side of the landing pad. It might have once been stables and a corral. Alas, when Jelena investigated further, she didn't sense any horses in it. They'd probably moved out centuries ago, sometime before the castle had been repositioned to its current altitude.

"A lot of weaponry on those walls," Thor observed, focusing, as usual, on different things than Jelena. "And forcefields on all the windows. The stone walls are reinforced, as is all the machinery under the castle, including a big generator. It takes a lot of power to keep that hover system working with so much weigh atop it. There are some shuttles in a smaller courtyard in the back. If we have problems and can't get back to this one, they could be an option."

"Assuming someone left the keys in the ignition," Masika murmured.

"We're eschewing keys on this mission," Jelena said. "We have Starseers along."

"Oh, right. I noticed that Blondie opened a locked door."

"Blondie?" Erick protested.

"She's given you a nickname," Jelena said. "That must mean she's developing a fondness for you."

"Ah?" He sounded faintly bolstered by her observation.

Maybe she should keep such comments to herself, lest he think he might have a shot at pursuing a relationship with Masika.

The shuttle settled onto the landing pad with a soft thump. Thor stood up.

"Are we getting out right away?" Erick asked.

"Let's wait and see if anyone comes out to inspect or unload." Jelena pulled her staff close in case they needed to leave in a hurry. "I bet the sommelier stayed up late to oversee his shipment's arrival in person."

"A lot of people are up late," Thor observed.

Yes, the humans on those ships might have been dozing, but Jelena sensed numerous men and women up in the castle. Some were closed away in bedrooms for the night, but many weren't. She judged two hundred and fifty to three hundred people in the dwelling. The population of the place surprised her, but she supposed the fact that the Vogels kept a sommelier on the staff and ordered this much wine at a time indicated a sizable household. Some people were in a barracks, and she imagined those being security guards or even a small mercenary company. She'd always thought of the core planets as well protected by law enforcers and the military, but maybe Arkadius wasn't as secure as she expected, at least for those living on their own private islands.

"Maybe they're planning a party with their wine," Masika said.

"They can't be that eager for it," Erick said. "Nobody's running out to unload the cargo."

"I wonder how long the shuttle waits for its boxes to be unloaded before deciding nobody is home and taking off." Even though Jelena figured that would take a while, she patted around and picked a way toward the hatch. If nobody was paying attention to the shuttle, it seemed a good time to slip out.

"The men in the barracks are all awake and alert," Thor observed. "And there are guards on the walls manning the artillery weapons."

"Yeah." Jelena didn't like that the people here were expecting trouble, especially since she assumed it had to do with her team.

Clumps and grunts sounded as Masika, Thor, and Erick followed her to the hatch.

"Let's head for that barn first," Jelena said, sensing a side door in the structure, one that led to an alley that ran between the castle and the outer wall, a route that might let them bypass the wide entrance gate.

"There aren't any horses in it." Erick rested his hand on the hatch handle. "Someone may have liberated them long ago."

"Then I'm glad for them. We'll go visit anyway."

A soft clunk came from under Erick's hand, and he pushed open the now-unlocked hatch. He only opened it a few inches at first, so he could peer into the courtyard. Jelena ducked and looked under his arm. She trusted her senses, but they didn't allow her to see in the same way that her eyes did, so it was easy to miss things.

Despite all the people in the place, the well-lit courtyard was empty, the modern landing pad with its blinking lights seeming out of place adjacent to the old cobblestones. As Thor had said, guards stood atop the wall, manning the big guns. Their focus was outward, however, rather than down into the courtyard. Men's voices and an occasional thump or bang drifted out from the barracks building at the side of the castle. The barn stood dark and empty.

Jelena hopped out first, her staff in hand, and ran in that direction. She climbed over the fence and ran for the wide doorway—it was open to the night, and she glimpsed vehicles and tools rather than stalls and hay bales. She almost crashed into an invisible forcefield blocking the entrance, but her senses warned her of it a second before she reached it. She halted at the same time as someone's hand clamped onto her shoulder. Thor. He and the others were right behind her.

"I see it," she murmured, turning to run around the corner of the barn instead.

The stone wall loomed up to the side, providing them shadows and shelter from the eyes of the men at the guns. Their focus might be outward, but that didn't mean one of them wouldn't glimpse movement in the courtyard. For that matter, an alarm might have gone off if she'd run into that forcefield.

"Nobody's noticed us yet." Thor had released Jelena's shoulder, but he eased past her. "I'll lead."

She glowered at his back. Just because she'd almost run into a forcefield didn't mean she couldn't lead. "Do you know where we're going?"

"No, but neither do you."

"Maybe we can find a directory," Erick said. "Castles come with directories, right?"

"Ostberg could lead," Thor said, "but then we'd be looking at his shy butt."

Jelena almost tripped. For some reason, it startled her when Thor made jokes. Maybe because they were infrequent and his delivery was so deadpan she sometimes misunderstood them.

"My shy butt is safely enrobed at the moment," Erick said, "but I haven't found the directory yet."

"We're trying to find a spot where we can hide for a while near the Vogels' bedrooms," Jelena said. "I think they'll be more susceptible to ghost stories if they're woken from their sleep."

Thor looked toward the night sky. Clouds had swept in, stealing the stars and a great deal of the visibility. If not for her senses, Jelena wouldn't know those three ships were out there on patrol.

"I'll try to locate their rooms," Thor said, leading them along the wall and toward the castle. "But I doubt they're sleeping."

"My plan involves hunkering in some closet or fireplace until after they fall asleep."

"A fireplace?" Erick murmured. "Sounds even tighter than the shuttle cab."

"Old castles always have big fireplaces in the pictures I've seen."

Thor paused, lifting a hand and waving for them to press themselves to the wall. Jelena flattened her back to it reluctantly. They hadn't yet slipped into the side passage between the castle and the wall, so they would be visible to anyone striding through the courtyard.

Noise came from above, soft footfalls and the banging of a holster against someone's thigh. Jelena sensed two men approaching along the wall, guards with weapons. If they leaned over the side and looked down, there weren't nearly enough shadows to hide her team.

They won't see us, Thor spoke silently, *but don't move.*

A clang came from the front of the castle, followed by the sound of a winch pulling up chain. The portcullis being raised.

A man in a suit strode out the front entrance with two armed guards in combat armor to either side. Jelena's stomach sank. Combat armor? These people were definitely anticipating trouble. Her hopes of scaring the Vogels into compliance through haunting were dwindling, unless they could hide in a fireplace for a couple of days until the castle had been searched and the idea of intruders had been dismissed. But they didn't have days. Leonidas's surgery was in the morning, and Alfie was back in the ship waiting for Jelena to return to care for her.

The sommelier, Thor informed them as the man in the suit headed for the shuttle. Whoever had come out last had thought to shut and lock the hatch. Good. But a locked door wouldn't fool the man if he'd been warned about stowaways.

The sommelier opened the hatch with a hand to a print reader, but the armored men quickly pulled him back and sprang forward, pointing blazer rifles into the shuttle's interior. Lights came on inside, and they scanned the cargo, first with their eyes and then with a handheld device for reading life signs. Jelena was glad they hadn't waited to get out.

Two more armed and armored men strode under the open portcullis. While the others hopped into the shuttle and searched it, these two looked all around the courtyard. One man's helmet turned toward Jelena's team, and she held still. It seemed impossible that he could miss seeing them, but he did not raise an alarm—or the rifle in his arms.

You're handy to have along, Jelena told Thor.

Yes.

And modest.

Someone called down from the wall, and the two guards turned their attention elsewhere.

Come. Thor continued along the wall, this time at a run.

If Jelena and the others made noise, nobody heard it. They slipped down the passage between the castle and the wall, a passage lit better than Jelena would have preferred.

Thor stopped at a side door in the stone castle wall. It appeared to be made from simple wood, but she sensed a forcefield behind the wood. There was a handprint sensor panel on the wall next to it.

This leads to the kitchen and garbage collection area. Thor lifted his gaze toward the outer wall as footfalls sounded above them again. Another guard. His focus was skyward. For now.

Thor? Jelena touched his arm.

Ida Vogel's bedroom suite is three levels above and there. Thor pointed toward the back corner of the castle. *She's in there and talking on a comm console. The brother's suite is down the hall a ways, and he's there with his wife. His grown son and their children are also in bedrooms there. The sister may be the easiest target. All the adults are awake, but you may need to do your ploy now.*

Uhm. Jelena felt naked and vulnerable in the well-lit passage, especially with all the people passing along the wall. *It'll probably take some time. I was imagining doing it from a dark, quiet hiding spot inside.*

I'll keep anyone from seeing you, but I suggest you take as little time as possible.

"What are we doing?" Masika whispered, not privy to the telepathic conversation.

"Standing guard while Jelena haunts people," Thor said.

"Ah." Masika patted the rifle in her arms, apparently having no trouble with the notion.

"And Erick," Jelena said.

"Pardon?" Erick asked.

"I need you to come along for the haunting, in case the Vogels are harder to fool than dogs."

"Oh, lucky me."

Jelena put her back to the wall and sent her senses in the direction Thor had indicated. She breezed past the auras of numerous people on the way and eventually found Ida Vogel's suite. She was the lone occupant. That should be useful for her scheme, but Jelena took a deep breath, nervous now that it was time to enact her plan.

Can you tip a few things over in her room, Erick? And make a few ominous noises.
Yes.

Jelena focused on Vogel herself, trying to get a sense for the woman and also to put herself in her shoes, to see the world as she saw it. The castle and the wall at her back grew dim in her awareness, and she found herself looking down at a desk, a holodisplay up and papers under her hands. Old hands, the skin creased and less elastic-looking than her own.

When Vogel heard a noise and turned in her chair, frowning, it was as if Jelena heard it through her ears. Vogel's first thought was irritation at being interrupted rather than alarm, and Jelena sensed that the woman wouldn't be easy to scare or intimidate.

Erick caused a wind to stir and moan through the room. Vogel got up to close a window overlooking a garden in the rear courtyard, but paused in confusion when it wasn't open. Unlike the exterior doorways, her windows weren't guarded by forcefields. They were almost as old-fashioned as the castle itself, with glass panes and wood shutters. She checked the other windows in her suite and stopped at a planter that had tipped over, spilling dirt.

A shutter banged open behind her, and she jumped and spun toward it, alarm flaring in her mind for the first time. The shutter bumped erratically against the wall. Mentally bracing herself, Vogel walked toward it. She tried to close the window, even though it wasn't open. The moan sounded again in the room.

Her heart was beating quickly now. She strode toward her desk and comm, intending to call someone. This was the time to act. If more people came into the room, it would grow harder to scare them.

Jelena tapped into Vogel's mind and created an illusion for her. A black-robed figure with its hood up appeared in the air in front of her desk, or so Vogel believed. She gasped and stumbled back, glancing toward the door.

Make sure that's locked, Jelena told Erick.

Already done. I'm a professional at haunting.

That doesn't have anything to do with your little brother's certainty that there are ghosts, does it?

I'm sure I don't know what you're talking about.

"Ida Vogel," Jelena made the illusion say, the voice deep and ominous. She hoped she was doing a good job. Since manipulating people wasn't one of her strengths, maybe she should have given this task to Thor. No, it was her plan and up to her to make it work. "You have slain Starseers." The voice rang with accusation. "You have slain many."

Vogel stared at the apparition. She was surprised at its appearance, but not at the accusations. At that moment, Jelena knew that she wasn't unaware of what the underlings in her corporation were doing. Jelena almost faltered in her plan. Was she letting the woman off too easily? Should she ask Thor to…

No. She wasn't a judge, and she certainly didn't have the right to use a friend as an executioner. What a cowardly act that would be, even if it were somehow justified.

"We are aware of the wrongs you have done to our people and the universe as a whole," she said through the apparition's shadowed mouth and straight into Vogel's mind. "Some considered sending assassins to avenge the deaths of the slain. But your company does some good for people, so we have decided to give you another chance."

Vogel glanced toward the door again and edged that way.

A powerful gust came out of nowhere and sent her stumbling back to her place. Erick's work. The shutters banged an ominous rhythm against the walls.

"You will no longer house animals in your laboratories and experiment on them, nor will you have people killed so you can harvest their organs."

Vogel winced at the first accusation, but she scowled at the second. "That's only temporary so we can fulfill our orders. The jealous Regen Sciences bastards blew up our production lab and all the organs we had growing."

"Temporary murders. How acceptable."

Vogel continued to balk, silently protesting that they didn't order any murders, only paid for the acquisition of bodies of a certain age and type.

"Do you not believe that offering a reward for the dead would encourage desperate people to commit murder?" Jelena had her apparition say, the voice thundering in Vogel's mind, and she sensed the woman's unease at having her thoughts read. Good. "You will cease your criminal and morally reprehensible practices," she added, trying not to feel weird for lecturing someone older than her grandfather. "Morally reprehensible" was the kind of thing *he* would say. "You will personally fly out to your laboratories and give these orders and ensure they are followed. If you do not, my people will come for you. I assure you, we have the power to bypass your security systems and your troops."

Erick knocked another planter over with a timely crash that made Vogel jump and stare at the shattered ceramic and dirt on the floor. Real terror welled within her now. Jelena knew it was petty, but she couldn't help but feel satisfaction.

She was debating whether she should mention Masika and experiments on young, desperate people—and was also thinking of the ghosts she'd thought to bring into this—when the suite door crashed open.

Jelena's concentration faltered, and her illusion wavered. A man strode in with two guards at his back. Ida Vogel spun in relief toward him, recognizing her brother.

Thor blurted, *Watch out!* into Jelena's mind an instant before another presence stormed into Ida's head. Not Erick. Who—

A hand seemed to snap around that bit of consciousness that Jelena had sent into the sister's head, crushing it, then lashing straight through the wall and into her head.

Pain ricocheted through her skull, and she stumbled back, awareness returning to her body as she crashed against the wall. Her head struck it, and the words, *He's a Starseer!* rang in her mind before she blacked out.

CHAPTER TWENTY-ONE

Jelena woke to an alarm blaring and lights flashing. She lay on her back on the cobblestones, still near the castle's side door. Erick knelt beside her, one arm under her shoulders. He patted her cheek for what she sensed wasn't the first time.

"Jelena, are you with us? We have to get out of here."

"The brother's a Starseer," she rasped, trying to sit up. Something warm trickled from her nose. Blood?

Erick helped her up. Masika stood a couple of steps away, her rifle ready as she alternately looked one way and then the other and finally toward the wall above them.

"I know. I didn't realize it until too late." Erick helped her to her feet.

She gripped his arm and leaned against him, not sure her weak knees would support her. Her head throbbed, her brain feeling swollen and too large for her skull.

"Where's Thor?" Her gaze snagged on the door—it was open now, the wood ripped from the hinges, the forcefield down.

"He went after the brother."

"He's storming the castle by himself?" Her concern for him—and disbelief—gave her some strength, and she growled, forcing her knees to firm up. "We have to help him."

She didn't make it more than a half a step to the door.

"No, we don't." Erick pointed up. "Hear that noise? That's for us. He said to get to one of the shuttles, prep it, and get the hells out of here."

"And that he'd catch up?" Jelena scowled, wanting to go help him. She sensed men running through the corridors of the castle, men in combat armor. Yes, she'd seen Thor battle such men before, but how many could he face at a time? And who was this Starseer-trained brother? How much power did he have? She rubbed her temple. That attack hadn't come from a novice.

"Probably." Erick kept an arm around her and steered her toward the back of their alley, the direction of the rear courtyard garden and those other shuttles. "Mostly he said he was going to kill that bastard."

"That wasn't the plan," Jelena mumbled, but after making sure someone had grabbed her staff—Erick had it—she let herself be guided toward the shuttles. As much as she wanted to run in and help Thor, he was probably making the distraction they needed if they were going to get out of there. And she was the only pilot in their group. Logical, but her frustration battled with that logic. To leave now would be to flee without accomplishing anything. The sister would realize it had all been a ploy, that some Starseer had been in her home, threatening her, and that it hadn't been a ghostly apparition that she needed to fear for the rest of her life. Unless Thor killed the sister and brother, what would truly change in the corporation? And even then, wouldn't the company go on, directed by the son or some chief executive officer?

"When he saw you hit the wall, Thor was too pissed to pay attention to the plan," Erick said.

"Guess it's good to know he cares."

It was less good to know he might be going on a killing rampage.

"A little faster, if you can. Or I'm going to have Masika throw you over her shoulder and carry you."

"*Masika* will do it?" Jelena forced her weak legs to greater speed. "Not you?"

"She's stronger than I am. And—" He broke off with a curse.

They had reached the corner and could see out into the garden. Jelena sensed the shuttles on a pad beyond the hedges, benches, and flower beds, but it did not matter. Six men in combat armor were stomping across the grass toward them. Other armored men pounded out a back door in the castle, splitting up, and running in several directions.

Erick released Jelena, shoved her staff at her, and stepped out with his arms raised. Masika jumped past them both, firing straight at the men's chest plates.

As the troops started to return fire, a wall of energy slammed into them. The men stumbled sideways, but several of them got off shots. Sensing Erick was busy attacking, Jelena forced her aching mind to work and created a barrier to protect them. She could only extend it partially, though, since Masika was firing, and she didn't want to deflect her blazer bolts back at her. Jelena almost ordered her to stop, especially since her shots seemed reckless, hitting foliage as often as their enemies. But when one of the benches flew up and slammed into a man's back, Jelena decided Masika's attack might be more premeditated than it first appeared.

With the alarms wailing, Jelena couldn't hear much so it was only her Starseer senses that warned her of a threat from behind. She spun and found two men looking down from the wall and pointing their rifles.

Reacting on instinct, Jelena spun her barrier to the rear and thrust it upward. It struck the men as they fired. They and their weapons flew backward, falling off the wall on the other side.

With a sickening jolt, she sensed them bouncing off the ground and off the island completely. They would fall all the way to the ocean below, and she had no idea if their armor could save them from such a great drop.

Four men charged around the front corner of the castle and sprinted down the alley toward them. Jelena scarcely had time to shift her barrier to block the passage before they opened up fire.

A boom sounded behind her, and Erick stumbled back into her. The jostle almost caused her to drop the barrier, but seeing those crimson blazer blasts streaking toward her face gave her the focus of the sun gods. She kept it up, and the bolts bounced off.

Behind her, Masika shouted a battle cry and raced out from the protection of the castle. Erick had been hit, and pain radiated from him, but he snarled and stomped out after her.

The troops in the alley reached Jelena's barrier and had to slow down. She thought she had them blocked, like a cork in a wine bottle. Then one sprang onto the wall. He tried to run around and over her barrier. She shifted it to cover the space up there but was too late. He dropped down as the others kept firing, meaning she couldn't simply drop her barrier and reconstruct it right in front of him.

The man leaped for her, and she was forced to drop her barrier anyway. She jumped to the side so his body would block her from his colleagues' fire, and whipped her staff up to block him. Instead of shooting, he sprang toward her again, as if to bury her under his weight.

He was fast, his movement enhanced by that armor, but she was used to sparring with and avoiding attacks from Leonidas. She dodged to the side, just enough to avoid his outstretched arms, fully aware that his comrades were biding their time to get a shot off at her. She jumped back in close before he could whirl and snatch at her. She struck him in the side, feeding her energy into her staff. His armor didn't give—no surprise there—but lightning crackled, the air lighting up as branches arced around the man.

The intense brightness of it startled Jelena, making her squint. Wait, that wasn't all from her attack. The entire sky flashed white, sending strange highlights through the clouds.

The man stumbled back, for more reasons than one.

Jelena rushed after him, even though she sensed that Erick and Masika were fighting out in the garden and needed help. She couldn't simply run away. She had to keep the man between her and the others, or she would be easy target practice for them.

She jabbed her staff toward him again. This time, he parried the blow, using his rifle like a fencing foil. But the lightning erupted again, as happy to branch up his rifle as his arm.

He dropped the weapon, roaring with anger and pain. But he wasn't done yet. He leaped at her, once again trying to bury her and perhaps pummel her to death while he was at it.

She planted the butt of her staff, using the cobblestones to brace it, and angled the tip so that it caught him full in the chest plate. She poured her energy into it, and sparks leaped as more lightning streaked up, curling all about him. A branch flicked into his faceplate like the popper of a whip, and the Glastica cracked. The man yelped and stumbled back, reaching for his face.

Jelena took the chance to jump away, throwing her barrier up behind her again as she raced into the garden to join the others. Erick and Masika were fighting back-to-back, he with his staff and mental power, she with her blazer and physical power.

Once again, white light flashed overhead with the brilliance of all three suns shining in the sky at once. It came from high above the castle, or she might have suspected Thor was responsible. This time, the ground shuddered along with the light.

"To the walls!" someone cried over speakers.

A black ship—an imperial stealth Fang—streaked past overhead. Only then did Jelena realize the castle was under attack. She barely had time to register it or ponder who it might be—not the Alliance in that old imperial ship—before blazer fire hammering at her barrier brought her back to the moment. Some of the guards might be obeying the order and running to the wall, but the ones in the garden weren't ready to give up their nearby prey yet.

As Jelena reached Masika and Erick, a thunderous boom sounded, not from above but from the rear of the castle. Something large and brown flew across the garden and landed with a crack on the landing pad by the shuttles. A door.

Thor ran out of the doorway, looking toward Jelena's group, his eyes intent and utterly fierce as they met hers. Blood smeared his cheek—it didn't appear to be his—and his hood had fallen back. He gripped his sword, crimson rivulets running down the blade.

Out of nowhere, a guard leaped a hedgerow and pointed a rifle at him, nearly point blank. Thor barely glanced at the man before he was hurled upward and backward like a boulder launched from a catapult. The guard flew over the wall and disappeared.

The troops fighting Erick and Masika, as well as the men firing at Jelena, saw that and halted their attack. Jelena wasn't sure if some command had come in over their helmets, or if they were horrified—terrified—by Thor's deadly display of power. Whichever it was, they all turned and ran for the front of the castle.

Not slowing, Thor ran onto the trampled grass of the garden. "I told you to get to a shuttle," he barked at Erick.

"Yes, and we're working on it."

"You made it ten feet." Thor flung his hand toward the side of the castle.

"We made it at *least* thirty."

"Come on." Jelena stepped between the men and nodded toward the landing pad. "If the way is clear—"

Another boom erupted, this time from above as two more of those Fangs flew past, dropping bombs. More white flashes lit up the sky, and then a great shudder wracked the castle.

"The forcefield is down," Thor said over the clanging of alarms, alarms that had grown louder and more intense, with a shrieking wail joining the bleats.

"Let's go shuttle shopping," Jelena said, racing for the landing pad and trusting the men to follow her.

They sped out of the garden, skidding on the cobblestones of the main walk as they spun around a corner. A bomb slammed into one of the unprotected castle towers. Stone flew in all directions, raining down on the courtyard. Jelena ran faster. They would need time to start up the shuttle and figure out how to override whatever security was on them.

Thor caught up with her and ran at her side, that same determined and fierce expression on his face. He didn't say anything, but when a guard leaped out from behind a shuttle ahead of them, he sprinted instead of slowing down, and charged right at the man. Their foe got his rifle up, but Thor's sword whipped across, glowing an eerie blue as it sliced the weapon in half.

Jelena attempted to run around the fight so she could get in the shuttle and start it up, but a blast of hot air slammed into her. At first, her confused mind thought it was some Starseer attack—had the brother evaded Thor?—but realization came in the next second, as the shuttle lifted off scant feet from her. She checked with her senses and found at least a dozen occupants inside, some of them children. The Vogel family? How had they reached the shuttles without her seeing them run past? An underground escape tunnel?

It hardly mattered now. As the guard brawled with Thor, the craft rose into the air. Another bomb slammed into the castle, and Jelena curled her lip at the shuttle. She could understand wanting to get the children away, but it seemed cowardly for the adults to flee, leaving their troops behind to fight and die.

"Who in all the suns' fiery hells is attacking the castle?" Erick yelled, grabbing Jelena's elbow and propelling her toward a second shuttle.

Glad there was one, she could only shake her head and run toward it on ground that shifted and bucked under her feet. Something bounced and tumbled past her. A rock from a destroyed tower? No. She caught a better look, and her gut lurched. That guard's helmet—and his head.

She wanted to snap at Thor—did he have to *behead* them?—but there wasn't time. And how much could she truly protest when he was protecting her? All of this had been to protect her—or at least their group—she reminded herself as she flung open a shuttle hatch and raced for the pilot's seat. She'd only talked him into coming along to see Leonidas. All this help he was giving them was a gift. What would have happened if he hadn't been there when she'd stumbled into Starseer Vogel?

"I need a lock picker," she barked as she slid into the seat and waved her hands over the controls, controls that stayed dim instead of responding to her. Another handprint scanner waited in the center of the console. It flashed red when she patted it.

"On it." Erick flung himself into the seat next to her, resting his palms on the console and closing his eyes.

The ground lurched under the shuttle, and something snapped deep within the platform the castle rested upon. The entire structure could fall out of the sky any second. Would it be karma if Jelena plummeted into the ocean far below after sending those guards to that fate?

More booms came as black Fangs filled the sky, hurling bombs at the castle. While Erick worked, Jelena sent her senses upward and was amazed and appalled at the battle going on high above. While those Fangs attacked the castle, four bigger ships wheeled and banked, exchanging fire with the three vessels that had been on patrol earlier.

"They must have had some sense that this was coming," Jelena muttered, realizing that all that alertness hadn't been related to her group, after all.

"We're in," Thor said behind her as the side door shut.

Masika raced up behind their seats, gripping the back of Erick's. Thor merely slumped against the closed door, looking weary for the first time. Looking *human* for the first time.

"Done." Erick leaned back, and the view screen and control panel came to life.

Jelena had already familiarized herself with the console, and her fingers flew as soon as they could.

"Is that Regen Sciences?" Masika asked, squinting through the view screen at the Fangs.

"I only know that the Vogels knew these were rivals, and the attack wasn't unexpected," Thor said.

"Regen Sciences," Masika affirmed.

Thor's voice grew distant as he spoke again. "More ships are coming down from orbit. Alliance military."

"Sounds like a good time to leave," Erick said.

"Working on it." As Jelena ignited the thrusters and lifted the nose, something slammed into the top of the shuttle. Metal crunched loudly, and she flinched and almost piloted them into a tree in the garden. "What was *that?*"

She growled as the shuttle responded sluggishly.

"One of the towers," Thor said.

"The *remains* of it," Erick said.

"*Most* of it."

They shared short glares, and for a ludicrous moment, they reminded Jelena of the children they'd once been, always arguing with each other. Then Thor's face grew weary again, his chin drooping to his chest, his blood-smeared jaw dark with beard stubble, and she saw the man once more, the man she didn't know as well as the boy she remembered.

Abruptly, the view of the damaged castle, the walls, and the garden disappeared, plummeting out of view. Jelena gasped in horror, sensing the fear of the dozens—no, *hundreds*—of people who had been left behind. She had the presence of mind to pilot the shuttle away from the battle still going on above them, but she could almost hear the shrieks of the men and women as the castle plunged ten thousand feet. It hit the ocean so hard, it flew into pieces. Jelena tried to lock down her senses so she wouldn't feel the people die, but it was too late. She knew right away that nobody had survived that.

Her hands shook as she flew the shuttle away. She tried to tell herself that the carnage and death would have happened whether they had been there or not, but tears ran down her cheeks and guilt filled her heart. She had never experienced so much death before, and she knew she would never forget it.

Thor came to stand behind her as she evened out the shuttle's flight and set a course for the beach where they'd left the *Snapper*. His face looked even wearier than it had a moment earlier, his eyes beleaguered.

You felt that, she thought to him. He would have had to—he was more powerful and better trained than she. *All those people dying at once,* she added.

Yes. He rested a hand on her shoulder, though he looked like he needed support as much as she.

I imagine that's what war is like, all those people dying at once. All those people dying, period. She'd heard her mother's stories, of course, and very occasionally some from Leonidas—he rarely shared that part of his past—but this was the first time it all felt real to her. It chilled her anew to think of the deaths she and her friends had been responsible for the last couple of weeks. And for what? To save some animals? To get Masika out of an unpleasant situation? It was hard to say it was worth it. *How can you want that?* she asked, thinking of war again.

Thor lowered his hand, frowning. *I do not want war.*

Isn't that the whole point of your training? What you plan to do? You want the empire back, right? There's no way that's going to happen without a war. A big war.

War is not what I want. It is not what anybody wants. But to roll over and accept the Alliance as my master is unacceptable. More than that, it would be sick after all the atrocities they committed to take down my family and the empire. I made a promise to my father, one I intend to keep.

With war?

He looked down at her through lowered lashes. *Maybe I'll use guile.*

Is that what you used in storming the castle? She gave the sword on his belt, retracted once again, a pointed look.

No, but I was angry.

Because she'd been hurt? Jelena wasn't sure whether to feel pleased or worried that seeing a friend get hurt could drive Thor into a rage. When he raged, people died.

I know some of the Vogels made it out. Did the Starseer brother?

No. Thor glared defiantly, not at her but at the view screen, and then walked to the rear of the shuttle and sat down.

Jelena couldn't fault him for killing the man, especially since her unexpectedly powerful foe might have killed her if Thor hadn't rushed in, but she wondered again how many people had died who wouldn't have died if she hadn't made the choice she had back on Alpha 17. And would some of those Vogel children, perhaps the grandchildren of Luca Vogel, find out Thor had been responsible for killing him and want revenge someday? Jelena rubbed her face. How easy the spiral into war and atrocity.

"You all right?" Erick asked quietly, glancing back at Thor, then meeting her eyes. Masika had also settled into one of the seats back there, and she stared morosely out a porthole.

"I will be." Jelena forced herself to concentrate on the route ahead and nothing more.

"Good. I'd hate to think Thorian can rub his broodiness off on you when he's fondling your shoulder."

"That was hardly a fondle."

"Oh? It was a long touch. Like fifteen seconds."

"You were counting? Are you developing voyeuristic tendencies?"

"No. I was holding my breath and hoping you'd shove his hand away. He's way too dark and sullen and blood-covered for you. Leonidas would never approve."

Jelena resisted the urge to look back and see if Thor was paying attention to the conversation.

"I don't think Leonidas minds blood-covered men," she said, welcoming the distraction that the conversation offered. "Considering how often he's been one."

"Being a blood-covered man and wanting one for your daughter, even your step-daughter, are different things. I assure you, he wouldn't approve."

"Would he approve if we found someone to fondle *your* shoulder?" she asked, preferring to deflect the jibe than consider the seriousness lurking behind it. Besides, it wasn't as if Thor was sticking around, nor had he done anything to suggest fondling was on his mind. No, *war* was on his mind. Unfortunately. The entire universe, certainly the Alliance-run part of it, would be happier if he *could* be distracted by fondling.

"I don't know about Leonidas, but *I'd* certainly approve." Erick gazed wistfully out his own porthole instead of looking back at Masika, as Jelena thought he might. "Do you remember where we parked?" he asked.

"Yes. I'll get us there as soon as possible. We have a surgery to attend."

EPILOGUE

Jelena sat in the auto cab, wedged in between Thor and Erick, silently urging the robot driver to go faster. Morning had come, two of the system's three suns gleaming off the windows of skyscrapers and elevated trains, and she wasn't sure how long they had until Leonidas's surgery. She'd gotten the hospital address from Austin, the only one who'd stayed aboard the *Star Nomad* to watch over things while the family was gone. Someone must have come by to pick up the twins.

Jelena wasn't sure because she'd chosen to dock the *Snapper* at a different port, in case the Alliance was looking for them. The rates-by-the-hour junkyard-slash-parking-lot she had chosen promised discretion. The tacky sign out front said so, and she hoped it proved true. Laikagrad was on a different continent and far from where Sunset Island had gone down, but news traveled quickly around the globe and throughout the system.

But she would worry about that later. For now, she just wanted to make it in time to give Leonidas a hug before he went into his surgery. If someone was waiting to arrest her when she got out, so be it.

"I can't believe you're going to wear that get-up to the hospital," Erick said.

Jelena plucked at the unicorn-head gold necklace dangling against the pale blue blouse she'd changed into and almost answered before she realized he was talking to Thor. Erick, who had also changed out of his black robe and wore beige cargo trousers and a T-shirt proclaiming his affinity for thrust-bike races, clucked his tongue at Thor.

"You look like death's apprentice," Erick added. "Dying people are going to think you're there for them."

"I've been traveling light," Thor said, flicking a baleful glance at him. "And Jelena didn't suggest that there would be time to shop for hospital-friendly clothing along the way."

"I didn't know you'd want to go on a shopping trip," Jelena said. "I'll be happy to stop with you on the way back. Maybe we can get you something bright and perky." She didn't presume to pluck at his black sleeve, but she did eye the sword, pistol, and knife attached to his belt. Would he get past hospital security with any of that?

"I don't think deposed princes are allowed to be perky," Erick said. "They're supposed to be gloomy and broody."

Thor's eyes narrowed.

"Yes, like that," Erick said.

I'm glad you're coming, Jelena told Thor silently, *but I am concerned there will be trouble.*

You think Leonidas will pick a fight with me?

I think the Alliance will if someone reports seeing you.

They will not see me.

Jelena wasn't so sure. He might be able to diddle with people's minds, but what about security cameras? *Are you sure you don't want to go back and stay on board until Leonidas gets out of the hospital?*

I am certain.

She did not argue further. She honestly believed Leonidas would be pleased to see him, and just in case his heart transplant wasn't a permanent, long-term fix, Jelena wanted to make sure Leonidas saw everyone he wished to see while he could.

The cab stopped at the hospital's main entrance, and Jelena pushed the glum thought from her mind. Eager to see him and gauge his health for herself, she hurried up the walkway and through the doors.

An angry bleeping sounded when Thor walked through, and her concerns leaped back into her mind. Why had he brought all his weapons? She paused to wait—and look around for cameras—as two uniformed men approached him. Erick rolled his eyes. Thor kept walking, exuding calmness, almost indifference. The security guards' steps faltered, and their eyes took on glazed expressions. One reset the door scanner.

"Must have been a false alarm," the other muttered.

"Yes," his colleague agreed woodenly.

If Masika were there, she would have pointed out how creepy that was. And possibly commented on Thor's level. But she'd volunteered to stay aboard the *Snapper* and let Jelena know if trouble showed up. She was probably worried about people finding her again too. They would definitely find someone to remove her tracking device before leaving Arkadius. Jelena hoped that, after the chaos of the night, the Vogels wouldn't realize that Jelena, Erick, and Masika were indeed still alive, but they might grow suspicious if their scanners showed a supposedly dead woman roaming the system.

The person at the front desk was helping someone else, so Jelena tapped her earstar. "Mom," she told it.

A moment later, guitar twangs, singing, and the sounds of a boisterous crowd came over the built-in speaker. Jelena assumed the device had misunderstood and connected her with someone else—though she could not imagine who—but then her mother spoke.

"Jelena?"

"Yes, Erick and I are here. And an old friend." Jelena lowered her voice. "Uhm, is Senator Hawk there?"

Thor was several paces behind, but his eyes sharpened, as if he'd heard that.

"No, he was here earlier, but he had to go to a meeting. His wife and Wren and Jay are still here. Tommy is cooking."

"In the hospital? Is that allowed?"

"Not usually, but Leonidas made a comment about the uninspired food here while Tommy was standing nearby. That prompted a..." The music in the background swelled in some enthusiastic chorus. "Well, if you're here, come on up. Seventh floor, room 12. And 14."

"Leonidas is so big he warranted multiple rooms?" Jelena headed for the elevator.

The woman at the desk looked in her direction and opened her mouth, but something distracted her, and she frowned down at a holodisplay. When Jelena met Thor's eyes, he gazed blandly back at her without comment.

"We've actually got the end of this wing to ourselves. Senator Hawk waved a few fingers, since Leonidas…well, this may be more my fault. We've assembled a sizable and somewhat rambunctious entourage. You'll see. He can't wait to see you."

"Did Dad already have the surgery?"

"He did. Early this morning."

Jelena was disappointed they hadn't arrived in time, but relieved that everything sounded like it had gone well. Presumably, there wouldn't be a party going on if he were on death's doorstep.

On the seventh floor, Jelena, Erick, and Thor stepped out of the elevator where they almost crashed into Maya and Nika and Senator Hawk's two boys—they were all running down the hall at top speed. A ball was involved, and it flew through the air, bouncing off a wall not far from Jelena's head. A female android carrying stacks of sheets cleared her throat loudly and pointed toward an open door at the end of the hall, one that music floated out of. She wore an impressively beleaguered expression considering androids usually didn't adjust their facial features.

"Jelena," Maya and Nika blurted together, ignoring the android. They leaped at her, flinging their arms around her.

Even though it had only been a few weeks since Jelena had seen them, a lot had happened since then, and she returned the hug enthusiastically.

"How's Dad doing?" she asked.

"He's down there. We'll show you." Nika stepped back and tugged on her sleeve. "Wren and Jay, go get Jelena some kabobs. And get Erick some too. And, uh—" She squinted dubiously at Thor.

"That's Thorian," Maya blurted, then grinned shyly and waved at him.

"Maya," Thor said, inclining his head.

Jelena felt strangely pleased that he recognized the twins and even remembered their names after so many years since their last visit.

"Thorian?" Nika asked, squinting up at him. "He's gotten…" She looked at Jelena, needing help finding an appropriate word.

"Broody," Erick supplied.

Thor sighed.

"Let's go see Dad." Jelena extended her arms to wave everyone down the hall.

They stepped into Room 12, the one with the open door, and found two empty beds shoved to the side, and a band set up. Two guitar players strummed next to two holo players, one tapping at virtual piano keys, the other drumming very enthusiastically for someone without real sticks. Jelena recognized two out of the four musicians. Admiral Tomich was one of the ones strumming a guitar while singing a song about cowboys and spaceships and lost loves, an odd choice since he was happily married these days, as far as Jelena knew. That was his eight-year-old son at the drums. Jelena didn't recognize the holo piano player, but she thought the other guitarist might be one of Leonidas's younger brothers. She remembered the older one had come to the wedding, but he wasn't close to them and that was the only time she had seen either one. Maybe having a family member nearly die could bring relatives back together.

Senator Hawk's wife, Dr. Suyin Tiang, mother of the twins' playmates from the hall, sat with a couple of Mom's cousins that Jelena remembered meeting a few times. She balanced a curly-haired, brown-skinned toddler on her lap. Jelena had never found Suyin as fun and interesting as Hawk—probably because she worked in a clinic and didn't have pilot stories to share—but Jelena was glad she was here instead of her husband. She trusted Thor wouldn't consider attacking Hawk's family. Maybe seeing the children would even give him a reason to rethink his list.

"Jelena and Ostberg!" Uncle Tommy called from another corner where he'd set up a portable grill. He waved sauce-covered tongs at them. His wife Tanya, a plump and cheerful woman, was acting as assistant kebab-maker. She smiled at Jelena while she slathered marinade all over the meat cubes and strung them on sticks.

Jelena hadn't seen either of them for more than a year and waved heartily. "Those are vat meat cubes, right?" she asked, alluding to an old argument. For years, she'd been trying to get Tommy to switch from using real animals for his concoctions in favor of meat grown in vat factories.

"Of course!" he said with a cheerful wink, which she was fairly certain meant he was lying. Cheerfully. "And there are cookies. I promise no animals were harmed in their creation."

"Excellent." That, she believed, at least.

"Cookies," one of the boys blurted and raced to a basket. Maya and Nika trotted after him.

"There went our escort," Jelena said, glancing over her shoulder.

She expected Erick and Thor to be behind her, but only Erick had walked in. Was Thor lurking in the hallway? Maybe he didn't *want* to see Hawk's children and rethink his list. Or maybe he wasn't interested in walking into a gathering of people that would be strangers or near strangers to him. Of those here, only Leonidas and Jelena truly had a history with him. Poor Thor. Did he have anyone he considered family anymore?

Mica and Yumi, her mom's friends who had been among her original crew on the *Nomad*, were sitting near the grill in chairs that looked to have been dragged in from a waiting room. Yumi wore a blue robe similar in style to a Starseer robe and had her long black hair clasped back. There were a few strands of gray in there now, but she grinned and waved enthusiastically to Jelena. Mica, wearing a business suit, might have looked staid and proper, but her short, tousled blue hair assured she would loathe being called such. She waved at Jelena, too, then crooked a finger for Erick, her former engineering apprentice, to come over to talk.

Erick complied, snagging a cookie from a basket on the way, and also said a few words to Uncle Tommy. Erick peered through a partially opened side door as Mica asked him a few questions about the state of the *Nomad's* engines. Jelena sensed her mother and Leonidas in that side room, so she headed over, waiting until later for cookies. She'd already delayed far too long.

"Mom?" she asked, poking her head through the doorway. "Dad?"

Mom rose from a chair and locked her in a hug before Jelena had time to do more than register that Leonidas was in the bed with monitors behind it and wearing a dreadful blue smock—or was that a nightgown? Then her face was buried in a shoulder, and all she could do was lift a hand toward Leonidas while returning the hug with her other arm. Mom was a couple of inches taller than she, and strong from training with Leonidas, so there was no escaping her hugs.

"I'm fine, Mom," Jelena said when it was starting to look like she'd be a permanent fixture attached to her mother's chest. "I'm sorry it took so long to get here. We had some delays."

"Yes, we heard about them from Brad," Mom said, sounding dry, but supremely relieved too.

Jelena gulped. Admiral Tomich had been giving her updates? How much did the Alliance know—how much had Tomich shared? Had he looked them up after Erick had asked him for information on Thor's location?

Mom finally pushed her back out to arm's length. Her red-brown hair hung in a tail over her shoulder, and her eyes were moist. Jelena winced. She hadn't wanted any of this to make Mom cry—she would have preferred most of it not even get back to her.

"I expect to hear more of the story from you—you've been awfully quiet and evasive in your videos, my dear. Which has led us to assume you were doing naughty things."

"Not naughty." Jelena lifted her chin. "Noble. At least, that was how it started. Since then, well. Uh, I guess I can tell you the whole story later." Hopefully without further wincing.

"You better. Leonidas and I have been making decisions about your future, or at least the next couple of years, based on these reports that have been filtering in, but I'll let him tell you about it."

Er, her future? Her future where she was trapped on the *Nomad* and not allowed to ever touch another freighter or go off on her own again?

"How are you doing, sir?" Erick asked. Somehow, he had slipped past Mom and made it to Leonidas's side first.

"Going out of my mind from all this enforced bed rest," Leonidas rumbled. He must have been referring to the days leading up to the surgery, since the actual event had been that morning. "I would much prefer to be out battling pirates. Or throttling mouthy engineers."

Erick blinked. "Was that comment for me? Or my little brother?"

"Yes."

"Ah."

Erick looked faintly worried until Leonidas gripped his arm and asked, "Did you take care of my daughter and her engine out there?"

"I tried, sir. The engine was most agreeable. Jelena..." Erick looked back at her, and she sensed him torn between wanting to be loyal to her and wanting to be loyal to her parents.

She propped a fist on her hip, ready to stick her tongue out or punch him, depending on how he finished that sentence.

"Has a noble streak," Erick finally said, "and a good heart. And a total disregard for self-preservation, local and Alliance laws, and staying away from entities larger and more powerful than she is."

"I *know* that," Leonidas said, "but did you take *care* of her?"

His eyes glinted as he looked toward Jelena. She sensed he didn't truly believe she needed someone watching over her, at least not in the capacity of protector, but he liked razzing Erick.

"I...think so, sir. We survived a few tough scrapes."

"Who knew tough scrapes would be involved in a simple freight run from Orion Moon to Alpha 17?" Mom murmured.

Leonidas, with his enhanced cyborg hearing, had no trouble catching the question. "Well, she is *your* daughter."

"By blood, yes, but *you're* the one with the good heart and the noble streak. I'm sure we can blame you for giving those to her."

Erick shrugged at Jelena, not looking like he knew what to make of this conversation.

"Isn't it great when parents talk about you like you're not there?" she asked him and came around to the opposite side of Leonidas's bed.

His gray hair was a touch longer and scruffier than usual—he'd kept it military short for as long as she'd known him—but his color was good, and he only had a couple of tubes and wires attached to him, so she found that promising. The corner of a heart monitor was visible through the big V in his gown, the only outward sign that something interesting had happened to that particular organ.

"Do you have a neat scar?" she asked him, not sure how to touch on the mushy stuff, such as that she'd worried about him, and worried that she would be too late and would have to live with knowing she'd chosen some lab animals—and Thor—over hurrying to his side. But they'd always had a relationship where trading quips was more the norm than sharing heartfelt feelings. Besides, as a Starseer, she could sense his true feelings. She hoped he understood hers.

"A fairly unimpressive one. My battle wounds are larger and more garish." He lifted a bare, burly forearm to display a faded jagged scar running from elbow to wrist. "Enemies rarely take the time to seal the wounds they give you before running off."

"I've noticed. Most enemies are exceedingly rude."

"I concur."

"You didn't bring your tassel hat to your surgery?" Jelena asked, referring to a gift he'd received on a mission several years earlier. It was hideous, but neither she nor Mom had let him throw it out. One didn't throw away gifts, after all. One should take them out from time to time and appreciate them.

"Should I have?"

"Probably," Jelena said. "Your hair is looking rough. I see now why you keep it so short. No need to comb it."

"Huh, my secret is out."

Erick looked at Mom. "I thought they might have a deeper conversation given that he could have died out there. And she could have too, if we're honest. Would they be acting any differently if I wasn't in the room?"

"No, this is how they share their feelings, whether there are witnesses or not."

"It's unlikely it would pass muster with a writer of drama vids."

"Extremely unlikely." Mom fluttered her fingers at Jelena. "If you two don't hug, I'm going to tell Tommy to withhold the cookies."

"From *both* of us?" Leonidas sounded truly alarmed. "I'm a recovering invalid. Isn't it torture enough that I have to listen to that pained crooning in the other room?"

Despite his complaining, he was pleased that so many people cared enough to be here for him. Jelena also sensed that he didn't mind the singing quite as much as he pretended. He was glad people were enjoying themselves and relieved that the outcome hadn't been different.

Jelena swallowed and drew back from his mind, uncomfortable at the thought of him contemplating his own death.

"I can tell Tomich to play livelier songs if you want," Mom said.

"Just push the cookie basket in here and shut the door."

Mom snorted, but walked out. Whether she intended to put an end to the crooning or not wasn't apparent, but she did set the cookie basket on the table by the door. Jelena thought she heard a protest from Nika.

Jelena wasn't sure how to hug someone in a reclining position, but she bent down to obey her mother's wishes. Besides, Leonidas deserved hugs.

"I'm glad you made it," she whispered, blinking away tears. It was much easier to keep tears from forming when talking about hats and haircuts.

"I'm also glad you made it," he rumbled, patting her on the back. "Though once everything has returned to normal—" he tapped his heart monitor, "—we're going to have to have a family discussion about the future. For you and for the *Snapper*."

Jelena straightened and gave Erick a concerned look. "Are we not going to be allowed to run more freight? I may have promised someone a job. And, uhm, I'm trying to talk someone else into staying with us for a while." She wondered if Thor would stop lurking in the hallway soon and come in. There was another entrance to this room if he wanted to avoid the shindig next door. "If we're not keeping the *Snapper*, do you by chance need a strong, burly security guard who also paints? Have you thought about redecorating the *Star Nomad*? She does wonderful murals, even though she's glitter averse."

"We owe money on the *Snapper*. We're trusting that she can successfully run freight for years to come so we can pay her off and make the family business more profitable, so *someone* can go to the university if she wants." Leonidas raised his eyebrows toward her, but he didn't say more—they'd had this discussion before. "And so Maya and Nika can go when they're old enough. So, the *Snapper* stays, even if we have to talk Mica into creating a new ident chip for her." His eyebrows twitched upward, and Jelena sensed that he knew far more about her adventures than she'd wanted to burden him and Mom with. "And find her a captain," he added quietly.

Jelena bit her lip. "You don't think I can…" She stopped. What had she done to prove she could captain a ship? Oh, she'd gotten the cargo there on time, but since then…she'd been far too independent for someone working for someone else, and she knew it. But that was because she didn't want to run freight for a living. She wanted to help people—and animals—and she wanted to figure out a way to make herself known in the Starseer community, so she might be accepted and not ostracized. She still didn't know how she would do that, but felt the two goals could possibly be linked.

"I think she could make a good captain, sir," Erick said.

Jelena nearly fell over.

"Oh?" Leonidas asked.

"She *did* get the cargo delivered," Erick said. "And even though she's created a few problems that may cause ongoing issues, doesn't every captain need some time to settle into his or her role? Aren't a few hiccups to be expected? And how better for her to learn from her mistakes than by having to live with them? I'm sure she'll think twice in the future before rescuing animals without thoroughly researching the people or company holding them."

"It would have been more reassuring," Leonidas said, "if you'd ended that sentence earlier."

Erick smirked. "We both know she's not going to stop rescuing those in need, furred, skinned, and otherwise."

"Yes, and I'm concerned about giving her a ship to facilitate that."

"Again, people are talking about me as if I'm not in the room," Jelena muttered.

A thump came from beyond the closed door that led to the hall, like someone bumping an elbow against the wall. Or maybe hitting it with a fist. Jelena sensed Thor out there and also her grandfather. She wasn't surprised he was here, too, and hoped to see him soon. She wondered what Grandpa and Thor were talking about. And whose fist had struck the wall.

"You could hire a stranger with a fancy résumé to captain the ship," Erick said, "but then you'd have to pay the person. Jelena is apparently working for an allowance still."

Leonidas snorted. "I didn't know you were concerned about her being underpaid."

"She owes me a pack of *Striker Odyssey* cards. And a cape."

"A cape?"

"With sequins and sparkles," Jelena said.

She wasn't sure which one of them appeared more horrified.

"We thought we'd see how the first voyage went before talking salaries," Leonidas said, then met Jelena's eyes.

She perked up. Was she to be included in the conversation now? It was odd and a little disconcerting to have Erick act as her character reference—though she supposed she should be glad he was speaking in her favor. Just because he'd been to the university and was six years her senior… He didn't seem much more mature to her. A mature person did his laundry and folded his clothes, didn't he?

"Your mother thinks we should give you another chance, but based on a few things we've heard, we may need to keep you out running freight for the border worlds for a while. You would be less likely to run into Alliance patrols out there—we understand there was a mishap on Upsilon Seven that our insurance might not cover."

Jelena blushed and studied the floor.

"You would also be less likely to cross paths with core-planet corporations with long reaches. It would be a good idea to keep you out of sight, out of mind with the enemies you've already made."

"The hope is that those enemies believe we're dead," Jelena said. "And Masika and I have already been discussing a paint job for the *Snapper*."

"Masika?"

"Jelena doesn't limit her rescuing to animals," Erick informed him.

"She's super strong," Jelena said. "I told her you'd give her tips on needlepoint."

"I see. A painted ship might not be enough to keep you safe if you're regularly in the shipping lanes that Stellacor uses. So…the border worlds." He held out a hand. "If you're interested."

Jelena blinked. Was she being offered the job of captain? Or at least another chance to prove herself?

"You *will* pay for the fuel and repairs that may be required due to any side trips that you undertake."

"Er, with my allowance?"

"Going forward, we'll pay you a share of the profits earned from your runs. Just so you know, we intend to keep the *Snapper* too busy for side trips." His eyes narrowed. "Independent freighters don't earn money unless they're picking up and delivering cargo."

"No side trips at all?" She'd delighted at the idea of being a captain and choosing her own destiny, but she had always imagined doing things more noble than delivering bags of rice and boxes of cereal. How else would she obtain the notice of the other Starseers in the system? But she didn't want to cut ties with her family—and it wasn't as if there was another way she could afford a ship of her own. "What about vacations?"

"I'm sure you'll have some downtime now and then," Mom said, stepping back into the room. "That's the nature of the business."

Downtime sounded promising. She would just have to find a way to finance personal missions taken on during downtime. "A share of the profits" didn't sound like piles of money to her.

"I think you're also going to get an extra engineer," Mom added. "Feel free to use him however you wish."

"Austin?" Erick asked.

"We're going to hire someone a little more seasoned. And a little less determined to find ghosts on the *Nomad*." Mom's lips thinned.

"You want him to come find ghosts on the *Snapper*?" Jelena asked.

"Maybe you can keep him so busy he'll forget about that hobby."

"Doubtful." Erick exchanged a dubious look with Jelena. "He went camping at the graveyard in town when we were growing up. He was always trying to get photographic proof of paranormal activity."

Mom acknowledged this with a waggle of her fingers and continued speaking to Jelena. "You may also want to look for someone with a medical background more extensive than yours. As we've recently learned, things happen out in the Dark Reaches, and having someone who can help in that area is a good idea." Mom came in to hold Leonidas's hand, smiling at him and nodding toward the hallway. She must have known Grandpa was out there. "Grandpa has said he'll continue your teachings over the sys-net, for both of you." She looked at Erick as well as Jelena.

"Does this mean I'll be able to hire people?" Jelena thought of Masika, but also of Thor. Was there any chance she could talk him into staying on the ship with her crew instead of pursuing his vengeance mission? It seemed unlikely, but maybe she could be persuasive.

"Yes, a couple of people if you need them," Mom said. "Maybe some security specialists with combat armor."

Jelena thought of Thor with his sword.

"It's likely you'll run into trouble out on the border worlds, even if you're not going on…vacations." Her eyes tightened with concern, and she gave Leonidas a long look.

Jelena's senses told her that Mom wasn't crazy about this idea. She wanted to keep Jelena home and safe with the family a little longer. If not that, she would have willingly let Jelena go off to study at a nice university on a safe core world. This new enterprise worried her. Surprisingly, Leonidas had been the one who'd argued to give Jelena some independence and to let her try again.

"Makes sense," Jelena said. "Maybe I can find an Uncle Tommy. A chef *and* security officer."

"That would be *wonderful*," Erick said, a hand to his chest.

"Then Erick wouldn't need to take ludicrous risks to get a pizza back to the ship."

"Everyone should have an Uncle Tommy," Mom said, "but it's not that easy to find people with that combination of skills."

"Maybe I should go sample some of his kebabs now," Erick said, drifting toward the door. "And pack some up to take with us."

"That does seem wise."

The hallway door opened for the first time, and a red-faced Thor walked in stiffly. Grandpa came in behind him, wearing denim, flannel, and a goofy hat with a broad brim, his own face affable, especially when he spotted Jelena. She should have brought him a new hat from Upsilon Seven. Years ago, Mom had asked him to stop wearing a Starseer robe all the time, since it alarmed the customers loading their cargo onto the ship, and he'd discovered a love for cowboy attire. At least he wasn't wearing the spurs and chaps today. Jelena was fairly certain Mom now regretted making snide comments about the Starseer robe. After all, robes didn't jangle.

"How are you, little one?" Grandpa asked, coming over to wrap an arm around her shoulder.

"I'm well, all things considered."

Grandpa regarded her, his brown eyes knowing, a faint smile visible through his neatly trimmed silver beard. If he and Thor had been arguing, it wasn't evident from looking at his face, but Jelena wouldn't be surprised if he'd expressed disapproval at the way Thor was using his gifts. Unfortunately, they didn't know each other that well, and his disapproval might not mean much to Thor. The only one here who might have more luck swaying Thor than Jelena was lying on that hospital bed.

Leonidas turned his head, his eyes widening at Thor's entrance. He and Mom might have learned a lot about Jelena's adventures, but it seemed this aspect of them wasn't in the reports they'd received.

"Have you sampled the cookies yet?" Grandpa asked Jelena.

"*I* haven't gotten to sample the cookies yet," Leonidas grumbled, though he was still looking at Thor. Actually, he was looking him up and down, probably wondering why the prince was dressed like death. No, that wouldn't be true. He'd seen the news. Or, if not, Mom would have shared it. Right before she commed Jelena to tell her to avoid Thor.

"Has your doctor deemed it acceptable for you to eat sweets in your delicate state?" Grandpa asked.

Jelena almost snorted because Leonidas looked about as delicate as a brick lying there, but she reminded herself that he'd truly had a close call and looks could be deceiving. Even big, burly cyborg looks.

"If he hasn't, I'll have words for him." Leonidas made a fist.

"Careful, you'll pop your heart monitor off," Jelena said.

Leonidas opened his fingers and gestured for Thor to come to the side of the bed. He was currently lurking just inside the doorway, looking sullen and wary, though that was more because of whatever Grandpa had said than anything Leonidas had done, Jelena was sure.

Grandpa nudged Jelena and nodded toward the inside door. She balked, wanting to listen in on the conversation. Did Grandpa think Leonidas might talk some sense into Thor? Jelena wasn't sure about that. She didn't think Leonidas would approve of assassinations under most circumstances, but he must have reason to detest the same people Thor was going after. Would ten years have stolen his desire to see the emperor avenged?

Grandpa cleared his throat, and Jelena reluctantly headed for the door.

"It's good to see you, Thorian," Leonidas said, his tone strangely grave. Jelena was relieved he didn't call him "my prince" or "Sire" or something like that. Leonidas had once served the emperor closely, after all, and judging by occasional comments over the years, he wished the empire had never fallen.

"Colonel Adler. I'm glad you survived your surgery. And the last ten years of having such a rambunctious daughter."

Jelena had almost exited the room, but she balked again at this.

Leonidas's eyes twinkled. "Jelena's not so bad. Have you met the twins lately?"

"Briefly in the hall, but not really since they were three or four and painting your combat armor case."

"Ah, yes. The year they decided stickers weren't sufficient. I've never understood why the girls all wanted to decorate my armor."

"To make you look less fierce and scary," Jelena said. "Good people don't dress like walking deliverers of death." She squinted at Thor instead of at Leonidas.

Grandpa cleared his throat again and this time, gave her a mental nudge as well as a physical prod.

Sighing, Jelena stepped outside where the music had turned from spaceships and cowboys to sailing the high seas of Outer Trason as a pirate. Despite the different lyrics, the song sounded similar to the other one. Mom hadn't managed to increase the perkiness factor of the music. Rather surprisingly, and alarmingly, a few of the older set were dancing in the center of the room. Not *all* older. She spotted Austin, looking every bit as gangly as Erick and twice as awkward, stumbling over his feet as he danced with Yumi. Had Uncle Tommy spiked the cookies with alcohol? Could that be done?

"What is it you think they're going to talk about that they need privacy for?" Jelena asked after Grandpa pulled the door shut behind them.

"I do not know, but young Thorian needs someone he respects to speak with him and hopefully set him on another path."

"He had Dr. Dominguez and a bunch of Starseer tutors. I'm sure he respected at least some of them. And that they tried to talk him out of doing foolish things." At least, she was fairly certain after their visit to Halite that Dr. Dominguez didn't approve of the assassinations. She had no idea what all those other Starseers had been after, other than that they were supposedly imperial loyalists. The man on the couch had seemed decent though. "He's stubborn," she added.

"Perhaps, but Leonidas saved his life long ago, so he owes him a debt, yes? And since then, they have been apart so much that in many ways, Leonidas will be a stranger to him. Young people are less likely to defy those they don't know well."

"I'm not sure Leonidas is going to tell him to find another path. They're from the same place, and they have the same outlook and feelings about the empire. Or they did once."

Grandpa's face turned uncharacteristically grave. "If he does not tell him, I do not know who will."

Jelena thought about mentioning that she'd tried, but she doubted she had changed any of Thor's opinions, so what did it matter?

"It is not the assassinations that bother me so much, though I find that tactic disturbing of course, but it is how they have been training him." Grandpa shook his head. "From our brief conversation, I know they brought in *chasadski* tutors, and he uses some of their tactics."

"*Chasadski?* Like Tymoteusz?" Jelena thought of Thor's comment about back doors into people's minds. She'd known that wasn't a normal Starseer tactic.

"Yes."

Though he appeared grim, Grandpa squeezed her shoulder and found a second cookie basket to visit.

Jelena chatted with Mom, Yumi, and Mica for a few minutes, and managed a smile when she learned that her only other Starseer acquaintances, Abelardus and Young-hee, were on the way. But as soon as she sensed Thor leaving Leonidas's room—again through that direct door to avoid the crowd—she grabbed a couple of cookies and skewers of meat and stepped into the hallway.

It was empty except for Thor. His face wasn't as red as it had been after his chat with Grandpa, but he didn't exactly appear cheerful. Jelena hoped he didn't regret coming.

"Are you all right?" she asked.

His mouth opened, but he didn't answer right away, as if he hadn't expected the question. And here she'd thought he knew her every thought before she spoke.

"I'm fine. I'm glad Colonel Adler came through his surgery admirably."

"I think you can call him Leonidas. He's been retired for a while."

"I keep hoping he'll want to come back and serve in my army one day."

Something that seemed far less likely now. Jelena grimaced at the thought that Leonidas was getting old. Prematurely, yes, but old nonetheless.

Not wanting to dwell on that, she replied with, "The army you're going to raise after you finish getting rid of people you don't like?"

Jelena wondered if anything Grandpa or Leonidas had said had made him change his mind.

"The army I must raise if I'm to reestablish the empire."

"Would it be horrible if the empire remained in ashes? The system is doing fairly well these days under the Alliance government."

Thor curled a lip. "The part of it that's protected by the Alliance. They've only been able to establish their rule on five planets and a dozen moons. That leaves a huge part of the system in chaos, or ruled by the mafia or opportunists or corporations far shadier than your Stellacor. Under the empire, ninety-five percent of imperial subjects knew they had nothing to fear from thieves and murderers."

"They were too busy worrying about the repercussions of speaking their minds in a totalitarian government that didn't allow free speech."

"You were eight when it fell. What do you remember of it?"

"What do *you*?" she challenged. "You were only ten, and it's not as if you were living a normal person's life."

The android nurse came around a corner carrying trays of food, and they both stopped speaking, not that the android would likely care or report the conversation—or the speakers. Jelena wanted to change tacks anyway. This wasn't the argument she'd wished to have.

"The Alliance almost caught up with you on Upsilon Seven." She saw the indignation in Thor's eyes and the way he opened his mouth to protest, but she pressed on. "Even if you're determined to go back or continue on down your list, maybe you should give it a break for a while. Wait for them to think you're done, and then they'll lower their guards, and you'll have an easier time of it when you start up again." She couldn't believe she was giving him advice on his assassination plans. Not that she wanted him to "start up again." She just wanted to give him a reason to stop for now. And then... well, there was plenty of time to change the future.

"And do what? Go back to Halite for more training?" He spoke the words with distaste. He must not be monitoring her thoughts or he would have known what she had in mind. Maybe he was too preoccupied with his own thoughts.

"Not unless you miss the rabid apes and your puzzle and underwear collection. Erick informed me that the underwear was unremarkable. I'm sure we can find you something better at any clothing store."

"*We?* You and Erick?"

"We both have eclectic tastes in fashion, and we'd be happy to share our shopping expertise with you. How do you feel about sparkles?"

Thor rubbed the back of his neck. Maybe Erick's asteroids and space-ships pajamas would be more his style.

"It just so happens that I'll be running freight out among the border worlds for the foreseeable future. It might be a good place to go to avoid the Alliance. My parents suggested I hire some security specialists. They were thinking of someone with combat armor, but you might be sufficient."

"*Sufficient?*" His eyebrows flew upward.

"Barely. I don't suppose you can cook. No? What about doctoring skills?"

He stared at her.

"Well, maybe we can find one other person who can do both those things." Remembering the food in her hands, Jelena held up the kabobs. "Meat cubes on a stick?"

"I…" He was still staring at her. He'd either just noticed her stunning beauty, or he had no idea what to say to her job offer. "I'm supposed to be planning a resurgence of the empire, ridding the system of my father's old enemies, and amassing an army."

"You can't do that from the *Snapper?* My parents promised we'd have vacation time now and then."

"I'm the *last* person you should want on your ship. You think the Alliance won't be after me, given the people I've killed?"

"We can dodge Alliance soldiers at the same time as we're dodging the Stellacor bounty hunters who will be after Masika as soon as her aluminum foil armband falls off. Think of the convenience. Two groups of brutes avoided at the same time."

"You're spaced."

"Does that mean you accept my job offer?"

"I…"

Goodness, she was doing a good job of rendering him speechless.

"I guess I could go along for a while," he mumbled. Such heartfelt enthusiasm.

"Wonderful." She gripped his arm, unable to contain her own enthusiasm. She hadn't truly expected this concession.

"Well, I crashed my ship. I'm without many other transportation options for the moment."

"Couldn't you just steal one?" She thought of the way he'd waved his way past the security men. Then she wished she hadn't asked the question, since it might put ideas into his head.

"*Steal?*" He lifted his chin. "Imperial princes do *not* steal."

"But killing people is acceptable?"

"Killing loathed enemies is always acceptable. Ask your father." Thor nodded toward Leonidas's room.

"I see." Jelena should probably let Thor go back to the ship while she returned to Leonidas's side, but curiosity made her linger. "What did you two talk about?"

"Senator Hawk."

Huh, had Grandpa telepathically told Leonidas about Thor's plans? If not, she didn't know how Leonidas could know. Unless he could simply guess at the people on Thor's list because they had, in a way, betrayed him too. From the stories Jelena had heard, he and Hawk had started as enemies, and it had been having Tymoteusz as a common foe that had forced them to work together.

"Senator Hawk and how he has cute little kids and a wife so you shouldn't kill him?" she asked.

"More or less."

"Did Leonidas have opinions on the rest of the people on your list?"

"No."

So, Grandpa's thoughts that Leonidas might talk Thor from his path hadn't had any merit. She wasn't surprised. Jelena kept herself from thinking that it would be up to her to change his mind, but only because he might be monitoring her thoughts now.

"I'm going to go spend more time with Leonidas and my family," Jelena said. "I assume you aren't planning on staying."

"I'd rather not put Admiral Tomich in a difficult position."

One where he would have to put down his guitar and singlehandedly attempt to capture him? Yes, that would be awkward, but she doubted that was the *only* reason Thor didn't want to join the shindig.

"Then I'll see you back on the ship later?"

He hesitated, and she thought he might have changed his mind already, or that he hadn't meant it before, but he ultimately nodded. "Yes."

"Good. Here, take these." She thrust the kebabs at him, this time, successfully foisting them off on him. She gave him the cookies, too, amused by the image of him standing there in his black ninja outfit, all scarred and fierce…with a pile of cookies in his hand. "Until we find a security chef of our own, all we've got is food that comes out of boxes, pouches, or cans." Alas, fresh fruits and vegetables were few and far between on space stations, and she had never been impressed by the half-hearted terraforming that had been done on those border worlds. Produce was at a premium when it was available at all. "You'll want to enjoy your chance at real food."

"You don't think they'll have pizza on the border worlds?"

"I'm not sure we can count on Erick always being able to get it to the ship. He may not want to risk another suspicious bump on his stomach."

"Ah." Thor headed toward the elevator, giving her a long look over his shoulder as he went.

Jelena wasn't sure if it meant he thought she was spaced or if he thought he was in for strange and interesting times if he went with her. Either way, he was likely right.

THE END

29028289R00188

Made in the USA
San Bernardino, CA
11 March 2019